RYAN LEONE

ANTI HEROES

GORILLA CONVICT

ISBN 978-0-9800687-5-7

Printed in the United States.

Jacket cover art and design by Avery Smith. Jacket photograph licensed under Creative Commons.

Book typeset in JAF Lapture by Albert Kapr and Tim Ahrens.

Gorilla Convict Publications (St. Louis)
www.gorillaconvict.com

In loving memory of Ryan Leone, whose words live in these pages and our hearts — Palabra!

FOREWARD

It did not take long for me to realize that Ryan Leone arrived in this world with a special talent.

About five seconds.

Ryan was born at 5:02 p.m. on a pristine summer day (August 3, 1985) in Framingham, Massachusetts. As his father, I was present and vividly recall that as he disembarked from the womb, he simply looked around the room, taking in everything and analyzing this new experience. From the start Ryan was taking measure of his surroundings.

Ryan's interest in literature and film quickly took root. As an infant, I read to Ryan nightly; at first, he did not understand the words but viewed the accompanying pictures and wove his own story. Soon he understood the words and begged me not to stop; often our reading sessions would go on well beyond an hour.

By the age of nine, Ryan began writing stories himself. We heard about a youth writing contest at the local Barnes and Noble bookstore. Ryan's entry, presciently titled "Why I Suck Blood," won first prize for his age group. No surprise, given the book's first sentence: "The menacing evening skies were adorned with howling moon dogs."

Ryan's love of stories turned to another medium. At the age of three his favorite movie was *Ghostbusters*. He memorized large swaths of dialogue from the movie and put together several Ghostbusters outfits from common household items. By adulthood, Ryan was a film aficionado, with a vast knowledge of film and many high-profile friends within the film industry.

It did not surprise me that Ryan's writing would make its mark as an adult. If Ryan's destination was no surprise, his journey certainly was.

Like many of his contemporaries at the outset of the

the 21st century, Ryan began experimenting with drugs as a teenager. The remaining 22 years of Ryan's life was marked by constant trips to rehabilitation facilities (more than 20 by Ryan's count) and multiple incarcerations for non-violent drug offences (eight cumulative years). When Ryan ultimately passed away on July 2, 2022, it was from cardiac arrest apparently driven by pneumonia, not, as reported by some, an acute drug overdose. Yet, his long-term drug use most likely compromised his heart.

Ryan wrote *Wasting Talent* while incarcerated at the federal detention facility in Oxford, Wisconsin. At one point, Ryan gave me a near final manuscript which I promptly read and rendered a mediocre product. About 400,000 copies and 915 Amazon reviews later (62% five stars, 4.3 average star rating), it appears my judgment was totally off course.

Ryan had a premonition about an early death that we often discussed. He repeatedly said that he was prepared for death but had two nagging regrets: not being available for his two sons (age four and two at the time of his death) and several outstanding projects that were this close to completion.

The ever creative Ryan seemed to always have ten or more projects progressing simultaneously on his docket. Three were at or tantalizingly close to completion when he died: *Florida*, a completed screen play that Ryan wrote with his close friend, actor Nick Stahl, *Idiot Savant: The Savage Life of Ryan Leone*, a documentary marshalled by noted documentarian Seth Ferranti, and Ryan's long awaited second novel, *AntiHeroes*.

The documentary was essentially complete at the time of Ryan's passing but the decision was made to reconfigure the documentary given the shocking turn of events. It is scheduled for release during the fourth quarter of 2023. Likewise, *AntiHeroes* was largely complete, and following some light cleaning and editing, is now available for the public.

I frequently told Ryan that he was in a unique position as a writer. He was, at once, a supremely talented writer and riveting storyteller, but also someone who had witnessed first-hand the darkest side of life, whether it was the horrors of deep addiction, the unspeakable failings of our prison system, or simply the stark reality of life on skid row. I believe that Ryan's greatest gift was his ability to bring these harsh realties to life, speak the truth about the most highly marginalized among us, and to ultimately leave his mark on that beautiful world he first scrutinized on August 3, 1985.

The "real" Ryan, as only a father could know, was a man with a huge, loving heart, an inherent gentleness, a passionate commitment to social justices, and, above all, as a fervent anti-opioid crusader.

We all leave earth eventually and we can only hope that we leave behind a strong, meaningful legacy. Words are forever and a large part of Ryan's legacy inhabits the pages that follow.

Ryan's mother Diane and I could not be prouder of our only child and take extraordinary comfort in knowing that his legacy endures in *AntiHeroes*.

Enjoy!

Frank Leone
Santa Barbara, CA
August 2023

INTRODUCTION

What's with writers and prison? They tend to go. Good ones do, anyway. O. Henry did 5 years on an embezzlement charge. Dostoyevsky only did 4, though in fairness he did them in a prison labor camp in Siberia, and only after his death sentence had been commuted. Oscar Wilde did hard time in Reading Jail and wrote a fine poem about the place. Chester Hines and Voltaire lived some 200 years apart, and yet both saw times when it seemed as though they couldn't keep their asses out of jail. A similar thing happened to Cervantes. Cervantes wrote *Don Quixote* while he was locked up, and there's plenty of more examples. I'm not even close to done going through the writers that everybody's heard of. A few more right fast: Ken Kesey, who did 5 months in county; Dashiell Hammett, who served fed time. Jean Genet loved him some jail. François Villon was a career criminal who barely got out of being hanged. He wrote *Ballade Des Pendus*, and the court was so moved by the eloquence of his contrition as to spare him the rope. And let's not forget Albertine Sarazin, who took matters into her own hands and escaped from prison. She was doing 7 years for armed robbery.

So fuck, I guess. Isn't it fair to say there could be a correlation? It isn't as though the names above are just some nobodies, secondary to the real talent. On the contrary, they're all legends, said to be among the best to ever do it. Of course, correlation doesn't necessarily mean causation. Just saying, What it seems like is maybe a writer could do worse than to get locked up.

Take a writer who's boring, for instance. There are plenty, so pick one. Make it a learned writer, for that matter. Wouldn't such a writer as the one you're thinking of be better off in jail instead of at large, carrying on and boring the shit out of everybody, fucking the game up? Is there any reason to doubt that a boring writer might learn something useful while incarcerated, or get ideas for some characters, at least? There will be all types of people locked up in there, and some of them will be just as boring as the learned writer, no doubt. The lion's share of them will have a story to tell, however. Like, you can spend even just a few days in jail and you'll hear mad stories. If you're the type that actually listens to people when they talk, then there'll be a lot to be picked up from them. Pay attention to their timing. Pay attention to how to get to the point. Pay attention to what makes a thing believable, what makes it real.

Perhaps I'm biased. Probably I am. Then again, I'm not so sure. I mean, okay, I do seem to fuck with writers who've been to prison, and yet at the same time it isn't even like I do it on purpose. A lot of them I'd fucked with before I ever knew that they'd been locked up, and some of them I'd fucked with before I ever was locked up. Only since did I try and think about what that might have to do with, what qualities the time can instill in a writer– or further instill, anyway. What came to mind was a certain type of humility, the one that's comfortable acknowledging that there's no reason why the reader ought to give a fuck. It deals with that by getting straight to the point, running things fast, and keeping them moving, with no yammering. This certain type of humility—unapologetic, yet self-aware—often times is what's behind that approach, and not many things can instill this type of humility in a writer like getting dragged by the law and thrown away for some years will, as it's a rare bird that can go through that without doing some honest-to-fuck soul searching. It doesn't end with the sentence either. The sentence is more like when it begins. Being around a hundred or so prisoners in a cellblock or in a pod, in a housing unit or in a dorm–prisoners who've been told in no uncertain terms that (a.) they're in seriously deep shit and that (b.) their lives are for all intents and purposes over, in as much as their chances of ever amounting to anything have dwindled down to less than one half the square root of fuck all– in an environment such as that, it isn't wise to go around like you own the place, not unless your goal is to coax somebody to kick your stomach until you shit yourself. Most everybody tries to avoid that, so most everybody learns a certain respect, what conditions you to observe others with a more focused attention to reactions, however small. You learn to read people, and you can learn what makes them tick, individual by individual, as need be. You study characters, and you get to know what makes a character a character, versus somebody who isn't at all interesting. Everything's about respect, and it translates.

There are two approaches to telling a story: Tell it on the level or tell it down. Tell it on the level and you're cooking with gas. Tell it down and nobody finishes the book, if they ever picked it up in the first place. Allow me to get to the point though, because it's time to get to the point of all of this now, and the point is that in your hand you've got *AntiHeroes*, by Ryan Leone, and it's the newest addition to the cannon of convict writers, plus it goes hard, too: written on the level, all gas no breaks. Frankly, I was caught off guard by how cold it is.

Ryan's cold. I'll put it to you like this: If you fuck with William S. Burroughs, you'll fuck with Ryan Leone; if you fuck with Hunter S. Thompson, you'll fuck with Ryan Leone; if you fuck with hood books, you'll fuck with Ryan Leone; if you fuck with James Paterson, you'll fuck with Ryan Leone. You see, he covers a lot of bases, only he makes all of that his own and lets it run fearless.

Nico Walker
Oxford, MS
April 2022

For Karina—

For sticking with me through
prison, addiction, and mental illness.

For giving me Nikko and Weiland.

I get to fall back in love with you
every time I see your features
on their angelic faces.

And for Paul—
(1982-2019)

"I'll see you on the
dark side of the moon ... "

ANTIHEROES

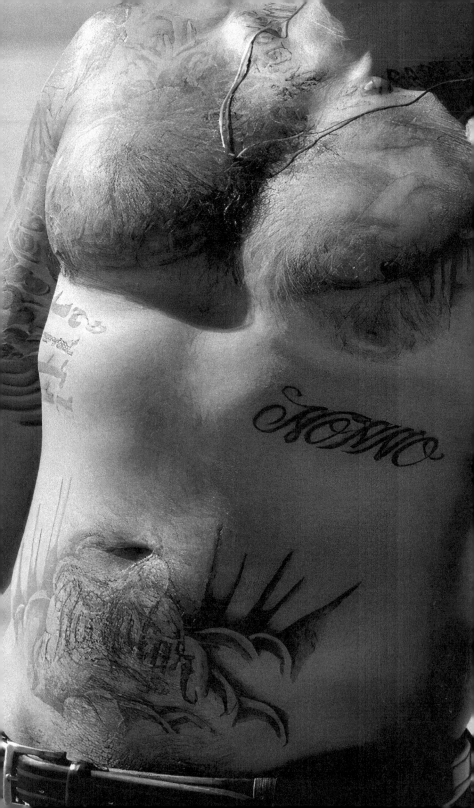

1

REAL FUCKING HELL

LOS ANGELES 1989 — 2017 : : IRAQ 2004

"But the human mind, when it reaches the bottom of the abyss, must bounce back or disintegrate entirely."
— Eddie Bunker

Gnner's thousand-yard stare had always attracted the sluttiest women at Alcoholics Anonymous meetings. His eyes were possessed by perpetually blank pain. The women salivated over his lack of emotion.

Gunner wasn't traditionally good-looking. He was rugged, unshaven. There was a grotesque scar peering out of the corner of his left eye. AA women associated his rough aesthetic with danger and spontaneity. He represented adventure. At least that's the lie they would tell themselves. They wanted to be choked. They wanted their hair pulled. Most of them weren't even real-deal alcoholics; they just had daddy issues and would use meetings as conduits to form toxic, co-dependent relationships or to get their rocks off for the night.

And goddamn, Gunner looked the type, like he had yanked his fair share of ponytails in his day.

Gunner had been rendered socially inept and couldn't pick up the simple hints that women wanted to sleep with him. He didn't even think he was fuckable. He didn't realize that being invited back to their house to "have coffee" really meant that the silent contract of sex had already been agreed upon.

And sex was a liability for Gunner. The embarrassment would always lead to an incident.[1] Recovering alcoholics had a different dynamic than normies. They were aggressive compared to the few gentle and submissive women Gunner had been with before he went away.

His mom had been an adult film star for a couple of years. They lived in the San Fernando Valley, just north of Los Angeles.

She could never be a star like the other girls. Freebasing cocaine uglified her beyond repair. The enamel on her teeth had sizzled away, leaving her toothless, except for a few rotten stumps.

She was emaciated with obscenely over-sized fake breasts; it had given her a hobo hunch and waddle. (She may as well of rolled shopping carts down the fucking street — she was that unsexy.)

There was a niche market for raggedy women, but it was more of a gimmick than anything else. *The Shelter Jizz Dispenser, Pregnant Welfare Whores of the Anal-bian, Cum Guzzling Butt Sluts from Outer Space (part 3, 4, and 8)* and in her latter cannon, a well-known, underground Danish film: *Kučke Beskućnice Jedu životinjsko Govno za Lijek*[2]

But eventually she turned to the streets and what little stability she had been able to provide Gunner vanished.

There was the blur of faceless, violent father figures. He remembered his mom dragging their luggage down the street as one of her Devil-grinned exes chased them with a machete in broad daylight.

Gunner was around prostitution, dope, and a flurry of naked depravity. He was raped by a used car salesman. That was a face he would never forget. The details haunted

---

1   See Also: The Rough Childhood
2   Translated roughly to "Silly homeless bitches eat animal shit for drug fixes."

him throughout his tortured life. He could still see the exact rash of razor cuts on his bald head. He could still smell his body odor, later in life he realized low-grade marijuana had the exact same nasty stench as that pedophile.

Gunner's mother knew that he was being molested but had turned a blind eye because she had owed the man money for drugs.

It wasn't long before she had pawned most of their possessions. She realized how valuable her son was to some of the meth-head perverts she interacted with. Gunner was the only thing she had left to sell. Somehow the fact that she was HIV positive circulated around town and nobody would pay to fuck her anymore.

She would drop Gunner off at a mobile home park and a heavyset man would grab Gunner by the wrist, drag him into his trailer, and rape him.

At first Gunner would cry.

A lot of men refused to pay when it happened.

His mother wouldn't be able to buy her dope. She'd beat her only child until he was drooling blood and babbling apologies.

Eventually, he learned to cry internally.

Trauma removed linear coherency from his childhood memories. He could only remember fragments — most were too disturbing to ever discuss out loud.

There were occasional glimpses, smells were eerily transportive, but he would have no idea how old he had been or what else was happening in his life when certain events occurred.

There were a few very vivid nights.

His mother took him to an enormous house in the middle of nowhere flanked by looming mountains. They pulled up to a gate. She rolled her window down and pressed a button on an intercom box. The gate slowly swung open.

Her Volvo went up the long gravel driveway to the

front of the house. It looked like the entrance to a castle. It was the biggest home they had ever seen. They sat silently except for the rattling fury of torrential rain.

His mother chain-smoked cigarettes. She kept the windows rolled up. They sat enveloped in the cancerous haze. So fuckin' what? It's cold.

She usually talked to Gunner like he was some eager stranger at the bar.

But she remained quiet that night.

The door to the home finally opened and Gunner saw a man in a porcelain mask. It was painted like a Day of the Dead woman, a blacked-out nose, ornate webbed patterns spinning from its chin. He had seen this kind of mask on the Mexican television channels.

Gunner was more fascinated than scared. He had been raped and beaten so many times that a mask like this didn't elicit concern.

The person came and opened the passenger door. The mask was much more detailed up close, and he could tell that the man behind it was abnormally tall. He was black-clad: a sweater, pants, and combat boots. He crouched down, face-to-face with Gunner. The eye holes were dark, teasing shadows — impossible to see the real eyes.[3]

Gunner remained stoic and calm, watching rainwater race down the man's mask.

His mother leaned over him, "Half up front?"

The man stepped back and said nothing, standing tall, ominous in the heavy downpour.

"I was told a thousand up front. A thousand after six?"

The man took a plastic wrapped stack of money out of his pocket and handed it to Gunner's mom. She licked her lips, making no effort to conceal her excitement as she counted the money.

---

3   Real lies.

She folded the grand and put it in her cleavage.

"Go on, Greg. Have fun." She said, "He's a nice guy ... it'll be great."

He looked like the kind of man that butchered people with chainsaws. Gunner had been raised by TV. Perhaps he was a cannibal. He saw a show about a serial killer that ate people and cut them up and made penis pies that authorities eventually found in his refrigerator. He had been an extremely quiet guy.

He hopped out of the car voluntarily.

Death carried a rumor of relief.

His mother drove away.

Gunner followed the man inside. It seemed endless and massive. The house had booming acoustics. They walked down a hallway. Flickers of distant candlelight illuminated the corridor. Framed photographs were obscured by the bounce of their walking shadows.

They went to the living room. There was a long wooden table with a child in a wheelchair wearing the same porcelain mask. His hands were cuffed to the wheelchair. There was a plate placed in front of him.

There was also a woman tied to a chair. Blonde hair spilled out the sides of her mask. There was a plate in front of her and two empty chairs on each side of her.

The woman and the child said nothing. Their heads sagged. They refused to look up.

It was possible they were already dead.

Penis fucking pies.

The room was empty except for the table and a few wooden crates scattered across the floor. The man walked up to a crate and took out a porcelain mask and some rope.

He walked up to Gunner and placed the mask on his face.

"Hello, Martin," the man said.

Gunner was confused. That wasn't his name.

The man leaned down and put his mask up to Gunner, making kissing noises as he mimicked pecking him on the cheek, "I've missed you terribly. My, my, my!"

He took Gunner by the hand and brought him to the chair next to the woman. He wrapped the rope around Gunner's waist and pulled tight, tying him securely to the chair.

"And now we eat our chow, ladies and gents!"

Gunner looked at the woman and child. They kept their heads down and didn't say a word. He could tell that these people were terrified of the tall man. He got up and started walking to each plate and taking off their covers.

There was a pile of gore in the centers; it was dim in the room, but Gunner could recognize various body parts. There were furry limbs and marble-like eyes — it looked like badly mutilated roadkill. It smelled putrid, the distinct stench of burning hair and fried flesh; Gunner mustered all his strength not to vomit.

"How was your day, Barbara?"

Gunner realized nobody could eat except for the man. Everyone else had their hands restrained.

"Barbara, your day, how was it?"

She had her head down and was staring at her lap.

"Fine," the man said, "You're still upset about the other night. I understand. I'll just tell you about my day then, hun. I finally tracked down Father Gary. You know what he told me? That I was a Voo-doer. I laughed at him saying it. I did. I had never heard such an idiocy. Voo-dooer? I am the motherfucking antichrist!"

The man slammed his fists down on the table. There was the banging of fallen dishes and cups. His voice boomed and reverberated throughout the house.

He tilted his head at the ceiling and shouted, "You hear that, you old fool! The fucking antichrist!"

The shouting frightened Gunner. It reminded him of

getting beaten by his mom or her boyfriends. He finally put his head down like the others at the table. The idea of being killed by this lunatic suddenly felt imminent and he realized he had pissed in his pants.

There was a warm current trickling down his leg, and he wondered what would happen if the man saw it.

He didn't notice. He was making slurping noises. He was pretending like he was devouring whatever heap of death was on those plates.

"*Mmmm*," he said, "You are an exceptional cook, darlin'—it got me to thinking that instead of you taking the kids out for Halloween, we just stay in and watch some spooky movies together. There's a lot of crazy drivers out there tonight and that damn awful rain. I can bring Father Gary down here and we can slow cook his ass in the fireplace, watch his skin fry right off."

He waited for a moment and then—

"Oh, now of course you can, sweetie," he said.

Gunner realized that he was having conversations with himself. He would answer his own questions. This scared Gunner even more. This guy was legitimately insane. Some fates are far worse than death. He focused on keeping his head down and the man eventually got up and walked away.

He raised his head slowly and caught the woman doing the same thing.

"How—" she began but the man had returned, and they both put their heads down once more.

Gunner peeked up to see a guy in his early twenties, tied to a chair, being dragged into the dining room by the man. He was thrashing and stomping his feet desperately. His face was strained; his screams muffled by the duct tape covering his mouth.

"Can I get an amen, Father Gary?" He asked and laughed at his own joke.

He placed him at the table with the rest.

"I told the fam that we would stay home tonight, watch horror pictures, worship the devil, and roast your holy ass in our fireplace. My wife and my boys are just gonna love it. We gonna Voo-Doo-Doo you."

He laughed once more, "And I got a surprise for you that they don't even know about! But it's going to be ... what you say ... riotous? Yeah, downright riotous."

He left him tied to the chair and hurried out of the room.

Once he was certain that he was far enough that he wouldn't hear, the young man said, "Hey, hey — one of you. Hurry and listen."

The woman and Gunner both raised their heads to see him, the duct tape was now below his mouth, as if it had never been secure. He had just let it appear that way.

"You know who this sick fuck is?"

The woman trembled, "Do you?"

"Yeah, I do but it's a long story and you need to listen to me. Right now, he thinks you're his family. They were killed in a car crash — look, it doesn't even matter. He's going to kill you, okay? Unless you listen. He's part of some fucking Santeria cult thing. Black Magic and rituals and sacrifice and shit. But he's mentally ill. Extremely mentally ill. And we can use it against him. He thinks that you're his wife and kids and that I'm the priest that accidentally killed them."

He took a long breath.

"Listen," he looked around frantically, "He is in some sort of self-induced trance. But when he snaps out of it, he'll kill you. You need to play his game. Like me, I call myself Father Gary because he thinks that's who I am. Call him honey, he thinks you're his wife. And kid, you call him dad. Not daddy, call him dad, okay? Get him to untie you. And then untie me. I will fucking kill him. He's dangerous. He's killed—"

The man walked back into the room.

He was holding a tied-up teenage girl in his arms. Silver tape was wrapped cruelly around her mouth. She was pale from exhaustion and shock.

He placed her at Father Gary's feet.

Father Gary managed to get the loose duct tape back to his mouth. It looked secure. He looked down at the girl wrapped in rope. It was his fiancé, but he remained motionless, panicking silently, his eyes widened from concern.

"Found this girl at the old priest's hideout, little apartment in Reseda. He's been living with her to try and conceal his devotion to Christ from me and the peoples. It's his sister or something important to this celibate old wizard fuck. I'm going to make him eat her, alive, as he burns in the fire. You know what you've done. Fraud! You ... you fake fucking miracle chaser. You con artist, ass fucking clown."

"Dad," Gunner said, and the man tilted his mask.

He was stunned and perplexed to hear his son speak after all the time he had waited.

"Dad, I missed you."

After all the sacrifices he'd offered.

The tenderness was palpable. His *dad* seemed to slide across the room and swoop him up in a single, precious Polaroid embrace.

"Yes, Martin. My wonderful, wonderful boy!"

"Hunny, untie me too, will you?"

He untied Gunner and went for his *wife* Barbara.

The mouths of their masks touched in a placid kiss, and she whispered how much she missed him.

"I missed you too. I truly, truly did."

She looked at the fake Father Gary and he motioned with his head for her to come towards him. She nodded slowly.

Gunner saw this and said, "Dad, I'm thirsty."

The masked man stopped hugging his wife and turned towards his son.

"Got anything in the kitchen for me, Dad?"

"I'm sure I can find something for you."

And then everything faded to black.

It couldn't have been a dream. He could recall the details of that freakish night more vividly than anything else he had ever experienced. He just couldn't remember how it had ended.

His memories became kaleidoscopic.

He saw luminous, stained-glass windows. They depicted sacrificial scenes with daggers and ribbons of ruby-red blood.

He was naked on the floor of an altar. He could re-member exactly how cold he had felt, hugging his knees, shivering with abashment.

Masked people swayed above him chanting.

He woke to a familiar pulsing leak.

... *Dooh ... Dooh ...Dooh ...*

His mother's studio apartment was rundown. She nev-er had the money to get anything fixed.

They had placed a bucket on the ground to collect the drips. ... *Dooh ... Dooh ... Dooh ...*

The sound comforted him.

He had no idea how he found his way back. It seemed so far away the night before.

The apartment looked the same as it always had. There were clusters of trash and cigarette butts everywhere. A conspicuous square space on the dresser, free of dust, re-minding Gunner that his mom had recently pawned their only television set. She did that a few times a month.

There was an old pornographic poster of her from some foreign adult magazine that nobody had ever heard of. Her head was missing, torn off by one of her drunk jealous boyfriends. (Gunner had always assumed.) She was licking her own nipple or at least the tattered half of it. She looked good for a fake-titted-headless-torso. Better than she did as a crackhead with a head.

A cockroach scuttled across an empty pizza box.

Gunner was confused. The night had evoked a dream quality from the start. Eventually, it turned inescapably nightmarish. There was no way that it had all just been in his head.

... Dooh ... Dooh ... Dooh ...

No, he just didn't remember the end.

Gunner went to the kitchen. He opened the pantry to find box after box of grits. It was the only food they were given, aside from canned goods at the food banks they went to on Sunday morning in Pasadena. His mom refused to waste cash feeding her child. He ate grits nearly every meal.

He searched for a cooking pot; most had his mother's drug paraphernalia or pieces of trash stuck to their centers. He'd find lipstick-stained glass tubes; Chore Boy, Brill-O, copper colored if they were new or bunched up and blackened from smoking crack. He found bent spoons and used condoms and hypodermic insulin syringes.

He had almost stabbed himself with needles several times. His mother had been diagnosed HIV positive a few years before. She also had the Genotype One (*El Uno*) strain of hepatitis C. It was the hardest to treat because it was the most resistant to treatment. Legend had it that the virus had mutated in desolate parts of Mexico and had made its way to the United States by infecting American hookers that had been exported to service horny cartel workers dwelling in the jungle. This was the kind of bedtime story Gunner was told throughout his childhood.

If he had been pricked by one of her dirty needles, he could easily catch one of her communicable diseases. It was no place to raise a nine-year-old little boy.

But it was the only home that he knew.

He found a clean pot and poured a couple packages of grits, added pond-colored water from the sink, placed the stove on low and looked for a spoon to stir the grits. There were none in the drawer. His mother often used them for drugs; he was used to finding them bent on the nightstand in her room. She would be mumbling next to it, quasi-conscience, with a syringe sticking straight up, out of her arm — the surrendering flag of another fallen soldier.

Gunner knew that his mother wasn't home because she wasn't blasting music. This was a trick poor people employed in small homes with limited privacy — music became cloaks, so he didn't have to hear her screaming from sex or getting slapped around by one of her wasted boyfriends.

The living room was in its typical disarray.

Gunner froze.

He couldn't believe his eyes. His mother was hanging from a beam on the ceiling. Her body was limp and swinging unevenly, back-and-forth, like a creaky pendulum. She was bloated, morbidly inflated; mouth slack, as if she had been frozen, mouthing the letter O. Gunner hated that he immediately thought of a blow-up sex doll as he cut the sheet and her body tumbled to the floor.

He hated that even at the end of her life she had been reduced to a sexual object.

Her body lay lifeless on the floor. He felt nothing — absolutely fucking nothing. He was already immune to emotions.

He lacked empathy. His mother had thrown him to the wolves. It was her fault that he was nine and sociopathic. It was easier to look at her dead than when she had been alive.

His mother had been a cold, cold bitch.

Gunner knew that he had to clean the drugs and paraphernalia before he called 911.

He turned around and shrieked. He placed his hand over his mouth. There was a porcelain mask propped up on the mantel above the fireplace. Day of the Dead, the same mask from the night before.

Definitely not a dream.

He wasn't sure if his mother had committed suicide or if one of those freaks had drugged him, killed his mom, and then left him there alone, traumatized and unreliable.

It created a lifetime of confusion and self-doubt. Gunner was introverted and shy.

Practically mute. Fortunately, there are plenty of people that appreciate a person who would rather listen than talk.

Cindy was one of them: a traditional bimbo. She was heavyset but viewed her fat as a voluptuous asset. Her face was a damaged shell of a distantly pretty girl; failed marriages and liquor binges formed a map of imperfections across her swollen face.

Gunner had bumped into Cindy while he was hovering above the coffee and cookie table after an AA meeting. He could tell by her obnoxious voice that she was from the middle of the country.

"I've never seen you at the 5 o'clock."

Gunner gave his signatory blank smile.

"I myself can't f'in stand book studies. They are so damn boring. And I don't get to hear myself talk!"

She was pleased with this. She thought about it and howled at herself.

"Whatever works?" Gunner said.

"Oh, totally! I don't have another one in me. Swear-ta-god, man"

"Yeah. Me, either."

Cindy had powdered sugar peppered across her chin. Gunner noticed and thought better of saying anything, he didn't want to make things more uncomfortable than he already felt.

"Hey, listen," she began, "I know we literally just met each other ... but once you've met one of us sickies, it's like you've met us all. Am-ah-Right?"

He shrugged, sure.

"I'm new to the area and had to take the bus here. I live in Woodland Hills. You got a car by chance?"

"Yes," Gunner said.

"Nah, ah! Would you be a doll and give a lady a lift?"

"I can do that for you."

"No shit. Fantastic, really. You're a complete lifesaver."

Cindy talked mostly about herself in the car: the boring job as a data entry specialist; the obligatory jabs at her ex-husband; "the gay" as she would refer to him.

She also complimented Gunner on the immaculate condition of his Jeep Cherokee.

"I read somewhere that you can tell how considerate a male lover is going to be by the way he takes care of his automobile."

She tried.

But it was clear from Gunner's monosyllabic responses that aside from the ride, the only thing she could get out of him was some anonymity-protected NSA dick.

If that.

"I know 'The Doctor's Opinion' was the selected section tonight, but I never understood the big words and the fancy old-fashioned way the book was written. It was written like a zillion years ago ... I need help with it. You wouldn't mind helping me read through it?"

"That's cool," Gunner said.

"Love the way you say that. Dang. Just love it.

They moved into the bedroom with purpose. Gunner had honestly thought he was sitting on the bed to translate the message of the Good Doctor to Cindy.

But Cindy had other ideas.

She took her shirt off. Rolls of fat sagged over her jeans like uneven pillow stuffing. For such a large woman, Cindy had genuine finesse in the way she had ripped her clothing off and glided towards Gunner; in one fluid motion. This was a move she had down smooth. Cindy's tits were swirled with marbled stretch marks. She smelled sour. It was a combination of body odor and the distinct stench of boxed and forgotten holiday decorations.

The smell reminded Gunner of the used car salesman. One of the men that had raped him.

Cindy kissed Gunner and he kissed her back. It was uncomfortable and more like a nibble than an actual kiss. She purred accordingly. He closed his eyes because he already knew how it was going to end.

Cindy had peeled off his white undershirt. He was covered in cheap tattoos. The kind that a man would get in prison or maybe even the military. Cindy didn't care which, it meant danger and it turned her on even more. His body was hard and chiseled. She could feel years of muscle tissues as she traced ornate striations across his body.

Gunner squeezed his eyes. He was taking painful strides to concentrate and try to get where he needed to go.

But it was too late.

Cindy had already started to tug on his belt. She reached for his cock and then gave the 'disappointed look' that Gunner dreaded but expected.

She cupped his flaccid package and began to gently massage it.

"Want me to suck your dick? I don't usually go down on ..."

Someone that I'm not actually with. Gunner had finished the rest in his mind simultaneously. He wondered if women knew how often this sentence prefaced a blow job.

Gunner sat on the bed frustrated and abashed.

"Did I do something wrong?"

Gunner shook his head.

"Wanna watch a porno or something?"

Gunner shook his head. "It isn't your fault ... it's mine. It's me."

"I used to be a nurse's assistant. I know how to stick my finger up there and stimulate your prostate gland—"

Gunner cut her off, "I'm good,"

Cindy went to touch the conspicuous scar under his eye. From the angle she was sitting it looked like a fleshy teardrop.

"Did something, like, happen to you?" she said.

Gunner winced and swatted away her hand from his scar.

"I think I should get going now," he said.

"Hon, it's okay. A lot of us are damaged. Especially in the rooms. We can work on it ... together. We're in this together."

"We just met."

"But we're the exact frickin' same! Promise. I can't get off either. I can't cum. We're the same."

Gunner shook his head, knowing how truly wrong she was.

Gunner had seen his mother sexually humiliated in front of him many times before he was old enough to understand what it meant. There was the Armenian landlord that would bend her over the kitchen counter and insist that Gunner watch him fuck her when she was late on rent. This was when he was seven or eight.

And then there were innumerable rapes and molestations.

After Gunner's mother died, he had spent the remainder of his childhood and adolescence in state-run facilities. He was already labeled oppositional defiant as an eleven-year-old. This was the precursor to antisocial behavioral disorder or sociopathy. Gunner had an extremely strong adversity towards authority figures.

He had been placed in a foster home a couple of times. He tried to stab one of his foster parents because he claimed that they were Satanic. He set fire to another couple's home, claiming they were trying to sell his organs on the black market. He was just being a kid! He was deemed violent and an unusual threat to the community at such a young age.

The most problematic children are raised by the state in extremely poor conditions. He was raped a few times in these institutions but eventually started fighting back. He used a makeshift knife to slit the throat of a perverted staff member.

He was incarcerated in juvenile hall and later California's Youth Authority, which was the equivalent of a combative and dangerous adult prison. In many ways CYA was worse. Juvenile thugs lacked the principles of adult convicts and acts of violence were much more arbitrary.

He got into methamphetamines as a teenager. The group of teens that used speed had a lower set of social standards than other people his age.

Gunner was accepted because he was quiet and incredibly intimidating. His reputation preceded him. He had slit the throat of an adult that tried to sodomize him. This made him a local legend amongst the bad kids.

Gunner won fist fights and backed up his friends in full-out brawls. They went around shoplifting from stores and vandalizing properties for fun. Crystal meth had allowed him to appear more sociable and outgoing.

He dropped out of high school like most of his friends. Everyone was signing up for the military because they knew they'd be spending their years in state penitentiaries if they just stayed in their hometown committing petty crimes and smoking meth.

Gunner had accumulated felonies as a minor and he was precluded from joining the army.

But then it all changed instantly.

The entire country was galvanized when terrorists hijacked commercial airlines, killing themselves, along with a large amount of innocent people, after intentionally crashing into the World Trade Center and Pentagon.

We were going to war.

The army was waving minors' records and low-level crimes.

The military had started out as a relatively positive experience for Gunner. Getting off speed and away from his dead-end friends had allowed him to flourish. He was one of the superstars in basic training. He hardly talked and he had "that goddamn retard strength" as his drill sergeant had called it.

At eighteen, he was in a military airplane headed across the world, staring mindlessly out of the oval-shaped window ... seeing the true expansiveness of the globe for the very first time in his limited life.

But war is hell. Real fucking hell.

Gunner had fallen from a helicopter and subsequently pissed blood for a month. He had watched a member of his platoon (a friend) get shot at close-range; his head splintered into a gory stump right in front of his eyes.

He realized that real violence looked fake.

Fake violence wasn't bloody enough.

Television and films couldn't possibly convey the penny-well, manure stench of a massacre.

The paranoia was omnipresent on both sides of the

war. How many times did the boys see a car bomb mangle someone's face and render it uglier than a ghoulish Halloween mask?

Too many to count, that was for sure.

They would constantly check their peripherals like crack fiends. Gunner and his friends would venture into Pakistan and pay for pussy. They did this to sustain their sanity. This is how Gunner started smoking meth again. Although he had been raised in the sleazy shadows of the drug world, he was now worldly enough to know that doing drugs, especially while he was committed to fighting for America, could be perceived as a weakness and would be looked down upon.

He kept the meth-use to himself.

There were always young Pakistani men that would lead Gunner and the rest of his squad through a courtyard to the brothels. Children would kick cans down the dusty pathway and pirate-looking men would be playing cards, smoking skinny rolled cigarettes.

One day, after he had sex with a Pakistani prostitute, he saw her smoking out of a thin speed pipe. From the rich chemical smell, he could tell that it was potent. He had asked her if he could have some and she surrendered the pipe as if she had done something wrong.

He showed one of the short pudgy Pakistani men outside in the courtyard. He nodded at Gunner, very professionally, and pulled a decent size bag of meth from his pocket. Gunner paid him in U.S. dollars. As he was leaving, he saw the man backhand slap the woman.

Gunner knew that he had gotten her in trouble.

Oh well, he was used to shit like that.

The war had been incredibly scary, and speed offered him a portal to escape. The real trick was finding times to smoke it alone when he was back at the barracks with the rest of the boys.

The days in the sweltering desert were draining and the men always welcomed 'lights out' so they could fade into thin and temporary cocoons.

There was a concert of throaty snoring and nasal exhaust. Gunner would tip-toe to the corner of the barrack. He found that the best system for covert meth-smoking was to light a candle. This allowed him to block the light by towering over the flame and only using it when he had to heat the spinning puddle of the pipe's center.

Gunner got this system down and would smoke by himself at night. The crystal meth in Pakistan came from Dubai and was some of the cleanest he had ever smoked. He didn't know it then, but he was smoking peanut butter crank — which had become a delicacy in the states. He stayed up for many days in a row, the paranoia of the surrounding war had fleeted temporarily; instead, he spent his time within his head: the hyper-loop of memories, mostly about his mother.

Then one night everything changed in a literal flash.

The sound reminded him of a bottle rocket, a thunderous roar trailed by an intense sizzle.

The bunker had been hit by a bomb.

The candle went out.

Gunner didn't even know how long he had been up, but it was long enough that it was already difficult to discern between reality and audible misfires in his mind.

His heartbeat whined in his ears.

The dust suffocating in the pitch darkness.

He had no idea how close the enemies were. He needed to remain quiet. They were probably right outside.

He lay still like a possum, but his thoughts were dizzied
by notions of fight or flight.

And he was tweaking, after all.

It was impossible for Gunner to know how much time
had gone by. There were no windows in the bunker and
meth has a funny way of making time stand still entirely.
He thought everyone had died instantly, that smoking
meth in the corner over the candle had saved him. *And I'd
also like to thank methamphetamine for making it possible
for me to be here tonight. Thank you speed.*
He had crawled on the floor at some point and felt a
liquid that he assumed was paint, it had the exact same
consistency; he had always really loved hand painting in
foster care, rubbing the paint across the paper, making
awesome shapes.

He followed the trail in the dark.

It led him to what he thought to be an amputated human arm. It fucking stunk. It was impossible to tell what
it was without light. He felt fuzzy hair but there wasn't
a hand attached; that's what threw him off. He pulled at
dangling scraps at its end. It came off easily, like chicken
skin, and that's what made him realize he was pinching off
stringy flesh from an arm.

The violent thought made him vomit.

He had followed a trail of blood.

He heard the first whisper when he was hunched over. It had startled him because he clearly heard someone say, "Mommy!"

For a moment, he thought he heard chanting.

Gunner didn't know who or where. He was dehydrated. He had been awake for a few days, perhaps longer. He was certain he had heard "Mommy" and he felt oddly comforted by it.

"Ma?" he said, weakly.

Nothing.

He would occasionally brush against rubbery gore and squirm as he crawled over bodies in the direction of the whispering.
It made him sick to his stomach. He finally found a flashlight and fumbled to turn it on.

Everything was worse than he had imagined.

There was a disturbing collage of butchered torsos, imploded skulls like abandoned lobotomies, and body parts sprayed across the destroyed bunker in a bloodied tornado of twisted carnage.

Perhaps a penis pie, too.

The whispers became clearer and turned on him, "Gregory, your mother is a no-good whore!"

He heard the chanting now. He heard it.

This scared him. He tried to turn the flashlight off ... but it went on strobe-mode by mistake.

The light flickered rapidly as the whispers and hums became a shrieking crescendo.

"We fucked your mother, Greg-ory. She loved it! She's an entire snake pit of diseases!"
The pulsating of the flashlight, the nightmarish images, and the screams about his worthless whore of a mother all hit him simultaneously — in some hellacious disco rhythm.[4]

Gunner was exposed to the nihilism of his drug addicted mother ... He witnessed the unspeakable ... He suffered marathon sexual, emotional, mental, physical, and spiritual abuse ... And found his only family hanging from the ceiling.
But it was the tornadic horrors of meth psychosis in Iraq ... up for multiple days ... deceased members of his platoon haunting him from butchered limbs ...

That had finally been too much.

PTSD rendered his dick useless.

USELESS!

Impotence = incidents.

---

4   A nude seizure in the fiery pits of hell.

2

THE JOURNALS

HOLLYWOOD, CA 2017

"That, I realized, is the great beauty of dreams: the devil may inevitably find a way to jerk you off, but you can always wake up before he makes you cum." – Jim Carroll

Mikey May woke up suddenly. He couldn't remember exactly but his heart thudded, he knew that he had escaped from some cruel and vicious nightmare.

His girlfriend's arm was draped over him. It was pale, mottled with track marks and lumps. She was cold. He pushed her, with more force than he intended, she folded and rolled easily off the motel bed.

He jumped down and kneeled over her listless body. He touched her face and pulled away in a flash — as if he had been zapped by electricity.

Her skin seemed colder than before.

Mikey was naked.

He crouched over her, groaning panicked babble. He looked around the motel room. There were stolen DVDs everywhere; hypodermic syringes, empty pizza boxes, junk food ...

"Jessica!" He screamed, "What did you do?"

He continued to survey the motel room and then he saw

the candle. It was on a dresser below a television mounted to the wall. The wick was lit. Globs of wax had melted and cascaded down into a deformed mess at its base. They bought these candles at the 99-cent store and used them to cook heroin on metallic spoons. Junkies called them "hourglass candles" because they took exactly one hour to melt all the way down.

She must have woken up and decided to do it. They had argued the night before. They could do their shots before bed and figure it out in the morning. Or they could wait until the morning, do their shots then, take the stolen DVDs to the pawn shop, and go and score their dope comfortably.

Mikey was the introverted of the two. He was the planner. He approached their heroin addiction and theft routine as systematically as an accountant. Jessica pigged out. From an outside perspective she always seemed more optimistic ("Don't worry. We'll figure it out."), but in truth there was never enough heroin on the planet to satiate her obscene appetite. So whatever logic she presented was always to do as much as possible in the moment; never seeming to understand the consequence or implications of poor planning when you have a four gram a day habit.

Calling 911 was pointless.[5]

She never had a good complexion and her pock marks looked hideous against her pallid, trout-blue skin.

Her lips had faded to a ghastly, ripe purple.

She wasn't breathing.

---

5   There's a small window after an opiate overdose, where someone goes into respiratory arrest, shallow breathing can be saved by CPR or an antagonist medication like Narcan (Naxoxone) — but that window is 20 minutes at the most.

He used his thumb to open her eyelid and saw a butter-scotched iris, a very distant yellow, as if infected puss had rendered her eyeballs a sickly, lifeless mess.

She was dead.

Mikey placed two fingers on each of his temples. He applied pressure for a moment, he wanted to shut his thoughts up. He was just starting to feel dope sick, it was very mild, but the anxiety reverberated achingly throughout his mind. He closed his eyes and squinted again, but his racing thoughts refused to be hushed. The horrific discovery of his dead girlfriend and the taunting inevitability of withdrawal was enough to make anyone snap.

He needed something.

He walked up to the candle and inspected the bent spoon laying on the mantle. Jessica was always a sloppy user, the kind that would hastily prepare her dope and often leave enough on the spoon for another, equal sized shot.

But she seemed to have had purpose. There was hardly anything left on the spoon. There was a small, crunched up piece of cotton. It looked charred, stained with dark goo from the Mexican black tar they had been shooting for the last eighteen months. There was enough to do a shot, it wasn't going to get Mikey high; but it would help keep the withdrawal heebie-jeebies at bay for just a little longer.

He refused to look at Jessica's discolored body on the floor.

Mikey was at the point of his addiction where it was nearly impossible to find a vein. He started stabbing and prodding himself with the 29-gauge insulin syringe. It was dull and barbed, which made it even more difficult. There was nothing on his hands; although they looked caked in dirt, it was dried blood from making holes with the needle and not being able to find a vein to inject his dope into.

He propped his leg up. He felt around. He had sores; most had been calloused into island-shaped scar tissue. Just poking the needle in was excruciating. He finally tilted his head toward the mirror and examined his jugular vein. It had an even track on it, a dark line that went all the way up to his face. He stuck his finger in his mouth and watched his neck halfway inflate, just enough to poke at an area that looked the least used. He jammed his dull needle into the jugular vein and could see blood blossom in the barrel of the syringe; the blood looked a bit too bright, it was a cartoon-shade of red. This was the sign of an artery.[6] That's the one way you could tell: the brightness of the blood.

It was hard for Mikey to hold his breath. He was a heavy cigarette smoker. He decided to push the plunger down anyway.

He knew immediately that he had hit an artery.

There was a boiling sting, a fiery rush coursing through his throat and head. He instinctually tossed the syringe. Mikey screamed in agony. He fell on the floor, got in the fetal position, his eyes rolled back into his head, possessed by insidious pain.

If you hit an artery on a limb, that pain essentially goes all the way to its front, a hand or a foot. Blotches of white skin appear; it looks like the beginning of a terrible burn, but the rash subsides eventually. Your feet or hands take on an animal balloon quality, swelling up wildly.

Mikey always told Jessica that Pink Floyd was talking

---

6   YOU DO NOT WANT TO INJECT ILLICIT NARCOTICS OR ANYTHING FOR THAT MATTER INTO YOUR ARTERIES!

about the same "swollen hand blues" they would get from accidentally hitting their arteries.

There was no way of knowing if that was true. Mikey told Jessica a lot of shit that wasn't true, just for the fun of it. Their junkie lives were that monotonous.

Mikey had never hit an artery by the throat. He saw spots and then total darkness.

He crouched up slowly, he found it difficult to find mid-balance in total darkness.

"I'm blind!" he screamed "I'm goddamn blind!"

He started crying furiously. He thought about how ridiculous the motel room must look: him naked screaming about going blind, Jessica, also nude, dead from an overdose on the ground. The typical wasteland of gas station food and drug paraphernalia surrounding them.

"I'm fucking blind!" He screamed again but they were at the kind of spot where it was 24-hour chaos. Shouting, music blasting, arguments, fucking, fighting, and everything else you could imagine. It was the kind of motel where the silent rooms were suspicious and creepy.

Nobody cared.

There was way worse shit being yelled than "I'm blind."

It was too much for Mikey, he began to stumble, with animistic flight across the room until he hit his head against the mirror. It cracked but it didn't shatter. Mikey's forehead bled immediately from a deep cut. He ignored it, instead he felt for the sink faucet and turned on the hot water. He doused his face. Shook his head. Still darkness. He cried once more. But he continued to submerge as much of his head as possible into the warm sink water. Warm compressions help take bulging abscesses down, so perhaps the heat would have the same effect.

At this moment, he wanted to commit suicide.

Jessica was dead. He was blind. It was hard to imagine their life could get any worse the day before but it, like, really fell apart today.

This was a new low for them.

The idea of killing himself soothed him.

Suddenly he was very tired. He lowered himself to the bathroom floor and curled up, drifting into a deep, immediate sleep.

When Mikey woke up, he was still on the floor. Again, his heart thudding, and he knew he had forgotten some bad dream. The events leading up to his crashing were so outlandish, they didn't even feel real, he thought about them, he could see just fine now, he smirked, and then he saw Jessica's dead body: ghostly, gaunt. He was back in reality. His head throbbed. He grimaced, sensitive to the light.

He rose to his feet and used his hand to shield his face from the cheap motel lamp. He walked over to where he had thrown the syringe and picked it up. He had no idea how long he had been passed out. But he had never felt this kind of headache. His brain felt like it had been stabbed by a jagged icicle, painful shivers pulsating throughout the inside of his head.

The barrel of the syringe was filled with blood. He pressed the plunger, nothing came out.

It was stuck. The blood had coagulated.

This was a recurring issue for an IV addict, sometimes you pull the trigger up to see if the blood registers, just because you see blood, doesn't mean that the needle is securely in the vein. It can be a balancing act and there's angles that need to be maintained. It's easy to become dislodged and then you miss the shot. The effects are much milder than mainlining.[7]

And it stings and creates scar tissues that essentially hides and destroys veins. Abscesses are a frequent consequence from missing a shot.

Mikey was sick. Jessica was dead. His head felt like it had been bludgeoned. And now this: he didn't even have a goddamn decent shot.

He pulled the plunger of the syringe off and dumped the clumpy, sludge into the spoon and recooked it. He could see blood clots staying solid in the spoon, but this was all he had and there was no fucking way he wasn't going to do it.

The bloody mixture had a hard time getting drawn up for a second time in the syringe. He wondered how much dope had been lost, coagulated, and recooked. The needle point had become even more barbed and it was almost impossible to stick it in any potential vein; Mikey was tearing holes in his arms, hands, and legs, thick blood rolling out of each failed attempt. It was a voodoo doll massacre above the sink, smeared blood making a horror movie mess across the counter. He was out of strength.

He snapped the needle off, and ripped his pants down, using the barrel and plunger to boof the shot.[8]

The anal membranes act as one of the biggest veins in the human body. It isn't painful.

But it's demeaning. After everything, he simply surrendered, bent over and boofed the coagulated shot up his ass.

He felt nothing just as he had suspected.

There may have been a slight placebo, but his eyes watered from a barrage of yawns. This was the onset of heroin

---

7   Injecting directly into a working vein.
8   This is when you push the drugs into your asshole.

withdrawal. He tried not to look at Jessica. He didn't want to look at her.

He didn't want it to be real.

Mikey lay on the bed and turned on the television. It was some flashy, Hollywood inside scoop show; all the glitz and glamor to hypnotize him into utter mindlessness.

There were two hard knocks on the door. No housekeeping announcement. Possibly police or a probation/parole sweep. Mikey froze. There was the body, which was obviously a major issue because he never called 911. It would be challenging to explain the situation.

But there were also the stolen DVDs. Those were a big deal at that moment, especially for Mikey May. They were really cracking down on petty theft and he had been busted on eight separate occasions. The last time he stood in front of the judge they had consolidated all the charges into a felony grand theft case. The judge wanted to give him one year for each incident. He ultimately gave him drug classes, that Mikey of course failed, and an eight-year suspended prison sentence. This meant if Mikey was arrested one more time, especially with his signature stolen DVDs, they were going to send him straight to a hardcore California penitentiary. He already had a warrant so if it was police on the other side of that door he was completely fucked.

He didn't respond, he slowly got off the bed and threw a sheet over Jessica's corpse. He then tiptoed to the bathroom. He was appalled when he saw his own face. It had a much bigger gash on his forehead than he realized; when he had blindly run into the mirror, and his eyes, presumably from hitting the artery, were now completely red. They had the same color as Campbell's tomato soup. But they weren't just blood shot — they were blood soaked and enlarged. The gash on his face and the demonic eyes made him look ridiculous — like some cheap, morbid villain.

There was another knock.

"Yeah?" Mikey asked

There was nothing.

Mikey walked to the door quietly. There was a diamond-shaped peephole. He looked out and saw the owner of the motel, a short Indian man, leaning against the door.

Mikey opened it. The owner looked at his grotesque face and tried hard not to react. But he was clearly startled. Mikey stuck his head out of the tiniest sliver of the door he could leverage, without revealing a glimpse of the inside of the motel room.

"You're late," the man said. "Late by a lot."

"You know my girl's mom always sends the check around the 9th, you're the first person we pay, my guy."

"Mike, it's already the 24th. What do you want to do to me, huh? I have a business. I got family."

"Of course. But like how long we've known each other. We've been here nearly a year. I know sometimes our monthly is late, but you don't got problems from us. You know the money eventually shows up."

"I'm tight right now. I need payment today or I'm going to have to ask you guys to go. I can give you until 11:00 a.m. tomorrow."

"11:00 a.m.! That's what we have been fucking reduced to? We don't even get no special checkout time, bruh. After being in your slummy fuck-wad, fuckhole for a long as we have? We never complained about the dead cockroaches in the coffee machine or the cum stains on the comforter that your housekeepers never cleaned. I felt like I've been fucking my soulmate on top of some crusty jizz-nest for the last year. She deserves satin—shit—we both deserve satin, man."

"Are you fine, Mike? You don't seem fine."

"We never bitched about any of it. You never got no noise complaints, no overdoses, no domestic disturbances, no police ... I'm a model tenant, man. And I gotta check out at eleven in the morning what, like, I'm some fat-faggot businessman hurrying away from his affair?"

"The money today or you check out at eleven. I'm sorry Mike. Hard times it is for all."

"That it?"

The short Indian man just nodded. There was a certain stoic quality to motel owners. They all seemed to have the same, apathetic dark beads for eyes.

There was no soul behind that gaze.

Mikey closed the door. Dope sickness was brewing inside of him. He knew that he had to figure out something quickly. He had been busted stealing DVDs so many times that the store owners dubbed him "the DVD bandit" — there were surveillance photographs taped to several registers around town.

DVDs were his favorite thing to steal because they were small, a new release went for $20, and he could fill a backpack with fifty of them. Jessica would return them and get store credit. They'd wait outside store parking lots and sell the store credit to prospective customers. And most of the local pawn shops took shrink wrapped DVDs.

There was no way Mikey could try to return the DVDs himself. He'd go straight to jail. He had just gotten out a couple of weeks ago. He met a heroin addict named Charlie while he was locked up and they had exchanged numbers. Charlie was a low life and would love an opportunity to hustle up some dope. More importantly, although Mikey had just met him, he was certain he was one of the only people he knew that wouldn't care that there was a dead woman in the motel room.

Mikey found his number written on one of his journals and called it from the motel phone.

Charlie's dad picked up. Charlie was like 37. No shocker there. Mikey explained that he had an easy lick for him. Charlie said he'd be right there.

Mikey still ignored the fact that his girlfriend lay dead, draped by a sheet, on the side of the bed. There wasn't enough heroin in him to numb out the situation but he was caught in a limbo — the dope sick preamble is largely in the mind, a dizzying assault of anxiety; panic to get more dope; knowing comfort can only be achieved by getting more; the terrifying realization that it may be impossible to get more, right-fucking-now; the torturous passage of time... being stuck in a shattered, drafty hour glass ... each heroin-saturated cell in your body swirling down a vortex below your feet, like granules of fuel that incapacitates your body once it runs entirely out.

Mikey wrote feverishly in his journal as he waited for Charlie. The way he had every day of his life since his little brother had vanished. It had been 15 years and Mikey was now 23 but he made a vow to stay in contact with him through the conduit of his journaling.

Scott was a year younger. He worshiped Mikey, who was a fantastic older brother, and would explain everything to Scott. He wrote stream-of-consciousness style before bed or when something major in his life happened; like losing his girlfriend Jessica to a heroin overdose. He internalized his life and as it became more interesting, Mikey knew that someday his journals would be published, and he would be considered one of the most important writers of his generation.

He seemed to lack any other ambition and his wealthy parents would fight with him about it:

"Yeah," his dad said, "and what are you going to do in the real world? The one that requires, you know, money and basic life skills."

Mikey pointed to his stack of journals.

His father bellowed, "Your journals. You're a drug addict. There's nothing more boring than being a drug addict. I look at that stack and I see the hobby of a daydreamer. But you don't have any realistic dreams, Michael. Just the ones that exist in La-La land. Go to trade school. Anything. Go through the damn motions. Prove to me that when I pass, I'm not leaving my fortune to some hippie hedonist."

"Jim Carroll," Mikey said.

"Huh? Who the hell is Jim Carrol?"

"He was a very well-known writer, poet, and musician."

"Big shocker, never heard of the guy."

"They made a movie based on his diary writings.

It was called *The Basketball Diaries*. It starred Leonardo DiCaprio."

"Right, about the basketball kid who ends up letting old homosexuals blow him in bathroom stalls so he can get his dope fix."

"Dad," Mikey began, "if that's all you got out of that film it says a lot more about you than it does about anything else."

"Don't psychoanalyze me. Your hero was a queer prostitute. And it doesn't even shock me. You go out of your way to be edgy, always have. You used to wear your baseball cap backwards like a little punk and now with all the goddamn tattoos. You wonder why you always go to jail. You've said that to me. And the reason is because of your inherent irreverence to class. Scott was the opposite of you. Even as a young kid he was obedient, he respected his parents, something you still haven't quite grasped."

A tear slipped its way out ... Mikey had been high on heroin ... He stuttered, "Don't ... don't talk about Scott ...

don't ..." — and suddenly his sadness combusted into rage, "Fuck you for that!"

Mikey's father got up to leave his room. He adjusted his tie. He rotated a couple kinks out of his neck, and he turned to Mikey, "I wish it would have been you instead of Scott."

It was the most evil and sincere his father had ever looked.

He finished writing and put his journal in his backpack. He had hundreds of journals stashed at his parents' multi-acre property.

Nobody knew the secrets and insights that these journals contained ...

Mikey didn't check on Jessica. He imagined her face had already been uglified like a mummy. And the urgency of scoring more heroin eclipsed any other thought except grabbing his backpack and walking out the motel door.

Charlie was in the parking lot. He was driving, what was obvious to Mikey, his mom's soccer minivan. He was bumping Smash Mouth and flashing a big goofy grin at Mikey. This trap house motel was occupied mostly by *eses*, killers, prostitutes, drug dealers, and perverts. The sight of this dumb motherfucker singing "All Star" in a minivan reeked; like he was law enforcement or a target to get robbed — Mikey didn't want to be associated with either of those profiles and quickly got in the van.

Mikey had come to realize that a lot of dorks with large and intimidating statures inhabit county jails and prisons. Charlie was generally quiet, there was pain and misery in his demeanor. He had sun bleached blonde hair and his skin was perpetually tan in an unhealthy way. This was a common trait amongst convicts who spend years, if not decades, frying their unprotected skin out on prison yards.

There were moments when Charlie would try to be funny, like singing Smash Mouth. But they were always embarrassing and missed deliveries. He was an awkward tough guy. He told Mikey he had been adopted within the first five minutes of meeting him. He also saw Charlie break an inmate's jaw for playing a prank and throwing cold water on Charlie when he was in the shower. He got out, completely naked, dick out, and upper cut the guy that did it.

Mikey had never seen his jaw split in three places, blood burst out messily, and there was a triptych of bone fragments protruding from his chin, cheek, and upper lip.

It was one of stranger things Mikey had seen throughout his incarcerations. There's something about naked brutality that you can never forget.

"So what's the lick, comrade?" Charlie asked.

"You don't really talk like that when you ain't locked up right?"

"Only to comrades, comrade."

They exchanged smiles for different reasons.

"I'm like dying right now," Mikey said, "You sick?"

"I'm okay. I did a cotton like an hour ago. It seems to be holding me. So what's up man, for real? What's this plan?"

"Easy ass little come up, man." Mikey started pulling DVDs out of his backpack. "You just gotta return these. Get store credit. We'll sell it to someone on the parking lot and I'll make the call to the Devil"

"The fuck's 'the Devil'?"

"I don't know, my connection, some fat pisca," explained Mikey. I call him 'the Devil' because he's got a tattoo of the devil and I don't remember his real name. But his shit's good. $60 a gram. Cheap."

"Why don't you call him the beaner then?"

"Because I call him 'the Devil'," Mikey said, "That's why."

"And all I gotta do is return them DVDs there?"

"That's all you gotta do, comrade."

"I don't gotta beat nobody up on Christmas Eve; I think J.C. would approve."

Awkward joke. Mikey didn't laugh. He was struck with momentary sadness. He didn't realize it was the day before Christmas. Jessica and Mikey had a toxic relationship, but they were both big on holidays because they had strained relationships with their respective families. They usually couldn't afford to do much for each other. They'd eat at a place like Chili's and go back to whatever motel they were staying at, take MDMA, watch porn, and fuck all night.

It was tradition.

Charlie came back brandishing the store credit receipt like it was a winning lottery ticket.

"It fucking worked!" He exclaimed.

"Of course. I keep my habit going from boosting DVDs specifically. Let me get the receipt. I'm gonna go turn it into cash."

"Wait, how do I know you ain't gonna just take off with the money?"

"You fuckin' serious right now?"

Charlie considered this for a moment and apprehensively handed him the receipt. It showed Mikey that Charlie wasn't to be trusted.

Shady people always have the most irrational trust issues.

"Be back in like five ... Don't trip."

The receipt was $100. He was hoping to get $80 so that he could get two grams from The Devil. Heroin is sold in 'packs' — meaning the more grams you get, the cheaper the dope. A single gram is $60 but a two pack is $80. Jessica and Mikey were doing four grams a day — so sometimes they did the DVD thing twice. Mikey figured he'd just give Charlie a gram for running around and doing this with him and he'd be happy. He could figure out the rest once he could think straight.

It didn't take Mikey long to find someone that was willing to give them cash for the credit. It was a young Asian kid that said he was going to spend $100 anyway, so he just gave Mikey the full hundred.

It was the first luck he caught that day.

Charlie was shocked that he was able to get the money that quickly. And now they had enough money for cigarettes and fast food. Mikey sold his phone a few weeks before when he was in the heat of a crack addiction clearance sale. It will strip you of all your material possessions quicker than any other drug. He used Charlie's phone and the Devil's number went straight to voicemail. This was very unlike him. He could see the panic rising in Charlie when he realized it wasn't going through.

"Voicemail — fuck — He never does that, either. I don't think his phone has ever been off."

"What are we gonna do then, slickster?" Charlie asked.

"You don't got a connect?"

Charlie shook his head. Another red flag: what heroin addict doesn't have a heroin dealer?

Mikey tried again and it went to voicemail.

"I got another guy but it's more expensive. I honestly don't care about paying more. I'm sick as fuck."

Charlie nodded, "Yes. Call."

Mikey dialed the number and Andy picked up.

"Hellllooooo?"

"Andy, it's Mikey."

"No way! How's my favorite hot, tan dude?"

Charlie whispered, "He a fag?"

Mikey nodded.

Andy had an almost exaggerated lisp.

"Sick, Andy. Real sick, dude."

"Sick enough to get buttfucked? Joking! Joking!"

Charlie grimaced and Mikey thought about him singing Smash Mouth and rolled his eyes.

"No buttfucking today, bud. What can you do for $100?"

"I'm doing grams for a hundred."

"Damn, Andy, my other guy is doing G's for $60."

"Then go to him, this ain't no fucking swap meet Mikey. Besides it's powder. It's worth it. Trust a fly bitch."

Charlie whispered, "Dude just called himself a bitch?"

Mikey nodded at Charlie and put a finger to his own mouth, "Where do you want to meet?"

Charlie made a perplexed look.

"Come on, you know where. I'll be there in 30."

Mikey hung up and told Charlie to go find a parking lot to kill some time. The mind is powerful, just knowing he was going to get something quelled his nerves, he was finally able to stop squirming and sit still in the passenger seat.

"So, uh, we're buying dope off some faggot, man?"

"Yeah, but he's cool. He's always got good shit."

"What kind of faggot is cool?"

"This one I guess."

"He ain't never tried and gave you a hummer or whatever?"

"No, dude. Andy's cool. He's just a normal guy and knows I'm straight."

"Let's rob the cake boy. Shit, we can make it like he doesn't even know you're in on it."

"Why don't you have your own hookup?"

Charlie laughed, "Cuz I jacked all of em'."

"Exactly. Andy doesn't push crazy weight or anything. I bet he doesn't even have a six pack on him. He smokes the shit off tin foil, flips a little on the side to smoke for free. Not even worth it."

"Hey, man, you brought me in on this, you're getting me high, it's whatever. It's cool. But if you change your mind and you wanna take that queer's dope, I'm with it. I have a .38 in the trunk."

"Fuck, really. I have a warrant."

"It's all good brother, as do I. As do I."

They were both covered in cheap, ashy looking tattoos.

Cops can spot prison tattoo work a mile away. Mikey's dad was right about that. For a second, Mikey had almost forgotten that poor Jessica had died that morning and her body was still at the motel. He wasn't worried about getting in trouble over it. He was just sad, or as sad as a brain running on mere dopamine fumes could possibly be.

The more Mikey was around Charlie the more he didn't trust him or like his energy. Charlie had never mentioned Mikey's appearance: the huge gash across his face and his bloody eyes. They had been in county jail together just a few weeks before and Mikey looked drastically different. The fact that he wanted to rob Andy, the homophobia, the skinhead slang Charlie just wasn't his type or guy. He preferred the more emo-type, wanna slit my wrist because my daddy yelled at me, variety.

The tough guys were exhausting to get high with.

Mikey directed Charlie to the mall where he always met Andy. It was the same routine: walk through the mall to the other side and Andy would pick him up and drop him off on the other side. This way he had a full peripheral vantage point and could see if he was being set up or followed by cops.

Andy drove a new Range Rover and was dressed in preppy clothes. He looked nothing like a heroin dealer. He was a crystal meth smoking gay kid, hypnotized my constant paranoia, but safe and always managed to fly under the radar. He didn't like to make talk when they were in the vehicle because he feared wires and listening devices. He was playing some sort of Euro house music that Mikey thought sucked.

Andy pulled up to a curb to let Mikey out. And before he drove away, he signaled for him to walk back to the driver's seat. He handed him a small folded up paper package. Mikey already got the heroin from him, so he was confused.

Andy smirked and said, "Merry Christmas. I'm hip to y'all's get down."

And then he drove off. Mikey unfolded the paper and saw two capsules full of the white powder — MDMA — Andy remembered Jessica and Mikey's Christmas ecstasy tradition and for the first time Mikey cried. The dope sickness had almost eroded entirely once he had the baggie in his hand, terrifying anxiety no longer disorienting his thoughts.

It was a real cry. She was really gone.

He composed himself. He knew Charlie couldn't see him like this. For all he knew: Charlie was already planning on robbing him. He got in the van.

"You get it?" Charlie asked.

"Of course. Do you have water?"

Charlie looked in the back of the van and felt down by his feet. He shook his head. There was a McDonald's right in front of them, so they went to the drive through and asked for a free cup of water. This always elicits a strange response from the Macdonald's workers. They do as they are told but you can see judgment, from their placid, emotionless eyes.

They got the water and went and found a parking spot.

Charlie had insulin syringes and a spoon in his glove box. Andy wasn't lying. It was the good kind of Coachella heroin; considered the best in all of California. It's Earth brown but when you blow on it or add heat it turns to a glassy black. This heroin had killed people Mikey knew so he was encouraged that it would be an impressive quality.

Mikey dumped a decent amount on the spoon and spit some of the McDonald's water. He was an expert at estimating the right amount of water. Some junkies measure it with the syringe, but Mikey was way too impatient for that. He placed the flame of the lighter under the spoon and watched the dope sizzle and bubble, the wafting aroma of vinegar filling the van. The smell was pungent. Mikey broke a cigarette filter off and took a piece of the cotton out, placing in the spoon.[9] Charlie and Mikey drew up healthy shots, usually black tar was black in the barrel of the syringe, but this dope came back an oily gold; a testament to its purity, as its water soluble and darker coloring is indicative of adulterants.

Charlie was able to hit on the first or second try, on one of his bigger veins in the crook of his arms, a sign he hadn't been doing IV drugs for very long. Mikey had to shoot up in his crotch, legs, neck, arm pit, etc. Only obscure and painful options were left for Mikey. He found a small vein on the underbelly of his wrist, always sketchy because it's like a minefield of arteries and fragile veins. It hurts and you must press the shot in very slowly or it will blow the vein out ... but he got it. Pins and needles fluttered through his body orgasmically, there was a cozy rush of warmth, and his racing thoughts scattered back into whatever echoing chamber they were screaming from.

"Damn, little buddy." Charlie said, "Whoa now."[10]

"It's good. I know."

"I need a piece. I gotta have a piece of this. This is the best fucking *chiva* I've ever done, man. I'll pay top dollar. Find out how much a piece."

Mikey was hesitant to call Andy back. He didn't trust Charlie and he didn't want anything bad to happen to Andy. A piece was 25 grams. If Andy was selling grams for $100, the pieces were probably well over a thousand. Mikey couldn't imagine Charlie having that kind of money. But

---

9   The cotton is so that the tip of the needle doesn't hit the metal of the spoon because it will barb it instantly. A barbed needle makes the shots less precise and much more painful.

10   Red flag 5: involuntary Elvis impersonations.

Mikey thought of the guy who had gotten his jaw broken in three places, the bloody sliver of bone that had torn his lip wide open.

He called him. Andy was naturally spooked. It's always suspicious to meet up with a drug dealer and then call them fifteen minutes later asking for 25 times the amount you got the first time.

"I got some Christmas money," Mikey said, "I was thinking of saving myself some money this holiday season and wanted a full one."

"$800," Andy said. Mikey nodded. It wasn't on speaker, and he was glad because that was a price that was realistic. Junkie optimism kicked in and he thought Charlie's parents might have money. He couldn't base their entire portfolio on Smash Mouth and minivans.

"You have a room?" Andy asked.

"Yeah."

"It's too much to bring to the mall. And it's going to be a little while. I'd have to go get it. But I can do it if you want it."

Mikey whispered a thousand to Charlie and he gave a thumbs up. Mikey told Andy it was on. They had to kill some time, so they ended up going back to Mikey's motel.

"Charlie, I forgot to tell you about my chick."

Charlie chuckled, "I didn't know you liked girls."

"She's dead."

"What you mean? You bone dead girls?"

"No. I mean she fucking went out on me. Died."

"When?"

"This morning."

"The fuck?"

"I didn't want you freaking out when we got there."

"What? Your dead old lady is at your motel room!"

"Yeah, I was sick. I wasn't gonna deal with that shit sick. You know?"

"You realize how much of a bust going to that room is for us?"

"Nah, man. People OD there every day. Someone got stabbed to death the other night and the cops only showed up for a noise complaint. Dude was screaming as he lay in a pool of his own blood. Buncha people saw it and cops only got called cuz he was dying too loud. Place is off the hook. Got nothing to worry about."

Charlie was shaking his head.

"There's a sheet around her. Nobody goes in the room. We can shoot dope safely. And Andy will only do a full piece like that somewhere private. I already told him I had this room."

"You are a crazy, crazy bastard!" Charlie said.

They got to the motel room and Charlie felt better. There was a topless girl pepper spraying a pizza delivery guy on the first floor.

Mikey wasn't lying; mayhem was common.

When they got in the room Mikey looked over and saw Jessica covered in the sheet. It made him feel queasy, because it was a dead human body of someone he was in love with and because of the flippancy he approached the situation with earlier. And now he was having company over. This was the kind of barbaric disregard for human value that serial killers surely felt.

Charlie pointed, "That her, man?"

"No, it's some other random dead woman I have in here."

"Damn, for reals?"

"No! Jesus. Would you hang out with some dude that had multiple dead women in his motel?"

"Depends, I guess. If they had money and dope. I'm not gonna hate on the lifestyle, know what I mean?"

"I can't even look at her. Love of my life, man."

Charlie walked up and knelt above Jessica's body, he lifted the sheet slowly, "Goddamn!"

"What?" Mikey asked.

"This bitch is bad! Shame. Hot ass little body on her ..."

Mikey exhaled and didn't respond. Charlie disgusted him. He just wanted to get as far away from him as possible, but he was also tired. He didn't feel like boosting more DVDs or finding someone to return them. Charlie buying 25 grams was the best-looking prospect for keeping his habit fed.

He could figure out the rest tomorrow.

"You got the rack for the piece?"

"It's in the van."

Charlie could tell Mikey didn't believe he had the money.

"What, you want me to show you that I got a thousand bucks?"

"We just have to have it counted out before he gets here. He's paranoid and doesn't like a lot of conversation. How much will you break me off for hooking it up for you?"

"I don't know, a half gram or some shit."

"A half gram! That some kinda inside Nazi joke? That won't even get me to the morning."

"Relax little buddy. I'll give you a few. Three grams seems fair for all the energy it took to make a two-minute phone call for me."

Mikey closed his eyes and nodded.

Charlie left the motel room and went down to his van to get the money. Mikey was surprised that he had it in an envelope.

"I got a union job, man."

Mikey went to the nightstand and picked up the motel phone. He called Andy and told him that he was ready and which motel room they were in.

Andy said he'd be there in fifteen minutes.

Mikey and Charlie did another shot while they were waiting. Charlie hitting his vein easily and Mikey almost in tears, poking himself frantically, looking for any trace of blood. He could smoke it, but it wasn't the same. He could shoot the shot right into his muscle, but it left painful lumps. He wasn't good about picking up new syringes, so he got a lot of abscesses.

Sometimes he'd have to go to the hospital and get them lanced. It was an incredibly painful process. Some judgmental nurse, nearly always judgmental, would inject a local anesthetic into the infected area with a horse-sized needle, the abscess would already be pulsating from the pressure of puss and bacteria under the skin, a large needle going into those multiple times was horrific. Mikey would scream as the nurse used a scalpel and cut an incision, painfully squeezing the puss out until it was completely drained, and then using tweezers to pack the abscess with strips of sterile gauze. He had scars all over his body from these procedures. He tried to be as steady as possible, not to miss the shot, but lately he'd been more reckless. He just wanted to numb himself out. He didn't care if he got another abscess. He found a vein in between his middle and index finger and pressed the plunger slowly so it wouldn't blow the vein out.

Mikey resented people like Charlie who were newer to their addiction and still had mostly painless options of places to shoot up into. He looked at Charlie, he was picking his nose and flicking boogers onto the wall next to the bed. These were the kind of places and people that addiction invariably exposed him to.

There was a knock on the door. Mikey went up and checked the peephole. He saw Andy holding a Chinese food bag and he let him in.

Andy's eyes immediately darted to Charlie. He was intimidating, even cozy and half-conscience on the bed.

Charlie got up and took the envelope out of his pocket.

"A grand, right?" Charlie asked, he was towering over Andy, five inches taller than him at least.

Andy nodded and gave a displeased look to Mikey. He knew the rules. There wasn't supposed to be dialogue during their transactions.

Mikey shrugged.

Charlie fanned out the money — ten hundred-dollar bills. "Now let me see what I'm getting."

"You guys just did it. It's the same," Andy said.

"I don't know you. It's a lotta money for me to be spending. Put it on the table and let me just make sure everything is copacetic. Seems like a fuckin' reasonable request to me."

Andy was becoming more visibly frustrated. But he started towards the table, he didn't see Jessica's body on the floor, and he tripped over her, he fell to the ground, and her head poked out of the sheet. She was ghostly white, golden spittle caked around her mouth, eyes open — that butterscotch death color, eyeballs more swollen now. Andy was horrified, "What ... the hell ... is this?"

"She went out this morning. I was sick all day and couldn't deal with any of this shit until I got right. It's okay."

Andy's voice was trembling, "Oh my gawd. She's dead Mikey! Wrapped in a goddamn sheet! What did you guys do?"

Charlie pulled a .38 from his waistline and pistol-whipped Andy. He connected to his cheek, and it collapsed instantly from the impact.

Andy wavered a little bit before falling on top of Jessica's body. Blood was everywhere, splattered on the white sheet and puddling quickly on the floor next to his head.

"What are you doing?" Mikey screamed.

"He was throwing a hissy fit as if we had killed her. What was I supposed to do? I ain't going to prison over your lady dying because this tweaking faggot got spooked out."

"So, you just kill him?"

Andy was making strange facial twitches. It looked like he was trying to sneeze; his face contorted from pain, disbelief.

Charlie walked up and bludgeoned him three more times with the butt-end of the gun. He groaned until there was a gurgling sound and then ...

Complete silence.

Andy's face was now unrecognizable, replaced by pulp and gore, his eyes crooked, body limp next to Jessica.

"Now he's fucking dead," Charlie said.

Mikey was muted by shock.

Charlie took the Chinese food bag out of Andy's hand and pinched out a chunk of the primo heroin.

"Here, man," Charlie said. And handed him some dope, "I threw an extra gram in for the drama. So that's about four grams there."

Mikey wanted to scream at him.

He had known Andy since they were little kids. They went to tennis lessons together. Andy was a nice guy, addicted to drugs, but he had a big heart. Charlie took his life because he didn't want to pay for the dope. They had a real problem now. The plan in Mikey's mind was to leave Jessica in the room. The housekeeper would find her. It would be ruled an accidental overdose. Andy's savagely beaten body was a different story, it changed everything. Now a murder had been committed.

He couldn't stay here overnight.

"We'll dump the fag. I know a spot by my parents' house. I saw dark clouds forming earlier. It's going to rain the next few days. It's the perfect time to do this."

Mikey just looked at the two bodies. He still couldn't bring himself to say anything. There was blood everywhere. He wished he had never called Charlie.

"What about the blood?" He finally asked.

"What about it?"

"When they find Jessica, they are going to realize that

all this blood belongs to someone else. There's going to be an investigation. It's going to point back to us. Goddammit, why did you do this shit?"

"I gave you an extra gram. Chill out."

By now the puddle of blood next to Andy's head had become dark and dense. He didn't think it was possible to clean it. He knew from television shows that police use a black light and can see the blood even if it has been cleaned.

Suddenly, there was a succession of loud knocks on the door.

Charlie looked at Mikey, "You expecting someone?"

Mikey shook his head. More knocks. He quietly walked to the door and looked through the peephole. He saw a large man in a studded leather jacket.

He recognized him.

"Oh, shit," Mikey whispered. "It's Gay Chris."

"Gay Chris?"

"Andy's boyfriend. He's a heroin dealer too but he doesn't get high. He just gets younger guys strung out and starts controlling their lives."

Mikey continued to look through the peephole. Gay Chris had a round face, clean shaved except for a perverted, sleazy soul patch.

He knocked again louder. Gay Chris was notoriously jealous and abusive to his boyfriends. There had been several occasions Mikey had met him with Andy, and he had a black eye or busted lip.

"I know you're in there, you little ho!" he yelled.

Charlie grabbed his .38 and started walking towards the door. "I'll pack this dude out too."

"I can hear you in there Andy!"

"Step away from the door. Let me handle this."

Mikey refused. Charlie had already stirred up enough bullshit and he wasn't going to allow him to inflict any more damage to this situation.

The knocks were getting more frantic. Charlie was getting more agitated. Mikey didn't have time to think so he just opened the door and stuck his head out.

Gay Chris looked at him, "What happened to your face? Where the fuck is Andy?"

"I'm fighting with Jessica; he's helping me calm her down."

"Bullshit."

He pushed the door open roughly and Mikey fell over. Charlie had the gun pointed at Gay Chris.

"Close the door," Charlie said. "Come on in."

He did as he was told. Mikey was standing by the table staring at the ground. He couldn't stomach to see anymore death today.

Gay Chris finally saw the bodies next to the bed. He was stoic. But he didn't stop looking.

"I can already tell you're a lot tougher than your boy was," Charlie said, "Mikey says you might got some dope. I sure hope you do and can appreciate the seriousness of this here situation."

Gay Chris said nothing. He continued to look at the bodies.

"Don't go shy on me now. You were talking all that crazy shit. I'm a businessman. You have something, we can negotiate you living or not."

Gay Chris made some sort of throat clearing sound. His eyes burned with fury as if suddenly leaping back into reality — overtaken by anger.

He started charging towards Charlie.

The gun was shaking in his hand, "I will pull the motherfuckin' trigger. Step back!"

Gay Chris tackled Charlie and the gun scuttled across the carpet. They were fairly equal in size, but Charlie curled up in a ball and didn't even fight back.

Gay Chris punched him repeatedly until he was fatigued, wrists flaccid, knuckles too sore. He had mostly hit Charlie on the back of the head but there was blood trickling down the side of his face.

Mikey looked at the door. It was a perfect time to escape all of this.

"Don't even consider it," Gay Chris said, "Where is the dope that Andy brought you?"

He leaned down and grabbed the .38 from the carpet, "You murdered him for eight hundred bucks. You fucking ended his life for your sorry little habit."

He was pointing the gun at Charlie, who was shivering, beaten, curled in the fetal position. He made soft whimpering sounds.

No shock there. Another bitch masquerading as a bully.

"He has it," Mikey said and pointed to Charlie.

Gay Chris grabbed Charlie by the throat. He made exaggerated choking groans. Tears streaming down his crumpled face.

"Where's the H you stole from my boyfriend?"

Charlie weakly pointed to the Chinese food bag that was on the bed. Gay Chris pistol whipped him in the mouth, and he squealed. Pieces of broken teeth spilled out of his mouth in a current of thick, syrupy blood.

"*Jus' phil me then!*" he screamed.

Mikey was petrified but laughed at the irony.

Gay Chris gave Mikey a sharp look, "What are you laughing about?"

"I have spent the entire day with this parasite. The homophobic asshole now has a lisp. It's funny. Despite the circumstances, I found it funny. That's all. No disrespect."

Gay Chris chucked. "That is funny. So ... like, I'm going to just assume that this guy killed Andy. You had no part in it?"

"Man, I swear to God. I had no idea he was going to rob him. He showed me the money before I even called. Andy was my childhood friend. I would never hurt him. Jessica OD'd this morning. It's been a day from hell."

"I believe it, Mikey. It isn't your style anyway."

"So where does that leave us then?"

"Help me tie him to that chair. I'll let you go."

Charlie's eyes expanded with terror. He could only imagine what kind of torture awaited him.

"Thank you," Mikey said, "I'm sorry about Andy."

"I'm sorry about Jessica."

Charlie was babbling incoherently until he fainted and slumped over. Gay Chris tried to pick him up, but he was too heavy — Mikey walked over and helped put Charlie in a chair next to the table.

"Go rip some strips out of a sheet." Gay Chris said as he fished through Charlie's pocket and found the envelope full of cash. He took the bills out and held them up to the light. "Fakes."

"Huh?" Mikey asked, busy with the sheet.

"He planned on robbing Andy the whole time. These are some low-quality fake bills."

"He's a scumbag. I'm sorry. I didn't know. I thought I was making a couple hundred bucks from the deal and now I regret it all."

Mikey handed him the pieces of sheet and Gay Chris tied Charlie to the Chair. He bent down and took one of his shoes off. He rolled down a jaundiced looking sock and scrunched it up, stuffing it in Charlie's mouth.

The stench of his own foot snapped Charlie awake. The sock had already turned dark red from absorbing so much of his blood.

His eyes were bulging, as if he was being strangled.

He thrashed in his chair, terrified, as Gay Chris laughed at him. "Ain't so big and bad now, are ya?"

Gay Chris opened the Chinese food bag and took about ten grams out. He handed Mikey the glob, "Just go, man."

Mikey thanked him and took out a pack of cigarettes from his pocket. He took the cellophane wrapping and placed the dope inside of it. He had managed to come up with fifteen grams for the day. He hadn't had a day like that for a very long time.

Jessica would be proud.

He didn't look back at her when he closed the door.

The room was in a fake name: Mike Baer. Probation and parole sweeps were one of the most common ways dope fiends got busted. Police would routinely check motel logbooks and see if there was any low hanging fruit. Mikey had a warrant, and the cops knew that he was dating Jessica — she was the Chief of Police's niece.

The local cops were overzealous towards Mikey because of it.

The rain outside of the motel was viscous. The usual antsy speed freaks were nowhere to be found. Mikey was concerned about the journals in his backpack. There was nothing to protect them from the water. The cellophane from his cigarette pack was weak and holes ripped in them easily. He was concerned about his dope.

But these were modest concerns.

He knew how badly he had fucked up this time.

He started walking towards his parents' house. It was a forty-minute walk up into the hills. He was shivering but didn't know if it was from the cold or the spinning confusion of his mind.

He had tried to clean up, get sober, several times. There had been rehabs and the Methadone and Suboxone and AA meetings. There was a point about a year before he met Jessica that he had ... just given up. He was frustrated. He didn't want to be a fucking junkie anymore, but he legitimately couldn't stop. It was a horrible lifestyle that people often perceived as selfish. That's what self-torture looks like on the other side, some piggish act of gluttony, when it's the opposite: being so broken that you avoid pleasure at all costs because you have tricked yourself into believing you don't deserve it.

He was carrying around heavy secrets.

The journals were the only way he felt that anyone would ever understand them. He clung on to the fantasy that one day he'd be a famous writer and every mistake he made up to that point would be forgiven.

Suicidal ideation had started whispering to him the first couple of times he had to kick heroin cold turkey on a county jail floor. He would stay up for a week at a time, saucer-eyed, electrified by withdrawal. Mikey would vomit until he was so weak, he could only drool yellow, stinky bile on himself. Inmates yelling about the odor, guards laughing at the rich kid, curled up on a shit-stained blanket, clawing at memories from a distant life.

It was a glimpse of actual hell.

Those moments would make him miss his parents and question himself. He didn't know if he was a good person anymore. His mind told him that he wasn't and very few people ever told him that he was. He knew that his heroin addiction had become a burden on his family. Everyone told him how selfish he was; killing himself would end the suffering for the few remaining people that cared about him anymore.

Mikey was a disappointment, a failure, a drug addict.

There was also the secret.

It consumed him, a cancerous vulture looming behind his life, making it impossible to ever feel normality or any genuine sense of happiness.

He told his journal about it many times. He wrote about it to try and temper its power, but it continued to haunt him. He tried every drug until he had found heroin. It didn't erase his past, but it slowed the racing thoughts down enough for him to pretend that it wasn't real.

Mikey knew that this secret would catapult him to places beyond his wildest dreams. Everyone would know who he was. Some people would feel sorry for him. It would upset others. But he knew it would be impossible for it to be ignored and he had written so much that he would be celebrated as a real writer. The content wouldn't matter once people fell in love with the flowery language that he had used to express himself.

He didn't know what was going to happen with Jessica and Andy. He was certain that Gay Chris would murder Charlie. The fact that Jessica's uncle was the Chief of Police would put incredible scrutiny on Mikey. He would be arrested and charged with multiple counts of murder. He would spend the rest of his life in prison; and then nobody would ever read his journals.

None of it would matter anymore. His life work would be dismissed as the ramblings of a maniac. For instance: nobody took the Unabomber's manifesto seriously because the guy was a complete fucking psychopath.

The secret within the journals was the one thing that had given his trashed life hope. He loved Jessica, in an abstract romanticized way, as much as you can love someone when you don't love yourself. Heroin makes meaningful relationships impossible, like trying to sustain a life in a reoccurring dream, when you know you will wake up from it at any moment.

Addiction curses every relationship.

The d i s s o l u t i o n is inevitable.

But when you're in the blind mania of a codependent torrent, the person you think you love seems as important as breathing oxygen. The thought of it being over is an ugly echo, warning shots from the vast emptiness that heartbreak traps every unfortunate within.

He was going to kill himself. He decided.

Torrential rain fell from the sky, freezing water ran down his face, making his teeth rattle. But he smiled.

He was tired and he was finally going to have some peace.

He thought about a suicide note and figured that he didn't need it. There were thousands of pages from his journals that could explain everything more lucidly than the way he felt at that moment. He had around fifteen grams of heroin and he could eat most of it and do one final shot. It would be painless. He would just go to sleep and never wake up again.

He just had to get the journals. They were hidden on his parents' property. It had been several months since he had spoken to his family. Their relationship had always been combative. Mikey was the oldest of their two sons and they had favored their youngest Scott. It was almost as if they didn't want to be parents anymore after Scott had gone missing. There was never a body recovered and there was no evidence that he had been kidnapped. They had given up hope of finding him several years after his disappearance and by that point Mikey had already turned to drugs.

Mikey's mother had become paralyzed by sadness after Scott went missing. His father was embittered and mean. He had given up on trying to get Mikey to go to college or trade school. He ridiculed him for wanting to be a writer. He was old-fashioned and success found outside of a conventional trajectory seemed implausible to him. They hated the druggie criminal that their son had become. Mikey hadn't lived with them for many years, but the police showed up at their home every time he had a warrant, which seemed to happen with increasing regularity.

The last time he had seen them was the previous Christmas. He had shown up after being up for a week on a crystal-meth binge; emaciated, his face hidden behind ruby-red clusters of acne sores. His parents didn't mention it, but the disdain was painfully obvious.

It was Christmas Eve again.

He figured that it was the best night to show up to his family's home unexpectedly. He had a plan in his mind, but his father's temperament was unpredictable. If something were to happen — he wanted to make sure that there was a clue for the world to find his journals.

There was a park by his parents' house. It overlooked the cityscape and had a trail to a hidden area with a cave. He had a 9 mm stashed in it. When he first started dating Jessica, he carved their initials into a tree along the path. He decided to leave his backpack in the cave and take the gun. The journals were full of mostly monotonous junkie shit: his day-to-day of stealing and shooting dope. But it had an entry about Jessica's death. He wanted to make sure that the truth was protected in the cave. He could see his parents simply throwing his journals away after he killed himself. He knew that someday someone would find the backpack and know what really happened to Jessica.

The trail was slippery from wet mud, but he eventually made it to the cave. It was a unique rock formation that had an enclosure. It was about 15 feet long. He had fucked Jessica in there many times when they were homeless. It offered protection from the rain and Mikey used his lighter to illuminate a page. He wrote the date and explained the location of the other journals at his parents' property. He put the backpack in the far corner of the cave, mumbling a sort of prayer. The gun was in a paper grocery bag. It had a full clip. He tucked it in his waistline and continued to his parents' house.

The neighborhood was jolly with holiday spirit. There were Christmas lights and decor on every home on the block except for his parents.

Their house was completely dark; a forgotten candle that had been blown out many years before, by the wailing sigh of melancholy.

The home emanated loss.

Mikey's mind was spinning. He was in a manic fit. He knocked on the door. He was going to stick to his plan and get the journals.

His father opened the door, "Mikey, what the hell happened to your face?"

Mikey forgot about the gash and blood-soaked eyes.

"It's nothing."

"And you're soaked. Are you just getting out of jail or something?"

Mikey was trembling, cold, "No ... I just ... It's Christmas and I wanted to see you and mom. That's all."

Mikey never said stuff like that. His father studied him incredulously.

"Where's your partner-in-crime? I thought you two were connected at the hip."

"She's back at our place. Can I come in? It's freezing out here."

"Michael," his father wagged his index finger at him "If I let you into our home and I catch you stealing from us again ... I will call the police. Do you, ya know ... dig that?"

Mikey nodded and his dad let him in.

The house was massive. There were marble floors and spiraling staircases leading upstairs.

"You look awful. Go to the restroom and try and clean yourself up before your mother sees you. Unbelievable that you manage to show up looking worse this year than you did last year. You know ... the damn cops were here last week. Still stealing video tapes?"

Mikey didn't answer.

"Clean yourself off. You can spend the night in your room. Jessica cannot come over. I repeat she cannot. And don't you dare do drugs here. K?"

"Okay."

Mikey went to the bathroom.

He was already feeling sick and due for another shot. He wanted to make sure that he did one before he tried to get the journals. He had a feeling his father wasn't going to let him into the lower garage easily. They were in a box, hidden deep in a wine cellar that he didn't think anyone, aside from himself, even knew existed.

It was very hidden.

He was going to kill himself in that lower garage. This way he knew the police would take the journals. It would only be a matter of time before they were published.

Mikey would be dead, but he grinned wide at the thought: everyone would know the truth and admire his syntax and diction and lexicon. There would be tattooed portraits in his honor. Biopics and documentaries would be made on the misunderstood artist.

Literary critics would honor him posthumously.

He would be a motherfuckin' legend.

He had some old syringes and spoons stashed in his bathroom. They were under vanity towels that never got washed. He took the cellophane bag out of his pocket. Only a little moisture had dampened his dope. He took out a huge glob. He wanted to do the final shot in the garage but there's nothing greater than a junkie dueling with the threat of death. It had been a while since he had done a reckless shot.

If it killed him, he was ready for it anyway.

He filled up the syringe with 90 CCs of pitch-black, lethal looking heroin.

Mikey examined his jugular vein in the mirror. He didn't want a repeat of earlier and the syringe was almost completely full. It was imperative that he get it right the first time he registered blood, or he was going to run out of room.

He stuck the needle in several times before he saw blood slowly fill the remainder of the barrel. He pushed the plunger down. There was so much dope in the syringe that he had to push hard to get past the resistance.

He was at the 10 CC mark when ...

The rest happened quickly. He was groggily awoken to pounding on the bathroom door. He was sitting on the toilet; he didn't remember how he got there but he was fighting to keep his eyes open.

"Police! Open the door!"

He had obviously overdosed but he was coming out of it. He knew that cops were on the other side of the locked door, but he was in a state of paralysis: both physically and cognitively.

There was a thud against the door, and he knew it was a foot kicking. His eyelids closed involuntarily, and he forced them back open. He saw the bag of dope on the counter next to the spoon and needles. Mikey grabbed the bag of dope figuring he had to eat the dope. But his head sagged heavily. Instead, he just shoved it in one of his other stash spots.

The door swung open. Mikey opened his eyes weakly. There were two cops with their guns drawn.

"Hands up, Mikey."

Mikey's equilibrium was inverted, the room was spinning, he saw the cops and tried to put his hands up, but he slouched over, falling off the toilet.

One of the cops approached him and didn't see Mikey yank the 9 mm out of his waistline.

"He has a weapon!" one of them yelled.

There was a lot of commotion. More cops entered the bathroom.

He closed his eyes, only for a split second, and then pointed his gun in their direction.

He tried to tell them to leave him alone, but he went out again, drifting into momentary unconsciousness, this time dropping the gun.

It made a loud clanking sound on the tile floor.

He was tackled by multiple officers, and he felt the cruel, familiar grip of handcuffs.

And then darkness once more.

3

THE RISE AND FALL OF COLLIN MCFADDEN

NY 1980 : : Texas 1988 : : Pacific Palisades 2017

"Eventually we all have to accept full and total responsibility for our actions, everything we have done, and have not done." – Hubert Selby, Jr.

Collin McFadden hated people of color. He always had. It was a very frequent topic of discussion when he was a little boy growing up in Upstate New York.

His family would call minorities "free loaders" and ridicule the emerging trend of progressive social safety nets that were purported to help struggling families and single parents.

"These Carter ideologues," Hubert McFadden would say over family supper, "They think it's okay to siphon my hard-earned money to support these blacks and Hispanics. It's called elbow grease. It's called getting a damn job. It is not my responsibility, as a successful American taxpayer, to support these worthless ... you know ... animals. I earned the fortune that I've amassed. Me, I did that. Nobody else. I certainly didn't need the government holding my hand. And that's why I honestly believe that Ronald Reagan will make this country great again."

It was true that Collin's father was rich but earning it was giving him way too much credit. He was born into a wealthy family that had been part of a financial dynasty. His father before him had founded McFadden and Crow, one of the premier investment banking firms of the East Coast.

It didn't matter how hard Collin tried in life. In fact, he didn't have to do a thing. An office plaque with his name had been created the day that he was born. He was a sub-par student who had a propensity for drinking heavily — albeit not very well. He was reckless, sloppy, and his belligerence always got him in a lot of trouble.

Or as much trouble as a rich kid can get into.

Money has an effortless way of laundering sins.

He had attended the Brady Academy, arguably the most prestigious boarding school in the United States.

Collin didn't understand the word no. As a child, if he hadn't gotten his way, he would throw a stomping tantrum. If there's anything his parents truly loathed, it was when Collin or his younger sister cried. It was an irritant for them so they would give in, just to shut them up.

He attended Texas A&M and was no stranger to controversy. He had painted a black face one year for Halloween. He walked around doing minstrel show imitations of illiterate black men. He wore overalls and puffed on a stogie like a real asshole. He had been suspended until his father worked out a deal with the school.

Collin was overweight and always had an entitled personality that most women couldn't stand. In college, women are more attracted to looks than money and Collin was an annoying, fat racist fuck.

The rape allegations came out his junior year of college. He was guilty of it, too. He had taken a girl back to his dorm room. She was drunk and kept asking him for nose candy, slurring it tiredly. Collin didn't do drugs, his drinking problem was bad enough, but he knew she wanted some cocaine to snort. He had a druggie room-mate who wasn't home, so he took a Quaalude from his sock drawer, crushing it into powder and cutting a couple of uneven white lines on a Garth Brooks LaserDisc.

He rolled up a $5 bill and handed it off. She snorted both lines and winced from the burn. This isn't coke she had thought before waking up to Collin on top of her. She was disoriented but still disgusted by his bare chest. He had elderly man boobs. They sagged like the deflated sleeve of foreskin. He smelled old and awful: a poorly negotiated compromise between Brut cologne and ripe body odor.

She tried to speak, and he said, "Shhh. It's okay. It's okay."

The barbiturate had strained her eyelids, but she could tell that he was sodomizing her. It really hurt. She could only catch fluttering glimpses. It animated him ominous-ly like the flipbook of a rabid cartoon. She could see the webbed red rash of alcoholism spread across his nose. And his hairy arms. She would never forget those nasty hairy arms and moles.

Collin had intentionally drugged and raped the girl. She thought of him as she sat in the shower and hugged her knees. There was audible dismay as blood from her rectum swirled down the drain. She thought it looked chunky, thick. It had the messiness of a surgery. She want-ed to keep this to herself because she knew the parade of attention that would ensue.

Her roommate knew something was wrong because her normally expressive eyes were puffy and dull; she seemed oddly detached. She finally broke down and told the room-mate every single detail. The police were called but they didn't arrest Collin McFadden. They seemed almost offended that she would try to file a complaint against a family that resembled a twisted, Evangelical version of the Kennedys.

It certainly wasn't a family that would allow such a horrendous lie to ever surface in court.

The girl's roommate was enraged and pushed the issue with the administrative side of the college. Mr. McFadden was called in and they presented the allegations to him in front of Collin. They alluded towards expulsion but had predictably mitigated the term by calling it an "involuntary transfer."

Collin was biting his thumb nail, the way he would when he knew he was about to be scolded by his verbally abusive father.

Hubert McFadden asked if his son could leave the room for a moment so that he could speak privately with the administrators.

Collin heard them arguing from behind closed doors.

The college eventually expelled the girl that Hubert McFadden's son had raped, as well as her roommate, under the pretense that the girls had conceptualized an elaborate hoax aimed at destroying one of their favorite students.

Later that fall, seemingly out of nowhere, the school's library had been renamed "The McFadden Learning Center."

That's just the way shit was when you contributed tens of millions of dollars in donations.

Collin's father was more upset with the fact that he had a sexual encounter with a black girl. The thought made him sick to his stomach. It was the kind of thing that would destroy the family prestige if it had ever gotten out. He just couldn't wrap his head around the fact that he had done ... *that*. Lord knows that his own father would have taken out the belt if he had so much as attempted something as downright filthy.

He insisted Collin be tested for diseases: blood test, urine analysis, and a cotton swab up his trembling urethra.

He took Collin out of school and made him go to a residential treatment center for what he said was alcoholism.

"Father, you need to get me out of here. It's filled with a bunch of loser drug heads. I don't belong," he said over the phone while he was away.

"You know what you've done."

"And what am I to tell them? That I'm in rehab because I made love to a black girl?"

"That's exactly why you're there, Collin. You can't possibly associate love with a primate. You've jeopardized the family legacy. You are a disgrace! Enough!"

He was never allowed to go back to college. His father made him stay in treatment for a year and then moved him out to Los Angeles to be the CFO of one of his many shell corporations.

He hated that black bitch for what she had done to him. It created a silent, reoccurring vendetta toward minorities for the rest of his life. It seemed like his innocence had been hijacked because some woman had claimed she didn't want his sex.

He just didn't see what the big deal was. He had pulled the ol' sedative and anal sex stunt many, many times without incident.

But he tried it on one black cokehead and his care-free college life was dismantled in what felt like an instant.

He married a woman named Susan that he had met at a Republican fundraiser dinner in Sherman Oaks. They both loved what George W. Bush and Dick Cheney had planned for the country. Susan wasn't a prize by any standards, but she laughed at his tasteless jokes and seemed to tolerate him enough to get married and create the life his family wanted him to be living.

Collin's father passed away when he was in his mid-thirties. It felt as though an incredible weight had suddenly dissipated. Never again, would he have to feel like a dwarf or social reject, belittled by the artificial standards of the upper-class elite.

He had inherited billions; the exact amount had never been revealed to anyone. He technically didn't need a participatory role in the company but there was no way he was going to give up the empowerment he felt in that position of authority. Collin loved to tell overqualified black men that they wouldn't be a good fit for the company. There was an orgasmic rush he felt when he fired someone, especially if he knew that they needed the job to support their sorry little families.

The animals and peasants.

McFadden bought a beautiful Victorian home up in the hills. He impregnated his wife twice and she never recovered her figure. Her body had always disgusted him, but it was a legitimate source of public embarrassment after she popped out the kids. He had hoped that people would assume that she was his sister when they were out eating somewhere. He often wondered if she knew how much she turned him off. Surely, she had noticed that he wouldn't make love with the lights on anymore or that he had insisted on violent, and what she hoped had been, unrealistic pornographic films.

He loved his children for the simple fact that he would one day be able to perpetuate the same tyrannical fervor his father had used to torment him throughout his life.

Collin McFadden was a man that loved going on work trips. He would stay in five-star hotels, calling for room service, drinking bourbon by the pint, and ordering black call girls from the internet like discounted pizzas.

He enjoyed greasy barbecue baby back ribs. He was one of those men that failed cotillion classes as a young man.

He had never quite learned how to eat without revealing the glutinous manners of the barn animal that he truly was.

He wore a bib and made the hookers crawl on the floor nude, as he chewed with his mouth open. His fingers were ugly, stumpy. He would smear blotches of brown sauce on their faces and call them primates until they quivered with humiliation.

He would drink himself into oblivion and wake up the next day, dehydrated, with only vague fever-dream memories from the night before.

One night he was in San Diego and called up for a girl. She had been late. He was infuriated when he opened the hotel door and saw a white woman in her forties. She introduced herself as "Amber."

Amber stood in the door frame with what he absolutely knew to be a faux fur coat. It was covered in a tacky cheetah or leopard print; he couldn't tell the difference between the two, but he had always associated the patterns with the clandestine agreements of sexual commerce.

"You're not ... a negro," he whined.

She batted her eyes, biting her lip for a practiced beat, "I can be anything you want me to be, sweetie."

"What I want, is for you to be a damned negro."

"Like a slave? Because, truth is, I just want you to own me forever and ever and ever."

Collin took a pull from his bottle, considered this for a moment and then nodded a concession, ushering Amber inside.

He was unshaven and his beard was peppered with flunked dignity. He looked nothing like George Clooney, just another overweight slob that she had a lifetime of experience with.

"Aren't you a little bit old to be a whore?"

"How old you want me to be?" Amber tried again.

She had the annoying musicality of a cheerleader and Collin was irritated by it, "What I'd like you to know, is that I think you are a worthless whore of a woman. And that you are quite physically repulsive. I wouldn't even rape you if you were the last piece of cunt on earth. Understand me?"

Her face was tired, worn. It was obvious there was a forgotten soul dancing somewhere in the corners of her brain, memories of when she felt young and unbroken.

But she had perfected the art of poker-lips long ago.
She just smiled sexily at Collin.

"Strip."

"Make me," she played along.

To Collin this was the first right thing she had said. It served as an invitation to be rough. He had been visited by thuggish pimps a couple of times in the past when he had gotten carried away with a whore.

Fucking animals and peasants. Primates. Apes.

Collin walked over to her. In his mind she wanted him to grab her throat. He squeezed it hard. She choked and made a passive gagging sound, "I said strip, bitch."

Amber slid her tube top down. She didn't wear a bra and her tits were perky, clearly silicone. In fact, they were much too firm for the expensive gummy bear implants he had wanted to get his boring, fat wife.

"Like these?" She asked innocently. Collin had already put his bib on. He was making canine noises — chomping at strips of rib meat.

"Pants. Take them off now, old sissy slut."

Amber bent over and peeled off her thong. Collin noticed a c-section scar across her stomach as she jiggled her ass at him. It was the same crescent blemish that his wife back home was so insecure about.

This pleased him.

"Does your child know what his insufferable jizz-rag mother does for work?"

Amber slowly ascended but kept her head down. He could see that he had struck a chord. Her flat lips had sneered for a moment like a folded card hand, exposed by mistake.

She tried to laugh but it came out choked, dry.

"Hey, man. You have something I can drink? I'm real thirsty," Amber asked.

Collin's chin was caked with dry barbecue sauce.

He used the bib to rub it off.

"Aw, you're thirsty, are ya, mama?" He taunted.

Amber nodded and Collin picked up his bottle of bourbon. He teased her with it, "You want this?"

"Please. Yes. My mouth is real, real dry."

Collin splashed bourbon onto the carpet in a zigzag.

"Then you crawl on that filthy carpet, and you lick it up."

Amber exhaled and lowered herself to the stains of liquor on the carpet. She had to get with a new service. These last few clients had all been completely vile like this.

"Just pretend it's my asshole. I want to watch you lick it. And do it nice and slow."

Amber gave a noncommittal taste and grimaced. It was salty and sweet from God knew what.

"Lick, it. Think of that loser kid of yours."

Amber swiped the carpet with a broader stroke and gagged.

She had experience with forced foul tastes.

She closed her eyes and did what had to be done.

"What I'd give," Collin said with laughter, "For him to see how worthless and disgusting his mother truly is."

Amber made a 180 degree turn on her stomach and continued to lick the carpet robotically.

She looked up at Collin, "You like it, daddy?"

"I Know you sure as hell do!" he bellowed, "Nastiness! Pure fuckin' nastiness!"

The evil energy emanating from Collin was palpable. He was howling with psychotic glee; flecks of prime rib stuck in his teeth.

He looked like some deranged cannibal.

He didn't realize that Amber had grabbed something that had been concealed in her asshole.

She made a tight fist around it like a magician performing a coin trick.

"Can I have a real taste now, daddy?" she asked.

"Master."

"Can I have some of your drink, master?"

"Master Mac to you! You filthy, elderly whore!" He screamed and hurled the bottle towards her.

It missed her head by a quarter of an inch, rolling on the ground, bourbon spilling out.

She picked it up and feigned a swig. She gulped a few times for effect. She put her fist to her mouth and slipped the small balloon inside.

The taste of her own ass didn't bother her anymore. It seemed dull when compared to the deluge of disgusting flavors from that carpet.

She folded forward and coughed, making herself gag and dry heave.

He was slurring, "What the hell's the matter with you?"

Amber turned her back to him and spit the balloon out into her hand. It was quick and went unnoticed. She snapped at the latex with her mouth and wiggled the capsule into her palm.

"Hello," Collin said, "Hello ... mama?"

She put the tiny pill capsule into the bottle of bourbon. There was roughly a quarter of liquor left, just enough for it to dissolve unnoticed.

"I don't know," she said, "I'm real sick."

"Oh, for Christ sake, give me my damn booze back then." Amber went to stand up.

"No, no, no. Crawl to me, mama."

She did as she was told and handed Collin the bottle.

"Worthless," he sputtered.

Collin took a pull from the bourbon.

Bingo.

"I'm not paying. You can tell your nig—"

Suddenly the room took on a strange static. It looked like bad tracking on an old VHS tape. He blinked and it got worse. The entire room was tilting and heavily distorted.

"Whoreee," he slurred coarsely, "Fuck$_{in}$—"

Collin McFadden slumped over.

Barbecue sauce was smeared on his face. He looked like he had already been beat up.

Amber sprang up.

"How you like me now?" she laughed.

She went to her purse and grabbed her cell phone. She typed a text message with her thumbs and waited.

There was tapping on the door, and she looked through the security hole. It was Bethany. Her hair was bright green and her body was disproportionate.

She looked like a circus clown in the watery distortion of the peephole.

Amber let Bethany in.

"Dahling, you look absolutely marvelous tonight," she said, strutting in with her Gatsby accent and attitude.

Bethany was transgender but always maintained some level of masculinity. She had a Burt Reynolds mustache. She wore plaid pajamas and an oversized hooded sweatshirt. Her green eyelashes were stiff with the same shade as her stringy hair.

She looked like a man trying to look like a woman and what resulted was a truly unique music video creation.

"Why thank you, love," Amber said, "Where's Moo and Emerald?"

"You know them high-maintenance hoes," Bethany said. "They're getting some goodies at the vending machine."

"Oh, but of course they are."

She closed the door and they walked towards Collin.

"Geeze, this man is ... amazingly hideous," Bethany said.

"You don't even know the half of it. He's a real pig."

Bethany gasped, "A cop?"

"No, just a foul pig of a human."

"Why is he wearing a bib and eating ribs? That's like so passé."

Amber shook her head, "Real fucking creep."

Collin's head was sagging. He snored obnoxiously.

"I'm sure that's what you say about me behind my back."

"Of course not! You're a total babe, Beth."

"You're a solid bitch, know that?"

Bethany walked up and they started french-kissing.

There was a succession of knocks.

They broke free.

"And there they are," Bethany said.

Amber walked up to the door and opened it. Emerald and Moo walked in. They were both transgender. Moo had dyed purple hair that went past her waist. Emerald had short brown hair, boyish qualities that were offset with eccentric multicolored makeup.

They were both chewing on Payday candy bars.

They acknowledged Amber and Bethany as they walked through and stopped at Collin. He was out cold.

"My, my," Moo said, "Look at this creepy fuck wad. Waltzed right out of a Sears catalog."

Bethany and Amber nodded.

"Wallet?" Moo asked.

Amber went up to McFadden, crinkling her nose, as she patted him down. She fished his wallet from his back pocket. He opened his eyes and they rolled into his head. He was out cold.

She threw the wallet on the bed. Emerald grabbed it and slowly removed his California driver's license, "Collin Mc ... Faggot?"

"Huh?" Bethany said.

"His name is Colin McFadden," She giggled, "Sounds like Collin McFaggot, kinda."

"Where's he live?" Amber asked.

"Shit," Moo said, "I know this street. That's up high in Bennington Canyon above Beverly Hills."

"So, he's rich?"

"You better believe it. I've gone to some rather interesting parties up there," Emerald said.

"I'm certain you have."

They all laughed.

"The one good thing about Placone's agency is the clients. Every single one of them has real dough, man," Amber said.

"Okay, snap-snap ladies," Emerald said, "You know what to do."

Moo dumped a backpack out on the bed. There was a video camera in a small nylon case, a Warhol-looking revolver, a pair of handcuffs, and a few latex masks of former U.S. Presidents.

Bethany took her pajama pants off. Her cock dangled out proudly, "I get to be Nixon."

"No, Clinton," Emerald began, "Remember the bet: You said that Elvis sang 'Crazy Little Thing Called: Love' and of course it was my zero drama, baby mama Freddy Mercury who sang that spine tingling opus. You're Clinton for the next three."

"Fuck!" Bethany exclaimed, "I hate Bill Clinton."

"Grow up dear, we all do,"

Moo and Emerald took their pants off as well. They walked up to McFadden as Amber started videotaping.

"What's with the bib?" Moo asked.

Bethany and Amber looked at each other and laughed.

"Good fucking question. Great question."

Amber took the camera out of the carrying case. The ladies looked truly frightening. Moo was Nixon, Bethany played Clinton, and Emerald as Hubert McFadden senior's fave: Ronald Reagan.

They had large fake breasts and left their tops on. Dyed

hair peeked out of the masks; penises resting on their re-spective crotches.

Moo grabbed the handcuffs and they approached Mc-Fadden. Drool was now spilling out of his mouth. His chin was messy with barbecue sauce.

"This guy seems so odd," Moo said.

"Aren't they all?"

"Well, yes. It's the food with this one."

"He said something about you," Amber said.

"About *mwah*?" Moo asked, studying him.

"Said my kid was a loser."

"And how did he even know you had a kid?"

"My scar," Amber said, "But for the record you're a far cry from a loser. And I love you more than dope, even!"

"Love you too, Mom. Geeze, this guy is real a piece of work, huh?"

"Yeah, baby. He is."

"You guys are too adorable," Bethany said, smiling.

Moo cleared some phlegm from her throat and spit on McFadden's face. He made a soft reactionary moan and twitched. It sounded almost sexual. He was knocked out.

"I'm going to start recording now," You guys do y'alls' thang."

Amber held Collin's license and read it to the camera:

"Collin McFadden. Date of birth: April 19, 1970. Fifty years old ..." Amber read and continued with his home address.

It was a truly bizarre sight. All three of the girls had thin female bodies. And decent-sized dicks. The president masks were ominous with clown-colored hair spilling out of them.

They wore no pants and began to rub Collin's body.

"This is what happens when we find a sexual predator in his natural habitat," Amber said in her faux-Australian accent, "Very dangerous, very elusive. On the prowl for endangered shemale cocks!"

All the girls started laughing. Bethany was licking Collin's face. The Bill Clinton mask had a hole that she could poke her tongue through.

Moo stood up on a chair. Her penis was right in front of Collin's face. She flexed her arms like an emaciated Popeye.

"Can you pee, hon. That would be so good to piss on this fat asshole's face."

Moo shook her head. "I can't go pee on command like that."

Bethany said, "Well, I sure as fuck can."

She stood on the table and kicked over the steel platter. Baby back ribs flew onto the floor. It seemed like Collin tried to mumble something. Bethany aimed her penis at Collin and urine started trickling out.

"You need to get your prostate checked girl," Amber said.

Bethany continued to piss on Collin. He flinched a bit and opened his mouth like a yawn. Urine dribbled from his lips.

She turned to Amber, "Why?"

"Because it ain't supposed to come out like a lawn sprinkler like that. That's why."

"Ever thought it could be from my chronic buttfuck condition?"

"Touché," Amber said.

Bethany's urine splashed Collin awake gently.

The piss stung; his eyelids squinted with pain.

"*Whaaaa*," he groaned.

Moo tilted her Reagan mask at Collin, "Hi-ya, McFaggot."

Collin was very impaired. He thought that he saw Ronald Reagan with huge tits and a ... cock looking at him.

There was a delayed reaction and then it suddenly hit him. He was catatonic from fear.

Who were these goddamn animals?

"Who ... who ... are you?"

"Just your friendly neighborhood sketch balls. Just passing on through," Emerald said.

Collin was weak, "How do we—"

"Know each other?" Moo finished for him, "Well, we don't really 'know' each other. We're not in some Woody Allen movie or nothing like that. Pretty much you ordered a hooker, and you insulted my mother and now we are extorting your punk ass."

It was obvious that he understood what was going on. He was trying to swat the freaky hoodlums away from him, but everything seemed weighted down and slower than normal. He was an overweight man, but the date rape drug made him feel a thousand pounds heavier.

"What we want," Amber said, making eye contact with Collin, "Oh hey, hi, it's me, the elderly whore. We want a million fuckin' dollars in crypto, or we show your family what you do in your spare time. How you pay trannies to piss in your fat ass mouth."

Collin's anger was muffled by another long groan.

He started to nod out again. The girls all stood around him so that Amber could record them with Collin.

He suddenly burst awake and put his hands around Moo's throat. She squealed and started to cough.

Bethany tried to get him off her, but McFadden seemed to have superhuman strength out of nowhere. He continued to choke Moo. He ripped the Ronald Reagan mask and he saw her for the first time. Her eyeliner running from sweat.

She looked like some demented children's doll.

"Get off her!" Amber screamed.

Collin continued to strangle Moo.

Bethany and Emerald jumped on him.

McFadden was gargantuan.

They couldn't get him off her.

Bethany ripped her mask off. The moisture from under the latex sent makeup running down her face like the silk of an expensive scarf.

Amber had never used a gun. She always had a girlfriend

that took care of that kind of shit. She was shaking when she grabbed it and aimed toward Collin.

Life was being released from Moo in a slow prism of morose and pale colors.

"Get off of her!" Amber demanded.

Collin backhanded Emerald and she fell to the ground. Bethany was elbowing his face. It didn't seem to hurt Collin. It only annoyed him. Moo had mere seconds before he was going to strangle her to death.

Suddenly, a thunderous **BAANG** roared through the room ...

A gunshot.

Collin was clipped from behind as Bethany dove out of the way.

He screamed in agony and fell off Moo.

Her gasps became a violent, coughing fit.

There was blood everywhere. It looked like war paint when mixed with the patches of Collin's brown barbecue sauce.

"What did you do to us?" Bethany screamed.

Collin was bent over. There were pools of blood puddles expanding around him.

He clawed furiously at the carpet, trying to regain some semblance of balance.

The drug was already wreaking havoc on his equilibrium and the throbbing wound sent it completely over the edge.

"I did what I had to do," Amber said calmly, "I couldn't let him murder my Moo-Moo in front of me like that."

"You know how fucking loud that shit was. It reverberated throughout the entire hotel. I'm one hundred percent certain of it."

"Spell 'reverberate'," Amber said, grinning.

"It ain't no time for bullshit, girl. Me and Moo got warrants anyway. This is the last place in the world we should be right now."

Collin was spitting up dark blood. It reminded Amber of the movie *Jaws*, when the shark had crunched down on the grumpy sea fisherman, and blood had oozed up from his stomach, as he slid down the tipping boat and into the water to his death!

It wasn't great white shark bad, but it wasn't looking good for the creep either.

"Mom, pack up the shit, please," Moo said in a newly rasped voice.

Collin tried to push himself up, but he was much too fat. He fell on his face and sobbed.

He looked as helpless as a child.

Amber was throwing things hastily into the backpack.

"Get a towel, Beth. Wipe everything down for fingerprints, DNA, whatever."

Everyone was in shock. The proverbial music had stopped suddenly, every single sound seemed loud and startling.

Bethany, Emerald, and Moo put their pants back on. They were frantic and they began to wipe down every single inch of the hotel room.

The gunshot was loud, especially for it being the middle of the night.

"You think he's gonna die?" Emerald asked.

"Does it matter," Amber said, "I mean, we're screwed no matter what if we don't fucking split. We gotta go, man."

"You gotta delete all the footage," Bethany said.

"And why would we do that?"

Bethany pointed at Collin McFadden. By now some of the blood had dried and he looked like he had been tarred. He was just missing the feathers.

He was motionless, losing color rapidly.

"Because we don't need no evidence of what actually went down here tonight," Bethany said.

4

THE WATCH PRELUDE SIDE A

Northridge 1993 : : Los Angeles 2017

"In a closed society where everybody's guilty, the only crime is getting caught. In a world of thieves, the only final sin is stupidity." – Hunter S. Thompson

The country had been going through a massive recession and a lot of companies were paying employees under the table. This saved them a lot of money, but it also circumvented some of the more important regulatory rules set in place. This is what allowed Ritchie Francesca to work as a bus driver. They didn't run his criminal background check. If they had, they would have realized he was a piece of shit who had done federal prison time for distributing child pornography.

He had also been convicted of driving while intoxicated on three separate occasions.

He was a deadbeat. A fat drunk who hardly ever showered and spent most of his free time playing Dungeons and Dragons. At forty-two, he lived with his parents and only had one friend: a boy named Chun, a thirteen-year-old Chinese foreign exchange student.

Chun smiled a lot — most likely having no idea what was going on. But he continued to meet Ritchie every week at the picnic table in the community park.

Ritchie paid Chun after their tabletop sessions. Some

of them got intense, buttery stains would emerge under Ritchie's armpits. He got swamp ass too.

Chun wore Oakley sunglasses. And never broke a sweat. He had long, black bangs. Ritchie thought he was cooler than Bruce Lee.

And then one day Chun was gone.

Ritchie's only friend never showed up at the park again. Drinking had always given Ritchie some comfort. Losing Chun was the first real tragedy of his life. He started drinking himself to sleep each night. It was the only way to stop the incessant crying. In a lot of ways, he thought he may have been in love with Chun. In his mind, at least, Chun had loved Ritchie's flat-top. ("It's ... It's real cool," he once said.) He didn't seem to mind that he smelled like literal zoo shit or that he had adult necknie and backnie.[11] Ritchie had the kind of boils that would make people uncomfortable if they got too close to them ...

As if the zits could burst open at any moment, puss erupting out of his neck like some infected volcano, splattering every civilian in its immediate proximity.

Chun seemed to never notice the acne. He may have been the only person that ever actually liked him in his entire life. Ritchie was racing himself to the bottom of rum bottles. Getting belligerently drunk made him feel optimistic, like maybe he'd find Chun again and they could live in a fort together somewhere away from all the nosey grownups. Ritchie seemed to forget the fact that he was a 42-year-old convicted sex offender on the national registry. Booze helped him messily sketch a new narrative ... one far less ugly than the truth.

Ritchie was drunk every hour. He never stopped drinking. The delirium and confusion were becoming

---

11   Pimples on neck/back.

increasingly scarier. The blackouts became a regular occurrence. He wet the bed many times, but his mother would coddle him and tell him it was perfectly normal to have these types of accidents in his forties.[12]

On more than one occasion he woke up in the middle of the night, not knowing where he was, his pants around his ankles, at a playground or park. He couldn't remember anything, and he knew as well as anyone that it was possible that he had hurt some blameless child.

He was thinking about this and more while driving the bus one day. He blacked out, after drinking an entire handle of Malibu spiced rum, when he collided with a pedestrian.

He had slammed on the brakes. The sudden halt made the bus slide wildly, fishtailing, twirling in entire rotations as if the bus was suddenly weightless. It hit a parked Honda and the impact essentially accordioned the smaller car.

The bus looked like it might roll, it jerked a few times before finally straightening out and coming to a firm, dramatic stop.

Black smoke billowed from the engine.

Ritchie had passed out and when he woke up, he had no idea where he was, he felt nauseated, he spewed vomit all over his bus uniform and into his lap.

"The driver is hammered!" a woman screamed as the hip flask fell to the floor spilling out cheap rum. "He's freakin' drinking on the job. Unreal!"

"Ah, you hutchup, huh?" he slurred.

"You guys see that. The bus driver is inebriated! He blacked out, he's totally incoherent, and we almost just got in a fatal accident. This man needs to be reported. And jailed. There are children on the bus for Christ's sake!"

Ritchie slouched over, not caring about the children, and dozed off.

---

12   Spoiler alert: It's not fuckin' normal. Nothing Ritchie did was normal. He was a disgusting freak.

"What about the man we hit?" someone yelled, "What happened to him? Can anyone see him?"

"Right there!" A man sitting towards the back pointed, "He's in real bad shape from the looks of it. Call 911."

The battered pedestrian was sprawled out on the street. He was gurgling blood; a dark ring had caked around his mouth from what had already dried up. There was a large gash below his left eye, it was bleeding profusely, running down his face and forming a large puddle next to his head.

People from the bus jumped out and stood around him.

"He breathing?" a teenage boy asked.

"Yeah. See that red spittle. How it slowly inflates little red bubbles, but they pop right away ... that's from breathing. But the man got hit hard. I wouldn't be surprised if the worst of the damage are organs that are hidden from us."

"What are you an EMT or something?"

"Nah!" the man said, laughing. "I just watch way too much goddamn television."

"So, then, what do we do now?"

"Only thing we can do. We wait for the paramedics. Maybe we go tie the drunk bus driver up so he don't go darting off on us?"

The teenage boy gave a thumbs up and they headed back up into the bus.

A swarm of onlookers formed around the body.

It was the best thing that could have happened to Gunner. It became a widely televised and sensationalized case:

CONVICTED CHILD MOLESTER NEARLY SLAYS WAR HERO.

Gunner was okay considering he was hit by a fucking bus. (Driven by some sloshed pedophile!) It was as if the horrors of his past refused to let him forget. He would always have a sharp numbness in his lower back and the gash under his left eye would heal hideously.

There were ambulance chasers lining up to defend Gunner and he ultimately received a seven-figure structured settlement.

Rent covered for the rest of his life.

Ritchie Francesca received 15 years in state prison. It was a big local story, but it never made national headlines.

The transportation company filed for bankruptcy.

The problem was that Gunner didn't know what to do with money like that. He was a simple man and didn't require fancy things. His mother had taught him very little about what to do if he ever came into money.

He remembered watching her when she was having violent, demeaning sex with various Johns in their cramped apartment. She would look right at Gunner with pleading eyes.

One year they went to Big Bear with one of her boyfriends. A Mongol outlaw biker. There was a wounded deer in the middle of the road. Gunner must have been seven years old, but he never forgot those eyes. The deer was so beautiful.

The eyes were expressive and pained.

The look of betrayal.

Pleading eyes.

The deer didn't feel betrayed by Gunner's family. All they had done was find him lying in the middle of the road. He had already been hit. It was the realization that his life was over. The life that seemed inherently promised was so easily taken.

His mother's boyfriend took out his highly illegal Uzi

and peppered the deer with a quick succession of bullets. Arterial blood sprayed a brilliant mist across the fresh white snow.

The eyes became instantly vacant as the deer surrendered to its death.

He wondered why his mother's eyes never changed. They were begging eyes. Even when he found her dead, hanging from the ceiling, she pleaded.

Because she still felt betrayed.

"Greg, listen to me. My ma, your worthless fuckin' hag of a grandmother, taught me a few things. There are only three expensive items you'll ever need in your entire life. You need a nice car, a fancy watch, and a good pair of sunglasses. People treat you differently when you got money. That's how it goes. So, if you can make it seem like you got it, then you have the benefit of being rich without being rich. Understand me?"

Gunner nodded.

"Do you really understand? Or, no, you just got that stupid look. No wonder my boyfriends would rather fuck you than me. Look at you, you're such a little fucking twerp!"

Gunner nodded again. What his mother failed to understand is that he was already dead inside at nine years old. She would berate and humiliate him because that's how she had been treated by everyone else.

He reached his pain threshold much sooner than she would have expected.

She grabbed him by the chin, "Listen, you remember when I was filming that *Angela Anal* picture?"

"We lived in Northridge."

Gunner's mother, pleased that he was engaging now, let go of his face, "Yes. When we lived in Northridge. That's right. I had just had my first major part and know what? I bought a watch first. I had wanted this bitchin' Bulova watch. Ah, Greg, if you had seen this thing. It was a real beauty. I got the watch first. All the skanks I worked with were awe-struck by this fuckin' watch, man. I went to go buy a brand-new Mercedes Benz and they ignored me at the car lot. Why?"

Gunner stared at his mother blankly.

"Why did they ignore me?" she asked.

He shrugged. She flew into a rage.

"Because of my ratty ass clothes, that's why. Because the only non-thrift store items I owned were from men and you can only suck so many cocks at once. I know you know that. But the point is, these fuckers at the car dealership ignored me outright. They didn't realize that I had nearly seven fucking grand in the bank, man. And so, I went to another dealership and a guy attended to me. He paid attention. He didn't look at my tits. Not once. I suspect he was a faggot or something. He sure had the trimmed nails of a queer. I ended up buying a used Caddy. It was a real sharp car. And I asked him why he had given me any attention. My shell Adidas shoes had holes in them. I wore a big, baggy sweatshirt. He said the watch. He noticed the watch just like my piece of shit ma had said he would. People treat you what they think you're worth."

Gunner received his first settlement payment of nine thousand dollars and forty-six cents. He went out and financed an antique 1971 Rolex Cosmograph Daytona Oyster watch.

He hated sunglasses because the veil of shade summoned his PTSD.

He would periodically see soldiers' severed body parts, guts raining from red skies, and decapitated heads swimming darkly in a peripheral mirage.

Sometimes Gunner saw his mother's corpse in the reflection of building windows; badly burned, toothless, mouth slack with smoke swirling out of her dry, decaying lips. Sometimes she was hanging the same way he had found her when he was a kid.

For some reason, she was always nude when the apparitions haunted Gunner.

He refused to wear sunglasses, but he did lease a brand-new Jeep Cherokee and he got the watch.

The watch is what caught the attention of Cindy.

Gunner had left her apartment angry and embarrassed. He drove in silence, occasionally yelling at himself or punching the steering wheel. He was disgusted, shaking from the shame of erectile dysfunction.

It happened every time.

Every fucking time, now.

He knew that embarrassment could easily lead to an 'incident' so he would always go for a walk around the block to clear his thoughts.

He parked his jeep in the underground parking garage.

Gunner had established a walking route. He walked a few blocks, passing a strip mall. It was around midnight and the streets were essentially deserted, save the occasional person walking a dog or couples holding hands — which he absolutely disdained. Happy people made him want to puke his fucking brains out.

He wanted normality but he couldn't imagine a realistic pathway towards it.

The meetings helped but deep down he knew that his sexual handicap, the night terrors, and his violent outbursts were something he knew he could never properly manage.

He applied the principles of 12 step recovery to avoiding "incidents" but he was, what the people of the rooms would call, "a chronic relapser."

It had been forty-something days since the last one. He

lost track. This was a major accomplishment for Gunner. He would keep penciled tally marks above his bed but every time he relapsed; he would have to scribble them away again. His walls had many streaks of gray lead smears. Recovery was frustrating.

He couldn't seem to get it right.

Gunner always went through Loady Lane. It was a long and expansive alley that stretched behind the strip mall. It was near the local high school. Students would hang out there, sneaking cigarettes and smoking pot out of apples.

It was also a hangout for the homeless.

It was littered with heaping dumpsters and bags of garbage that permeated the alley with the rotting odors of trash. It reminded him of his mother. Her apartment always had a similar stench. She never washed dishes or took the trash out to the shoot at the end of the hall.

Loady Lane was abandoned except for a drunk hobo stumbling down the alley. He had a King Cobra 40 oz. drink peeking out of a crinkled brown bag. He wavered, spilling some of the booze as he grabbed an imaginary railing and fell.

He shouted at Gunner, "How the yell ya doing?"

Gunner was already upset. He hated to be disturbed when he was deep in his introspection.

"Just fine," he said.

"Ay, man. That watch is really fucking cool."

Gunner nodded and the bum put his hand on his shoulder. He could smell the malt liquor fuming from his putrid mouth.

Gunner shoved the bum.

He fell on his ass.

He looked up at Gunner, "What, man. I like the watch."

"It's fine. Just please don't touch me."

"Fine. Me too, yeah. I'm cool. Spare a couple bucks?"

Gunner shook his head, "Don't got it."

"Man, look at that watch. You think I believe it?"

"Have a good night."

The bum sprang up, stuttered, and got close to Gunner once more. "Come on. Don't be an asshole. Gimme a buck or two, I really need it."

"Get out of my face. Please."

"I need three fuckin' dollars to take a bus to my old lady ... You can gimme that. You can do that for me. Ya greedy rich bastard!"

He was standing in front of Gunner. He stood tall and confident for a man with a precarious equilibrium. He was the same height as Gunner, and they locked stares.

They both had blood-stained eyes for separate reasons.

"I don't want to hurt you," Gunner said.

"Oh! You don't want to hurt me. You don't want to hurt me! You think some spoiled rich twat can hurt me! Do you know what kind of hell I'm living in, man? Ya don't ... Because you're just a spoiled snob. And you probably came from some selfish cunt of a mother—"

Gunner didn't allow him to finish.

He hit him with a right-hook. It was a practiced punch that had precision and power. He connected and heard the familiar sound of a breaking nose, the nauseating crunch of a snapped branch.

Blood squirted out in an obscene cascade, rushing down his chin and on to the chest.

The bum folded forward and fell face first to the ground.

By this point Gunner saw red. He was in a trance of fury. The penny-well stench of death from the bunker seemed to sneak itself back into his mind. He smelled burnt hair and flesh. The distinct smell of spoiled meat, bittersweet, a barbecue of decomposition. He could see his mother's eyes ... as stoic and lifeless as butchered roadkill.

The cheesy soundtrack of pornography drowning out her screams. The grill of a bus: the boogers of trapped dead insects. His breath taken away from rape and trauma and militaristic hells.

He stomped incessantly on the bum's head. A pool of blood began expanding every time he kicked him.

His body would twitch, each spasm weaker than the one before until his body lacked any movement at all.

Gunner looked at the listless hobo. He didn't know if he had murdered him or not. It was certainly possible. He was much more focused on the massive erection that had formed beneath his pants. It was like a monster being resurrected for one more kill, when the audience wasn't expecting it, before the credits of a horror film.

He could feel his cock harden and it felt fantastic. He usually had a small bottle of lubrication on him — as it was impossible to predict when an 'incident' would occur while he was in active recovery.

He couldn't stand masturbation without lube. It was always very painful for him.

He knelt to the bum. He could have checked his pulse, but he knew that he had a very limited window of time. And that his cock would be even stiffer if he thought that he may have killed him.

Instead, he dipped his palm in the puddle of blood.[13]

He gave a cursory look around. They were alone in the shadows of Loady Lane. Gunner stumbled to the dumpster, nearly drunk from endorphins, he stood atop garbage bags and ripped his pants and boxer briefs off. He took his army dog tags out and rubbed them like a lucky rabbit foot.

---

13 Blood makes slick lubrication.

It was his ritual.

He closed his eyes and thought of Cindy. He jerked off ferociously, thinking of her cellulite cracked breasts. His cock was smeared and streaked with the homeless man's blood as he bit his lip and concentrated.

It usually didn't take very long for him.

The hobo slowly regained consciousness and couldn't fucking believe what he was seeing. Gunner was in a were-wolf-like episode and looked terrifying, rubbing his bloody dick under the milky puddle of moonlight.
"What ... the fuck ... what are you ... some sort of weirdo?"

Gunner came, howling into the sky like a lunatic.

"The ... fuck, man. Hey, keep your money."
As soon as he came, Gunner looked at the homeless man. His face looked unrecognizable. It was busted and bloody. There were teeth missing. This broke the trance. He had returned to reality. He looked at his bloody cock and hastily pulled his pants up.
He took a scrunched up $100 bill from his pocket.
"Um, sorry," Gunner said as he threw the money towards the homeless man.
He then ran as fast as he could through the alley of Loady Lane.
"Fuckin' weird-ass Republicans!" the homeless man grunted to himself, lines of blood dangling from his mouth.
He watched Gunner disappear down the alley.

5

PRETTY EYES

Los Angeles 2017-2018

"A paranoid is someone who knows a little of what's going on. A psychotic is a guy who's just found out what's going on." - William S. Burroughs

Brandishing a firearm, assault on a peace officer, resisting arrest, possession of heroin, possession of drug paraphernalia, felon in possession of a firearm, violating the terms of his probation and eight counts of petty theft ...

Mikey May received twenty years in California's Department of Corrections.

Also, an almost mockingly (Like, *ha-ha-ha* motherfucker!) paltry $200 fine.

Because some of his crimes were considered violent in nature, he would have to serve two thirds of his sentence before he would be eligible for parole. He was going to be in prison until he was at least forty years old.

The case became an instant phenomenon in the national media. Mikey's family had already been in the spotlight when his little brother vanished in 1987. And now there was this: Scott May's older brother, blacked out on a bender, a botched suicide attempt, a messy confrontation with cops ... and his girlfriend Jessica DuPont — Chief of Police's niece — vanished without a trace.

It looked really bad.

The news ate it up.

Picketers would stand outside the courtroom, holding cardboard signs: **WHERE IS JESSICA?** and **THERE'S NO SUCH THING AS COINCIDENCES.**

A frenzy of eager reporters would crowd and shout around Mikey; his head down, shackled and handcuffed, with correctional officers on each side of him, pushing his wheelchair into the courtroom.

Of course, everyone thought that the troubled addict had killed her and then tried to kill himself before the police had stopped him.

Tabloids had even hinted that Scott's disappearance should be re-visited with Mikey as a suspect.

There were the obligatory sensationalized headlines: **IS A SEVEN-YEAR-OLD CAPABLE OF COLD-BLOODED MURDER?** with some photograph of Mikey as a young child; distracted, pouting; made to look mischievous in the graininess of the old photo.

There was a lot of pressure to cooperate with law enforcement. They wanted to know what happened to Jessica. He kept his mouth shut. He didn't want to implicate Gay Chris.

There was no way of telling the police that she had died of an accidental overdose without explaining everything else that had happened that day.

They threatened twenty years, but Mikey's attorney assured him that it was a bluff and that it would ultimately be "about half that."

At the sentencing hearing, he had whispered to Mikey, "You've already mentally prepared to do a real term. You need to accept whatever he says with grace, take a deep breath. You'll be fine."

Mike had no friends or family at the hearing. Heroin is a plague for the people that care about the addict, rationality eventually evacuates each one; there are only so many lies someone can hear — there's a universal threshold when it comes to betrayal.

The audience was comprised of reporters, jurors, and curious spectators.

There were loud gasps throughout the courtroom when the judge handed the sentence down...

Twenty. Years.

Fuck.

Mikey's eyes were vacant. They looked glued open; shock had taken away his ability to blink. His ribs were broken. He slouched crookedly in his wheelchair and chose not to make a statement after his sentence was announced.

The guards wheeled him away, he remembered how loudly the swinging doors slammed shut behind him; the reality of the free world discarding him like he was some worthless piece of fucking trash.

Police detest cop killers or anyone that is charged with anything violent towards an officer. They hated Mikey before he had been charged with assault because they believed that he had murdered the Chief's niece.

Mikey couldn't remember the first night in jail.

He must have told the guards that he felt suicidal because he woke up the next day in a suicide watch cell. It was 8 x 10 with plexiglass in front instead of bars.

He had no idea where he was when he opened his eyes. He was wearing some sort of weighted dress. He was naked underneath, and it was freezing. There was an inmate sitting in a folding chair looking at him. That's one of the few jobs you can get while serving time in a county jail: suicide watcher.

Oh, he was locked up.

The inmate assigned to watching him was Hispanic. He had Aztec tattoos covering the top of his shaved head and a thick paint brush mustache. He saw that Mikey woke up but didn't say anything. He just studied him as if he was a wounded insect, squirming under a magnifying glass.

Snot rolled out of Mikey's nostrils. He felt goose pimples sprout up, forming a rash on top of his arms. And suddenly, he felt sharp, stinging pain from the many times he had been too frustrated to find a vein and muscled a shot into his ass cheek. It would burn momentarily and then form a hard lump. The heroin would numb the pain so he wouldn't notice when he was high.

But he hadn't done heroin for nearly 24 hours.

Dope sickness erupted violently throughout his entire body. He was shivering, it felt like slushy ice was flowing through his veins. Abdominal cramps folded him forward, and he swayed with his head down, eyes closed, trying to combat the nausea.

Opiates make you constipated. Mikey would shit once or twice a week if he was lucky. It wasn't normal shit either. It was painful, hardened egg-shaped shit that junkies called heroin babies.

But withdrawal opens the floodgates of bodily malfunction. There's a deluge of discomfort, the mental anguish of panic; the body temperature fluctuating from sweaty hot to frigid cold. He was trying not to vomit by finding the perfect angle to tilt his head.

It was like being seasick.

There was something subtle brewing inside his digestive tract. It felt like the soft hum of a motor, but from experience, he knew that it could turn volcanic at any moment, shit would spew wildly out of his asshole until it became so tender and raw that a simple fart felt like a goddamn dagger ripping apart his anal spokes.

He was in a very delicate situation. Sudden movements, or his head sagging at the wrong angle would elicit vomit or diarrhea. He sat with his eyes closed, hoping for his symptoms to become more manageable.

Mikey thought about everything that had happened leading up to him being in that cell. His memories were hazy and had a dream quality; without the buffer of heroin, he felt the heaviness of Jessica's death. He winced thinking about the brutal violence that had left the motel room splattered in blood and he was sad for himself; sad that things had turned out so fucking bad for him.

He thought about being a little boy and tried to imagine what that version of himself would think about his life today: wearing a dress, paled from heroin withdrawal, stuck in an Aquarium-looking cell as some gangbanger watched him with childish fascination.

There was only one thing he could do ...
Masturbate.

His body was so depleted of endorphins and dopamine, it was the only way to summon whatever he had left in reserve. Heroin has bizarre effects on sex. In the beginning of a run, it's impossible to cum. It doesn't matter how hard you thrust and pump, you simply can't finish. Eventually, it kills your sex-drive all together. After a while, all junkies become asexual. Injecting dope becomes the orgasm. Dope sickness creates a paradoxical issue: you cum in mere seconds. And that's without a full erection, there just needs to be a little bit of blood flow, half-way engorgement, and you can have sex or masturbate.

Jerking off was a lifeline and Mikey had done it in jail

covertly many times. He had devised a technique where he would use a reverse grip, his hand backwards, as he propped his knee up and made a tent with his blanket. The reverse grip would hide any movement. He could masturbate, late at night in a bunk, or in a tank full of other inmates. He would feign a cough when he was done to mask the sigh of cumming.

It offered momentary relief.

Suicide watch was a unique challenge for clandestine masturbation. Mikey looked up and saw the Hispanic inmate with the same dumb look, staring at him, taking his job as suicide watcher way too seriously. Opening his eyes, even for a second, had amplified Mikey's withdrawal symptoms.

He felt so awful that he didn't even care about jerking off in front of the inmate. He was wearing a dress. Or whatever it was. And it would be nearly impossible to do it without him knowing. But he didn't give a fuck. He stuck his hand down to his crotch and closed his eyes as he tugged. He started to feel better. His mind went somewhere else, a pornographic collage, all the things that turned him on. His dick was as hard as it was going to get. It wasn't very stiff, in fact, he wouldn't even be able to have sex with it as flaccid as it was. It was just enough for him to jerk off. It felt heavenly for a few seconds and then ... he came ... and he was propelled instantly back into withdrawal.

"Hey, fool," the inmate said.

Mikey opened his eyes and saw him smirking.

"I do that shit too. I beat off too, fool."

Mikey nodded.

There was a lot of awkward sexual stuff like this in jail. Different cultures all melted together in an enclosed microcosm. There were closet homosexuals and flagrant homosexuals. But there was no such thing as locked up love.

There was an almost evil, sexual undercurrent that swept through every institution. Mikey didn't know how to respond. Who says shit like that? *I beat off too, fool.*

He was too sick to think too much about it.

Suddenly, Mikey's stomach imploded. He didn't make it to the metallic toilet. Shit oozed out of him, rushing down his legs. He got up and tried to make it to the toilet — the movement made him dizzy. The cell felt like it was spinning ferociously. It made him projectile vomit as he stumbled to the toilet. The rumble made his chest hurt. The acidic bile burned his throat. It was a horrible sensation to puke and shit simultaneously. Mikey felt like he was a puppet being tugged in a dozen directions by some deranged puppeteer.

The inmate said nothing. He just watched.

Mikey sat on the toilet. He began to sneeze repeatedly, an interesting rarely talked about symptom of heroin withdrawal. He was having a sneeze attack. It turned to sharp, thunderous coughing, and finally dry heaves. His stomach had been emptied out from both ends.

A tiny amount of bile drooled from the corner of his mouth burning his lips. It was warm. His mouth had turned white, caked from vomit and spittle.

Mikey cried again. Aside from crying when Andy handed him the molly in the parking lot, he probably hadn't cried in ten years. The emotive dissonance of heroin prohibited it. People need to cry. It's a release. It's part of being human. He forgot what it felt like. The tears burned as they rolled down his cheek. Every inch of his body ached. Even crying hurt.

Day two of kicking heroin is much more severe than day one. He knew that he was in for torture the following day. He couldn't sleep. There was crusty shit and puke all over himself. He had tried to clean himself off in the sink, but the water felt like razor blades. The stinging sensation of cold water was so overwhelming that he could only clean himself so much.

The night seemed to go on forever. He had restless leg syndrome, which was the worst part of kicking for Mikey. His legs became rubbery causing excruciating discomfort and pain. It made him thrash, tossing and turning all night. His legs felt like they were trying to split apart. As if the bones were trying to escape and bust right through the seams of the skin.

Another inmate had replaced the first one. He looked similar: hispanic, tattoos, paint brush mustache. But he wasn't silent.

Mikey wished that he was.

"Are you fine though?" the suicide watcher asked.

What kind of fucking question was that?

Of course, he wasn't! He looked like an exorcism was being performed on him.

"Hey, fool, you fine?"

Mikey didn't answer.

"My uncle does that shit. That negro. That's some bad shit right there, fool. It'll destroy your life. I think you should, like, how you say, consider ... you should consider letting Jesus Christ be your lord and savior."

Mikey looked at him.

He was wearing an orange jumpsuit. He had 818 tattooed on his cheek. The last thing in the world Mikey wanted was some dude in jail telling him how to live his life.

"Come on, dawg. We'll do a prayer. He listens. Ask Him

for you not to be sick no more."

Mikey was shaking. He was on the verge of collapsing. His body wanted to shut down and this guy wanted him to pray.

"Come on. Get up, fool. God will listen!"

Mikey got off the bunk.

He knew this guy wasn't going to give up. He walked towards the plexiglass in front of the cell. There were little holes poked throughout for ventilation and so people on each side of the glass could hear each other speak. There was also a meal-slot that was opened three times a day for meals.

"Good. Put your hand up to the glass."

Mikey was so weak he didn't even know if he could do it. He put his hand up and the inmate matched it with his own hand.

"God, we are here today, because ..."

He looked at Mikey. "What's your name?"

"Mike."

"We are here today because Mike wants to do good, God. He is sick of not doing good and he wants to do real good. Please help him. Please look out for him. Also, God, help me out with my trial. This fucking bitch said I broke her nose. Sorry for the bad words but I'm mad, God. Thank you and amen."

Mikey took his hand down.

He missed the other suicide watcher. He wasn't going to be able to handle the faux-Christian for too much longer — he didn't know what time it was, it felt like the middle of the night.

"Wood, where you from?"

"Here," Mikey said weakly, "L.A.."

"That's right. Alright. Me too, fool. I'm from Monte Flores. The *bootahs* fuckin' got me, dawg. My girl said I broke her nose and shit. I'm looking at some real time.

Like years, fool. So don't trip. You don't gotta kill yourself or nothing. What they got you on? Like a DUI or some college crime white boy shit or what?"

"I don't even know my charges. I barely remember getting arrested."

"You ain't here on some weirdo shit though, right?"

Mikey was sick. It was extremely difficult to talk. It required more energy than he had to expend. He had become a pro from doing so much time and he knew that his paperwork was somewhere in the cell. He wanted to shut the inmate up; he was also curious about what new charges he had picked up.

"I'm going to find and show you my paperwork and then I have to rest," Mikey said.

The inmate nodded.

Mikey went to his bunk and looked at his linen roll. They always give you a small hygiene kit: a small bar of Bob Barker soap, a disposable razor, a small translucent tube of toothpaste, a small white toothbrush, and a black comb. They give you a county jail rule book and there's booking paperwork that says when you were arrested and what your charges are. It's a salmon-colored paper and easy to spot.

Mikey found it in the pile of linen.

His eyes expanded when he saw the charges. The drug stuff wasn't a big deal but the brandishing a firearm to a police officer and felon in position of a firearm could easily get him ten years by itself. He had an eight-year joint suspended sentence from all the petty thefts he had been arrested for. There was no bail. It just said, probation hold. — which didn't matter because he had nobody to bail him out anyway.

"What's it say, fool?" the inmate asked.

Mikey walked over and slid the paperwork through the meal slot. He took cheap reading glasses out of the front pocket of his jump suit and started reading.

"Damn, homie! I thought I was fucked! No wonder you wanna kill yourself. I don't blame you! I'd fucking kill myself too!"

"Pretty sure you aren't supposed to say that to me as suicide watcher."

"Fuck this job, fool. They give me a bag of Columbian coffee. Not even Tasters or Folgers. I don't care if you die. I'm pretty sure I get my coffee no matter what."

This guy was bi-polar.

"This is like ten years, maybe more, dawg. Damn"

"It's more. I already had eight years over my head. Joint-suspended sentence. I'm fucked."

"Damn, fool. Pray. God looks out."

All the talking had exhausted Mikey. He felt like he had to take a shit. He ran over to the toilet — nothing came out. It was just gas, howling loudly into the toilet bowl.

He flushed the toilet several times to eliminate the odor. In an institution this is called a "courtesy flush."

He could feel his stomach rumble and didn't feel safe getting off the toilet. Mikey put his head down and continued to fart and courtesy flush. He was wide-awake but had been up for over a day. He nodded out on the toilet. His body shut down. It was the kind of quasi-sleep you get in a car or airplane. He could hear things, but his body was physically sleeping.

"May!" someone shouted.

He had no idea how long he had been out.

He looked up and the inmate was gone. There were five guards standing in front of the cell.

A guard said, "You got a visitor."

He opened the meal-slot and put an orange jumpsuit inside of it.

"Get dressed in your jumpsuit."

Mikey had a bad feeling about this. Suicide watch was always 72 hours. There were no interruptions and certainly no visitation allowed. He had never had five guards escort him to a visit. This was something else.

He took his suicide dress off and put the jumpsuit on. It had buttons lining the front and a folded collar on the top. He also had flat orange canvas shoes.

"Back up to the meal-slot and place your hands behind you so we can cuff you."

Mikey did as he was told. He felt wobbly. And walking backwards reignited his nausea. He placed his hands behind him and stuck them through the slot. He felt the cuffs go on his wrists. Dope sick, the cuffs felt colder and tighter than they usually did.

"Now step forward."

There was a loud unlatching sound and the plexiglass door slid open. It was in a magnetic track — it thumped when it opened entirely.

A guard got on each side of Mikey, grabbing his arms, and the others followed. They walked down a labyrinth of corridors.

Mikey saw tanks full of inmates; some on pay phones, some playing cards or slapping down dominoes on metal tables. The jail was extremely loud and had the unique, rancid smell of every county jail: feet, perspiration, trans fat farts, withdrawal, body odor ...

They took Mikey to an interrogation room.

He had frequented the jail many times throughout the years, but he had never seen this room before. One of the guards unlocked the door with a huge brass key. And they brought Mikey into the room. There was a table and a chair on both sides.

There was a man in a tie sitting in the chair on the other side of the table. Mikey didn't recognize him. He looked like a cop.

He was bald and slightly overweight. He had a mean stepfather goatee and looked flustered.

"Sit down, Michael," he said.

Mikey looked at the guards and they nodded. He sat in the chair. His hands cuffed behind him.

"Can we get those cuffs off of him?"

One of the guards walked over and did as he was told. Mikey was only slightly more comfortable.

The dope sickness was all consuming.

"You know who I am?"

Mikey shook his head.

"Martin DuPont. You dated my niece."

Mikey felt like he was going to shit. He just nodded at him and concentrated as hard as he could on not having an accident, right there, in front of everyone.

"Jessica is missing. Now, listen, the girl has had serious issues for many years. She has a criminal record. Everything from drugs to theft. She's gone missing many times before. I don't know if you knew this, but I raised the girl. My brother, her biological father, is a real piece of shit. He's a pervert. I'm sure you get the idea. I never blamed Jessica for becoming an addict. Her mom ran out on her when she was a kid and my brother abused her until we found out about it; she was only seven years old. She had a tough life. I knew she was dating you. I know your background, the drugs and theft, same as hers. I never cared too much. Junkies date junkies. Long as you weren't hitting her, I figured it wasn't my business. You guys are both in your early twenties. I hadn't given up on her. Young enough to turn it around. The night you were arrested, you were out of it, but in the police reports it says you told the officers that you were trying to commit suicide and that you only pointed the gun at them because they had stopped you. You must have been feeling really low that night. Perhaps you had made a mistake that you didn't think you could get out of. Whatever the case, the next day there was a call to the homicide detectives, the motel room that you and Jessica had been living in was covered in blood — that's the way it was first described to me. But then I saw the photos ..."

Martin reached below the table and retrieved a briefcase.

There were manila envelopes inside and he shuffled through until he found one that had "motel" written on it. He handed Mikey the envelope. It was thick. Mikey opened it and was shocked to see the state of the room. There was blood all over the walls, ceiling, and carpet. There had been no effort to clean it.

He couldn't believe the massacred condition of the room.

"There were no bodies found. I say bodies plural because that's a lot of goddamn blood. The owner of the motel called because he saw your face on the front cover of The L.A. *Times* this morning. Your case has gotten a lot of attention because of your little brother's disappearance. The owner of the motel said you guys have lived there for a little over ten months. We know you were staying there under a fake ID. He never heard you guys fight. But he said you were acting strange the day of your arrest. When he approached you about rent, your forehead was freshly cut open, still leaking blood. He said he didn't see Jessica once that day and he usually did because she liked to smoke cigarettes out front. He didn't see her and then the housekeeper found all this blood. Now, I don't want to jump to any extreme conclusions, I ain't no Scooby Doo, but come on, this don't look too good for you, bud. The owner said you were agitated and angry that day, very unusual for you, he said. You had a wound. And then you try and kill yourself ... Jessica nowhere to be found ... and your motel room looking like the goddamn Manson murders. So ... tell me, Michael, where the hell is my niece?"

Mikey farted.

It was a breezy horse-like fart. He was thankful that it was dry. There were a couple of snickers around the room.

"Sorry, I'm kicking heroin. It's hard to control my gas. Listen, Mr. DuPont—"

"Marty," he said.

"Marty, I don't know where Jessica is. I didn't kill her if that's what you're implying."

"Jessica was like a daughter to me. Your story, the 'I don't know' bullshit isn't cutting it. You know something. You know enough that you wanted to take your own life. You're facing incredibly serious charges. I am the chief of police. I can snap my fingers and your case disappears. I just need to know where she is or if she's dead."

"I don't—"

"Know," Marty cut him off, "I don't know, I don't know. Yes, you fucking do know, you little fucking hype. I can make this case go away or I can make sure you get twenty years in prison. Twenty years for a convict that killed the chief of fucking police's niece. You don't need no conviction. There's solidarity in the force. Twenty years of torture for you. Let's try again. Where is my niece?"

The room was spinning. Mikey's body temperature was swinging like a drunken pendulum: hot to cold, cold to hot. There was a siren going off inside of his head. It was anxiety and panic, colored red and Dodger-blue, swirling and flashing around his brain.

He felt light-headed, like he was going to faint at any moment. Marty's threats didn't scare him. It felt like things couldn't possibly get worse than they were at that moment.

Boy, was he wrong about that!

"Earth to Michael ... where the fuck is Jessica?"

"I. Do. Not. Know," Mikey said.

Marty signaled to one of the guards. He walked up to Mikey and handcuffed him once more.

"Take him to the stairwell," Marty said, and then he turned to Mikey, "You want to play games? We have tons of games for you. And we always win. We are the law, Michael. I will get answers out of you. You'll tap out. You ain't tough."

Mikey wanted to tell him to go fuck himself but he was too weak. He didn't know where the stairwell was, he expected he was about to get severely beaten by the five guards ushering him down the long, dark corridor.

Mikey started coughing. It turned to dry heaves again. His stomach was completely drained of fluids. He closed his eyes. There were guards on each side of him. They held his arms, nearly dragging him because he was so fatigued.

They finally stopped.

They were in front of a large steel door. The stairwell he presumed. One of the guards jangled a key from a large ring and opened the door.

They were at the top of a steep stairwell.

The guards pushed Mikey and he tumbled down the stairs violently. He was handcuffed and had no way to brace his fall. He wasn't expecting it, he rolled down forty or fifty stairs, and when he reached the bottom, his head hit the floor, knocking him out cold.

He woke up to batons hitting him.

He was being jumped by the five guards. There was blood everywhere, blackened by the shadows of the poorly lit stairwell. He didn't know if it was from the batons or from falling down the stairs. Warm blood stung his eyes.

The guards didn't say anything while they beat Mikey, they just made grunts and breathed laboriously, like hurried backseat sex with a prostitute.

It was very primitive and grim.

Occasionally, there was a cracking or crunching noise. Mikey had all his ribs broken, he moved his tongue around until he felt a loose tooth, he applied a light amount of pressure, and it spilled out of his mouth.

There was the distinct taste of blood oozing down his throat, an extreme copper taste as if a handful of dirty pennies had been liquified and forcefully swallowed.

There was a staccato rhythm of screeching, noises you'd hear during an indoor game of basketball, the guards' boots against the waxed concrete floor.

"You must think you're a real bad motherfucker. killing women," a guard said, "You bad?"

Mikey was so dizzy and disoriented that he just nodded in agreement. He was bad. He was coughing up pellets of bloody phlegm.

Another one said, "Why don't you square up with someone your own size?"

Mikey was squinting, concentrating on an incoming fart. He didn't know if it was going to be wet or dry, he mustered all his strength to hold it in. The guard took this as defiance.

"I'm going to uncuff you. I'm going to give you a free-bie. One on one. Huh, tough guy? Huh?"

Mikey felt a knee on his back. His face was cold against the dusty floor. The handcuffs came off and he wanted to just curl up, but he knew that he was going to keep getting beat up regardless.

He was certain that he was going to be killed by the guards. Being thrown down a flight of stairs handcuffed should have killed him.

He attempted to stand but his broken ribs wouldn't allow it. He staggered forward and took a pathetic swing at a guard, missing by a long shot — he slipped on his own blood, falling back down, hitting his chin hard against the floor.

The guards cheered with amusement.

"Pussy," one said, spitting on him.

"Did you just try and hit an officer?"

Mikey couldn't muster any energy to look up.

"That's assault on a peace officer, brother. That's what ... like five ... six years that'll be added to your sentence."

His eyelids finally collapsed. He could hear laughter and echoes and finally ...

Silence.

That's how he wound up in a wheelchair for his trial. And why he was charged with assaulting a guard. There were no cameras in the stairwell.

Although it felt like it lasted forever, the heroin withdrawal eventually subsided. It took a month for Mikey to start sleeping normally again. This was the post-acute-withdrawal phase and the aching discomfort of his ribs being broken made it nearly impossible to relax.

The national press stayed obsessed with Mikey until the trial was over. It had made him a celebrity prisoner and he couldn't be with other inmates in the general population. They kept him in a solitary confinement wing of the jail called Northwest-ISO.

There was a bunk bed, a metallic toilet with a connected sink, a small metal desk and a round stool attached to it. There were no windows to the outside, except for a small one on the door that guards could peek in when they made their hourly rounds.

He was allowed an hour of recreation daily. He never went. It was a small cage, slightly bigger than his cell, with sunlight splintering through its razor wire top. He didn't like to be reminded of the outside world. He preferred to stay in his cell and immerse himself in a novel. He was allowed a phone call once a month, guards would roll a phone with a long chord down the hall to each cell in the isolation-wing.

Mikey had nobody to call.

His parents had written him a scathing goodbye letter, essentially disowning him as their son. Even Mikey's parents thought he killed Jessica. Fuck, even his attorney thought he killed her. He asked him several times, straight up. Mikey would just look at him. And the attorney would say, "Alright, alight, alright ... you don't know anything."

Periodically, one of the guards that had jumped Mikey would walk down the hall. They never looked at him if they were alone. They weren't as tough by themselves and they knew it — or maybe they felt guilty for nearly killing Mikey and then charging him with assault.

Most guards are impressionable and carry a wolf-pack mentality. After being around hoodlums, gangsters, thieves, junkies, and seasoned convicts ... they became just as institutionalized as the inmates themselves.

Prisons and jails are ideological breeding grounds for: racism, homophobia, misogyny, xenophobia, and hatred.

Guards aren't immune to the moral pollution of incarceration. They become just as dangerous and demoralized as the criminals.

And then they go home at night.

It's no surprise that domestic violence rates are disproportionately high for correctional officers — or the occasional headline in the local newspaper, that they apprehended some hick prison guard for slashing some guy's throat or strangling their cheating wife.

Mikey became aware of that double-edged sword the night that they beat him half to death in the stairwell. Their story was that he had somehow gotten the handcuffs off himself and brazenly attacked one of the guards.

He then tried to kill himself by taking a swan dive down the staircase. It didn't kill him. And he got up and started assaulting the guards again. They had no choice but to defend themselves with batons. Nobody bothered to ask them why they had batons in the first place. It wasn't normal for correctional officers to have them. Batons, shields, gas masks, mace spray tanks, and percussion grenades were all part of riot gear. Every jail has them, but they are rarely ever used and reserved strictly for big scale disturbances.

Everyone was so preoccupied with Jessica's disappearance and the subsequent vilification of Mikey that they didn't question the absurd, totally unrealistic, outlandish story.

Mikey sat in that county jail for a little over a year. Finally, one late night, a guard opened the meal-slot, "May, gather your shit. You're catching the chain. You're going to prison."

He knew that he would probably be in solitary confinement for the rest of his prison term because of the high-profile nature of his case. Inmates hated him too. The newspapers had painted him as some elusive, girlfriend-killing dope fiend, who only got halfway caught.

Guards would escort Mikey to the showers when he was in isolation and inmates would throw trash at him.

"Scumbag!" they'd shout and an apple would narrowly miss Mikey's head.

He knew that he was in trouble when the guards and convicts all hated him. He had 19 more years to survive. The notion of killing himself, he thought in retrospect, was largely due to the gloominess of his heroin addiction — a seemingly endless cluster of claustrophobic fog. He didn't see a way out. It wasn't like prison was rainbows and cupcakes. But at least he no longer felt possessed by the demonic forces of hard drugs.

The guard came back a half hour later. Mikey knew the drill. He put his hands behind his back, bent down, stuck them through the meal-slot and he was handcuffed. In special housing units like isolation, this was the only way that inmates were handled.

He had put his possessions in a big, translucent trash bag. He had 94 journals covering the months of incarceration. That was all. The guard grabbed the bag and escorted Mikey through the jail. He didn't look back at the cell he had been living in for the last year. These were memories he cared very little about preserving except for what he had written.

It was the middle of the night.

Probably three in the morning. That's when they did transportation to state prisons. He knew that it was Thursday. That was chain day. He wondered if they would put him in a holding tank with other inmates. It had been so long since he had interacted with other human beings, save the occasional guard or nurse.

He wondered if he was in danger.

He knew a lot of people wanted to hurt him.

The guard put him in a small, single man holding cell. It was usually reserved for severely drunk and disorderly people that were just getting booked in. There was a bulletin board with advertisements for different bail bond companies. Mikey was bored and examined each one. They were gimmicky. Some were satirical, spoofs of easily recognizable films. There was one that showed a ghost in jail, it had the *Ghostbusters* font and it said **WHO YOU GONNA CALL?** with the number written in big, neon letters. There were ads that seemed directed at college students or first-time offenders.

A photo of a scared kid in a graduation gown, he was

gripping jail bars and had some Brutus-looking convicts behind him, looking horny and ready to pounce. It said: **THERE'S A FIRST TIME FOR EVERYTHING!**

There were ads of voluptuous women in bikinis and there were others with nerdy, realtor looking men. There seemed to be an ad for every demographic.

There was a small advertisement towards the bottom of the bulletin board: **CHUCK'S LIGHTNING QUICK BONDS.** There was a man in a plain white t-shirt and two crudely drawn lightning bolts poking out of a cloud. It was meant to appeal to the white power types. Nazi shit. Clever.

6

ANIMALS AND PRIMATES REDUX

Los Angeles 2017 - 2018

"If you like the way things are, then all cops are good cops. If you don't like the way things are, then all cops are bad cops." - Charles Bukowski

It was many hours later when McFadden opened his eyes. He didn't know where he was but the pain in his back was debilitating. The parts that weren't throbbing were numb. He looked around and saw the hotel room in complete disarray.

The fairy thugs. The fucking animals.

McFadden was able to stand but only for a moment before he collapsed. The memories from the night before were vague and hideous.

They took on a carnival quality in his mind.

The faces of former Presidents, limp cocks, and something that looked like elephant skin, but he simply couldn't remember what.

He saw his wallet on the floor. Thank goodness. He remembered a camera with a blinking red light. He made a weak sound, his anger impotent from fatigue.

This was a real predicament. He had no idea how he would explain this to law enforcement. It would surely make the news that the son of Hubert McFadden was mugged in some fancy hotel by anarchistic queers.

It was obvious that he had been shot but impossible to tell exactly where, because his entire body was poked by painful pins and needles, as if he were one giant limb that had gone to sleep. It hurt.

He needed immediate medical attention and feared that he may be paralyzed.

He pulled himself up to a chair and it seemed to offer tepid circulation. He was able to move but it proved to be extremely difficult for him.

It took him forty minutes to stumble around the room and make sure he hadn't left anything. He opened the door and shielded his eyes from the sudden flood of daylight.

His head was pulsating. He had never experienced a hangover to this degree and the light was torturous. He held onto the guard rail of the balcony, hoping he'd avoid seeing anyone as he made his way down to the parking lot and to his car.

A housekeeper was humming as she pushed her cart full of toilet paper and cleaning supplies. She bobbed her head gleefully, like she was reciting some feel-good song in her head.

Then she saw Collin McFadden and shrieked.

She put both hands on her mouth and forced it to stop leaking sound. Her eyes widened, staying enormous as she slowly stepped backwards with her cart — not taking her eyes off McFadden.

The barbecue sauce and blood had made a repulsive crust on his skin. The fact that he was heavyset made him look like some malevolent blob.

It was clear that something horrific had transpired.

He was relieved that it was only some Mexican. The dumb bitch probably didn't even have a green card. He swayed past her, his arms flailing from the disorienting effects of whatever he had been dosed with the night before.

The maid concentrated on holding her scream. She kept pulling the cart and didn't take her eyes off the crazed man. White people could be so odd and scary.

McFadden made it to the parking lot before blacking out entirely.

He was found asleep in his car by a couple of police officers. That fucking brown maid had surely called them.

The drug had rendered him a groggy, self-righteous asshole. "Don't pretend as if you don't know McFadden and Crow, the premier investment banking firm of the East Coast."

"The mission statement of your company don't answer the questions we're asking. Again, why do you have a fresh bullet wound?"

He was having a difficult time keeping his eyes open. His head sagged and chomped at an invisible object.

One of the cops was black, the other Latino.

He couldn't stand to be on the other side of their authority.

"Why in the hell does it matter? I was mugged by some goddamn animals!"

"By whom, sir? Who mugged you and where did this happen?"

"Enough! I certainly don't need to explain myself to you. I am the victim here. And you work for me! You are civil servants." He paused and looked directly at the black cop. "Well, civil slave in your case. So, don't you dare question me, boy."

McFadden didn't remember anything after this. He woke up in a hospital. His entire body was engulfed in burning pain.

He screamed. It was high-pitched and hollowed. He didn't recognize the sound; it was completely unobstructed; after a moment, he realized that he was missing all his teeth.

He had always associated the subtle taste of dental work with money and greed. But this was very strong. There seemed to be a whole lot of blood trickling down his throat.

It made him gag.

There was a cop sitting in a chair reading *Guns & Ammo.* He lowered the magazine for a moment and watched the hideous toothless man cough up blood; he shook his head with obvious disdain, getting back to his reading (or perhaps just looking at the photo spread.)

It was clear as day that the police officer was upset with McFadden, but he honestly couldn't remember much. He knew he was in some sort of trouble because his left ankle had a handcuff around it, shackled to the bed.

But goddamn, he didn't realize how much trouble he was truly in. He had been charged with driving while intoxicated, resisting arrest, and assault on an officer.

He was bailed out immediately and picked up by the family attorney. He handed McFadden an ice-cold Dr. Pepper for his swollen face.

The attorney said, "It's not looking good, Mac,"

McFadden tried to speak but could only make gurgling, fluid noises.

"Susan made you an appointment for the dental situation ... It's the press though, Mac. They are painting you as some evil, racist ... damn oligarch. But you were brutalized by the police. I'm gonna make you the white Rodney King. The cosmetic flaws of this case are absolutely mind boggling. You were clearly in a state of emotional duress after a traumatic armed robbery for Christ's sake! And you were parked. I'm not sure how they are going to prove that you had intent to drive after you had been drugged against your will — but like I said: the press. It has been on all the major networks. I hate to be the one to break this to you, but Susan is sick, Mac."

McFadden was silent but his eyes gained intensity at the mention of her name.

"Colon cancer and it isn't a good prognosis. It's terminal. She wanted to tell you, but the press found out before she had the chance. They are saying that you were obviously robbed in a prostitution arrangement gone bad. They've been propagating that nonsense non-stop. The heir of one of the largest financial institutions is out paying for sex while his wife of ten years is withering away from cancer. It doesn't look good and it's getting a whole hell of a lot of attention. We have been working with a publicity agency. A very, very good one. They specialize in damage control. We were able to get you out under the pre-trial condition that you would abstain from alcohol and attend Alcoholic Anonymous meetings. Public opinion is important here. It isn't as much the assault. It's that these thug cops have alleged that you had used racial slurs before you had brutally attacked them. They are claiming that this vicious number they did on you was self-defense."

McFadden whined incomprehensibly; his face paled from the severe pain buzzing beneath his jawline.

"Mac," the attorney began, "We will prevail. We don't play by the same rules as the mere civilians do, you got it?"

McFadden tried to talk and made a grunting noise.

"If you need to tell me something, save your strength, write it on a piece of paper,"

The attorney grabbed a notepad from his briefcase and handed it to McFadden with a pen. It was difficult to lean over to the nightstand next to him. But he was determined.

He wrote: *They videotaped me. Trying to frame me. Make me look homo. Get it taken care of.*

McFadden slammed his fist on the nightstand and groaned.

"Okay, yes, Mac. I will get it taken care of. I always do. You rest. Leave it all to me."

McFadden had to get a hybrid set of implant veneers. The fake teeth were large and perfect. They looked goofy on his piggish face.

The permanent snarl gave the appearance that he was always smirking.

It didn't match his crude personality. It was hard for his wife to get used to. It seemed inappropriate and disingenuous as he stood above her hospital bed, defending himself against the hooker allegations.

"Of course not, Susan," McFadden said, "How you would ever believe some second-hand rumors from lib-tard news sources is beyond me."

She couldn't get used to that stupid plastered grin.

She whispered weakly, "I know what you've done, Collin. And you're a real son of a bitch, you know that?"

McFadden really hated to hurt her feelings to this degree. It was a real irritant for him when she was puffy and exasperated. Susan was instantly uglified when she was sad.

God, it absolutely fucking disgusted him.

"Your children will never forgive you for this!"

It turned out to be true. Their children were young; six and twelve; but they seemed to be aware of the collective negative energy that was now directed at their father.

There was a mob-frenzy of news reporters and a flurry of flashing cameras from the overzealous press. McFadden had never felt so ostracized in his life. He had become one of the most hated men in the country overnight.

The advent of cell phone video recording had illuminated

police brutality and exposed violent, racially charged attacks. It was rare for the public to side with the police.

But the press had vilified Collin McFadden. He had become a caricature of an aristocratic scumbag out partying with hookers, while his wife was on her deathbed.

He was surprised that he enjoyed his first Alcoholics Anonymous meeting. It was full of a bunch of arrogant assholes just like him and nobody judged anyone else — they were too busy in narcissistic rants about themselves.

In many ways the meetings reminded McFadden of the self-absorbed holiday meals he shared with his extended family when he was growing up.

McFadden cringed when he heard the word God, but he was amazed how much he related when a fellow drunk would talk about the angry, self-loathing hell that their minds were enslaved in before they had decided to get straight.

For the first time in his life, he felt a genuine sense of belonging. He quit drinking and gained forty pounds. He had those silly teeth implants that made him look like an Orwellian farm animal, but he was committed to a life of sobriety and had become a nice person — totally cured of his inherent racism.

Of course, that wasn't true. This was about pussy. He had met a woman when he had to get his court card signed to prove that he was attending his pretrial mandated meetings.

"I'm Collin ... M," he said, as she scribbled her signature on the paper.

"Hello there, Collin M! I am the court card lady! I hope that you are getting something out of the meetings. You know, it really doesn't matter how you get to these rooms, what matters is that you stay long enough to allow the miracle to occur."

McFadden was staring at her tits. Curvy cleavage beneath the V of a blue blouse — impossible for a pervert to miss.

She noticed his gaze and blushed.

"Can I ask you something?" she said.

"Shoot."

"You lift weights? You must. Your arms are really, really huge."

McFadden laughed incredulously and couldn't stop blushing. He already had that permanent moronic smile from the veneers, this made his teeth wolfish.

He looked like a straight-up psychopath.

He couldn't remember the last time a woman gave him a compliment without collecting a damn invoice. In fact, his wife Susan, was the only woman that had ever seemed to like him for who he truly was, and she turned out to be a beach whale.

He wished that nasty bitch would just hurry up and die.

The court card lady became McFadden's reason to choose the sunset meeting at the Alano Club. He detested the San Fernando Valley, but this woman would make his heart skip a beat and was well worth the trip. He stunk himself up with Brut cologne and even started wearing t-shirts to meetings — which was out of character, but he wanted to appear "wild and crazy" to this treasure of a woman.

She reminded him of the girls that he would have a crush on when he was in grade school. The ones that didn't seem to know that he had even existed.

She was invariably flirtatious towards him, and he just couldn't figure out why. It didn't matter. He felt like he was a kid again and he needed that. Susan was declining, and his children had become annoyingly emotional and sentimental. It made him want to barf.

There had been an anarchist movement that originated

ANTIHEROES

in New York City a few years before. A bunch of jobless losers had rallied against capitalism and demonized the 1% — as if being successful was a bad thing. Those shoeless fucking hippies occupied Wall Street in a seemingly pointless tantrum of jealousy.

Drug heads. Animals. Filthy bums.

Racism in America found a renewed interest as soon as Donald Trump had become president. It created a divide. Racists felt comfortable crawling out of the shadows and the progressives had unified to counterbalance it. The fact that a plutocrat had spouted off racist remarks and subsequently attacked minority police officers, had made McFadden a perfect scapegoat in this rich versus poor climate where the old white man had become public enemy number one.

His face had become ubiquitous on television. Journalists and reporters hounded him relentlessly. It was ironic that the only place that he could find any solace was in the privacy of AA meetings.

McFadden took the court card lady out to get coffee after one of the many meetings they had sat through together. She laughed at his jokes as she sipped her coffee. He put his hand on her thigh and she didn't flinch. She welcomed it and ... in what seemed like a childhood wet dream: McFadden was in her apartment, she took his shirt off and traced his curvatures as if he was a sculpted statue and not in the flabby pre-stages of some auto-immune disease like he was; they had sex and he held on to her, nude in bed.

His sweat smelled awful — a wash of Brut and greasy fried chicken.

"I've never felt this way in my life," he told her.

The court card lady stroked his hair.

"What happened?" she asked. "On the TV. Why do they hate you so damn much?"

He closed his eyes and exhaled.

She immediately regretted asking him about this.

"You know who I am then?"

She giggled, "You're on the TV every day. Would be hard not to!"

"Then you know ..."

"That you got a wife and kids? Well, yeah, but I can't help who I like. And she can't be all that if you are here with me."

"She's disgusting. I think she's using the cancer thing to try and gain sympathy with my kids. She's a real selfish bitch like that."

"Well, what happened with all of it? With those police?"

"Oh, doll," McFadden began, "These animals, they were awful. A monkey and a wetback. They goddamn brutalized me arbitrarily, for no reason at all, other than I am white and filthy fucking rich — I swear on my children that the Mexican one even sprayed me with some salsa."

This made her laugh, "Salsa! You're a riot. It was mace that they sprayed you with. Or pepper spray."

She laughed again.

She couldn't tell if McFadden thought that it was funny or not. He had that creepy wolf look.

"Well, whatever the hell it was, it burned. That burn is what I remember most from that fateful morning," he said.

"What you need to do is fake it 'til you make it. Ever heard that term?"

"Of course, I have."

"You just can't talk the way that you do. You sound like a slave-owner from another century. What you need is some good PR. You need a black sponsor for the meetings."

This was a good idea. Alcoholics Anonymous is an organization that prides itself with its tradition of anonymity.

It's an old-school thing that was polluted by the media's obsession with this trust-fund blimp, who had attacked minority cops in some racial rage.

AA meetings were supposed to be products of an unspoken truce between the press and the people in the recovery community. That all went out the window with a case this high-profile; being seen with a black man was a no brainer, a must.

"And where would I find this black sponsor? Is there a black sponsor service I can ring up?"

There was an awkward silence.

She didn't find the joke funny.

"I know someone. Think it may be a perfect match for you. It's this old timer but he's a whitewashed black dude: educated, polished, all that. He's like that actor. I can't think of it. Aw, you know who I'm talking about, right?"

She was really having fun now, "Right?"

"Who fucking cares?" McFadden said.

It was uncomfortable for McFadden when he had to explain to the black sponsor that the allegations on television were fabricated lies and mistruths, nothing more. It made McFadden recoil in disgust, to willingly offer some animal any position of authority over him.

Baker was just as he had been described. He was affable and courteous. He knew some big words. Baker looked more affluent than McFadden. He had perfectly blended pepper gray hair. It looked distinguished. He wore reading glasses and had a gap in his front teeth that emanated an academia impression.

It took a while to get used to each other. It was hard for anyone to acclimate to McFadden's freakish smile and that insufferable air of superiority; he was the Monopoly man if he had manifested into some chunky, spoiled rapist.

The court card lady had her spell on McFadden. This had more to do with his desire to continue the affair than what his children or public opinion cared about him.

He would go to Baker's small apartment to do 12-step work or to read out of The Big Book. The sessions with Baker bored McFadden to death but he didn't care, he was in love.

He just stared blankly in a subdued daze, thinking about the woman's pillow breasts while this black man talked about finding a higher power.

"The only way that this will work is if you're honest with another human being," Baker said, his lips pursed like a bluff, "In this case that human would be me."

"I have been honest with you. I think I've been incredibly honest, in fact." McFadden said.

"Listen here, before I got sober, I walked around with a hell of a lot of baloney up in the brain. The guilt and shame and resentment. I was sick with alcoholism, and I just couldn't live with the person I had become. Ain't none of it got any better until I was honest with a person other than myself."

McFadden knew that Baker wasn't going to let him off without giving some concession and offering up a secret. He didn't want to talk about the trannie shit no matter what.

The damned tabloids often paid people for information and he could tell that Baker was relatively poor. His apartment had the perpetual scent of beef and shrimp flavored ramen noodles wafting throughout.

He was worried, however, about the affair with the court card lady. This would be the proverbial nail in the coffin if it had ever been exposed but he considered telling him.

"You're apprehensive," Baker said, "You don't trust me. I get that. I used to make excuses and rationify — that's not even a word but I'd co-sign my own nonsense is what I meant by it."

"It is not that. You've been kind to me. It's just very personal."

"You have a lot going on. Listen, Mac, I'm going to tell you something that I rarely ever talk about. Back when I was deep in it, stuck in the throes of a seven-year bender, I had been driving home late one night... I was real, real hammered and felt safer when I pulled onto my street. I lived in this suburban cookie cutter of a town. This was in Cleveland, now, some years back. It was a miracle I even made it back from the bar in the first place.

"Then I was pulling into my driveway and I ... I hit someone. I heard this disturbing thump; it skipped like a wet log on a record player. I could feel the body drag under my tires. I looked back and could see blood, Mac. The blood was spread out thickly across the concrete driveway. My neighbors had a young boy, couldn't have been more than five or six, and I knew that I had hit him. I wasn't sure why in the hell he was playing outside at that time, but I certainly didn't stop to ask questions either.

"I drove all the way here to L.A.. I had a cousin here and I simply acted as if it hadn't happened. I sobered up some months later and found God as it were. But the guilt. That guilt ate at me for years, Mac. I finally couldn't live with the secret and knew for certain that my higher power had my best interests at heart. I decided to tell them, consequences be damned. I went back to that town freshly sober, a new lease on life. My heartbeat raced furiously as I stood at their front door. And when I told them what I had done and that I was sorry — they cried. They cried and they hugged me. I had killed the family golden retriever. The dog, can you believe that?"

"Jesus, what a story," McFadden said.

"The point is that it is impossible to know what you have done and how the world will react until you get honest. And as the eighth step calls for, 'we made direct amends to such people wherever possible, except when to do so would injure them or others.' So, Mac, I really want you to search deep inside, and I want you to ask God to help with this, and I want you to be honest and relieve some of that damn self-loathing that keeps you a miserable drunk."

McFadden shuttered just thinking about telling this ape something so personal. He thought of the trannies and the sour, acidic taste of urine dousing his face.

But he had to tell him something.

"The court card lady," Mac said, "I'm fucking her and I'm in love. I am head over heels in love with Cindy. If my children find out or Susan or the liberal-biased press ... I am a dead man. A real dead man."

7

PRETTY EYES MASSACRE

"But this was what happened when you didn't want to visit and confront the past: the past starts visiting and confronting you." — Bret Easton Ellis

Mikey's mind was racing.

Mikey didn't have a lot of morals, but he didn't believe in snitching. He always thought that if you were to live outside the law you had to be honest. He also didn't think he was going to get twenty years in prison.

He had witnessed Charlie murder Andy. He never reported it and he never reported Jessica dying from an overdose. He didn't know if that made him an accessory to murder after the fact.

When he had left the motel, Charlie was barely conscious, and Gay Chris was incensed over Andy's death. It was impossible that he was still alive.

He didn't know Gay Chris that well, but he certainly didn't want to be responsible for giving him a life sentence.

He also knew how badly Martin DuPont wanted closure on his niece. The first year of his term had been the worst year of his entire life.

It all came down to what happened to Gay Chris. Mikey lived a life that was tormented by guilt from his childhood. He had explicitly detailed everything in his journals, but nobody knew that they even existed. He couldn't take more guilt. He wouldn't be able to live with himself if he gave Gay Chris a life sentence.

A guard had brought Mikey a paper jumpsuit. This is what everyone wears when they are being transported on the prison bus.

With this revelation, he had almost forgotten that he was on his way to a state pen.

Mikey had no idea what to expect with prison. He had only ever done county time. He was fairly certain that because of his status, he would have a similar experience in prison as he had in jail: alone in isolation. He was okay with that. He didn't consider himself a tough guy and he had only ever heard nightmare stories from his older friends that had done real time.

The cops were vindictive.

They did everything in their power to make his time as horrific as possible when he was in the county jail. He was put on a disciplinary diet immediately. It was something typically reserved for the worst, most violent, and untamable inmates; convicts who simply couldn't be punished enough to settle down. The kind that splashes cups of urine on guards when they walk by the cell.

Mikey didn't do anything like that but the first time the meal-slot had opened, a tray was slid into his cell with a single loaf in the middle of it. It looked like an enlarged hot pocket. He didn't know what it was, but it didn't look edible. It was burnt and it smelled awful. Disciplinary cakes are all the food that an inmate would be served that day, per caloric requirements of law, mashed up and put in this loaf that they bake in the jail kitchen. Green beans, milk, spaghetti, bananas, whatever was on the menu that particular day.

Mikey was too dope sick to eat anything in the beginning anyway.

He would just slide the tray with the loaf back each time

they served it. Once you're done kicking heroin you get "long gut" — an insatiable appetite. Junkies typically gain a lot of weight in early recovery because of this phenomenon.

Eventually, he started eating the disciplinary cakes. No matter how hungry he was, it never tasted okay, not even once. He had to force himself to eat it.

He hoped that Martin Dupont's vindictiveness wasn't going to follow him to prison. He was left in the single man drunk tank for several hours. Mikey had a lot to think about. It changed everything.

He looked out the tiny rectangular window of the room he was in and saw a line of inmates being patted down, shackled, and getting ready to get on the prison bus. He assumed that they would come and get him last. Sometimes when he went to court, they would put him in a protective cage in the front of the bus. Everyone wanted to talk to Mikey because his face was omnipresent in the papers and on the news.

The line of convicts was led outside onto the bus. They never came for Mikey. He found that odd. As far as he knew, there was only one bus that would take everyone to the reception center. You would stay in reception a few months until they figured out what prison you'd go to long term.

Another hour or so went by and a guard finally came for Mikey. He cuffed him and led him to the same wall he had seen the line of convicts getting shackled. There were a dozen inmates. Mostly Hispanic, a few black, a couple white. From doing county time and knowing ex-cons, he knew that prison was racially divided and that he was supposed to have solidarity to his race. He tried to nod at one of the other white guys and it seemed to spook him. He quickly turned away from him. Mikey had a bad feeling about this group of people.

They all looked a little off.

A guard came with a clipboard and did a rollcall. He said everyone's last name and the inmate would acknowledge it, "Here."

The guards patted them down and put shackles around their ankles. There was one big chain connecting all the inmates.

They were taken outside to a small bus. Mikey was on the chain next to a wiry Hispanic kid; he looked a little younger than Mikey. He was already covered in cheap tattoos. Corny stuff that almost made Mikey laugh out loud. He had **FUCK FAGS** on his neck. And dollar signs as tear drops.

Mikey turned to him, "Why are we taking a small bus?"

"You're a weirdo, right?" the kid asked.

"What you mean by that?"

"A sex 'fender."

Mikey shook his head.

"We're going to a super max for the sex 'fenders. This is, like, what ... the PC of PC. Like the worst in the system or some shit."

Mikey had a hard time asking, "So you're a ... weirdo?"

"Hell yeah, fool. Hella weird. You too?"

"No."

"That fucking sucks. Get prepared to see some way out shit. I been to this spot. It's looney."

"They have ISO?"

"They got the hole. But you probably gonna be in a two-man cell. We was all in ISO here in county but it's different there. You gotta fuck up to get to the hole."

"What you in here for?" Mike asked.

"Weird shit, fool. You got some pretty eyes. Has anyone ever told you that?"

That was the end of the conversation. Mikey was terrified. Ol' Marty DuPont strikes again. He had a feeling that he wasn't going to be alone in a cell and that things were going to get worse than he could have possibly imagined.

Mikey thought it might be time to tell him the truth. Maybe he could cut a deal. Maybe people would stop treating him like he killed the Chief's niece. Maybe it was time for the big reveal: his life work, the journals, the secret ... out there.

He would call his attorney. It couldn't get much worse. He heard that drugs were easily accessible in prison.

He could always kill himself if it backfired.

He was already infamous. There was an audience. It was actually a good time to drop the bomb when he had this many eyes on him.

There would be shock, only at first. But he knew that the secrets didn't matter as much as the beauty of his prose. People would read it for the shock value. It would be considered salacious. But then the literary critics would say, "Hey, wait just one Yankee minute, this kid has talent. This is lyrical and stylistically charming." And there would be sides chosen. People that support Mikey for his veracity. For his gift with language. And then there would be people that judged him for the secret.

It was time.

THE BALLAD OF MIKEY MAY — yeah.

He thought about wearing turtlenecks. Writer shit. Reading his work in front of filled stadiums. He thought about signing books (Even giving them away to fans that showed up and couldn't afford one — classy shit like that.) and meeting celebrities and touring and agents and adoring fans and magazine articles.

All that.

This is how he coped with the reality of being in a bus full of the worst sex offenders in the state of California. It was possible that he was going to get raped that night. The prospect of it all freaked him out and he tried to think about the famous writer stuff instead.

He started to hear fragments of conversations he wished that he hadn't heard.

"They gave me an enhancement because she was pregnant. So that's why they had given me the life. They talking 'bout manslaughter on the child. Like I killed two people instead of just her. Stupid shit like that ..."

"Life without? Or?"

"Life fucking without. They savage."

"Savage as hell, man. That don't seem right. The kid wasn't born yet. That's one body. Nah mean? They on that bullshit."

Mikey closed his eyes. He tried to escape this nightmare for the duration of the trip. He didn't even know where they were going.

A few minutes later, the kid next to him nudged him, "Yo, Pretty Eyes."

Mikey looked at him.

"You wanna cell up together?"

Mikey had no idea how to answer that.

"You never been to the *pinta*, huh?"

Mikey shook his head.

"I can tell. Usually, you go to reception. Don't matter if you're general pop or SNY."

"What's SNY?"

"Special Needs Yard. It's protective custody."

"Isn't that what we are? PC?"

"Nah, fool. Like I said, we're like super-duper PC. Like the charges we got are so bad that we would get killed in regular PC. That's rats, gang dropouts, fools that rolled it up over a debt, some sex 'fenders too. But our shit is really bad. Like killing kids, child molesters, fools that kill women."

"I didn't do any of that," Mikey said quietly.

"Then you pissed off the cops. Because this is a level four sex 'fenders yard. It ain't even part of the CDC. It's privately owned. But it's better to be honest. It's better, fool. No politics. There's trannies. It ain't all racist. No gang shit, well a little gang shit. Most these guys are doing all day."

"All day?"

"Life. Like they ain't got a date. They never gonna go home, fool. I don't got no date. It's a wrap for me. You?"

"Twenty years."

"Oh, you good then. You home already, but I done time with a lot of these fools. Unless you like getting buttfucked to wake up in the morning, I suggest you cell up with me. I won't do nothing like that if you don't want."

"We can choose our cellies?"

"I been here before. I got some juice with the COs. I can make it happen. You don't wanna cell up with some of these dudes."

He pointed to a huge black man with an afro, "Like that fool right there ... his name is Boogie. He will straight up buttfuck you, dawg. Every day. I was cellies with him in Chino. And every day I got buttfucked. And he's one of like a hundred dudes like that. So that's what I'm saying, you're the prettiest boy in here. They gonna be fighting to cell up with you. Cell up with me. I won't do nothing creepy unless I'm on a happy card."

"A what?"

"A happy card. Damn, you is brand new, Pretty Eyes. You know crystal meth?"

"Uh huh."

"People crush it up and put it in a spray bottle. Then they spray a greeting card with the meth. And they send it in. You measure it with dominoes. A domino-sized piece of paper is ten bucks. That shit makes me hella horny. Whenever it hits ... it's like a straight up sex riot in here. But people get all paranoid too. They think people are trying to kill them."

"What about black?"

"*Chiva* ... that shit is everywhere. It's easy to get. But it's expensive, fool."

"Like how much?"

"$400 for a prison gram."

"Damn! What's a prison gram?"

"It's like a .7 instead of a full gram."

"For $400? Damn! In L.A. it's like $60. A full gram too."

"This ain't L.A., son. But I can get that shit easy. When we touch down, I'll get you some. On the cuff. Just ask to cell up with me. My name is Bam-Bam. But tell the guards you wanna cell up with Jimenez. Or you gonna get but-tfucked by Boogie. I'm telling you, *pero*."

"What do I gotta do?"

"When we touch down. They are gonna bring us to R & R. They do our thumbprints and take mug shots. It takes fuckin' forever, fool. They gonna clear you for medical and make sure you can be on this yard. Like you don't got no enemies."

"What if I tell them I have enemies? Then, what, I won't have to go to the sex offender yard?"

"Nah, you don't wanna do that. Then they gonna cell you up with someone for thirty days until they transfer you to another weirdo yard. And chances are, to be completely honest with you, they gonna bunk you up with some rapist who knows the game. Some weirdo that wants to be alone in a cell with you. Alone with anyone. It's like being in the hole. But you don't wanna go to the hole on a yard like this. You'll for sure get buttfucked that way. That's like a guaranteed buttfucking, fool. Nobody will hear your screaming. It'll be bad, Pretty Eyes."

Mikey thought about his options. Bam-Bam was skinny and small. Mikey knew how to fight pretty well. Growing up, going in and out of jail, you learn how to defend yourself.

It's part of the life.

Bam-Bam was probably the scrawniest guy on the bus. If he tried anything, Mikey was positive he could kick his ass. The notion of rolling the dice and possibly being encaged with an enormous predator like Boogie freaked him out.

"Alright," Mikey said, "But no more calling me 'Pretty Eyes.' That shit ends right now. No sexual shit. None at all. I'm not into dudes. And you need to get me some dope like you said you would."

"Bet, fool. Bet! I can get you a paper of black no problem. Even tonight. I know the housing unit we're going to. I can even get you a binky so you can slam that shit. Wouldn't it be nice to do a little issue of black? First night on the yard and you gonna get all smacked back."

"Sounds too good to be true."

"When they take you out to do the medical and all that … there's this CO; name is Jones. Tell him that it's your first time and that you're friends with Jimenez. Don't call me Bam-Bam to the cops, fool. They don't like that. Say you wanna be bunkies with Jimenez. Jones is cool. He'll make it happen. I'll tell him too."

Mikey felt a little better. The lights on the inside of the bus were dimmed. The silhouettes of the inmates looked ominous in its glow. He would occasionally hear someone say something deplorable. Inmates bragging about how many kids they molested, war stories about gruesome butchered families; sorority houses broken into, college girls dominated and raped — vile, disgusting, nastiness.

He was convinced that he was in actual hell.

Like maybe that night he tried to kill himself he had succeeded. This is what he imagined it would look and smell like. Sex offender ghouls softly illuminated by the long, twitching light bulbs from the roof of the bus. He felt like he was walking some demented plank and when he got to the end he would be violently sodomized by a swarm of starving, pedophilic sharks. He would be ripped apart. And then he'd have to walk that same, unforgiving plank, again and again, every day for the next 19 years.

He was starting to regret every DVD that he had ever stolen.

Mostly, regretted keeping profound secrets in his journal. Secrets that were selfishly nestled between lined paper. Things he should have told the world about long ago.

Or the time he made his father cry, when he had been caught with his late grandfather's stamp collection, that he was getting ready to pawn. He could never forget the look of sadness and betrayal from his macho father. It was the only time he had seen him cry.

He had stuck a needle in Jessica's arm for the first time. She was snorting OxyContin when they had first met. He turned her into a needle freak; ultimately leading to her tragic death.

He regretted all of it.

He wished he had never become a drug addict. There was a good person beneath that filthy cloak of narcotics. He had hidden him for so long that he forgot who that person even was.

If this wasn't literal hell, it was certainly some karmic response that represented it. For the first time in his life, he felt genuine remorse.

The bus pulled up to the gates of the penitentiary.

There were triple row fences with coiling razor wire running along the top. The complex was gargantuan. There were rectangular cement buildings and stadium-style lights. It was like some massive, dystopian city surrounded by desolation and endless desert scape.

The gate opened and the bus pulled in.

There were correctional officers armed with rifles, standing in various gun towers. Stenciled warnings were emblazoned on the walls of the buildings: **NO WARNING SHOTS FIRED**.

The bus stopped in front of a building with an R & R[14] sign on its door. A couple of guards came out to greet the small bus load. One of them opened the door. He had a clipboard in hand and began the standard roll call; after making sure all the inmates were still there, they started letting each chained row off the bus. Mikey and Bam-Bam were in the first chain.

They shuffled, handcuffed and shackled, as they awkwardly went down the steps of the bus.

Guards looked at them with disdain. Mikey was used to glares from correctional officers, but he had never seen such overt loathing. It was also the first time he had been part of some interracial, sex offender all-star squad.

The guards took the inmates to a wall. They made them put their backs against it as they took the handcuffs and shackles off. Mikey's hand had gone to sleep, once his hands were free, he tried to shake the painful pins and needles away. There were red rings around his wrists where the handcuffs had been. Some guards are nice and will cuff an inmate loosely, while others cuff them tight enough to cut circulation off.

Mikey was treated as if he was a "weirdo" like the rest of the bus. It made him uncomfortable — having already been brutalized in the stairwell, he learned that guards could do whatever they want to you. You can scream and holler and yell, but nobody will hear you.

---

14   Receive & Release

Nobody cares.

It was a frightening realization: the guards were just as dangerous as the inmates. He had zero sense of security and knew that he could be raped, beaten, or murdered at any moment.

The inmates were moved to a large holding tank. It had jail bars as its entrance, a slab of concrete for sitting that ran the length of the tank, and a metallic toilet attached to a sink in the corner. The group of predators looked scarier in this light than they had in the dimly lit bus.

Mikey could feel eyes undressing him. He saw an old black man, with a salt-and-peppered afro, lick his lips and grab his crotch as he looked at Mikey. His tongue had a reptilian-esque tick, its tip would hiss out as he gazed lustfully.

Mikey looked at the floor. Bam-Bam was creepy, but he seemed the least threatening of the bunch. He was looking forward to getting in a cell and away from the other creeps. Charlie's photo popped up in his mind.

He was thinking of the night that Gay Chris had pistol whipped Charlie in an act of uncontrollable rage. Mikey had laughed about the lisp that developed from his teeth being smashed apart by the butt of the gun. It just wasn't possible for Charlie to still be alive.

Hope for the best, prepare for the worst.
Prison taught him that mantra.

It was easy to drift away into fantasies of freedom. He reminded himself that Charlie hadn't killed Jessica – she died from an accidental drug overdose. He wrote down exactly what had happened in the journal he had stashed in the cave by his folks' house.

He knew that Jessica's uncle, Marty, wanted closure on

her disappearance. Mikey wanted a sentence reduction or to be moved to a nicer facility.

He just had to find out if Gay Chris was still alive or not.

A guard came and got inmates one-by-one for brief medical and psychological screenings. This was to determine if someone was of reasonably cognitive ability and lacking any major medical issues.

Mikey was taken to a small room. There was a desk and folding chairs on both sides. There were a few cabinets that had combination locks on them. There was a poster on the wall of a viking petting some warrior horse in silver body armor. The poster said something about HIV/AIDS, but he had no clue what was happening in the photo.

An enormous Samoan nurse came waddling in.

The room was barely big enough to support such a large woman with Mikey. She huffed furiously as she asked the obligatory questions, "When was your last TB test? Do you have chest pains? Have you been hospitalized in the last year? Do you have hepatitis A, B, or C?"

"I have C for sure. And I have A or maybe it's B. Which one do you get from licking ass?"

"Hep A can be transmitted through contact with an infected person's anus or feces."

"Guilty as charged, right here," Mikey said.

He laughed at his own joke; she ignored him, obviously accustomed to sleazy men.

She took his vitals.

"Your heart rate is a bit high. You nervous?"

"It's my first night in prison, ma'am. Of course, I'm nervous. I'm petrified."

Mikey was seeking comfort from her.

She turned to him, "Then don't come to prison, ding-dong!" she said coldly, and yelled, "Next!"

A guard escorted Mikey to a cubicle office.

The psychologist was in his late fifties with a body that

seemed perfectly round — like you could roll him down a hill. His cheeks were flushed red. He had the evil, pebble eyes of a raven, magnified by his rim horned glasses.

"Sexual orientation?" he asked.

"Heterosexual."

"Do you feel suicidal?"

"No."

"Do you feel homicidal?"

"Uh, no."

"Thanks. We're done. Let the officer know."

"Wait ... That's it? What if I had said I was a bi-sexual murderer that wanted to kill some inmates and then kill myself?"

The psychologist took off his glasses. He rubbed his temples and sighed, "Nothing, really. I would just add it to your case folder. Were you serious about this?"

"No. I was just curious what would have happened."

He rolled his eyes and shouted, "Next!"

And Mikey was on his way.

He was taken into the captain's office who approved who would be able to stay on the yard and who couldn't. It was the last person Mikey needed to see before they gave him his clothes and linen and took him to the housing unit.

"Sit down, May — Mr. Fuckin' Hollywood himself. My wife and I see you on the television every single day. I told her you was coming here and she didn't believe me."

"Here I am."

"Why they got you at this fucked up joint with all the depraved sex fiends?"

"The chief of police thinks I had something to do with his niece disappearing."

"I told you, me and the old lady watch the news together and see you every day. That Dupont guy truly believes you did that shit. Me, I think everything they are talking about is circumstantial ... at best. It certainly don't warrant you being sent to a prison like this. This is a real, real bad place. Sick fucks lurking behind every corner."

"He's trying to break me to get me to talk."

"You got anything to say?"

Mikey thought about it for a while. He liked the captain. It seemed like he would be an easy person to talk to.

"I might have a few things to say that would clear up a lot of unanswered questions. I'm just waiting for the right time to talk about it."

"Well, hey, if that time ever comes ... you tell a CO that you want to talk to me. I'm the captain and my last name is McNamara. My friends call me Jay Mackie. Use my nickname and you'll get the VIP treatment."

"I appreciate that."

"For what it's worth, I think you're innocent. And for everything you've been through with your little brother and all ... honestly, I feel for you, son."

"Thank you. Can you cell me up with an inmate with the last name Jimenez? He's my boy from the county jail and I don't want to be celled up with any of these other creeps."

"You bet," he said, he looked around and made sure that they were alone, "Hey, can you take a selfie with me real quick? My wife would crap her fat trousers if I came home with that."

Mikey leaned in and gave an awkward thumbs up as the captain took a photo of them with his phone.

Mikey was taken back to the holding tank. There were only a half dozen inmates left. Most had already finished their intakes and had been taken to their respective housing units.

Bam-Bam was already gone. Mikey found a section on the slab of concrete and fell asleep.

He was woken up, a couple hours later, by a guard yelling his name. Mikey was now the only inmate left in the holding tank. The guard handed him a bed roll through the bars and unlocked the door. Mikey wasn't handcuffed but was instructed to walk with his hands behind his back.

They left the R & R building and walked along a pathway outside. It was a humid night for California. Gigantic stadium lights illuminated the entire prison grounds glaringly white.

The guard didn't speak a single word to Mikey.

There were large concrete rectangle buildings surrounding him. It looked industrial with tumbles of razor wire blossoming from the tops of endless chain-link fences. He saw multiple deserted recreation yards, a softball field, some bleachers, pull-up and dip stations, and a running track on the outer edges. None of it looked very fun, especially with the trigger-happy redneck standing in the gun tower with a rifle slung across his shoulder.

NO WARNING SHOTS FIRED was painted in bold black letters under the tower. It was the same sign Mikey had seen when the bus had pulled up to the prison. Some of his old junkie friends would tell stories about prison riots and the number of deaths that occurred each year from ricocheted bullets.

He couldn't believe they used live ammo. It was the kind of rumor he thought he would debunk when he finally made it to prison and saw things with his own eyes. The fact that it was real intimidated Mikey because of all the other stories he had heard about stabbings, riots, combination locks in socks, rape, race wars, getting jumped, guards brutalizing inmates without recourse ...

Twenty. Fucking. Years.

They got to the F building. The guard said something into his walkie-talkie and the door unbolted. Mikey followed him inside, his heart beating wildly with anticipation.

It was the classic prison setting that Mikey had seen in

the movies. There were two tiers. Metal tables and stools lined the bottom floor, it was used for indoor recreation activities. There were pay phones attached to the wall, televisions on pillars, and community shower stalls at each corner of the building. The unit made a horseshoe shape, cells on both floors.

There was a cop station in the middle that had two correctional officers sitting at a desk.

There were no inmates out.

They were in their cells. Mikey looked around and saw angry faces and curious eyes peering from cell doors.

Mikey walked up to the guard station and handed over his laminated ID card that had been given to him during the intake.

"They're on a lockdown," the guard said, "Some kind of minor disturbance. Think they are just doing an investigation and they'll let everyone else out a little later tonight. It's only 7:30 p.m. They don't do lights out until quarter to ten."

Mikey nodded.

"The captain already assigned a cell for you. I guess you asked for it or whatever. You're in 138. Walk up to its door and we can open it remotely from up here."

Mikey walked up to cell 138. It was dark.

He could see luminous, kaleidoscopic shadows, coming from inside of the cell and he knew that Bam-Bam was watching a floater TV. He had explained to Mikey that you could have your family order them from a package catalog. They sold plastic, translucent TVs so that inmates couldn't stash drugs or weapons inside of them.

You could only get an electronic package quarterly, but Bam-Bam told him that he always bought a floater right away — a used TV that inmates sell for cheap. Your booking number is supposed to be engraved in the plastic and guards periodically shake cells down. If they want to be an asshole about it, they can take your floater, which is usually grandfathered down from inmates that had been released, so they have their booking number scratched in them.

Mikey tapped on the square, plexiglass window and he saw Bam-Bam's kooky face emerge. He looked elated to see him. Mikey turned to the cop station and nodded, signaling that he wanted to be let into the cell.

There was that familiar, loud unbolting sound and the door opened on its track.

"Pretty eyes!"

"Hey, knock it off with that shit."

Bam-Bam laughed, "You're right. *Spenca*, fool."

Mikey walked in and the door slid shut behind him. He was surprised how large the cell appeared. There were three bunk beds stacked up and the ceiling must have been twenty feet high. There were a couple large lockers, a metallic toilet attached to a sink, a desk and stool. There was a window with diagonal bars running across it. It was a view of chain-link fences and coiling razor wire — that looked menacing in the glare of the stadium lights.

"How come there's three bunks?" Mikey asked.

At some point they are trying to make these three-man cells but that's not gonna be for a long time. For now, we can just use it as storage. And I got this floater TV too, *ay*."

"You get that black for me?"

"Come on, *pero*. Of course I did."

Bam-Bam took out a small folded up piece of paper, "It's a fifty. I'm waiting on the binky now cuz you told me you like to slam. I gotchu."

Mikey couldn't contain his grin. The little weirdo actually came through for him. Unreal.

"Can I sit on your bed?"

Bam-Bam nodded, "*Mi casa, su casa*, right?"

"Why's it so dark in here? I can't see shit."

"I get bad headaches. And when I get them, light

fucking kills me, fool. I just let the outside lights and the TV shine enough that I can see but my head don't hurt."

Bam-Bam handed Mikey the fifty of heroin as he sat on the bed. Mikey unfolded it and was shocked to see the size of it. It was a flake.

"Dude, this is fifty bucks?"

"Yeah, why, how much that be in the world?"

"You can't even buy heroin sacks this small but it's probably, like, three dollars' worth."

"I mean ... I can give it back. That was on the strength to you since you gonna be my new celly. But if it ain't good enough I can give it back."

"No, no ... thank you. I appreciate this. I guess it's just my first time in prison and I don't know how all this stuff works. I haven't done dope in so long that I'm sure this will get me lit. Especially if I can shoot it."

Bam-Bam took this in and nodded, probably only comprehending some of it. Mikey noticed that he was slow, probably had a learning disability, or maybe it was the language barrier.

"Alright, fool, here give me your sheets and I'll make your bed for you. You can just kick back and watch Telemundo. Bitches in bikinis eating pies. It's ... how they say ... with the function, fool!"

Mikey felt like his anxiety had run out of things to obsessively worry about. He was finally relaxing, feet propped up, watching perverted Mexican television, about to get high on heroin for free.

Sure enough, a woman with huge tits, wearing a bikini, ate a pie.

Mikey must have dozed off. Travel days in prison are always exhausting. He had no idea how long he had slept on Bam-Bam's bed. When he woke up there was an inmate at the door speaking Spanish to Bam-Bam. He was leaning into the side of the door, where there was a sliver of space before the wall. It was the only way you could talk to someone on the other side. Mikey didn't understand Spanish and had no idea what they were talking about.

Suddenly, a plastic pouch tied to a sheet came hurling into the cell from under the door. Bam-Bam dove down and grabbed it. He took something wrapped in toilet paper out. He stuck his hand back in the pouch and extracted a small single-serving shampoo bottle. He placed the items down on the cell floor and took a stack of mailing stamps out of his pocket. He put them in the empty coffee pouch and tied the sheet tightly around it.

He leaned into the crack of the door, "Pull!"

The pouch started moving, tugged by the sheet, until it disappeared under the cell door.

This was called fishing and it was how contraband and notes were covertly passed around the prison. The inmate that Bam-Bam was talking to was what was called a Porter in state prison. It was an inmate that swept and mopped the tiers in the housing unit. It was an important cog in the underground dynamics of prison because they were allowed to walk around the unit after lights out, on lockdowns, and early from count times.

Bam-Bam unwrapped the toilet paper and showed Mikey the binky. It was a makeshift syringe. Inmates would steal the rubber necks of the milk dispensers in the chow hall and tie them to the end of the body of a plastic writing pen. It had to be transparent and have the ink removed. Inmates would steal insulin syringes from nurses that had to deliver daily insulin syringes, or they would have them smuggled in through a contact visit.

"You know how to use one of these, fool?"

Mikey inspected the binky, "How do you push the dope in once you find a vein?"

"I'll show you."

Bam-Bam grabbed a plastic spork from his locker. A spork was a fork and spoon hybrid, very ugly, and usually only used in institutional settings.

"How do you cook it on a plastic spoon?"

"You don't," Bam-Bam said, "You just put the *chiva* in the middle of the spoon. And you use something to stir it up until it breaks down. I use a pen cap, but you could use your fingers even."

Bam-Bam took the flat square-shaped piece of heroin and put it in the spoon. He took some water from his sink and started stirring the dope with the cap of his ballpoint pen.

"You want it to turn, almost like, yellow. That's how you know it's some bomb ass shit."

Bam-Bam stirred, tiny brown flakes started breaking away from the piece of dope, "See that shit means it's cut. *Chiva*[15], *coca*[16], and *escante*[17] will turn to oil when you add water. If it don't break down or is any color except piss-yellow that means, it's been cut. Here in the *pinta* you are going to see a lot of dope dissolve brown, or you see these little dark flakes cuz the fucking *tacatos*[18] cut this shit with coffee. That's really your only choice right here, pero. You know?"

Bam-Bam continued to stir for another minute until the heroin was liquefied in the spoon. Mikey's stomach felt like it was boiling with the anticipation of getting loaded.

Bam-Bam grabbed a plastic coffee mug and started pouring a blue fluid from the shampoo bottle the porter had sent them.

"What's that shit?"

"I don't know the name but it's from the barber shop. It's the same shit they let the combs and scissors soak in,

15	Heroin
16	Cocaine
17	Meth
18	Junkies

fool. It's the only thing that will kill diseases and shit cuz we don't get no bleach.

Bam-Bam stuck the binky in the coffee mug and started cleaning it out, "There's some dusty ass *vatos* on this yard, dawg, I'm just trying to keep you disease free in case you give in to a buttfuck session at some point."

Mikey looked up and laughed a little, "Knock that shit off, bro."

"*Spenca.*"

Bam-Bam grabbed a Q-tip from his locker and tore off a piece of cotton. He threw it in the center of the spoon and began preparing the shot.

"You do this too?" Mikey asked.

"I do some drops every now and then, fool. But I don't do it all the time or nothing. After I hit you, I'll make myself some drops with the cotton, don't trip. When your body ain't used to it ... it don't take hardly nothing. You gonna be as high as a giraffe's ass."

"Giraffe's pussy," Mikey said, "The saying goes I'm going to be higher than a giraffe's pussy."

"Whatever it is, that's how high you're going to be."

Mike was transfixed on the process. He had never done heroin this way and it fascinated him. Bam-Bam put the tip of the needle in the bunched-up cotton and squeezed the rubber neck at the end of the binky. This created some suction and the small puddle of dope disappeared into the plastic pen body of the binky.

"Want me to hit you?" Bam-Bam said.

"My veins are blown out. I doubt you can find anything very easily."

"You never used a binky so it's going to be easier if I show you. You don't have a vein that comes back more easily than the others?"

The room was dark except for the multicolored glow of the television. "Can we turn the light on?"

"Nah, fool. I can hit you without the light on. That shit kills my head, *pero*. Come on."

Bam-Bam sat next to Mikey in the bed. He had the binky in his hand. He was inspecting his arms and hands.

"Alright but only because you paid for the dope. I doubt you can hit me. My veins are calloused. Sometimes it takes me hours. Literally."

Mikey felt a sudden sting on his neck. It happened so quickly that he didn't even realize Bam-Bam had shoved the needle in his jugular and administered the injection. By the time Mikey put his hand up to his neck Bam-Bam had already finished.

"Did you just try and hit my jugular?"

"I did hit it. I squeezed the shot in too. You're done, fool."

"That's impossible," Mikey said, as a wave of warmth began rolling through his body, every inch tickled and caressed by featherily static. His eyelids drooped, not even attempting to stay open. His anxious thoughts were obscured by the gentle embrace of nothingness.

It may have been the highest he had ever been.

Bam-Bam took drops out and did his own shot. He turned to Mikey, "Damn fool, you look like you're fucking about to die. You want to listen to my radio?"

Mikey didn't respond. He was paralyzed by tranquility.

Bam-Bam put the headphones on Mikey. His eyelids fluttered open for a moment before he nodded back out, zigzagging through vast corridors, guided by the melodies of Mexican love songs.

A coarse hand grabbed his face. His eyes burst open. Bam-Bam was standing by the door of the cell holding an icepick style shank. It looked like an elongated screwdriver that had been sharpened to inflict intense pain.

His eyes remained heavy, but he could see Bam-Bam

smiling, holding the knife. He looked like he had morphed into some sort of deranged lunatic, the kind that you can never come back from.

Everything was happening so fast. The hand was coming from under the bunk. It belonged to a very large black man. The nails were dirty and ungroomed. They sliced Mikey's face several times as he struggled to break free.

The Mexican music continued to blare. He had no idea what was going on. Bam-Bam had gone crazy and there was an African American boogie man hiding under his bunk, trying to snatch him, in some quintessential prison rape scene to a mariachi soundtrack?

It felt like a nightmare, but he knew it was happening. He thrust until the headphones fell off.

"What the fuck is going on?" he screamed.

The hand tried to cover his mouth. Mikey bit down as hard as he could, puncturing holes in the rough flesh. He tasted the warm sodium of blood as it trickled into his mouth. There was an agonizing groan from beneath the bed.

The hand recoiled.

Mikey sat up and locked eyes with Bam-Bam.

He hadn't broken his sneering, crazed grin, "Member when I said I wouldn't buttfuck you or nothing, Pretty Eyes?"

A huge black man rolled out from under the bed — Boogie.

"I never said my daddy would be able to keep his hands off you, fool."

"It's alright, baby boy," Boogie whispered.

Mikey had no weapon. Heroin was a major handicap on the reflexes. He wanted to give in and drift into a blissful, blank unconsciousness... but he knew his only chance of surviving was to force himself to stay awake.

He turned to Bam-Bam, "You tricked me into celling up with you?"

Bam-Bam shrugged.

"Oh, come now, the boy ain't smart enough to lure you

in all by his special needs ass self. It was mwah. I knew all the boys would be lining up to wife your pretty face. Let's be one, Hunny ... Boogie is the only alpha bitch on this yard. I see something I want; I get it. Now let me see what you're working with under them ugly ass jail pants, yuck!"

Bam-Bam thought about what Boogie had said and let out a delayed laughing response, "Alpha Bitch! Ay, that's fucking pretty funny."

Boogie rolled his eyes, "Bless that slow young man's little brain. I'm sure he's anxious to see it too. Your cock. Take it out for us. I promise that Bam-Bam will put the piece away. Ain't supposed to hurt ya! This'll be fun."

Mikey shook his head, "Nah. You're going to have to kill me before you make me do any gay shit."

Boogie blinked effeminately, "Excuse me?"

"You heard me, you fucking freak."

"Can't believe you said gay! Hunny, I have the bombest pussy on the compound. Bam, hold this boy for me, I'm going to have to teach him the old-fashioned way."

Bam-Bam walked up to Mikey and pinned him to the corner of the cell. There was very little resistance because Bam-Bam had placed the tip of his icepick in Mikey's head, hard enough to create a superficial wound but not enough for any real damage. It was to keep Mikey in place.

Boogie took a shank out of his waistline. It looked like a long, pointed kitchen knife. Something the killer in a slasher film would have, except the steel was heavily serrated instead of flat. It was made from a door stopper. In prison they call this kind of shiv a "bone crusher" because of its massive size. They are designed to inflict major injuries on their victims and are considered the most lethal makeshift weapon in penitentiaries.

The cell was silent. Bam-Bam kept Mikey stuck in the corner of the cell.

Boogie was nearly a foot taller than Mikey. He

towered over them. The steel of his knife glinted different colors from the reflection of the TV. He untied a string that had been keeping his pants on and wiggled his way out of them.

"Your turn, Pretty Eyes!"

Mikey shook his head. He refused to look down at Boogie's bare crotch.

Boogie moved closer, "Come on, baby. Take them filthy things off. Bam take yours off so he knows that it's okay."

He could smell coffee on Boogie's breath. Mikey closed his eyes. He could feel Boogie's face brush against him. It repulsed him. He knew that sudden movement would get him stabbed so he waited until Boogie groped him to lunge forward and attack him.

The cell was dark. Mikey could hardly see what was going on. He punched Boogie in the face, which didn't even make him flinch.

Bam-Bam stabbed him first. He stuck him in the thigh and Mikey wailed, collapsing to the floor.

Boogie tried to pin him, but he rolled away.

There was pressure in his leg, and he couldn't stand on it. He fell to the ground once more. The stab wound was excruciating, he had never felt such a sharp, deep reaching pain before.

"Baby boy, you are making this way harder than it needs to. Take your clothes off and show us a good time. It's a lot better than getting sliced and diced with our knives, right?"

Mikey curled up in the fetal position.

"There you go, fool," Bam-Bam said and knelt next to him, tugging at his pants, "Atta boy."

Boogie crouched down and started pulling at them as well — the material finally ripped, and they were able to tear his pants off.

Mikey was in state-issued boxers. He curled up as tightly as he could. They were already tugging at his boxers. He curled tighter to no avail, the boxers ripped, and he was completely naked. Mikey was shivering cold and embarrassed.

"Whoooo hoooo!" Boogie shouted. He started rubbing Mikey's leg, getting off on how uncomfortable it was making him.

Boogie was just about to reach his ass cheek when Mikey whispered something.

"What's that baby?"

Mikey whispered again, still inaudible; he raised his pointing finger up at Boogie, signaling for him to come a little closer to him.

Bam-Bam was at the window of the cell door, naked, making sure no guards walked by. It was possible he was jerking off, but Mikey couldn't be sure in the dimmed light.

Boogie smiled flirtatiously, playing along. "Yes?"

Mikey bit his ear and tugged as hard as he could possibly clamp down. Boogie shrieked. Mikey could taste the blood again, this time it was a profuse current rushing down from the side of Boogie's face.

Mikey tried to stand.

His stab wound was much more painful after the initial shock subsided. Mikey bit a huge chunk of his ear off, Tyson style, victoriously, and spit the bloody mess out of his mouth.

Boogie was screaming. Bam-Bam was muted from his fear of the combative (naked, too) situation. Mikey lunged towards Boogie's bone crusher and missed, falling flat on his face. Mikey's coloring had been siphoned out of him from the hole in his thigh; he felt like he was going to faint from losing blood too rapidly.

He thought he felt his shoulder burning. It felt incredibly hot. He realized that Boogie stabbed him in the shoulder multiple times. Mikey tried to run to the cell door and yell for a guard. He knew that he needed medical attention.

Bam-Bam and Boogie began attacking him from both sides. He dropped to the ground and curled up again. He was stabbed in the back of the calf, the ass cheeks several times, his hands and fingers, his forearm, the lower back, the rib cage, his groin ... many of his stab wounds overlapped.

Then everything went quiet as if the volume had been turned down for this horrible moment in his life. He could see the naked men stabbing him, but he couldn't hear any sounds. Mikey assumed that he was experiencing death.

There was so much blood on the cell floor that it started spreading and leaking out of the door and out onto the tier.

The shanks swung at him; whenever they connected his face twitched a tad from the impact.

It was irritating. Aside from that, he was concentrating on silent retrospection.

He thought of his brother Scott. His entire life had been dictated by the disappearance of his little brother. Nobody knew what had really happened ... except, of course, for Mikey.

It was the kind of thing that he couldn't talk about to anyone — so he confided in his notebooks. By doing so, he learned how to craft lyrical, awe-inspiring syntax.

Mikey explained the salacious secrets of his family for the entire world to read one day:

THE BALLAD OF MIKEY MAY.

He was going to be the best fucking writer of his generation, he thought, as naked predators viciously attacked him with their prison shanks.

The dream of being a celebrated writer carried him through a lot of low points. It was more about the implications of his journals being read. It would give his brother's life a level of purpose that Mikey couldn't even articulate. It was more of a feeling than something that could be explained.

He knew nobody was going to read his work if he died right there, naked, bleeding out on the cell floor of two lowlife rapists.

Mikey screamed and stood up. He wavered and stumbled and leaked blood out of his many slit-gashes. He screamed again and again until finally he thought he heard himself.

He was on a gurney. He had an oxygen mask covering his face. He was seeing square windows of cells scroll above his head. His ankle was shackled to the gurney.

He saw a guard next to him, "You're going to be alright, man. Hang in there. Be strong."

He could hear again. He must have slipped into shock when he was being stabbed. He couldn't remember how he had gotten out of that cell, but he remembered the captain's name.

He was ready to talk. He had enough.

"Jay Mackie!" Mikey screamed, "I'm ready to sing like a fucking canary!"

His voice was muffled by the oxygen mask, and he shook his head until it slid off, "Jay Mackie. Tell him I will snitch to Jay fucking Mackie! I will cooperate like a turd. I know where Jessica is! I know what happened to Jessica!"

The guard leaned down, "Cool it, okay. The whole damn unit just heard all that crazy talk."

It was too late.

The chanting began. Two words, over and over.
"The hell they yelling?" the guard asked.

Mikey knew.

"Pretty Eyes," over and over again like a drunken anthem.

Mikey was finally willing to tell the authorities the truth about Jessica Dupont.

He was hoping that it would be enough to get him the fuck out of this hellhole.

That wasn't the only secret he was getting tired of holding in. He knew things that would blow everyone's minds ... Seriously."

And he was ready.

8

SECRETS KEEP YOU SICK

INGLEWOOD, CA 2018

"The Jungle Creed says the Strong must Feed on any Prey at Hand, I was Branded a Beast and Sat at a Feast before I was a Man." - Donald Goines

There was a succession of knocks on Cindy's door. Someone showing up at her door always threw her for a pause. It wasn't the insecure taps of a solicitor, and it certainly wasn't the obnoxious banging of law enforcement.

Cindy knew both all too well.

She thought it may have been Gunner. She felt like she had won the lottery in that situation: Finally, a man she wouldn't have to physically fuck! Gunner reminded Cindy of some of the severely depressed, shower-phobic Johns she had met throughout the years.

The ones who were neurotic, wound up much too tightly for sex ("I don't know, I read that you could contract the genital herpes complex even if you were wearing protection. Not saying you have anything like that. I'm just saying. That I don't even know what I'm saying.") They would pay her to listen to them vent about their sorry ass lives.

She opened the door and was surprised when Baker came galloping in. He didn't acknowledge her.

He went to the leather sofa and sat down. He took out a Phillies cigar and ripped it apart, removing the stringy guts of tobacco onto the coffee table. Cindy hated when he rolled blunts because he always made a mess. But she knew better than to whine about it when he was angry. She didn't want him to "lose his cool" — his words for it, which sounded innocuous, but would often translate to hideous welts on her face or spitting her broken teeth out in the toilet bowl with a dark blue, bruise-sealed eye.

"They look like bloody pieces of Chiclets gum," Baker would say and laugh about it. "You hear me, bitch? Your teeth look like them certain type of gum. Chiclets or some shit."

He would laugh again, "What, you don't think I'm funny no more?"

She would agree and they'd share a laugh. Cindy did everything that she could to avoid Baker 'losing his cool.' His rage problems terrified anyone that knew him.

Cindy had seen him kill a guy just because he had rented the last copy of a movie he wanted. Baker followed him to his car and casually blew his head off with a .45. The guy's wife and children were cemented by shock and disbelief the instant they saw a gun brandished, they remained as still as statues; not even blinking when messy pieces of brain and gore were splattered across their frightened faces.

Baker leaned into the car and grabbed the DVD copy of *American Psycho* and a king-sized box of Milk Duds that the guy had bought for his family at the Blockbuster rental store. The guy would never know why he was murdered. Baker had asked for the film and the guy behind the register pointed out the guy that had beat him to it and snagged the last copy.

He shot the man in a congested parking lot, in front of his family, at three in the afternoon, on a Saturday. It was miraculous that he didn't get arrested for homicide that day.

Baker was wild and unpredictable. He was the personification of the motto **ZERO FUCKS GIVEN**.

Cindy slowly learned how to navigate his mental mind field. She had taken early missteps and felt the unforgiving wrath of his brutality.

He opened a clear baggie full of cannabis and poured some out on the coffee table. He leaned over and broke large nugs up into smaller pieces with his hands. He then placed the broken up weed in the shell wrapping of the Phillies, sucked on it — Cindy thought it looked like Baker sucking a thin little dick, but she knew better than to say something so silly — he lit the blunt and exhaled a thick white, coughing cloud.

"This fuckin' daddy's boy. I swear to God—"

"McFadden?" Cindy said.

"Yeah-huh. Now ... get this. This boy want to tell his bitch, you know, the one sick with the cancer, that he been fucking with you now."

Baker chuckled, coughing painfully, as weed smoke puttered out of his mouth.

His gapped tooth lost its charm. It had a snakish menace when he was out of character and not pretending to be a dignified, tax-paying, academic type.

"Why the hell would he do that?" Cindy asked.

"White people shit. Something bout' he don't want his kids feelin' a certain type of way about the situation. I had to listen to some Academy Award-type shit. Talkin' bout' how he was blinded by lust but confessing to his wife is the right thing to do for his kids' sake. Cryin' — all that dumb shit."

"Well, I am pretty fucking lust-able."

"Bitch, you fat as all fuck. Just because some simp dude into you, don't mean you the queen bee of the muthafuckin' stable."

Every man in Cindy's life had talked to her this way when she was growing up. She had learned to resent nice people because they were nowhere to be found when she was a little girl and really needed them.

She rubbed his shoulder, "I love you, daddy."

Baker swatted her hand away, grimaced, "I'm already knowin' bitch. Let's focus on the issue at hand."

"What are we going to do?"

"We move on him."

"How are we gonna do that if he's already going to fess up to her?"

"I'm on top of it. I went and seen his daughter today. Paid a little visit to the crib. She was playin' out front and I walked up and asked if her parents were there. She said they was and I told her I was some biblical ass nigga' from the heavens and that an angel named Cindy was fixin' to come down and be her new mommy. But that she had to tell her daddy about Cindy or shit wasn't never gonna happen. It'll fuck with dude's head, real good. See what I mean?"

"Oh, that's cold, daddy. That's real, real cold," Cindy purred.

"I ain't spend ten years in the joint reading for nothing. I know how these rich folk think. Speaking of which, what's army freak dude talking 'bout?"

"He can't get his dick hard."

"And?"

"He can't get it up and has a bunch of other mental problems. He's a vet, Iraq."

"Sounds a lot like that cat from Omaha. The fuck was his name?"

"Marcus."

"Yeah, Marcus. And he turned out to be a weirdo. He liked little boys and shit. We broke his ass off something proper. Dude's money right?"

"Brand new Jeep Cherokee."

"That's like under thirty racks. With the tax and the license. That a college kid car. That it?"

"Some blinged out Rolex."

"Rolex, what typa Rolex?"

"I don't know. An expensive kind."

"Holler at dude and find out what the type is. It's important. It has sentimental value for this dusty ass negro. For reals though."

"I will find out tomorrow and see if I can't get a better feel on what he's got in the bank. I have a feeling he's holding some wealth. The watch looks just as expensive as the Jeep."

"That's what I like to hear. Bonnaroo work, baby. You can suck my dick now. You've earned that. Slide on through."

Cindy loved when he called her baby. She just fucking loved it coming from such a gangster.

She bent down and unzipped his pants.

9

THE WATCH PRELUDE SIDE B

SOUTH CENTRAL, LOS ANGELES 1987 — 1997

"An emotional debt is hard to square." - Iceberg Slim

Baker was sentenced to ten years in federal prison in 1987 for conspiracy to distribute crack cocaine.

He was lucky that he had only caught a dime. The feds were handing out life sentences to appease the hysteria of a public that had seen crack ravage their inner cities.

Reagan had waged an insurmountable war on drugs, which was really an attack on minorities, or as snooty, faux-progressive sociologists would label "the dangerous classes."

The privatization of prisons and the proliferation of the prison-industrial-complex was emblematic of modern slavery.

It was about oppression and social immobility.

There was a 263% prison population expansion in California. New prisons on both the state and federal levels were being constructed at alarmingly rapid, unprecedented rates.

The advent of crack cocaine fundamentally changed the climates of the ghettos. You added baking soda to powder cocaine, and it would solidify into an intensely addictive and potent smokable form.

Brothers were out there getting paid. Much of the

youth was corrupted, making real money, for the first time in their underprivileged, opportunity-deprived lives.

Freeway Rick Ross was making a million dollars a day slanging coke in south L.A. while the government was supplying the Contras with illicit weapons and introducing crack to bad neighborhoods throughout the country. This created a shadow economy that the CIA used to fund clandestine geopolitical agendas.

Freeway Rick went to prison for 20 years while Oliver North, the imperialistic general, who had been balls deep in the Iran Contra scandal's butthole, went on to become the president of the NRA.

That's just the way shit was.

Baker had learned his history by reading everything he could while he was incarcerated. He spent his time hanging out with the most white-collar inmates he could find. He learned their lexicons and practiced their mannerisms.

Baker spent ten years of his life educating himself on everything needed to become socially chameleonic.

He became bilingual in the languages of the rich and the poor. In fact, he spoke both fucking fluently by the time he was ready to parole.

He just wanted to get out and burn white people.

Baker never knew his dad. He loved his mother, even though she was, as he would say, "a real bad hype." She would nod out on heroin in front of her three little kids. The younger ones running around with bloated diapers, completely neglected, smelling like urine and feces. She turned tricks to support her habit. Johns would come by the house; dark Indian men that worked at the 7-Eleven at the top of their block. They would come over and get blowjobs from his mom. She charged $5 and she did her sex work in a perpetual state of opiate withdrawal. She never had enough money to sufficiently sustain her habit.

Small balloons of dope were just a tease for an active junkie, but she was only capable of hustling a few of them up a day. She spent most of her time drooling on herself.

Baker would watch her go into their bathroom with a john. The toilet had been clogged for many months and Baker wondered how anyone could get their dick sucked in a small space with old fermenting shit wafting through the air.

She would then stumble out of the restroom, her nose constantly leaking dope sick snot. She would wipe it with the back of her sleeve until her nose was rubbed raw. Then she'd run down to the laundry mat where she could cop $5 of heroin from a tiny Hispanic man, who would spit a balloon from out of his mouth (Only English phrase he knew was "'Ank You" and he said it wrong after people would pay him.) Then his mom would run back to the house and go shoot up in her designated corner of the kitchen.

The kids would often find her with a tourniquet wrapped around her arm and a hypodermic syringe protruding from its crook. She would nod out and fall asleep standing up with lines of dry rolled blood from her many attempts to find a working vein.

Baker had seen his mother stand unconscious for six hours straight before. Occasionally she'd waver, take a clumsy step backwards, stagger a bit, catch herself, one eye closed, the other a fluttering little slit, until it finally gave up and closed all the way, plunging her into a deep, carefree standing sleep in the kitchen.

She'd wake up in the kitchen dope sick and panicking. She'd run around the neighborhood, frantically looking for a dick to suck, any dick, yelling it without a hint of shame.

She needed those five bucks bad, so that she could hurry and fall asleep standing up again.

Addiction sounded fucking insane to normal people.

Baker was generous when he had become "crack rich." He paid for his mom's habit so that she wouldn't have to sell her aging body anymore. He bought his little sister a Mercedes Benz and he made sure that the house was fixed up and the refrigerator was always full. He bought floor seats for him and his homies to watch the Lakers and they frequented the emerging hip hop scene of West LA. If you could afford to pop bottles and rent fancy cars and jewelry, you were always welcomed around the rappers and the high-class hoes that were trained to be their silent décor.

Baker was in his early twenties and having the time of his life. He would catch a flight to Vegas or go hang out in Miami for Spring Break. He could afford VIP at the hottest nightclubs.

One night he got in an argument with a random guy at a bar. It escalated and they pulled guns on each other. A standoff between two well-dressed black gentlemen ensued.

Baker didn't realize he was pointing his .45 at an undercover cop from Venice Beach.

The incident got broken up by security. The cop was embarrassed by the loud scene. He had come dangerously close to exposing himself.

He found Baker a couple weeks later and apologized for the previous exchange. "I get a little too fucking brave when I'm out there getting faded with the homies. Nahsayin'?"

"I'm already knowing," Baker said, "I'm the same damn way. Sometimes the alcohol works against brothers when it should be bringing us the fuck together." Baker put his hand out and they shook. "We straight, though."

"Hey," the undercover leaned down, "Since we travelin' down a fresh road ... My partner says you got some awfully fine work. I got money to spend with you if you'd be willing. I'm what you'd call a qualified buyer."

"Talk to me. What exactly is it you trying to do?"

"Man, I don't know. Maybe we could start out with a QP? What's that going at?"

"I usually don't break up the birds that small."

"Oh, I see, you only fuckin' with them keys. I guess I'm just some barnyard ass dude."

"Seeing as we almost shot each other over some words when we was on one ... I think I can make an exception. I'll prorate it. Zips are $650 all the way up on a full brick ... so that's, like — shit — $1,800 for a quad."

"Shoot that shit!" He drunkenly hooked his arm around Baker's neck, "How can we make it happen?"

"Tonight?"

"Yeah, nigga. Money don't sleep; why should we?"

Baker gave him an address for one of his safe houses. It was a townhouse in Gardena. One of his side bitches lived there with some baby. He had houses like this scattered throughout Los Angeles. This was the only one that had coke already cooked into crack rock. All the other houses had bricks of powder with cartel symbols engraved in their centers.

Baker had a driver take him to the new client. He went by the name of CJ. He told Baker that he was from Chicago and that he wasn't banging on anything. This was a relief to Baker. He was raised in a Crip neighborhood, but he didn't claim a set either. He was cool with Crips, and he was cool with Bloods. In prison there aren't those invisible lines. You are just black if you're black. There's some confused whites and Asians that claim to be black because of some fake accent. Those kinds of guys typically get stabbed in the pen. There's no point in setting over other gangs. It's you and the brothers versus every other race. It's indispensable for survival and nobody is concerned about what color bandanna people are flagging out in the world. Baker didn't see the point of beefing out on the street over gang shit either and preferred to do business with transplants like CJ.

He arrived at the front of the safe house around 2:20 a.m. on December 17, 1987. The lights were out. There were only a couple of rules that Baker demanded for the people that watched his safe houses. The living room lights were required to stay on. The house should never be completely dark at night. He had people on the payroll that would drive by and make sure the lights were on and make sure everything seemed okay from the outside.

The person assigned to living there couldn't be addicted to drugs. There were no guests allowed under any circumstance. Rent and utilities were taken care of by Baker. He gave them a thousand a week on top. He supplied his safe house watchers with unlimited food. Each house had the latest home entertainment system with VCRs, laser disc players, and a Nintendo.

Certain words were prohibited. For example: you weren't allowed to say the D-word (drugs) while in the house, and if you needed to talk any kind of business you had to go skinny dipping in the pool behind the townhouse with Baker or one of his appointed "lieutenants." These were preemptive measures to elude wiretaps and feds or anything else that was deemed unsafe.

One of the reasons Baker had managed to rise so quickly in the drug game was his insistence on safety and making sure his crew stayed out of cages.

"Tonya up on her post?" Baker asked his driver.

"She's supposed to be, sir."

"Would you knock it off with that proper bullshit. You ain't gotta talk to me like I'm your parole officer or some slave owner. I'm just the nigga that puts groceries on your family's table. You ain't gotta call me sir or nothing."

Tonya usually comes outside to smoke about once an hour. I haven't seen her tonight. And I've been here six or seven times."

"And you ain't seen her once?"

"Nope. And that's highly, highly unlike her."

"Damn, alright. You got a heater on you?"

"Of course. Aren't we mandated to be packing?"

"Shit, Tonya mandated not to be a dumb bitch, but it seems to me she's being a dumb fucking bitch. But I'm glad you is. I don't like it when my safe houses are completely dark. That's some nasty fuckin' juju, dawg. 'Totally bad vibes,' as the surfer dudes would say. I'm gonna go peep out the situation. Just promise me you gonna come up in there if that house swallows me up and won't let go."

"My word. I'll come blazing like a cowboy."

"Just being one hundred, that was gay though. Ain't nothing hard about cowboys. Don't they got them assless chaps or something hella wack like that in they all's arsenal?"

The driver put his head down defeatedly. He couldn't seem to say anything right to the boss.

"Nigga, I'm fuckin' wit you! I am just fuckin' wit you! Call me sir. Fuck cowboys in their butts. I don't give zero fucking fucks! Just make sure you come lookin for me if I don't come back and ... yo, what about — pop quiz — if the law shows up, what we doin?"

"Hold court in the streets."

"My nigga! That's right. If they ever try and arrest us, we go out in a parade of glorious bullets."

"And that wasn't gay?"

"Man, quit it with your homophobic ass. I'm going on in."

Baker had one of L.A.'s most effectual crack and powder cocaine distribution systems of the late nineteen eighties. He was flipping 250 kilograms of coke every week, that's ten million dollars, if you broke up the keys in individual grams.

Baker seemed paranoid to everyone, but he hadn't gotten caught. In the height of the War on Drugs, dealers would get arrested and nobody would ever see them again.

Baker was involved with the kind of weight that would

keep him locked up for the rest of his life if he was ever arrested with it.

He hired young, white college students to drive him around town or to run errands on his behalf. Police never question a black man being driven around by white people ("Don't look but I think he's someone. Probably in entertainment or sports.")

Baker rented safe houses with stolen identities. He had dozens of people working below him. There wasn't a single member of his crew that would be able to say how he was flooding Los Angeles with a quarter million grams of unadulterated Colombian cocaine each week.

He bought several tow trucks and formed a towing company. He volunteered his services to the police. (One of his dorky white employees did all the talking. His company would tow wrecked LAPD and Los Angeles Sheriff department vehicles — free of charge.)

"Just our way of saying thank you to the brave men and women that protect our city's streets."

Baker's staff monitored police scanners. If they heard that an officer was involved in an automobile or motorcycle accident, they would dispatch it to the other drivers through a radio system that Baker had installed in the trucks.

Whoever was closest would race over to the location of the accident and offer free towing and storage services to them.

Every police vehicle that his drivers towed were given a tally mark next to their name. Every Friday, Baker would give away a free kilo to the driver with the most tally marks.

They dubbed the game "Chasing Big Bird." At that time, the late eighties, a key of coke was worth thirty grand wholesale. You could get forty if you sold the entire kilo in grams.

It suddenly became very important to win stupid games each time they got the chance.

Police eventually became familiar with his company. By then he had purchased old police cars, SUVs, and motorcycles.

They would tow the replica vehicles from one safe house to the other. The drivers were never allowed to see more than one location. Cops were never going to suspect privilege-farting white kids, who were towing law enforcement vehicles, could be capable of transporting large quantities of cocaine.

The vast majority of Baker's clientele had no idea who he was.

Even Baker's most loyal customers didn't know he was making millions of dollars. He seemed like every other coke-dealing black dude of the 1980s in Southern California. He wore Velcro Reeboks and had a clunky beeper clipped to his turquoise jogging pants.

He didn't like the look of the dark house. Something seemed off.

He sat in the backseat of his driver's car with his head against the window.

There was familiar trepidation whenever he sold drugs to a new face. It was the one aspect of his operation that he was willing to take the risk himself on. He pretended like he was a small time dealer and would find and filter his new customers.

Baker took his .45 out and kissed it.

"Fuck it," he said, putting the gun in his back waistline, "Anything go down I'm expecting the gay cowboy shit, ya hear?"

The driver laughed. "Yes, sir."

Baker shook his head. The kid was a joker.

Baker got out of the car and walked up to the front door. He leaned over the pathway and tried to look in the front windows. The curtains were closed.

He reached for the front door knob and turned it. He

expected it to be unlocked. This settled his nerves a bit. If the door was locked Tonya had probably forgotten to leave the lights on.

There was only a half key at this house. He was going to go to the backroom and weigh out a quarter pound and then wait for CJ.

Baker unlocked the door himself. It was quiet inside. He turned the light on in the living room and noticed that books from the bookshelf had been knocked and scattered to the ground. The glass coffee table by the couch had been smashed.

He took his gun from out of his waistline. He wasn't sure if someone was there, but he knew that things weren't okay.

Baker walked gently down the hallway. He could see that the door to the master bedroom was closed. Light was peeking out of the bottom of the door.

He took a breath and gripped the .45 before swinging the door open and seeing a naked black man tied up with a gag in his mouth. The man saw Baker and his eyes expanded with terror.

"The fuck is you?" Baker asked.

The naked man mumbled from the gag in his mouth.

Tonya stumbled out of the bathroom. She was naked with her arms tied behind her back. She also had a gag in her mouth and had wide, nervous eyes.

"Kinda freaky shit is you on, Tonya?"

She yelled something, the gag making it incomprehensible. She knelt on the ground.

Baker was perplexed. He began to walk up to Tonya when he heard a man's voice coming from the bathroom.

"You know that feeling you get ...," it began.

CJ walked out, pointing a gun at Baker, "When you know it's a wrap? When you know you are about to go to jail for a very long time?"

Baker was silenced by shock.

"You should be feeling that right about now."

Men with DEA emblazoned jackets stormed into the room. Tonya was naked and shivering on the floor. There was shouting and commotion.

Baker dropped his gun. He was handcuffed and carted off to jail.

He didn't step foot in the free world again until 1997.

Everything had changed. L.A. had hit a nasty peak of violence in the mid 90s and it was finally mellowing down. Hip-hop culture had risen out of the fringes and was part of mainstream America.

The country was in an economic surplus because of the dot-com boom. It seemed that everyone was prospering. It was a celebratory time in America. Even the saxophone-playing president was secretly getting his dick sucked in the oval office.

The rich became richer. The middle class developed an upper and lower tier. And it was getting increasingly worse for the poor.

Baker's neighborhood had been savagely obliterated by the crack epidemic.

Families had protective bars on their home windows, imprisoned by the rampant crime and desperation lurking outside.

Many of the buildings had become dilapidated relics. They were abandoned and boarded with plywood; spray painted confessions were now censored by the shadows of old, forgotten walls.

Baker's sister had moved to Nevada. His mother had become addicted to crack when Baker had been sent away to prison. The very drug that afforded him all those fly ass Velcro Reeboks had taken away all his mother's teeth. She had already been battling heroin addiction for most of her life. Crack drove her off the deep end. She didn't even recognize Baker when he showed up from prison with a grocery bag full of his only belongings.

Baker's little brother still lived at the house. Obie had gone an entirely different direction. He was eight years old when Baker had gotten arrested. He never knew his father and he'd witnessed the horrors of addiction up close from his mom. He stayed away from guns and gangs and drugs. He took high school seriously and took care of their mother who would often go mad from crack psychosis. Obie had received a scholarship to the University of California Santa Barbara. Baker was proud of the kid. He knew that if his mom had her cognitive faculties that she would be proud of him too.

Baker was driving his '95 Cadillac Eldorado NorthStar convertible. Cindy was sitting in the passenger seat.

Cindy wore aviator sunglasses; her blonde hair blew wildly in the wind.

She had a stack of index cards.

"What is the fourth tradition?" she quizzed Baker.

"The fourth tradition ... um, each group should be autonomous except in matters affecting other groups or AA as a whole. That there is the anonymity thing."

"It's An-oh-nim-ity," Cindy said.

"The hell you mean, bitch. I said that."

"No, you said 'ANN,NIMITY.' That isn't how you say it."

This enraged Baker. He backhanded Cindy with all the force he could expend. Blood spewed from her nostrils.

She grabbed her face. "Sorry, daddy."

"Don't ever you think about correcting me, hear? Next one; worthless ass bitch."

She drew another index card at random. "Step ten?"

"Continued to take a personal inventory, and when we were wronged, promptly admitted it."

It was "wrong" not "wronged" but Cindy knew Baker was in no mood to be corrected.

"Another, less go."

"Step five?" she asked.

"Admitted to God, to ourselves, and to another human being the exact nature of our wrongs."

"Uh huh." Cindy said and accidentally dropped the stack of index cards on the floor.

"Come on, another. Hurry up."

Cindy was trying to pick the index cards up from the floor, but the wind had thrashed and scattered them.

Baker was smoking a cigarette dipped in embalming fluid and the smell was industrially rancid. His eyes had branches of messy broken blood vessels. He looked mad.

Baker grabbed the back of Cindy's head. He tugged on her ponytail and slammed her head into the dashboard forcefully.

"Ya dumb fucking bitch, always with that bullshit."

Cindy was sobbing and the dripping blood made her face look as if it were filthy. "I'm sorry, Daddy. Look at me! My makeup. It's ruined!"

"Ain't nobody give a shit about your makeup. It don't take away how fat and ugly you is."

Cindy just stared out the convertible at the car next to her. A young girl waved to her and she gently waved back as she wiped blood from her nose with a Kleenex.

They pulled up to McFadden's office. It was a huge building with fancy reflective glass. Baker parked in the underground garage, and they walked up to an elevator.

They were silent as they got in. There were men and women in suits, holding briefcases; the elevator was crowded. A black man and a chubby white woman already looked out of place in this prissy crowd. It was impossible for the businesspeople not to stare at Cindy's beaten face.

"The bitch fuckin' fell in the shower," Baker said, breaking up the silence. "Stay in yawl's own lane. Fuck!"

It seemed that everyone, including Cindy, looked at the ground simultaneously. They had to go up half a dozen floors before they stepped out.

The elevator ride was incredibly awkward.

McFadden and Crow Inc. was written in pretentious cursive on a polished brass sign.

They hurried past a secretary, sitting at a desk.

"Excuse me," she called after them. "You have an appointment?"

Cindy looked back at her, pleading but obedient.

Baker swung the door at Collin McFadden's office.

McFadden had his sleeves rolled up. He was hitting a gold golf ball into a flagged hole with a miniature putter.

He looked up and saw Cindy, "What are you doing here at my office?"

Then he noticed the blood. Then he noticed Baker.

"What are you doing here together? Did he hurt you? The hell is going on here?"

"Sit down. You racist, fat fuck," Baker said.

McFadden's face exhibited grave concern, despite his goofy grin.

"Did he hurt you?" McFadden asked.

"Just shut up, Mac." Baker said. "Just shut up."

"What is this? What do you want from me?"

"That depends a whole fuck of a lot on what you're willing to spend to make this go away, Mac," Baker said.

10

EXPECT MIRACLES

THE TWIN TOWERS — LOS ANGELES 2018

"Writing is something that you don't know how to do. You sit down and it's something that happens, or it may not happen." — Charles Bukowski

Jay Mackie stared at Mikey like a snake sizing up a rodent. Predator and prey. There was no doubt he would be eaten, it was just a question of logistics. Just how easy would this rat choke down?

"So, pray tell," said the captain with a certain giddiness out-of-place in an interrogation. It had the air of a Starbucks date.

Mikey just stared. Stared at his feet. Stared at the wall. Stared at his scabs. Stared into the abyss and the usual demons stared back.

There were consequences to snitching. In the prison hierarchy, it ranked below chomos. As Bam-Bam put it he was already housed in the Supermax of child molesters, girlfriend killers, and certified snitches. How could he sink any lower? What were they gonna do, house him under the fucking concrete? They might. He stared at the floor.

"Come on, Mike," the captain urged him with casual ease. "I know they say 'snitches get stitches.' But I say, 'snitches get riches, snitches get bitches.' Just look at that Whitey Bulger guy."[19]

---

19   Even in 2018 it was a poor example. Bulger made bank playing both sides of the law, but he would be fatally shanked in prison months later. He died as king rat of the most infamous informants. But

Mikey wasn't thinking about the potential riches, bitches, or movie deals. It was sheer survival instinct that caused him to mumble, "Whadayawannaknow, Cap'n?"

"Just call me Jay Mackie like my friends. Because when we are done we're going to be the best of friends." the captain reached over and gave him a jovial slap to the shoulder. "You a religious man, Mike?" Jay Mackie's eyes did not blink. He looked positively star-struck.

"Well, Jay-Mack, I've seen some things ..." Mikey's mind traveled back to those things. Fucked up hallucinations, twisted visions, strange premonitions. Nothing that convinced him of any one thing except that there was ... something ... the truth ... it's out there. His theology was a bit *X-Files* that way. But religious? His only stigma was the needle.

"I was raised Catholic," said the captain. "Just think of this office as a confession booth. Mike, it's time to get some things off your chest. It's time to ease the guilt. That pain in your stomach, that rumble in your gut, it'll go away — I'm your motherfuckin' Mylanta."

Once again the captain was playing the wrong card. Mikey was many things, but guilt-ridden was never one of them. The only pain he ever experienced was from withdrawals. He knew that kind of Bruce Lee kick to the gut.

Mikey started rambling, "There was this big-time dealer. I sold him an ounce of crushed-up water softener crystals and said it was DMT. I guess that was a pretty shitty thing to do."

It wasn't a confession. It had happened but Mikey wasn't sorry about it just like he wasn't really sorry about stealing DVDs or any number of petty crimes. He wasn't even sorry for pimping out Jessica once. He wasn't even sure sorry that she died in that dirty motel room. It was a rehearsed

---

Hollywood didn't care and the movies would immortalize him as a gangster legend — a real-deal antihero.

remorse, an insincere AA testimony, a little bait to lead the captain into thinking he'd harpooned his white whale. Mikey didn't know any 'big time dealer'. It was just a small-time street hustler. Mikey didn't even know his real name.

"They called him 'Rolex'," snitched Mikey. "He had a soul patch ... smelled like Campbell's beef vegetable soup ... tattoo of a Rolex on his wrist."

That part was true. The dude did have a crudely drawn prison tattoo of a watch. His dream was to have a real Rolex and when he got locked up he tattooed one on his skinny wrist as some sort of chaotic sigil toward his intention. He was gonna turn his life around and get that fuckin' watch.

It had sort of worked because he had gotten the Rolex. He had it for exactly 4 hours and 32 minutes before he pawned it for drugs. Four days later he sobered up and became aware of what he had done and robbed the shop to get his watch back. He had it until the next morning when he went back to the same store to pawn it again for more drugs. The owner counter-offered with a shotgun blast to the head.

The pawnbroker did his best to clean the remains of the junkie off his watch case but some of his brains and bits of skull still remained in a row of acoustic guitars directly behind.

"Rolex," chuckled the captain as he scribbled on a notepad. "That's good, Mike. What else you got?"

Mikey was so excited to have somebody listening to his bullshit he forgot he was talking to the guy in charge of keeping him locked up in that hell. He proceeded to ramble on with story after story.

It was all hazy recollections amid fleeting moments of coherence sandwiched between drug binges. Some stories weren't even his but stuff that happened to other people. Some was shit he just pulled off of crime shows. He even recited the plot line to *Die Hard* swearing he was there at Nakatomi Plaza that fateful Christmas Eve.

"Na-ka-to-mi," the captain sounded it out as he continued to fill up the notepad in cursive chicken scratch. "Gruber you said? Go on."

And Mikey obliged, just enjoying the sound of his own voice. After a couple of hours, the captain stopped him to order a pizza. He even asked Mikey what toppings he wanted and didn't object when the prisoner decided on pineapple and black olives. (Mikey's appetite was returning with a vengeance.)

While they waited the captain offered Mikey a smoke. It was an American Spirit Black with perique tobacco — a real man's cigarette that charred his throat while giving him much-needed f-o-c-u-s.

Three hours in Mike had finished the pizza and drained four R.C. Colas.

Four hours in, rumors about Mikey had already spread across the prison, from guard to convict, and kite to kite. Being in the captain's office that long meant that it wasn't a mere social visit. It could only mean he was in there spilling his guts. Now it was on their honor as convicts to spill his guts in return — status motherfuckin' quo in the dirty fishbowl.

Mikey didn't care. He had the captain's ear. He had cigs. He had pizza. He had soda. It was only a matter of time before he'd have everything else. Maybe even his freedom. It was a junkie pizza pie in the sky kinda optimism, but it always got him through.

Mikey took a drag, coughed, and got to his next story about accidentally injecting a whole vial of liquid LSD, losing his mind for three days, and managing to drive to a teepee motel in the middle of the desert.

"I'm pretty sure that's not a chargeable offense," said the captain.

"I was naked," said Mikey, hoping to score more points. "That's indecency, corruption. There may have been some children in that K-Mart. I'm sure they have security cameras."[20]

"Still ..." the captain trailed off while glancing at his watch. "We've been at it long enough and you need to be back in your cell for the night." He put away his completely full legal pad. "Got to file these notes."

Going back to the cell was the last thing Mikey wanted to do. Bam-Bam and Boogie would be waiting for him. Even though his mind was sharper than when he had checked in, he knew he couldn't face them in his condition. They would finish the job of carving him up and buttfuck him.

"I can't go back there. Can't I sleep ... " Mikey looked over at a couch. "What about in here?"

"In my office? I don't think that'd fly." the captain laughed. "What's the problem?"

Mikey paused. Telling stories about the streets was safer than snitching on your cellies. Mikey figured he was already too deep into it. He smashed his cigarette into the empty can of cola and sighed.

"Fucking Bam-Bam and Boogie. They're animals. Filthy. That damn mariachi music. I can't think straight."

"I'll make alternative arrangements for you," said the captain and called in the guard. After talking to the guard for a minute, Mikey was shackled up to be led back to his unit. Jay Mackie stopped him and pulled out his phone asking the guard to take their photo.

"Smile, Mike," said the captain. Mikey could only manage a crooked grimace. "That's great," said Jay Mackie as he inspected the photo. "We'll talk some more tomorrow."

The guard led Mikey back through hallways to his

---

20   Note: He had only been partially naked, wearing a pair of Ninja Turtle underwear. He didn't know where he got them until later when he found a wadded-up receipt. Evidently, he had also bought Twizzlers, a box of plastic spoons, and a *People* magazine.

lockup. Again the chomos and check-ins stirred in their cells and called out to him like ghouls from a crypt.

"Talk to the cops long enough, Pretty Eyes?"

"You a rat, Pretty Eyes."

"You gonna get busted. We gonna bust you up."

Mikey clenched his fists as the CO opened the cell door. "Step in, Pretty Eyes," the cop said with a snicker.

The prisoner scanned the cell like a little kid expecting a ghost to pop out from under the bed. The twisted mariachi music was still blaring out of the tinny radio. Boogie and his bunk bitch Bam-Bam had to be laying in the wait. If they were gonna get him, it would be while he was still chained up.

Mikey liked his odds a bit better than before. The H had eased the dope sickness, cleared his head, and left him somewhat optimistic. In a fair fight, he'd curb stomp Bam-Bam, but Boogie was no joke. He wasn't no limp wrist but a hulking homo thug.

But when the CO released him, the two ass amigos hadn't made an assault. This aroused even more paranoia from the junkie. He thought maybe they were just waiting for him to relax, looking for the spot, waiting, and then it would happen.

He wasn't going to let them fuck with him. If he was going to go down, he was gonna go down swinging. However it ended he was going to take it like a man.

Mikey dropped down and scrambled toward the bunk that Boogie had hidden under before. He scratched, swiped, and clawed at nothing but dust bunnies and shadows. Realizing that he had left his ass prone and exposed, Mikey quickly popped back up to his feet, racking his head on the bunk's rail. In a daze, he turned around, his head swimming with the static hum of the radio and the frenetic Mexican music.

Mikey raced over and did a sliding kick under the

opposite bunk. His foot slammed into the concrete wall behind. When he found no ghosts under that bed he began flipping the mattresses. Nothing but bedding floated down in a big heap.

The lockers. It was an illogical thought because Bam-Bam and Boogie's heads would barely fit in the small storage space, let alone their entire bodies. But Mikey was the king of illogical thinking and he rushed over. The music was swelling and he started to like it. Really, it seemed a perfectly logical soundtrack in this situation.

Their locks were gone and inside Mikey found only a few scraps of paper, a plastic spork, and a pack of chicken flavored ramen noodles. With their stuff cleared out, Mikey should've thought that the two were gone, but he couldn't relax until he made sure.

There was little else to check, but Mikey still got to work digging through the pile of bedding and flipping the mattresses again. He heard something hit the floor. They had left their dope rig which meant that they may have left ...

Mikey didn't finish the thought when his junkie senses started tingling. Baby, dope was in the room. (Go get 'em, tiger!)

That's when his investigation got really frenetic. Mikey forgot all about his cellies and began dissecting the room like a crime scene investigation on television.

He moved like a spider over the bed frames. He ran his fingers up and around the metal lockers, slicing his hand. He left a smeared bloody trail, across, up, over, around, and under the room like some fucked up Family Circus comic.

Maybe they had taken it with them? Bam-Bam had one of those all-purpose storage asses, always open for deposits.

Any doubt was pushed aside by Mikey's addict clairvoyance. There was that certain feeling that it was around, ready to manifest by sheer intention and force of will. It wouldn't be the first time it had happened like that.

Like that one time, he was sitting in a bar jonesing for junk. He only had enough change to buy a Coke and tip. He sipped it, trying to make it last until ... whatever was going to happen was gonna happen. He had a feeling.

Mikey was down to the last of his cola when an older man in a suit and fedora walked in. There were plenty of open stools but the man sat down next to him and tipped his hat.

It could have meant anything. Maybe he was just looking for bar talk. Maybe he wanted to bitch about his wife or cry about his kids. Maybe he was gay. Maybe he was a cop.

The bartender walked over and asked, "What'll you have?"

"Club soda and lime," the man answered and glanced at Mikey's ice melt, "Son, you need something?"

Mikey thought about ordering another Coke and continuing his wait. But the bar had been empty and this man had been his only company. He decided to roll the dice hoping the guy wasn't a cop.

"I was just thinking about how I'd love some Afghani black tar heroin." It was a moonshot but you 100% miss the chances you don't take.

The man simply laughed and ordered Mikey a water. "It'll do you good," he said.

As the glass of water was placed before him, Mikey was ready to give up. He drained the dirty glass ready to bounce when his plumbing started working and he got up to use the restroom.

The man reached out his hand, stopping him. "It was good to see you again."

Again? thought Mikey as he extended his hand. He couldn't count the people he had met and moments later forgot. They came and evaporated like ghosts.

The stranger and Mikey shook hands. He felt a small package pressed into his palm. Mike knew the drill and instinctively shoved the contraband into his pocket. (Prohibition-Era Street etiquette)

"You were going?" asked the man.

"To the bathroom, yeah —"

Mikey walked casually to the back. He was eager but he wanted to play it cool. He figured it might be some blow. Gay dudes always seemed to have the good blow. He could sell it for some tar easy.

When he passed through the bathroom door, he quickened his pace to the stall. The door was rusty and covered with a novel's worth of back-and-forth graffiti. The back of the toilet seat was missing to deprive druggies of a work surface. Everything was piss sticky and had a syrupy smell.

He pulled the package out of his pocket and couldn't believe his eyes. It was the best-looking dope he had ever seen.

Mikey couldn't believe his luck and thought about pressing it by asking the bartender for a spoon, but he didn't have any good needles on him. H of this kind deserved a fresh needle. It was a question of proper protocol.

There was also the question of payment. The man was probably waiting outside for Mikey to come back and settle up. There was no telling what it was worth. Even if the guy only wanted a dollar, Mikey didn't have it. He had tipped his last seventy-three cents hoping for the good karma it might bring.

Maybe he could grab a shaker of salt off the table and pawn it off as crystal or something. It was stupid because anyone passing out heroin of that caliber was a real player who could spot the difference.

But if the guy was a cop and he shouldn't offer anything in return. Mikey looked around the small restroom. It was too much to hope for a conveniently placed escape window like in the movies. He'd have to find another way out.

So he dropped down to the floor. If he could get to the door, he could get to the hallway, and then just maybe a back exit. The sticky floor gripped him like Velcro as he inch-wormed toward the exit.

Just another foot, thought Mikey when the door swung open and bashed him in the forehead.

"What the hell?" the bartender called out.

Mikey recoiled away from the door groaning.

"Hey, buddy," said the bartender. "You know, you can't sleep in here."

"Nah, bro. I'm good. I sometimes get dizzy when I piss." Mikey grabbed the edge of the grimy urinal basin and pulled himself standing—barely. "Is that other guy still out there?"

"No. Damndest thing. Didn't even finish his drink and left me with a scratch-off as a tip."

He held out the ticket and Mikey tried to work out the hieroglyphics of bells and cherries and lemons. "Is it a winner?"

"Damn straight. Five grand." The bartender held the door open for Mikey. "I'm closing early. It's my lucky day."

As they walked through the empty bar to the front the bartender mentioned something about having a guardian angel. Mikey gripped the heroin in his pocket and couldn't disagree. He'd find some needles too. He had that junkie faith. Lawd, he was a true believer.

Back in his prison cell, Mikey hoped for another miracle but he had ransacked the room and still had not found the stash. In frustration, he grabbed the radio and threw it against the wall. It splintered into clear plastic and the AA batteries rolled out across the floor along with something else.

Their stash.

Mikey tried to remember how Bam-Bam prepared the small flakes. He dissolved it in water and it had a brownish tint like it had been cut with coffee. (Or was that meth?) It didn't matter as he dropped in a wad of belly button lint and cotton he had found in the corner of the room. He didn't have the disinfecting blue liquid but decided to just take his chances with the dirty needle. He didn't know how much to take but decided to take his chances there too.

He searched for a vein, searched some more, searched some more, found it, hit it, and collapsed upon the pile of mattresses, bedding, and pillows. He was king of the cum-stained mountain. *If only I had some music*, he thought, and then laughed about the fucking radio.

Somewhere across town, Jay Mackie's night was just beginning.

It was a Monday night when he usually had his mystery-crime writer's group at Brewsin' Coffee. It was a collection of assorted weirdos and unwashed never-ever-beens doing a poor imitation of Agatha Christie.

They talked more about their dreams of getting published than they did any actual writing. But they mostly just drank coffee. They were so wrapped up in their re-tread train murders to never recognize the true genius that sat among them, transcribing his legal pads into a laptop, editing, and embellishing as the muse struck him.

The other fiddle-faddle in the group never got him. He'd never ever set a story on the Oriental Express. He told tales straight from the gutter — savage and sick. Truman Capote had to sweet lisp his way into prison to interview stone killers for *In Cold Blood*. As prison captain, it was Jay Mackie's day job. He was locked in there with the filth all day, every day.

Mackie listened to the prisoner's gossip, read their kites, opened their mail, and monitored their calls. When it came to the criminal underworld, he'd like to think he had his finger on its greasy pulse.

The convicts had all sorts of codes for drugs, women, and guns. The NOI dudes had their numerology and religious ciphers. The cartel had their ancient Aztec. The white-collar cons had cryptography. The dumbest pecker-woods had Pig Latin.

Jay Mackie did his best to interpret and fill in the gaps with his overactive imagination. His 'writer's gift' as he liked to refer to it. At Brewsin' Coffee, he was the real Hercule Poirot.

As far as he saw it, he didn't have to get the facts right. He wasn't trying to pin a case on anyone. He just needed source material for his stories.

Like a chef, he'd chop up their anecdotes, add a pinch of confessions, a dash of day room talk, and a spoonful of overheard confidential legal advice. All of this he would turn into half-baked crime stories.

He usually changed the names. "A convict named Poo-Poo, said ..." There were any number of Poo-Poos in the system. It didn't matter. But Mikey May, that was a name with real comic book alliteration—too good not to use.

He'd even had a few short stories published in low-print crime anthologies but received many more rejections. "Too sleazy." "Too grimy." "Morally defunct." It seemed absurd to him. A crime story that was too sleazy? What did they think criminals were? Was there a murderer that wasn't morally defunct?

As far as Jay Mackie saw it, he was in the third act of his life and was ready to emerge among his literary heroes. He at least hoped his nom de plume "Lee Henry Osmond" would stand among Capote, McBain, and Doyle.

He pulled out his cell phone and sent the selfies he had taken with Mikey May to his literary agent: **NEED TO TALK SOON. BIG NEWS!**

When he got home his wife had his bourbon waiting for him. "I got him," he said, hugging her firmly.

She backed away, uncomfortable with his sudden attention. He never hugged her. "Got who?"

"Flippin' Mikey May."

"Who?"

Jay Mackie showed her the selfie he took. He was all smiles but Mikey had that wide-eyed, junkie-in-the-headlights kinda gaze. "Mikey May," he repeated slowly for emphasis.

"Mikey who?"

"The guy," he said. "The guy from the television news. The one that killed his girlfriend. The chief's daughter."

"Oh, yeah," said his wife absently, "I remember that now but if you want a real story, you should see what was on the news tonight."

The captain slugged his bourbon. How quickly Mikey had become old news — another memory hole in the 24/7 news cycle. There was always another killer in the wings waiting for his five-minute dash through the media gauntlet.

Jay Mackie knew he had to get Mikey back in the headlines fast. That wouldn't be too hard if Jessica or her hacked-up corpse (preferably) were found.

The hard part would be keeping Mikey safe in the meantime. The kid was too soft for prison, let alone the hell hole they stuffed him in. They already pin cushioned him on his check-in. The captain had moved Bam-Bam and Boogie out but he couldn't keep that room free forever. There was always some new scumbag needing a cot.

He finished his drink and dialed an old military buddy that had gone into private contracting for the army.

"Harrison ... I need to call in a favor ... You still got that line with those psych guys ... I've got just the man for you ... He's wound up pretty tight ... No, no. I'm not expecting any miracles."

11

MEDIATIONS IN A CRISIS SITUATION

"Appear weak when you are strong, and strong when you are weak." - Sun Tzu

▌▌Baker, welcome to my office. Please have a seat." Collin McFadden pointed his tiny putter toward the chairs in front of his desk. Baker took one, but Cindy hung back.

She didn't make eye contact but acted like a whipped dog that had already been told twice ... and then a third time.

McFadden only experienced a twinge of cowardice. It was so minor that it only registered as a slight twitch of his index finger. He had been in tough negotiations before and he wasn't gonna get shaky — especially when the help got uppity. It was his office and he had home field advantage.

"Nice office," said Baker, looking around, "I mean I figured you had a nice office, but not this nice."

"Thank you," said McFadden. "Was there some AA business you wanted to discuss?"

"That's right, we need to talk big business to the business man, business man to business man" said Baker as he pulled out his .45,"Please step around the desk slowly."

"Look ... look," mumbled McFadden but he was coaxed by the gun barrel to walk the runway.

"Nice threads," said Baker through his smile, sizing him

up. "Now turn around and lift up the jacket so I can see the cut of that tailor made."

McFadden obliged, showing off the back of his trousers.

"Damn, Cindy. Whatchu think?" said Baker.

Cindy looked up from her phone and quipped, "Very nice."

"Any old tailor can make a suit for a skinny boy, but big and tall is a fine art. But you know the real tell of the man is his socks," said Baker. "Why don't you pull up those pant legs for me. Slowly, make it sexy."

Again, McFadden obliged, though he made no attempt to make it sexy. "See, no gun," he said as he showed off his ankles.

Baker simply clapped his hands like a toy monkey clanging cymbals. He turned to Cindy, "What'd I tell you? A businessman down to his socks." Then he laughed. "But McFadden your housekeeper done fucked up."

McFadden looked at the assailant, puzzled. Baker pointed the gun down at the businessman's feet. "See you got one black one and one navy blue one."[21]

McFadden raised his hands up like so what? and reached into his jacket pocket. Baker launched at him and grabbed his hand.

"My business card," said McFadden and handed Baker the antique white card with the basic-bitch Times New Roman font. "You got a card, businessman to businessman?"

Baker snickered and pointed his gun up at McFadden. "My card is right here, but since we on the subject a little professional courtesy is in order."

"Professional courtesy? You want some coffee?" asked McFadden.

"I'll take a root beer," Cindy suddenly found her voice and chimed in.

"Nah," said Baker. "You gotta have some big business booze up in this big business bitch."

---

21   Baker wasn't into McFadden like that. His routine was twofold: 1. Show dominance. 2. See if McFadden was strapped or wearing a wire.

"I'm afraid I have no cognac or strawberry daiquiris. Do you take scotch?"

"Only if it's single malt."[22]

He went to the cabinet behind his desk above his wet bar and pulled down a bottle. "McClellan's, okay?"

"That's good unless you got some of that Johnny Blue."[23]

McFadden paid him no mind as he sat three rocks glasses on the table. "You take some ice?" he said as he bent down to his mini fridge. He'd normally have his secretary make the drinks but he didn't want to involve her — this matter was way above her pay grade.

When he bent lower, he spotted an antique gun a client had given him. It was said to be priceless, a rare heirloom, one of a kind, yada yada. McFadden had stuffed it down here and forgot about it. He didn't even know if it could really shoot. He pocketed it as he filled an ice bucket. He placed a couple of the larger cubes in each glass.

He tipped the bottle and began to fill the glasses but before he could pour the third, Baker stopped him. "Just you and me ... Cindy is working."

McFadden looked over at Cindy. He didn't want to ask what kind of work she did. Maybe she was a professional punching bag.

Each man took a big gulp and stared eye to eye. The first one who talks loses, thought McFadden and he waited.

"So ..." began Baker, losing. "The long and short of it is you pay us and we don't wreck your family by telling them what you've been up to, which Cindy tells me has been substantial and often, if not pleasurable, at least for you."

McFadden simply leveled with him. "Wreck my family?" He laughed even harder. "That's like going to the ashes of someone's burned down house and threatening to

---

22 Baker didn't know anything about scotch, but he had heard the term 'single malt' in a movie before.

23 Johnny Walker Blue is a blended whiskey and not a single-malt as Baker earlier requested. He just knew that Johnny Walker Blue was an expensive whiskey, again from a movie he saw.

throw a cigarette on it. You want me to pay you for help doing something I already did?"

Baker didn't seem prepared for that response as he glanced dumbly around the room trying to think of what to say next, which was: "Fine, we gonna fuck up your entire world." He nudged Cindy, "Show him what we got."

Cindy held up her iPhone and started playing a music video.

"What is this?" asked McFadden. Then he saw exactly what it was. His hotel assault.

Bethany, the trans-girl in the Clinton mask was posturing around in a tank top, flashing up signs. It had been cut as a music video. Clinton rapped:

> Yeah, I'm Killary Klinton, spittin' rhymes in the mist,
> Got that HRT, my life is on twist,
> Used to be a bro, now I'm reppin' as a sis,
> Watch out, I'm not gonna miss.

"I've seen enough," said McFadden but Baker let it play a few more seconds while he laughed and clapped his hands like a retarded seal. "So, businessman, I'm gonna sell you the exclusive rights to this one copy for $100,000."

"One hundred thousand," said McFadden, mulling it over. He could have easily written the check and called it a business expense. It was a pittance. But he couldn't as easily forget about the humiliation. He couldn't forget about that song. The beat at least was catchy. He listened to the hook.

> HRT, Killary Klinton, mixin' up the potion,
> HRT, causin' commotion, fluid like the ocean,
> HRT, in my veins, breakin' down the notions,
> HRT, no more chains, this is my devotion.

"One hundred thousand is a little low, for a music video of this caliber." The scene was shown where the Clinton masked assailant was pissing all over McFadden's barbecue smeared body.

"Okay, two hundred," said Baker.

McFadden leaned back in his leather chair. "Thankfully you are a hustler, a con, and not a real businessman. You are trying to sell a Jaguar at Honda Civic prices. This is easily worth millions. I know a top hit when I hear it."[24]

"A tranny rapper?" Baker sneered. "Rap is about fuckin' bitches not being a fuckin' bitch."

McFadden simply pointed at the window. "The world is changing, my man ... you got to change with it or be left behind. You and these street hustles? Soon it's either dead or jail. You deal with drugs? Only a matter of time before big pharma runs you out of business with legalization. Extortion? Only a matter of time before you find someone that won't buckle like a belt."

"I got Cindy though—"

"Pimping and pandering? You got dreams to be Superfly?" McFadden laughed some more.

McFadden looked at Baker and then at Cindy. He asked her to play him the video once more.

"A hit song like this. I figure it's worth, say, five hundred thousand?"

"Half a mil?" said Baker with shock as McFadden pulled a large leather checkbook and set it on his desk. "It'll have to be put down as a business expense. Maybe promo music?" He turned back to Baker. "Do you have an invoice, or bill-of-sale for the ... video?"

"Bill-of-what?" Said Baker.

"You know, a b-i-l-l like those collectors call you about."

---

24   This was a lie. McFadden did not know a top hit when he heard it. McFadden hadn't listened to anything new on the radio. He simply listened to a heavily curated playlist of whatever was played at college parties. Now That's What They Call Frat House: Volumes 1 to 10, excluding volume 7.

"I pay my muthafuckin' bills," snipped Baker. "Besides this ain't official like that."

"Well why don't we make it official — real official — officially."

"What are you talking about?"

"Talking about you and me doing big business together."

"What kind of business?"

"The music business."

12
30 MINUTES OR LESS

"Man is not what he thinks he is, he is what he hides."
- André Malraux

Gunner paced in lumbering circles around Cindy's front porch. He knocked. He rang the bell. He banged on the glass like a zoo chimpanzee. He screamed "Cindy, I know you're in there." He yelled, "Open up!"

With no answer, he returned to his Jeep and stared at the second hand on his watch ticking and he got more ticked by the second. She hadn't been answering his calls all day.

"Stupid, stupid, bitch," he murmured. Gunner wasn't about waiting around any longer like a simp. He started up the car and moved forward only to slam it back into park a few houses down. Well, maybe just a bit longer.

He grabbed his junk through his blue jeans and stroked it. "Just a little bit longer," he commanded his dick. It had just started working again. It was time to put it to the test.

Gunner thought about just getting a whore. Cheap and easy. Hot and ready, like Little Caesars. He definitely wasn't above it but he didn't need a Desert Storm redux. He thought about that Iraqi whore that triggered the onset of the madness. Maybe he could just go to a bar and try his luck.

He was staring into the rearview mirror when he saw a Cadillac pull up behind him.

"Now who the fuck is this?" he said to the mirror. The mirror did not answer.

The car's driver had his head cocked back toward the ceiling, looking up at something. Gunner couldn't make him out other than his coal dark skin. The vet slowly reached over to the glovebox and pulled out his Glock while keeping his eyes locked on the Caddie behind.

Gunner thought it might be his sign to get the fuck out of there. Cindy wasn't worth getting jacked for. She had hit the wall and was barely a 4. On the positive side, she was semi-respectable. That was a stretch but at least she wasn't some crack whore. The likelihood of an STD was low, not that it mattered. They passed out antibiotics at the VA like candy. The biggest plus was that she was willing.

Just then, the man's head jerked forward where Gunner could see the whites of his shit eating, gap-toothed grin. He then watched as Cindy's head rose from the passenger seat. "You motherfucker," Gunner cursed as she wiped her mouth.

She didn't seem to notice him as she made a beeline to her front door. Gunner stashed the Glock in his pants and chased after her. "Hey! Hey! What the fuck?" he called out.

Cindy jumped and dropped her keys. "Dammit, Gunner. You about scared the shit out of me."

"Where have you been?"

"At work," she said. "My boss gave me a ride home. He's safe. I can trust him." The Cadillac pulled out and the driver waved at the two of them.

"Trust him, what? Not to veer into an overpass while you give him road head?"

"No fuckin' way," she said, "You take me for some kind of whore?"

The thought had just crossed his mind. It didn't matter. He was ready to just get it over with. Ease that tension and move on. Cindy was just an ice breaker.

"Just come in, honey," said Cindy. "I'm starving."

Gunner followed her drooping ass into her living room. He was also starving.

She dropped her bag down on the table. "So, whatcha in the mood for? Chinese? Pizza? Delivery options are limited in this neighborhood.

"You sure you don't want soul food?" Gunner sniped.

He thought he had found his domestic goddess. Someone just ugly enough that you never had to worry about guys trying for them. Someone who was beaten down just enough to have long given up hope for something better.

It'd take more than a fancy watch to attract some young gold digger. Someone with preexisting daddy issues could work — but what a headache. The best he could hope for was some roastie that had aged her way off of the cock carousel. They were ready to settle down and find someone to take care of them and their assorted mix-raced kids they had collected up like Beanie Babies along the way.

"Gunner, please calm down," said Cindy. "I had a really stressful day and I'm about to smoke a bowl. If that bothers you, you're welcome to come back in an hour." She pulled out an ounce of weed and set it down on the coffee table.

Gunner picked up the bag, opened it, and inhaled. It was piny with a hint of citrus and the right amount of skunk. The crystal trichomes sparkled in the light like a sugar frosted shrub. (If Gunner had known anything about cannabis he would have known this was some really dank shit. All he could think about was the smell of the used car salesman that had raped him.)

"Does your boss know you're a stoner?"

"Who do you think gave me this?" She put a thumb-sized nug into a large metal grinder, turned it a few times, and then packed it into a glass bowl shaped like Sponge Bob.

Gunner had enough self-respect to give the impression that he was weighing his options. He even got up and walked to the door. He even mumbled, "fucking addict."

He hated pot heads. He tried it once at a party. It was an oversized novelty bong and he burned his fingers trying to use it. Huffing like a homo on that glass tube did nothing but make him feel ridiculous and dumb — very dumb.

Meth was different. When it was good you felt everything more intensely. You fired on all cylinders. The only thing that came close to that kind of kick was the damn war.

"That's better," said Cindy as she exhaled a plume of smoke.

"Gunner, do you want some?"

"I don't fuck with that shit."

"What? Wow!" said Cindy and chuckled.

"What's so fucking funny?"

"It's 2018. It's legal here. Everyone fucks with this shit. Little elderly grannies fuck with this shit."

"Gimme that," said Gunner. He took a big draw to show that he was indeed cool but ended up just coughing until he went dizzy and almost passed out in a most uncool manner.

"Doesn't that feel nice?"

Gunner just murmured as his eyes glazed over.

"It's not going to make you relapse?"

Not a fucking chance, thought Gunner. "Hungry," was all he murmured.

"So circling back — Chinese or pizza?" She held up a couple of paper to-go menus.

"Pizza." Gunner plopped down on a chair. His head was swimming.

She dialed the number from memory and placed the order. "Thirty minutes or it's free," she said.

"Good, it'll get here fast."

"No," explained Cindy. "That's the thing it never gets here in thirty minutes. They have THE worst delivery so it's always free."

"So what do we do in the meantime?"

"We could watch the minute hand on your fancy watch or we could go into the bedroom and I could fuck your brains out."

Gunner wasted no time standing at attention. "Which way?"

"Your way, baby." She took his hand and led him down the hallway to her room. His massive hands were instantly all over her.

"Easy ... easy," she said, "We got more than thirty minutes."

Her bed was full of stuffed animals but it was the pizza boxes that caught his attention — many such piled high in greasy towers around the room. "Romeo's," they read. **THIRTY MINUTES OR IT'S FREE!** they bragged.

Since there was nowhere to sit or lay, Gunner just pushed her up against the wall and kissed her hard. His tongue waggled like a worm coring an apple.

Cindy gurgled, "*Mwahamagondon.*"

"Wha? What?" said Gunner pulling away from her lips trailing a string of thick spit.

"I wanna go down on you, baby."

She navigated the pizza boxes and pushed a plush cat and a stuffed bear out of the way to sit on the corner. He walked over to stand by her and she undid his trousers.

The whole time, she kept battered puppy dog eyes on him as she reached into his pants ... and then felt around, fishing for it. She finally pulled down his underwear so they hung down around his ankles. His hedgehog of unshaven pubic hair bushed out. Somewhere in the thicket was his little twig.

Cindy expertly parted the hair away until she saw his penis — like a robin's egg in a nest.

She took it into her mouth and began to suck with the centrifugal force of a Dyson vacuum cleaner.

Why isn't it working? thought Gunner. It was the damn weed. The bitch had sabotaged him.

In shame he pushed her away. It was harder than he had intended and she tumbled back into a pile of pizza boxes. He felt the slightest tingle in his junk as he watched her fall.

"It's okay," said Cindy. "I don't mind it a little rough if that's what you need."

Gunner thought about grabbing her up by the neck — choking an orgasm out of her. That might work. The weed had dulled his rage — it made him too easy going. "I just need a minute," he said, jerking his noodle uselessly.

Cindy said, "I need some music," and got on her phone pulling up an app. A heavy bass beat started playing out of her Bluetooth speaker.

"What the fuck is this jungle music?" said Gunner.

"It's 'The Chronic', baby."

"You got anything ... white?"

"I gotcha," she went back on her phone and soon the horns and sirens were replaced with heavy drums and aggressive guitars. Gunner was ready to go when some more rapping began.

"You like Rage?"

"I love rage," said Gunner. "Where the fuck is that pizza?"

"Chill, baby. It's only been about 31 minutes. It usually takes at least an hour. You can't rush free!"

Gunner clenched his fist. The song made him feel angry. But he wasn't raging against any machine. He was mad at the door, mad at the bitch, mad at his cock. He was rage against everything.

"If you're hungry, I got some peanut butter, you want a sandwich, no jelly though ... no bread either ... tortilla?"

Gunner did not. "Where is that fucking pizza?"

Across town the pizza delivery boy laughed as he looked down at the next order for Emilio Pinto. Beaner down to his name. Some hispanics tipped but many did not. It really didn't matter; he wasn't doing the jobs for the tips. Giving away free pizza didn't promote generosity anyway. Twenty percent of zero was still zero.

The delivery job was just to hide his real hustle as a

drug dealer. The magnetic "Romeo's Pizza" stuck on the side of his Honda Civic was cop camouflage. He could go anywhere, the hood, the city, the hills and the law never hassled him. He was a respectable, working man on a "thirty minutes or it's free" mission. Gangbangers, petty thieves, and drug addicts were another story.

His regulars had a code — they'd order pizza without sauce, cheese, or toppings — and pay with cash. Based on the size of the pie he knew how much weed to deliver to them.

"Got another one of those crazy crusties," his shift manager said as he slid the Pinto order to him. Crusties had become his bread and butter.

The delivery driver checked the order and saw that this wasn't one of his regulars. He didn't recognize the address, nor did he know Emilio Pinto. Maybe it was a pseudonym. It was okay — sometimes people would give out his connect details.

He grabbed the pizza in the cushioned red warmer and took it to the front porch, ringing the bell.

"*¿Quién es?*" called out a voice from behind the door.

"Pizza," said the driver.

"Pizza?" The door slowly opened and he saw a Mexican. "I didn't order a pizza."

"Emilio Pinto?"

He turned around and called out to someone inside. "Emilio, did you order a pizza, dawg?"

"Yeah," said another guy as he came to the door. He had a tattoo of the devil on the side of his neck. "Come in, come in. Don't stand out there. They'll kill you and buttfuck your corpse around here, fool."

Inside, the delivery boy handed over the box which the dude set on the kitchen table.

"That'll be $132.73"

"$132.73," Emilio slowly repeated. "For one pizza?"

"$22.73 for the pizza and $110 for the extra ... spinach."

"Fuck, did I order spinach? I hate spinach."

"No, spinach," said the delivery driver, as if to clarify. "Take a look."

Emilio opened up the box and saw the ounce of weed on top of the crust only pizza.

"I ordered that? I think there's been some mistake."

"I think there's been a mistake for sure, fool." He looked down at the pizza. "There's no cheese, there's no sauce. I was trying to get some meat. Don't you got sausage? You need to fix that online order shit. There was no Spanish option. It wasn't even in good English. It wasn't even good Italian."

He pulled it out of the bag and smelled it. "How much did you say this was?"

"One hundred, thirty-two dollars and seventy three cents ... plus tip."

"Tip, huh?" He tossed the weed over to his buddy. "Here's a tip, fool. Get here in thirty minutes — this shit is free."

"Fine for the pizza. I still need one-ten for the smoke."

Emilio pulled out his gun. "You know I could just rob your pizza slinging ass, fool"

"I could have killed you ten minutes ago," said the driver. His hand extended from a hole he had cut into the back of the pizza warmer. He was holding a pistol.

Emilio just laughed. "Pizza Boy is packing."

"Just give me back the weed. You can keep the crust."

Emilio turned to his friend, "Flaco, *trae la molta*."

Flaco went to a kitchen cabinet and pulled out what seemed to be fifty pounds of weed. "Look at what we got, fool. Do you think we need to take this from you?" He laughed and tossed the bag back at the pizza boy. The delivery driver didn't want to drop the gun to catch it so the bag just bounced off his chest onto the floor.

Emilio pulled off a slice of crust, dumped some salsa on it, and folded it like a taco. "You got guts but you're in the wrong business."

"The pizza business?"

"No, the weed business." He took a bite of the salsa crust. "It's all legal now, fool. Only people you can sell to are those too lazy or too paranoid to just go buy it. Could sell to the shops but they ain't buying either. It's flooded."

Flaco lumped the bag down on the table. "Shit, we can't even sell this. It's going to take us forever to smoke it all."

"You want it? We'll give you a good price."

The Pizza Boy and the gangbanger negotiated a wholesale price of $1,000 for a pound. The delivery boy only had two-hundred fifty, but Emilio fronted him the rest.

"So you see how you do?" said Emilio. "You bring me back the money and I'll give you another pound. We take it from there. You don't bring me back my money, we cut off your dick and shove it down your throat. *Chorizo*, fool."

The delivery diver put the pound into his pizza warmer along with the bag of weed he had brought. He went to leave but Emilio called after him. "Wait ... you forgot your tip."

He tossed the kid a small black package. "Marijuana futures are down, fool. You want to do this, you need to diversify. That's *primo escante*. Give some to your white boy friends. You'll see. They'll butfuck you all night long."

Back in his Civic, the teenager marveled at his luck. He had made a real street connection. It was just the thing to boost his career as an upcoming hip-hop artist. He would do for Santa Barbara what Eazy-E did for Compton. The pound of weed might get him enough to buy some beats and studio time.

He was thinking these things as he walked up to the next delivery. Their pizza was beyond late, but it had been late before.

This Cindy cunt ordered pizza at least four times a week. The worst thing she would do was bitch him out but he'd been bitched out many times before.

Suddenly he was grabbed in a choke hold from behind.

"Thirty minutes, motherfucker! Thirty minutes?"

"Chill, man," he managed to choke out. "It's free. Free. FREEE!"

The assailant grabbed the pizza warmer out of his hands and tossed it to the ground. A knife was pressed against his cheek.

"Why don't I slice you like that cold ass pizza."

"I got money," the delivery driver said. He pulled out a wad of one-dollar bills from his pocket and let them flutter to the ground.

"You see this watch? You see this watch?" He pressed the blade into his cheek harder. "Do you think I need your one-dollar bills? Do I look like I'm going to a strip club?"

"You don't look like anyone — I can't see a thing. What do you want?"

"I wanted a fucking. pizza. thirty. minutes. ago." The attacker stomped down hard on the back of the pizza boy's knee. He folded over like a sheet and collapsed. He was kicked hard in the stomach.

The kid squirmed like a maggot as he attempted to slither across the grass but a foot came down hard on the back of his ankle.

"Wait," said the voice. "You forgot your tip." He pulled out a wad of bills from his pocket and began to make it rain. Crumbled up five, tens, and twenties showered the battered boy like some fucked up rap video.

The pizza bot quit his job right there. *I need a new hustle*, he thought. Maybe something like liquor store clerk. Maybe underwater welder. Something safer. And then he passed out.

Gunner thought about stomping the delivery driver some more but he felt an unusual tightness in his pants. He looked down in shock to see the head of his unit poking at the denim.

Back in business, he thought as he collected the pizza

from off the ground. He was ready to return when he spotted a little package that had dropped out of the Pizza Boy's pocket. He knew immediately what it was, took a snort and lit up.

Go time.

"Did you get the pizza?" asked Cindy as Gunner came back to the bedroom.

"Yeah, but it's all fucked up," He opened the box. "Stupid kid didn't know how to drive or something. All the toppings slid off to one side."

"Whatever, it's free pizza," said Cindy. "FREEE," she squealed.

Gunner batted her hand away. "First things first," he said and dropped his pants. His tiny erection stood at attention.

"Later, we got time, baby," said Cindy, reaching for a slice, "I'm hungry."

But Gunner wasn't hearing any of that as he slapped her hand away and tugged at her pants that were too small and tight, giving her that half-baked muffin top.

"Okay, okay." She laid down on the bed and squirmed to get out of her pants, then her shirt, and finally her bra. Two saggy breasts popped out. Her nipples were giant greasy pepperonis. "You wanna hit it from behind?"

Gunner didn't answer but immediately started shoving himself in. She wasn't wet but his penis was small and her vagina so wallowed out, it worked in a fashion.

He began to drill her as she ate a slice of pizza. He finished before she got down to the crust. *Thirty minutes or less*, he thought and laughed. Much less.

He slapped her ass.

Then he punched it and red turned to blue. And again again — harder — watching it move like the ocean as blue turned to purple. And as emptied his veiny, withered sack he heard a sick whisper moaning, "Gregory ..."

13

SOMEDAY

WESTWOOD :: SANTA BARBARA 2018

"The sun will come out tomorrow. Betcha bottom dollar, that tomorrow, they'll be sun." - Annie

Mikey woke up in the hospital with his new buddy Jay Mackie bedside.

"Jesus, Mike," said the captain, "I thought we'd lost you."

"Wha ... What happened?" murmured Mikey as he opened his eyes. His body felt like an elephant was sitting on top of him.[25]

"You almost died." Just another day in paradise.

"Oh." Mikey yawned. He had almost died many times. "Wake me up when I really go."

"They had to use the Narcan. Had you died—shit—I don't know what we would have done ... probably would have to have faked your suicide." Jay Mackie chuckled at the thought.

"I don't think you'd been able to fake my suicide," said Mikey, "Anybody who knows me, knows that I'm too much of a narcissist to kill myself. Besides, I would have left a really long suicide novel. Fuck a note."

They both had a good laugh about that.

"By the way, I brought you something," said the captain.

Mikey perked up thinking caffeine, thinking sugar, thinking alcohol, thinking nicotine but mostly thinking dope.

"Flowers," said Jay Mackie, presenting a vase of yellow tulips bedside. "Sorry I couldn't find poppies." It was a bad joke that Mikey appreciated.

25   When you wake up from an overdose it is not uncommon to feel a brutal heaviness all over.

"I was hoping for drugs." It was the thought that counted.

"About those drugs ..." said the captain. "Where'd you get them? You had them in your ass, right? I told my wife you had to have stashed them up your crack!"

"Dope fairy," quipped Mikey. For all he knew, they could have fallen out of Bam-Bam's ass.

"Well, all's well that ends well." The captain reached into his laptop case and pulled out some paperwork. "I was reading over the administrative grievance you wrote last night but it seems you forgot to sign it." The cop pulled out a ball-point pen and held out a document for Mikey's review.

"I typed a grievance?" Mikey didn't remember writing anything but he'd been known to do crazier things on a drug bender. He didn't even know how to type.

Through cloudy eyes Mikey skimmed through the legal form — allegations of abuse, not addressing his psychiatric needs, psychological torture with loud mariachi music — it went on.

Sounded like his gripes but more succinct and to the point at only two very well punctuated pages. Had Mikey written the grievance it would have been ten times the length with a shit ton more exclamation points.

"So if I sign this then what? I get some free rec or more phone time?"

"Most likely you'll be transferred."

"Out of prison?"

The captain laughed. "Moved to a place better suited for your safety as befits your superstar status."

"It's not Supermax?" Mikey knew that's where they shoved all the home-grown, high-profile wackos like Ted Kaczynski and Tim McVeigh.

"No. Definitely not Supermax. You're not that superstar ... yet."

"Well, sign me up." Mikey scribbled his name as best

he could, harnessed to so many tubes and wires with his hands cuffed to the bedrail. The nurses had been unable to find a vein and stuck the IV right into his jugular. He looked like some kind of fucked up marionette trying to work an ink pen.

"Let me help you," said the captain as he maneuvered the wheeled meal tray over by the rail for a writing surface. He fetched some more paperwork out of his bag and set it down. "Now sign this one ..."

Mikey looked at the new form which was even more unintelligible and full of print so fine it would take a microscope to decipher it. The only word that caught his attention was Army. "The hell is this?"

"Uncle Sam is calling you to serve your nation. It's your golden ticket out of prison."

Mikey wondered if there was a war going on that he hadn't heard about. The military must be really desperate to want a drug addict.

"It's just a clinical drug study," explained the captain. "It'll be perfect for you. A nice little private hospital."

The only thing that registered to Mikey was the getting out of prison part. Given the choice he would gladly have accepted death overseas. All the better in the middle east with a direct line source to his vein. He signed the dotted line not giving a fuck.

"And here's the last of it for now." The captain placed another form before Mikey. "This is just a starter agreement until we can get a proper contract together covering comic adaptations, film options, sponsorships ... you know."

"Contract? For what?"

"Our book," said Jay Mackie with a smile. "I want to bring your story to the world."

This was news to Mikey. He had been waiting for someone to discover him, show interest in his writing, recognize him for a literary genius — that one big break.

He didn't expect it to be from a cop.

"I had planned to write a book someday," said Mikey.

"And that's what people say, 'Someday I'm gonna write a book. Someday I'm gonna do this, gonna go there, do that, fuck that girl.' Well, someday is today."

"But I've got this court shit to deal with."

"The only court you need to worry about is the court of public opinion and let me tell you, son, the news is roasting you alive out there over this Jessica business. Everyone sees you as just another white boy gone bad. We need to show them the truth about you."[26]

"But I don't have a laptop. I don't have my journals." Mikey offered up another excuse. He had thousands of excuses as to why he never wrote his great American junkie novel. But he would someday; someday he would.

"Journals?" The captain's eyes went anime with delight.

"I've already told my story," said Mikey. "I got journals, at least five hundred of them. It's all there. They just kind of need sorted and edited and maybe a cool cover and—" Mikey started heaving.[27]

Jay Mackie held up a blue vomit bag that was on the bedside table so Mikey could empty his flip-flopping stomach. Most of it got in the bag, but some splashed out on the captain's hands. "Journals?" Jay Mackie asked as he wiped off the puke.

"Yeah, I was trying to get them from my parent's house when I was arrested."

"Do I have permission to go there and get them?"

"Yeah, but they are hidden in my dad's wine cellar. You'd never find them without me. I'm very necessary."

The captain leaned back in his chair for a moment as if in thought as a nurse came in to check on Mikey. He

---

26   This was not true. The news had largely forgotten about Mikey.

27   "Sorted and edited" was to say the least about his work which totaled over half-a-million words, including some of his own invention.

handed the barf bag over to the nurse, asking, "Is the patient well enough to be transferred?"

"That would be for the doctor to decide," said the nurse as she glanced at the monitor on the wall. A concerned look flashed across her face as she adjusted the oxygen monitor hooked to his finger. "He's awake, that's good, but there's no telling what's going on with him. The initial drug screen showed enough in his system that we don't know why he's even still alive. Still waiting on the test results."[28]

The captain urged her to check with the doctor and then got on the phone. Mikey listened to half the conversation. "Harrison ... He's volunteered for the program ... It'll need to happen today ... Good, good ... Okay, we'll be there."

After hanging up the captain gathered up the crudely signed forms and told Mikey to, "not go anywhere." It was a sick joke as Mikey was shackled to the bed in a totally non-erotic way. (Unless you are into that.) [29]

Jay Mackie was gone for about forty-three minutes. "Okay, it's moving day, soldier. Pack up." There was nothing to "pack up" as Mikey didn't have shit, but the hospital gown loosely tied to his back.

Mikey stirred. "The doctor said it was okay?"

"Actually, he strongly advised against it." The captain lay down another form. "But it's fine, you just need to sign this saying that you are leaving against medical advisement."

"I'm what?"

"Don't worry about it, it's just a standard boiler plate, cover your ass kinda thing for the hospital."

Mikey scribbled his mark on the form. Soon the nurse reappeared with two large security guards flanking her. They were hired for their girth and not their IQ or muscle tone — just a couple of big boys who could manage a

28   Oxygen monitors are used to measure the oxygen saturation in your blood — it can drop dangerously low during an opioid overdose due to respiratory depression.
29   As an opioid addict, being cuffed to the bed was gratuitous torture for Mikey, as if tiny needles were piercing his flesh with every tug and pull.

mean mug and had enough smarts to fool a pre-employment drug screen.

"Just a second," the captain told them. He fished his phone out of his pocket and asked Mikey to smile for a picture, again in a totally non-erotic way. (Unless you are into that.)

She removed the IV and the guards unshackled him from the bed. They slumped him down in a wheelchair and they redid his cuffs and wheeled him out.

The nurses, patients, and visitors all looked at Mikey as he was rolled through the hallway like a Thanksgiving Day parade float. He tried to keep his head up about it.

Someday, he thought. Someday they'll look back and gloat about the time they saw **THE MIKEY MAY** live (barely) in the flesh (presumably). He treated the streaked linoleum like a red fuckin' carpet. They should be taking pictures, he thought. He turned to his right side—his best side—at least the side that wasn't that bruised up that day.

When they cleared the sliding doors out front, Mikey breathed his first, really good breath. Something about air that wasn't so clean and sterile. It smelled slightly of french fries, courtesy of the burger joint down the block and the fortuitous winds that one glorious afternoon under the California smog.

He and the security guards waited while Jay Mackie darted off toward the parking garage. They looked side-to-side, up-and-down like they were the secret service protecting the president. It made Mikey feel good to be so damn important. Maybe he could be president someday. It was a new era and with a stunning six pack and enough social media cred there was no telling what anyone could do.

Mikey was expecting a cop car or maybe an ambulance. He half-way hoped for a limo. Instead, he watched as Jay

Mackie pulled up in a Subaru wagon with a busted taillight and a peeling, sunbleached coexist bumper sticker.

The captain got out and rushed around to help Mikey into the front passenger's side. The security guys puzzled over exactly where to attach the cuffs to the family car.

"Maybe in the back with the child safety lock on?" suggested the guard with the just slightly higher IQ.

"Just cuff him around the seatbelt as best you can," said the captain, "He's too dope sick to run far."

The security dudes did their best to work the cuffs around the Subaru's seatbelts. Their work left Mikey with his arms crossed and legs bent like someone with cerebral palsy. "Good enough," said the captain, jumping into the driver's seat.

As they got on the highway the captain lit a cigarette and passed it to Mikey. "It's okay, you can smoke in here."

Mikey took a good drag. It was his second-best breath that day. The nicotine patch they glued to his tit just wasn't doing it. Nothing like a good kick in the lungs to let you know you are still alive. He coughed. Then he coughed again. It was his second-best cough that day. Damn, he was alive.

"Smooth," said Jay Mackie, sparking up his own, "So, which way to your parents?"

"My parents?" Mikey wondered if this was part of the drug study. Was it some kind of weird intervention? He hoped the fucked up situation might be some kind of reality television setup. How cool would it be if Ashton Kutcher popped out and screamed, "you got junked!"

"We gotta get your journals. What's a writer without his journals?" said the captain, "You saw my legal pads."

Mikey wanted his journals and wanted to somehow write himself out of the hell he had found himself in but mostly he wanted dope. "I think I'm gonna be sick," he said.

"You can't puke in here," said Jay Mackie. "I can pull over. Do you want me to pull over?"

"I need dope," said Mikey. It wasn't exactly a lie. The hospital had administered Suboxone but a dopehead always needs dope.

"I can't get you drugs right now," said the captain as he looked around. "There's a gas station, what about a Snickers?"

"I don't need a Snickers. I need smack, not a snack."

The captain pulled into the gas station parking lot anyway.

"Listen, I need you to be alert. I can't have you nodding off or fucking dying right now. We get those journals and then we can get your ... medicine." Jay Mackie took the cigarette out of Mikey's mouth and tapped the grandma length ash into a 7-Eleven cup. "Now, would you like a Snickers?"

"No," said Mikey. "But Skittles sure would perk me up."

"Skittles?"

The captain got out of the car, took a step toward the shop, and then looked back at Mikey. He went over to the passenger side window. "You're coming with me," Jay said as he started undoing the cuffs. It was totally unnecessary as it wouldn't have taken a Harry Houdini to get out of such loose confinements but it was nice not to have the dangling jail jewelry. The captain marched Mikey toward the entrance.

The wind whipped his hospital gown up. "My ass is showing," said Mikey.

"Just stand in front of me," said the captain and then added, "Now don't try anything."

"I'm trying not to show the world my ass," whined Mikey, as he struggled to wrap the gown around him. "If people wanna see this ass, they gotta pay." Mikey hated to be seen that way but at that moment he also hated not having Skittles. It was a real catch-22.

The two went into the store and despite Mikey's

protestations no one was even looking at them weird. No one was payin' to see that ass. A cop and junkie go into a convenience store wasn't even the setup for a joke in Los Angeles. It was just Tuesday and cops and asses were plentiful.

The captain looked through the rack of candy in front of the security glass window. "Starburst, was it?"

"Skittles. The blue pack. Tropical. You can have the gross banana ones." Even without the candy, Mikey was happy to be out at a convenience store. It felt so Tuesday.

"Okay," said the captain, grabbing the candy. "Anything else?"

"Scratch off number 14."

Jay Mackie looked at the scratch-off tickets behind the plexiglass. "That one is fifty dollars!"

Mikey shrugged. "As they say in AA, 'expect miracles'."

The captain looked at it for a moment before getting it along with the Skittles. "He's my crazy nephew," he explained to the clerk even though she didn't ask.

When they got back to the car, Mikey protested that he couldn't eat the Skittles if he was cuffed. The captain didn't bother locking him up again, only sternly warning him to not, "go anywhere or he'd blow his junkie brains out without a second thought."

As they drove to his parents Mikey thought about just jumping out on the freeway. Maybe if he tucked and rolled, he'd get away. But he also thought there was a slight chance he might end up as roadkill and the captain had promised him dope after all. Sometimes it was just the thought of that next fix that kept you going on a Tuesday.

Together they drove to Mikey's parents' house in Santa Barbara.

"That's the one," said Mikey, pointing to a sprawling Spanish Colonial mansion, its stucco walls and red-tile roof baked in the California sun.

The captain, in the manner of a Truman Capote fan-boy, spoke slowly and steadily into a small voice recorder. "An island of prosperity amidst an ocean of commonplace. How did this silver spooned cherub devolve into a wolfish marauder, forever hungry for the next fix?"

They stayed parked for a moment while the captain observed and finally, he said, "let's do this."

Together they walked to the door and Jay Mackie instructed Mikey to just keep his head low and say nothing. He knocked at the door and there was no answer. He knocked even harder — one of those loud knocks that only UPS or the cops can manage.

"I don't think they're home," said Mikey.

"You wouldn't happen to have a key?" asked the captain.

Mikey walked over to a flowerbed and picked out a large conch shell and shook it. Unsatisfied, he held it up to his ear and shook it again. "It was worth a try." Mikey shrugged.

The captain knocked again, huffed, and asked, "You used to live here. Ever sneak out? Know a good way in?"

"One that doesn't involve breaking and entering?" Mikey knew several ways in, the house had many fine plate glass windows. "Can't you just get a warrant?"

"That won't work. The detectives will seize those journals as evidence and we'll never get them back."

All the better as it would make the journals illegally seized and the secrets they held couldn't be used against him.

"Follow me." Mikey took the detective around back where there was a walled garden. "Boost me over and I'll unlock the gate."

Jay Mackie bent over and allowed Mikey to get on his shoulders, he straightened up his back to get enough reach to grip the top of the wall. The cop stood and Mikey was able to get almost enough leverage to climb over.

"Higher," he said. The captain grabbed Mikey by the ankles and thrust him upwards. The bone-thin addict had too much momentum and rolled over, falling behind with a hard thud.

After a few minutes, Mikey opened the gate as he picked thorns from his skin. "Fuckin' rose bushes," he said. "Scratched up my arms." The scratches were nothing compared to all of the track marks, blotches, shank wounds, and bruises. It was just one more thing on a big list of "things."

Mikey led the captain to a basement window below the garage. "The wine cellar's down here. You ready?"

The captain nodded and Mikey smashed the window out with a rock.

WHEEEETT ... WHEEEETT ... SQUAWWW ... SQUAWWW, blared the home security system.

Mikey paid it no mind as he broke away the remaining glass around the frame and lowered himself down. "Come on," Mikey urged the captain, "It's a rich neighborhood and the cops waste no time. That's how I got popped the first time."

That gave the captain a pause, as he was suddenly considering his course of action. "You get those journals and meet me back at the car. I'll be a block down."

Mikey picked up his pace and entered the wine cellar where there were racks upon racks of wine. His father wasn't even a drinker. He just liked to bring out that perfect bottle for holiday dinners or when they had company to show off for. That was very seldom and the bottles tended to pile up — especially those with low wine scores.

It was the sweet reds that never got drunk and so Mikey had learned as a child that he could drink all he wanted of those, taking care to fill them back up with cherry flavored Kool-Aid. Some wine had simply turned to vinegar and was stowed away in cobweb covered cardboard boxes, collecting dust. It was in those that Mikey had stashed his journals. He carefully collected them in a box and climbed back out the window.

The cops will be here any moment, he thought. He started to the gate but then he remembered he had stashed some of Andh's dope in the upstairs bathroom the night he was arrested. There was a chance it was still there.

He changed course and walked over to the backdoor. He stepped back and kicked hard. It took three tries before it broke, hanging loosely on the hinges. He pushed through and ran upstairs.

He fished around the back side of the toilet tank, until he pulled the package of dope out from behind it. He'd still try to get the captain to score for him, but it would be good to have a backup.

It was then that he heard the police sirens growing louder until they stopped in front of the house. Mikey crawled low to his old bedroom and peeked over the window ledge and saw the two cops approaching the door. "Shit," he said and looked again to where Jay Mackie's car was, not knowing if he should just make a run for it. The box of journals would only slow him down.

There was an even louder police knock at the front door. Mikey thought he'd better take the dope now because he wouldn't get another chance. He grabbed a spoon out of the kitchen and went to his mother's bathroom where she kept her diabetes needles and a BIC lighter for her smelly shits. He took one of her makeup cotton balls and hunkered down in the bathtub with the shower curtain closed. He knew he was bound to lose that game of hide-and-seek but it might give him enough time ... if only he could find a vein.

He almost had it when another knock startled him. "Fuck," he said. "Fuck you, Jay Mackie." The needle finally slipped in and Mikey rediscovered his reckless bravery.

In the face of his impending capture, Mikey tried to think of a good story. Unable to think of even a bad story, he thought he'd simply rat some more. "It was Jay Mackie. He set me up because he wanted to make money off a book deal. It was the cop!" he'd say.

But when he opened up the front door, he found no one around. The cop car was speeding away past the captain's Subaru.

Mikey ran over with the box of journals and tossed them into the back seat along with himself as he sank down to the floorboard.

"That took you long enough," said the captain. "I called dispatch, said I was out driving and saw a large black guy running down the sidewalk with what looked to be very expensive wine."

"Shit, then we'd better hide this," said Mikey, as he grabbed something out of the cardboard box.

"The hell is that?" said Jay Mackie, trying to catch a look in the rearview mirror.

"1947 Chateau Cheval Blanc. My father's best. Only to be opened on a very special someday. I figure that someday is today. We gotta toast my book."

"Fuckin' Mikey May," grumbled the captain. He started to say something else, but Mikey was already nodding off.

14

TRANSITIONING

"I cannot make you understand. I cannot make anyone understand what is happening inside me. I cannot even explain it to myself." - Franz Kafka

McFadden roared down the soulless highway in his silver BMW, barking into his phone like a mad dog at his attorney. "Yeah! I'm goddamn serious! I'm selling out!"

He slammed the phone down without waiting for the hapless attorney's reaction. The man's protestations would be predictable — don't do it, it's a mistake, blah, blah, blah. Meaningless chatter to rack up billable hours. The only thing that mattered was that he paid the corporate shill $1,000 an hour to jump through hoops when McFadden barked, and by God, he was barking mad.

The phone flew back up to his ear. "The board will be glad I'm gone. All those spineless bastards hate me. It's a brave new world and I'm a relic. Time to clear out. Just get me out and set up a new LLC." The attorney, ever the dutiful scribe, asked what to call it. "Call it Baker-McFadden Music. Call it Racist Records. I don't give a damn. Something catchy. You must have some drone in that ivory tower who can spin a phrase. Get it done!"[30]

Bloodshot eyes glued to the road, McFadden maneuvered into Boyle Heights, a forgotten neighborhood of L.A. that thrived with the echoes of past and future dreams. The wide avenues pulsated with life and color, a stark contrast

---

30   Note: In that "ivory tower," the only one with a shred of creativity was some poor slob wasting away in the mail room. The lawyers were about as exciting as a nun at an orgy.

to the sterile glass and steel landscape of his downtown office. Buildings, marked and scarred with graffiti, exuded an unfettered spirit of defiance, something that was long ago scrubbed clean from his corporate world.

His BMW's growl echoed off the weathered walls as he rolled down the neglected streets. He parked in an alley flanked by two crumbling warehouses, their façades inscribed with the raw artistry of local street rebels. The lawyer droned on about legal niceties and potential LLC names. McFadden tuned out the white noise, eyes drawn to the unpretentious warehouse Baker had told him about.

He killed the engine and stepped out of the vehicle, leaving the attorney's voice to ricochet off the leather upholstery. His polished Italian shoes scraped against the loose gravel as he made his way to the entrance, his crisp suit a stark contrast against the warehouse's unforgiving façade. He peered through a fractured window into the cavernous space within. It was a grimy, forgotten monument to industrialism, but to McFadden, it was a blank canvas. Fuck, it was everything.

"Here's your goddamn ivory tower," he sneered, his smirk disappearing as he ended the call. "Let's see how *Barron's* spins this." His voice ricocheted off the barren walls of the alley, swallowed up by the grime and concrete, as he imagined the music empire he was about to construct. In this new world, metamorphosis was king.

The glaring L.A. sun bled out, casting gold and orange hues across the skyline. McFadden stood in the shadowy expanse of the warehouse, an evening breeze carrying the symphony of the city — the blaring horns, raucous conversations, and stray chords from a lone busker's guitar playing an off-tune Oasis song

His mind was a storm of conflicting thoughts. The press, the public, his enemies, they'd painted him as a bigoted old-money relic, a monument to a bygone era, a crusty-old

white man. His past actions, fueled by arrogance and ignorance, had only added fuel to their fire. But now, he was on
a crusade to reinvent himself, driven by the white-hot rage
and insatiable ambition smoldering within.

Striding across the dusty, pockmarked floor of the warehouse, he felt a surge of something exhilarating, a sense of
liberation, if only for a moment, before his phone buzzed
again. He answered the call but shut him up before the lawyer could even start. "There's a warehouse at Soto and Whit-
tier in Boyle Heights. Get it leased and find me someone
who knows about recording music ... Yes, they should be
black ... Yes, I'm certain ... We need to get a studio set up."

He knew he was stepping into a minefield, that he'd
likely be met with skepticism and resistance. He would
have to learn, listen, and maybe even face ridicule and
rejection. But he was ready for it all. He was prepared
to evolve. It was going to be a bloody battle, but he was
staking his name, his legacy, his family fortune on it.

He took in the cavernous space once more, the bare
bones of his new arena. "Baker-McFadden Music," he
mused aloud, the unfamiliar name rolling off his tongue.
McFadden picked up a discarded can of red spray paint,
gave it a rattle, and tagged BMM on the wall. It didn't
work. He X'd it out with the spray can and next to it painted an even larger **TRANSITION RECORDS**.

He was fully aware that transformation wasn't just about
mindset and business ventures. His reflection had long been
that of a polished oligarch. It was time for a makeover.

Satisfied, he prowled down the throbbing arteries of
South Central, pulling up in front of a grubby corner bar-
bershop. The pulsating rhythm of hip-hop spilled out onto
the street, permeating the stagnant air. This was a forge of
style, a trendsetter, a place for a man to reshape himself.

McFadden stepped in, the sound of buzzing clippers and
the smell of shaving cream washing over him. Heads turned

at the sight of the white guy, eyebrows arching at the intruder in their sanctuary. Settling into a barber's chair, the torn leather pressing against his back, he braced himself.

The dome-headed barber looked at his pretty-boy locks of surfer hair, puzzled. "How do you want it?"

"Off," sniped McFadden. "Smooth as a newborn's ass."

He was known for his perfectly coiffed hair, a recognizable trait of his persona that he had since college. A symbol of his status, his privilege. As the barber's skilled hands maneuvered the clippers through his hair, each falling strand took with it the image of the man he used to be.

The insistent rhythm of a hip-hop track filled the room. "Who's this?" McFadden asked, his question halting the barber mid-motion.

"A kid who calls himself the Pizza Boy," the barber replied. "He's young, but he's got mad skills. His mixtape is making noise."

McFadden didn't hesitate. He whipped out his phone, dialed his attorney's number, and as soon as he picked up, commanded, "Find me the Pizza Boy ... No, I don't want a pizza ... He's a rapper ... I dunno, ask one of your diversity hires ... Ask Brennan ... Just get him."

The attorney, already accustomed to McFadden's abrupt demands, responded with a quick, "Understood."

As the clippers resumed their task, McFadden leaned back, a fire in his eyes. The beats of the Pizza Boy's music filled the shop, a sly smile dancing on his lips. This was just the beginning.

The barber's approach was unceremonious, even causing a slight nick with the straight razor, which was immediately followed by a splash of stinging alcohol. McFadden smirked, thinking, *reparations*. Leaving a hundred-dollar bill on the counter, he watched the old barber's eyebrows rise in surprise as if he'd never seen a tip before.

Ever the businessman, McFadden pulled out a silver

card holder and an ink pen. He crossed out "McFadden & Crow Investment Banking" and scrawled "Transition Records."

"I'm opening a music label and looking for new talent," he said as he gave everyone in the shop a card.

They eyed him even more confused but McFadden was already out the door. He paused to look at himself in the reflection of the dusty barber shop window. The shaved head and suit gave him a Lex Luthor look. It was still too corporate. He contemplated adding one of those iced out gold chains. It still wasn't right. He imagined the Twitterazi shouting in all-caps **CULTURAL APPROPRIATION**.

He sighed and then something else caught his eyes in the grimy, streaked reflection — a wig shop down the road.

McFadden didn't walk, he strutted down the cracked sidewalk towards the wig shop. Each step was a move closer to a new beginning. He stopped in front of the store, the windows cluttered with a myriad of mannequin heads showcasing wigs of every conceivable color, cut, and curl.

Inside, the aroma of synthetic hair, fresh out of their plastic packaging, filled the small space. The store was a vibrant sea of flamboyance, of self-expression, of people challenging norms, of colorful rebellion. It was everything

An enthusiastic shopkeeper, a tall woman in her late fifties with a head full of vibrant red curls, greeted him, "How can I assist you today?"

"I need a wig," McFadden declared, "Something ... bold."

The shopkeeper's eyes sparkled as she scanned him. "I think I know just the thing."

She returned with a wig that looked like it belonged on the cover of a glam-rock album. A platinum blonde cascade of voluminous curls with neon-pink streaks.

McFadden smirked, the sight of the wig both daunting and thrilling. This was a side of himself he'd never thought he'd explore, let alone embrace.

"I guess it can't hurt to try," he said, donning the wig. He looked at himself in the mirror.

McFadden didn't see the cutthroat investment banker or the intimidating figure he used to be. He saw the opportunity for change, a beacon of transformation ... enough to make him laugh from the gut.

He paid for the wig and a few others, thanked the shopkeeper, and, on a whim, asked, "You wouldn't happen to know a good place to shop for women's clothes nearby, would you?"

The shopkeeper gave a nod and directed him to a place just down the street, a store catering to plus-sized women.

Stepping into the store, he felt an unfamiliar shiver of excitement. The walls were adorned with clothes of all shapes, sizes, and styles. It was a place that celebrated diversity, a stark contrast to the staid black suit/blue suit uniformity of the corporate world he once belonged to.

He spent the better part of the afternoon browsing through the aisles, trying on different outfits, and reveling in the freedom of self-expression. Brightly colored blouses, form-fitting skirts, dresses that flattered his figure.

At one point, he even caught himself twirling in front of the mirror, the hem of a polka-dot dress swishing around his knees. He laughed, the sound echoing in the fitting room. He felt ridiculous, but he also felt ... free.

As he walked back to his car, arms laden with shopping bags, he caught sight of his reflection in a store window. A bold, bald woman with a spark in her eyes and a wicked grin.

Collin McFadden was no more. She was Colleen Mc-Fadden now, a woman ready to conquer the world in her own way. It wasn't going to be easy, he knew, but then again, he'd never been one to shy away from a challenge.

Back in the car, looking at himself in the rearview mirror, he couldn't help but chuckle. "It's going to be a wild ride, Colleen," he said to his reflection, adjusting the wig.

And then, with a sense of renewed purpose, she gunned the engine, ready to face whatever came next.

Her BMW roared to life as he floored the pedal, speeding towards her place. She had made a deal with Baker, and Cindy was part of the deal. Though she'd put up an initial resistance, a sharp glance and raised hand from Baker reminded her of her unfortunate position — like property to be bargained with. Subdued, she returned to her phone, engrossed in the never-ending scroll of social media.

Colleen's own phone buzzed with a new message from his lawyer: "Had to do some digging. Found your Pizza Boy." The message included a link to an Instagram account.

Clicking on the link, McFadden frowned at the sight of a scrawny white teenager. His follower count was an underwhelming 897. It wouldn't work. McFadden was certain of one thing: white men were on a diminishing timeline.

Pulling up at Cindy's place, the disconcerting glow of police lights greeted him. A car with a magnetic Romeo's Pizza sign sat in the driveway, surrounded by patrol cars. Colleen stepped out, her gaze falling on a figure being helped up by the police — a battered pizza delivery driver. The realization hit her like a brass-knuckled punch to the balls.

McFadden moved towards the police, a sense of urgency propelling him. "Hey! You there," he called out.

The cops swiveled around instinctively, their hands gravitating towards their weapons. One of them squinted at him. "Lady, do you know this kid?" he asked.

McFadden let out a laugh. "Are you kidding me? Everyone knows Pizza Boy."

The officer's face hardened. "Well, he'll be taking a little break from pizza delivery. We found a pound of weed in his delivery bag."

McFadden raised an eyebrow, "That's legal."

"Yeah," the officer responded, his tone dripping with

disdain. "But this," he continued, gesturing towards an unregistered firearm on the hood of the police car, "is not."

Immobile, McFadden watched as the so-called Pizza Boy was escorted away. "Kid, stay strong, stay quiet. I'll get you a lawyer."

Swiftly, she messaged her attorney, instructing him to arrange for a lawyer to meet the kid at the station. With that handled, she approached Cindy's door, noting the shiny Jeep parked in front of her place. She rapped on the door, waiting, before knocking again more forcefully.

A man, shirtless and adorned with military tattoos, swung open the door, his other hand busy buckling his pants. "Can I help you?" he grumbled.

"I'm here for Cindy," McFadden replied curtly, his gaze narrowing. "Who the hell are you?"

"Name's Gunner. Cindy's occupied. Who might you be?"

"I'm her woman, and if you've been messing around with her, you owe me."

The burly man frowned, "Owe you? For what?"

McFadden smirked. "For services rendered. You see, when you're with a whore, it's customary to pay a fee to her ... madame."

Silence hung in the air as Gunner's hands curled into fists. Suddenly, he lunged at McFadden, sending her tumbling down the steps and sending the wig flying. Gunner was on her in an instant, raining blows down with fierce intensity.

McFadden struggled to retrieve the antique gun tucked in her new designer handbag, but it was futile. Gunner's relentless assault had her pinned down, each hit rattling her consciousness.

"Call Cindy a whore again," Gunner growled, his fists momentarily stilling.

McFadden tried to call her a whore again but all that came out was a bloody gurgle and a broken tooth.

A police officer, having left the Pizza Boy in the back of the patrol car, rushed over. "Stop! Get off her!" he yelled.

Gunner seemed not to hear him or just did not care. His laser focus remained on the victim beneath him, his rage unchecked.

The officer unholstered a taser and fired. But Gunner, fueled by the meth and post-coital shame that coursed through his veins, barely flinched. His fists continued to find their mark, unyielding.

This is not good, McFadden thought grimly, her head ringing like a bell.

A pair of officers charged at Gunner, but with a single powerful swipe, he caused the cop to jump back. He seemed invincible, reminiscent of an enraged King Kong batting away biplanes.

Two additional officers joined the fray, wrestling to pull the raging hulk off McFadden. It took the combined strength of three law enforcement officials to finally subdue him, yanking him back and piling on handcuffs. All the while, Gunner spat obscenities and threats, promising a reckoning once he got out.

McFadden, meanwhile, lay sprawled on the steps, bloodied and battered, but alive. As she spat out a mixture of blood and saliva, she caught sight of Cindy peeking from behind the curtains of a window eating a slice of pizza. There was fear in her eyes, but also something else — curiosity, perhaps even respect.

Cindy emerged from the house, her eyes darting between McFadden, Gunner, and the officers. She stayed a safe distance away, taking in the scene. After a few seconds, she walked over to McFadden, stepping gingerly over his crumpled form.

"I see you've met Gunner," she said, a smirk tugging at her lips. "I guess you weren't expecting that, were you?" She handed him a kitchen towel and a frozen bag of peas.

McFadden coughed, wiping blood from her mouth. "Congratulations on your retirement. You are with me exclusively now. And if you ever see that motherfucker again I will bury you and him both."

As the police wrapped up the scene, one officer, a stout woman with graying hair at her temples, approached McFadden, who had the ice bag pressed up against his battered face.

"Mrs. McFadden, I wanted to speak with you about pressing charges," she said, holding a clipboard.

"Damn right, I'm pressing charges!" McFadden barked, taking off the ice pack to glare at her. "That lunatic nearly killed me. Do you have any idea how much this dress cost?" He motioned to his outfit which was now marred with blood, dirt, and Gunner's pungent sweat.

The officer nodded sympathetically, scribbling down some notes. "We're sorry for your discomfort, ma'am. If you could just give us a statement about what happened, we'll get the process started."

McFadden scoffed, but she began to recount the encounter, emphasizing every blow, every insult, every shred of indignity she had suffered. Her entitlement radiated like heat from asphalt. This was an offense not only against her person but against her status, her reputation, her dignity.

"And I want him gone," she said, pointing to where Gunner was now restrained in the back of the squad car, a smirk on his face, "I don't care how you do it, but I don't want to see his face again."

The officer nodded. "We'll do our best, ma'am," she assured her, but McFadden could see the skepticism in her eyes. She had been on the force too long to be swayed by tantrums of the affluent, but she would do her job nonetheless. She had to.

"Good. Because next time," McFadden continued, his

voice a threatening low growl, "I won't be so forgiving."

As the police hauled Gunner away, Cindy crouched down beside McFadden, handing him the wig. "What happened to your hair? Did he rip out your hair? That was your best quality."

McFadden placed the wig haphazardly on her smooth head and narrowed-eyed Cindy, her eyes flicking over her casual attire, the hint of satisfaction on her face. He could see the defiance in her eyes, the unspoken challenge. He smiled, relishing the new game that was afoot. This wouldn't be as easy as he thought, but then again, he liked a challenge.

"And what's with the dress?" Cindy said. "I mean it's nice but ... I didn't think you ..."

"Didn't think what?" said McFadden, "You were just another asshole that thought they knew me. Well, this is the real me and you can call me Colleen. Now we are going to go inside and see if you're worth all the trouble."

"Ok, Colleen." The name felt unfamiliar in Cindy's mouth but she was used to role-play. "You want to have sex? But you're a woman now?" she baited.

"I've always been a woman," said Colleen McFadden. "A woman and a lesbian."

15

THE JOURNALS REDUX

LOS ANGELES 2018

"In the room where our demons reside, we confront the possibility of our own salvation." - Unknown Author (Toilet Stall Graffiti)

Mikey stirred in a familiar bed in a familiar room. His old hotel room. He wondered if the whole thing was a twisted, unhinged dream. It had happened before.

He peeled his eyes open, half-hoping, half-dreading to see Jessica next to him. Instead, he heard a familiar voice. Not hers, but Jay Mackie's. The last voiced he wanted to hear.

The captain was dictating slowly into his voice recorder, "In the muted glow of the solitary bulb, the room unfolded like a chronicle of decay. The air held the stubborn perfume of stale cigarettes and cheap beer, a rancid miasma that clung to everything in its path. The crusty carpet beneath was silent, its faded threads weaving tales of forgotten memories. The pastel wallpaper, curling at the edges, bared its patchwork underbelly, a palimpsest of despair. The bed bore the weight of countless transient bodies, its sagging mattress echoing their whispered secrets. It was more than a room, it was a testament to human frailty, a cathedral of shattered dreams and missed chances."

Mikey grunted, interrupting the narration. "Jay Mackie, you are one wordy motherfucker." And that was saying something coming from Mikey who was a certified "real wordy motherfucker."

"Oh, good," said the captain. "You're awake. We've got work to do."

Mikey glanced over, eyes half-lidded, and spotted a smaller bald man with insectoid eyes and thick caterpillar eyebrows rifling through his journals. He looked like a shriveled, moldy orange.

"Who the hell is that?" Mikey croaked, his throat scratchy.

"That's Harrison, a ... doctor of sorts," Jay Mackie made a vague introduction.

Harrison, without raising his eyes from one of the journals, muttered, "Mr. May, how long did it take you to write all of this?"

"Dunno," Mikey shrugged, his brain still trying to swim out of the murk of sleep and anxiety. "That journal? A night, maybe. It's fuzzy. The rest. All my life."

The motel room door creaked open and a woman entered. She was a testament to faded glamour, her sequined dress frayed and dulled. Her synthetic platinum hair was piled high, contained by a sun-faded pink scrunchie, the garishness of her profession evident in her chipped nail polish and clumpy mascara-coated eyelashes. The uneven click of her broken stiletto announced her entry into the room.

"Who's this?" Mikey asked, disoriented. All these new people. Were they having a celebratory party?

"This is Laquinta, she lives here now. She let us crash for the night," Jay Mackie explained. "She's also booked for the whole evening; in case you need some ... company."

"If it's gonna be all three of you at once, I get extra," said Laquinta. "That's the deal."

"I'm good," Mikey managed, hauling himself up into a sitting position.

Laquinta claimed her spot at the end of the bed and

flipped on the television. She navigated the channels until she hit an *Everybody Loves Raymond* marathon, ignoring the protests from Jay Mackie with a dismissive glance. "Deal was, I get to watch my TV."

Jay Mackie, recognizing a losing battle, turned to divvy up the Chinese food. "Mikey, I didn't know what you liked so I got you General Tsao's or special fried rice. There's an egg roll in here too."

"Why the fuck are we here?" demanded Mikey.

Jay Mackie paused, a piece of gooey broccoli halfway to his mouth. "Our book, Mikey. It's important to revisit the scene of the crime. Thought it might jog some memories about Jessica."

"Need to take a shit," Mikey muttered, heaving himself off the bed in his stained underwear. As he locked himself in the bathroom, the cracked mirror reflected a ghoulish, lacerated, zombie version of himself. He'd have to start working on that six-pack someday ... maybe a spray tan.

When Mikey returned, Jay Mackie was arguing with Laquinta. "I just need the lights out for a minute. We've got work to do. That was the deal." He pushed the bottle of Cheval Blanc into her hands, asking her to go put it on ice.

The hooker eyed him and then the bottle. "Only because I've already seen this one four times," she said and turned off the *Raymond* rerun and took the ice bucket with her out of the room.

Jay Mackie was unloading a duffel bag full of gear until he found his blacklight. He flipped it on and the space became a grimy Jackson Pollock of stains splattered over the room – cum, blood, vomit, shit, piss, Chinese takeout, and the stench of desperation clinging to every surface — including the ceiling in defiance of decency and gravity.

Mikey swallowed hard, the memory of that morning tickling his throat like broken glass.

Jay Mackie prodded until Mikey relented, his trembling

finger pointing to a spot next to the bed. Under the black light, an ephemeral outline materialized — Jessica's last resting place along with Andy's in some kind of ghostly Twister game.

The captain started dictating into his recorder again, his voice was sharp and clinical. "The scene: a motel room that's seen more tragedy than its cheap, flaking wallpaper could bear witness to. A tableau of depravity laid bare under the ultraviolet, a phantom body marked by sin and secrets. The bed, a necropolis of stains — bodily fluids mixed with nameless filth in a grotesque abstract of human debauchery. Walls whispering tales of addiction and violence. The ceiling wearing a coat of desperation."

The sight rammed into Mikey like a demolition ball, smashing his carefully constructed sand fortress.

It was a junkie's nightmare relived in vivid luminescent paint. An unfamiliar pain stirred within him. Was it remorse or just more dope sickness?

"You promised me drugs," said Mikey. "I got you the journals now pay up. That was our deal." He just wanted to go back to sleep, wake up somewhere else, or not wake up at all. It didn't matter. "Just turn off that light," he demanded, his voice shaking.

"Yeah, no problem, Mike." The captain set the blacklight down and turned the yellowing room lights back on.

Jay Mackie cast a glance over at Harrison. "What do you think about ... medicine?"

Harrison looked up from his careful study of Mikey's journals. "How alert do you need him to be?"

The captain shrugged.

"Maybe just something to take the edge off?"

The bug-eyed man went over to a bag and started digging. He produced a bit of tan colored powder and carefully measured out a bit on a piece of aluminum foil. "This stuff is strong, Mr. May," said Harrison. "You'll want to go easy."

"Do you have a NEEDle?" asked Mikey, shaking.

"You don't use a needle for this," said Harrison, handing him a metal straw. "Just vaporize it and inhale through the tube. Again, take it easy, this stuff can kill you quick."

Mikey walked over to the table taking care to avoid the spot where he had left Jessica's corpse. He didn't know what to expect but he didn't care. It was drugs and he wanted to feel something other than what he was feeling — which was absolutely shitty. In that moment, dying would be preferable.

"Wait," said Jay Mackie. "Before you get your meds we got to talk just a little bit more about Jessica."

It was the last thing Mikey wanted to talk about but he wanted the drugs even more. His body was starting to ache and his fingers twitching. "What else do you need to know?"

"When the detectives came here there was no body." Jay Mackie's eyes narrowed. "Mike, what did you do with Jessica?"

"Just left her there with a sheet draped over her. I went to score some dope and then went to my parents. That's all I know." He started shaking, an emaciated marked up man in his underpants.

Jay Mackie nodded toward Harrison giving him the go ahead. "Just one drag to calm him down."

Harrison used a lighter to torch the bottom of the foil. As the flame kissed the small metal square, near invisible wisps of vapor began to dance and curl in the air. The drug's essence materialized like a phantom and the faint scent of pharmaceutical sweetness stirred the room.

Mikey sucked up the ghostly vapor into his lungs. His tremors stopped and a still calmness swept over him. He breathed a sigh of relief and sat down on the bed. Whatever it was it hit quicker and better than any heroin he had ever come across.

"Another?" he whispered.

"Okay, Mike. But first Harrison had a few questions about your journals."

Mikey's ears perked up at that. The drug's euphoria was taking hold and he began to feel giddy, but a part of that was just that someone was expressing interest in his life's work. "Yeah, sure. What do you want to know?"

Harrison held up a page out of one of the notebooks. "What's going on here?" It was covered by very tiny ink marks. "I'm afraid I left my scanning electron microscope back at the lab. I can't read this — old man eyes."

Mikey shrugged his shoulders. "I think I was just seeing how small I could write."

Harrison simply nodded in response and pulled another journal from the stack. He flipped through until he came to a page he had tabbed off. "What's this bit about a Hollywood A-Lister who took on the persona of Michael Jackson after he died filming a Pepsi commercial?"

Mikey just shook his head. "I ... I dunno. Maybe someone told me that?"

"Gotcha," Harrison smirked at Jay Mackie who looked none too pleased to find out that the precious journals were nothing more than incoherent junkie ramblings. The 'doctor' went back to the stack of pads and produced another page. "But this one was particularly interesting."

The journal entry was more legible than the others with a long string of numbers: 92-108, 132-130, 112-119, 102-99, 92-101, 81-96, 113-93, 110-113, 124-112, 107-102, 96-107, 95-111, 90-98, 100-93, 109-115 and so on.

"What's going on here?" asked Harrison.

"My locker combination? Social security? Wait that's too many numbers." Mikey shook his head. "I think I was just writing numbers for ... Fuck, I can't remember."

Jay Mackie crossed his arms tensely. "Listen, Mike. I risked everything for those journals and it's all ... unusable gibberish—"

"Not necessarily," Harrison cut him off with a smirk.

"What do you mean?"

"I sent a picture of this page to some NSA buddies for shits and grins," explained Harrison. "Real numbers nerds, they get off on this codebreaker stuff. Figured it'd be nothing, but—"

"A secret code?" the captain's eyes went wide.

"Not quite. You watch basketball?" Both Mikey and Jay Mackie shook their heads, and the doctor continued. "This page accurately predicts the final score of every Lakers game this season so far."

Mackie scoffed, "He could have just gotten that information somewhere, a newspaper, the Internet."

"You said you didn't get the journals until yesterday and you had him locked up before that?" The captain nodded and Harrison continued, "Well how would he write down the scores to the last few games while he was in prison?"

Jay Mackie looked puzzled. He was down for a mystery but not this type of Scooby-Doo shit. "Are you sure?"

"It'd be easy to find out, they are playing right now."

The captain quickly reached for the remote control and turned the TV back on. He scanned the channels until he found the game. It was the fourth quarter and the Lakers were playing the Bucks.

Mikey leaned back pleased with himself for doing something he didn't even remember doing. "Does this mean I get another hit?"

Jay Mackie nodded and Harrison scraped some of the powder off onto another tab of tinfoil, smaller than the first. It was hard to tell what a lethal dose would be, but when it came to opioid tolerance, Mikey had proved to be a real thoroughbred — a game changer.

As Mikey inhaled, Laquinta came back into the room spinning the wine bottle in a bucket of melting ice to chill it faster. It was an unlikely skill for her profession but the men in the room didn't seem to notice. Mikey especially paid no attention as he slunk back into the bed, his eyes half closed.

"You guys were holding out on me. You sent me out just so you didn't have to share your drugs." She was already worked up when she spotted the basketball game on the screen. "And I get to watch my shows — that was the deal."

"It's not drugs. It's medicine and this game is very important," Jay Mackie tried to explain but Laquinta wouldn't hear it.

"This is fucked up. I'm texting my daddy," she pulled out her phone and started tapping on it, her talon-sized fake nails click-clacking on the cracked screen.

Jay Mackie again tried to calm her. "No need to get your father involved. The game's almost over. Have a glass of wine. It's supposed to be the best."

She pulled it out of the ice bucket and said, "Hey Mr. Smart Guy. This is a red Bordeaux. It's not supposed to be chilled. It's fucking ruined!"

She hurled the $20,000 bottle of wine toward Jay Mackie. He ducked and the brown bottle hit the wall exploding into a Rorschach-like blotch of thick, viscous red wine adding another layer of stain to the room. The smell of sweet fruitcake, leather, chocolate, and coffee filled the room which added a noticeable improvement to its usual stale dankness.

"Jesus," cried Mackie. "Harrison, just give her some of the drugs ... er ... Mike's medicine."

Harrison shook his head and prepared a dose for the woman. Unlike Mikey she had already had it on the street and knew exactly how to smoke it.

"Give me that shit," she said as she torched the foil and inhaled the vapor. Her eyes went wide and then she hit the floor landing in the exact same spot where Jessica's corpse had once rested.

"Finally, some peace and fucking quiet," sighed Mikey.

Jay Mackie carefully stepped over her and sat down at the edge of the bed. "What's the score supposed to be, Harrison?"

The doctor was wiping drops of red wine off the journals. "If the pattern holds true, the Lakers should lose to the Milwaukee Bucks, 122 to 124."

The 4th quarter had just ended in a tie, 112 to 112. When overtime picked up, the Bucks' Eric Bledsoe came out hard with basket after basket, putting the Lakers behind.[31]

Jay Mackie had never watched an NBA game and wasn't even sure of the rules, but he was on the edge of the bed. As the Lakers rallied for a comeback and the overtime clock ticked down, the captain cheered on the Bucks, if only so that Mikey's cryptic premonition would prove true.

"Son of a bitch, we got a real Rain Man here," declared Jay Mackie as the final score ended up Bucks 124, Lakers 122. He slapped Mikey's leg in celebration, causing the junkie's eyes to lurch open.

"Did we win?" he asked.

"We lost and it was glorious," said Jay Mackie. "Jesus, Harrison. We gotta get to Vegas and make some real money. What's the score of the next game supposed to be?"

"The numerical sequence ends tomorrow, 83 to 83."

"Okay one lucky number left, we can still win big."

Harrison just laughed. "Jay, it's 83 to 83."

"It's a little low, so what?"

"No," said Harrison, shaking his head. "No NBA game can ever end in a tie."

"Why?"

"Cause those are the rules. Someone's gotta win. Someone's gotta lose."

Jay Mackie's face fell, his excitement deflated. "Damn

---

31   Note: Bledsoe had been fired from the Suns earlier in the season for tweeting "I don't wanna be here" which coincidentally was exactly what Mikey was feeling at the time, though he lacked a Twitter account to share his inner monologue with the world.

it, Mike. I thought we were onto something here." He ran a hand through his thinning hair, his frustration evident.

Mikey blinked, his drug-induced haze dissipating as the realization sank in. It seemed like fate was toying with him, playing a cruel joke in a twisted game of synchronicity.

Harrison chimed in, trying to lighten the mood. "Well, at least we know you have a talent for predicting basketball scores ... most of the time. We can work with you back at my facility in the morning and see what other special talents you might have."

Mikey slumped back on the bed, feeling the weight of disappointment settling upon him. The drugs, once a source of solace, now seemed to amplify his sense of emptiness. Mikey's only premonition was that all of this was going to end very badly and he wasn't sure there would be any winners when the smoke cleared. They'd be lucky for a draw.

"Oh, shit," said Harrison, kneeling next to Laquinta, his fingers pressed to the side of her neck.

"What is it?" asked Jay Mackie.

"She's dead, Jay," the doctor said coolly, as if he had seen it many times before.

"Not again," screamed Mikey as he leapt out of the bed and went for the door. He was done with this motel hell — finished, finally.

The police captain turned to tackle him but he tripped over Laquinta's cooling body and face planted on the sticky carpet. He watched in horror as Mikey's tighty-off-whities disappeared into the parking lot.

16

SAVAGE SYMMETRY

Los Angeles :: Bennington Canyon 2018

"We are what we pretend to be, so we must be careful about what we pretend to be." - Kurt Vonnegut

In the confinement of the patrol car, Gunner winced, the cold steel handcuffs digging into his wrists, tightened beyond necessity. The city lights flickered in the periphery as they drove towards the inevitable.

"Dammit," Gunner growled, anger and regret mixing in his voice.

"Enough," the policewoman at the wheel retorted.

"This is a sick joke," Gunner retaliated, his voice spiking with resentment.

"No, your actions are the joke. Assaulting a woman."

"Woman?" Gunner spat blood. "What woman?"

"The one you bludgeoned back there."

"That overweight clown in drag?"

"Mrs. McFadden identifies as a woman," the officer instructed, her tone sharp as glass, "What you did might be labeled a hate crime. That's up to the DA to decide."

"Hate crime? For roughing up some drag queen?"

"Assaulting a transwoman. There's a difference," she shot back, her voice cutting through his ignorance.

Through the labyrinthine corridors of the police station, Gunner was led like a sacrificial lamb to the slaughterhouse. His mugshot was snapped under harsh lights, freezing his defiant sneer for the record. His dirty fingerprints smeared on the cold pane, marking him indelibly in the system. It was another 'incident' in a very long rap sheet going back to his traumatic childhood.

Charge filed: assault. His rights were recited in a drone that mocked any sense of justice. The promise of a public defender felt like a slap — society's brand of mercy for those they deemed undesirable.

Then came the cell — a cold, sterile cage where even hope felt contraband. The finality of the heavy door slamming shut ricocheted within Gunner.

But in this gloomy confinement, company arrived in the form of a young, battered pizza delivery boy. His wide-eyed innocence was jarring, a stark contrast to Gunner's hardened exterior.

The kid was sitting on the bench with his legs folded up and his arms around his midsection — as if protecting himself from a terrible trauma. He was mumbling some lyrics under his breath, "My rage ... I'm a rat ... just a rat in the cage ..."[32]

"Jesus, kid. What the hell happened to you? You look like you got run over by a—" Gunner cut himself off when he looked down and saw the torn bloody Romeo's Pizza jersey.

"Just some asshole," said the kid, as he steadied himself and salvaged a bit of toughness. "It's nothing. It happens all the time. Almost shot him but he had help. There were at least three of them ... I think. Maybe four."

"Heavy is the head that delivers the pizza," said Gunner feeling a bit sympathetic. In the harsh fluorescent light the bodily damage from his frenzied assault was a patchwork of purple and blue bruises, streaks of blood, and caked on dirt.

"It's okay," said the delivery driver. "Some fat ugly rich bitch is bailing me out. Carol McFadden? Connie?"

---

32   The Pizza Boy didn't realize he was ripping off the Smashing Pumpkins — an oldies band from the 90's.

"Colleen McFadden?" Gunner had seen the name on the paperwork.

"Yeah, that's it," said the Pizza Boy. "You know her?"

"I'm locked up for beating the shit out of ... her."

"Sucks for you," he said. "She's supposedly got the best lawyers."

"Well shit," said Gunner crouching down in the cell. All he had wanted was a quick pump and dump with that Cindy bitch. Now he was so fucked. He didn't think his veteran status could save his ass even if he leaned hard on the Iraq war PTSD.

He had some money left over from his last settlement payment after he bought the Jeep and the stupid watch. It might be enough to get some kind of lawyer instead of a court provided lazy asshole. Then again it might be enough to just post bail and go on a serious meth bender and forget all about it.

"Hey, kid," said Gunner. "When you get out do you think you can get any more of that crank?"

"Crank?"

"Meth," replied Gunner. "Either way it was good. It fell out of your pocket when I beat the shit out of you."

The Pizza Boy's eyes went wide and he instinctively clutched his guts even harder. "You fuckin' piece of shit," he said at the sudden realization, "It was you!"

"Sorry, kid. Should've got that pie there in thirty minutes or less. I was hangry."

The kid just started laughing and then coughing and then mumbling, "it hurts, it hurts," gripping his ribs.

"So about the drugs?"

"Well, it just so happens I quit the pizza game. How much you talking?"

Gunner thought about it for a minute, doing rough calculations of other necessary expenses. "Maybe like four grand to get started?"

The Pizza Boy looked as if he was doing his own quick mental math and then nodded, "I can do that."

"The thing is I can't buy your product if I'm locked up." Gunner stood to his feet. "You said you are good with this McFadden. Get him ... er, her to drop the charges."

"I don't know," said the Pizza Boy. "I mean I don't even really know her."

Anything was worth a try as far as Gunner was concerned. He had just got his junk working again and he wasn't about to spend the next few years packed away with a bunch of dudes.

"What do you mean, you don't know her?" said Gunner, "She's bailing you out, right?"

"She's some kind of record mogul and I'm going to be the next big hip-hop star."

Gunner thought for a moment. It was hard to picture this broken delivery driver as any kind of superstar. But he thought he'd indulge, "I think you will. I can see it in you. But you know what every big star needs?"

"Bitches and hoes?"

Gunner chuckled. "Nah, kid. You need an entourage!"

"Entourage? Like that TV show?"

"Yeah, a posse, a gang, at least a bodyguard because people are going to try to test you. Someone like me will make sure no one can fuck you up ever again."

The delivery driver looked at Gunner as if sizing both the man and offer up at once. He nodded and said, "Deal. But you still owe me for that *escante*, four large."

"Deal," said Gunner. Four thousand was nothing compared to what he'd waste on a lawyer and bail.

The Pizza Boy worked a grin. "And one more thing — I get to kick your ass."

"The fuck you will," said Gunner. He could feel the rage gnawing at his gut.

"Fair's fair," said the Pizza Boy getting up. "If I'm going

to be a hood star, I need to have kicked someone's ass in prison."

"Fine," said Gunner, tucking his hands behind his back and leaning forward, "Hit me with your best shot."

The Pizza Boy's best shot sucked and barely registered. It was the same with his second best shot and third best shot. The fourth best shot finally made an impact but by then the delivery driver had tired and went back to gripping his ribs.

He wheezed, "If anyone asks, I whupped your ass. Deal?"

"Yeah, deal," said Gunner, "And when you get a chance, we need to get you a trainer. You hit like a bitch."

Up high in Bennington Canyon, Colleen McFadden drove to see her wife. Truth be told she was dreading the encounter. She instinctively slowed the BMW to a crawling 20 miles per hour. She had avoided her since the shit went down in the hotel and his lawyer dropped the Hiroshima sized bomb that she was dying of colon cancer.

She hesitated and punched in the key code to their house — their anniversary year. She half hoped Susan had taken the time to change it and save him the confrontation. But the *beep-beep* let him know that she didn't have the care or worry. He paused again and turned the handle.

"Susan," he called out to the empty echo of the spacious entryway. The only sound was a marble statue of a cupid pissing filtered water into a basin between two roman columns. It was his wife's half-assed attempt at interior decorating which was simply aping off of that *Lifestyles of the Rich and Famous* shit.

It was his housekeeper Bernita that greeted him. She moved with an arthritic shuffle and always had a feather duster in her hands that was more ornamentation than actually used. At this point in her years of service she had merely become a set decoration. She might as well have been a peacock or a lawn jockey.

"Mr. McFadden," she said, gesturing the feather duster.

"It's Mrs. McFadden, now," said Colleen. "Is the lady of the house home?"

"She in bed, Mr ..." She gulped. "I mean Mrs. McFadden."

"How pissed off is she at me?"

The housekeeper wrinkled her already wrinkled face and shook her head woefully. "You better talk to her. She's sick. She's tired."

Colleen McFadden turned to walk toward the stairs to their upper floor bedroom, when he paused. "Bernita, when was the last time you had a raise?"

She snorted. "Raise? I don't even know what that word means."

Colleen nodded. "So, I'll take that as too long. Whatever you are getting paid I'll double it — No. Triple it. Just call my attorney and I'll make it happen."

Bernita raised a gray eyebrow, as if not knowing how to take this uncharacteristic kindness. Finally, she said, "Thank you, Mr. McFadden."

He didn't bother to scold her for misgendering — she was from a less understanding age. "No, thank you for your dutiful service. I won't be around much more so please do your best to see that Susan gets the very best care and attention."

McFadden began the long trek up the grand staircase that spanned the three stories of their palatial home. Each step creaked slightly under the weight of past and present secrets, of the million unspoken words that had been kept locked away between her and his wife.

Her hand slid along the finely crafted banister, fingers catching on the intricacies of its carvings. Thoughts of her wife filled her mind. Their years together, their years apart. How little she had truly known her and how, in turn, she had truly known her.

Reaching the second floor, she walked down the familiar yet estranged hallway lined with photos that echoed memories of their life together. Some still brought a small smile to his face, others, a twinge of pain. Her steps were hesitant with new, pinching high-heels, almost unwilling to move forward, as she approached the door to Susan's bedroom.

A pang of nostalgia washed over her as she remembered the last time she'd stepped foot in this room — the room where they'd shared laughter, love, arguments, and eventually, icy silence. They hadn't slept in the same bed for decades now, a harsh reality of a marriage that had long since lost its warmth.

Taking a deep breath, she gently turned the doorknob and pushed open the door. The room was dimly lit, shadows dancing on the walls from the flickering candle on the nightstand. Colleen's eyes fell on the bed where Susan lay under the thin quilt. She looked like a horror movie prop.

She looked up, squinting in the dim light as the visitor stepped into the room. Her eyes widened in surprise, not recognizing the figure before her. Colleen wore a flowing burgundy dress, matching lipstick, and a wig of golden curls that tumbled down to her shoulders.

"Who are ..." Susan began, her voice barely more than a whisper before realization dawned on her. Her mouth gaped open like a trout plucked from the water. She looked at the stranger, really looked for the first time in what felt like forever.

"Collin?" she finally managed, her voice uncertain, her eyes searching. The room fell silent again, the tension lingering, as they both braced themselves for the conversation that was to come.

Colleen didn't blink as she looked at Susan, really looked at her. She was a shell of the woman she used to be. Her once vibrant hair was now gone, her skin pallid and lifeless. The glow in her eyes had dulled.

"What poor animal died on your head?" Susan said.

"You don't like it? I have others," said Colleen as she took off the wig and set it on the edge of the bed. Colleen ran a hand over her own bare head, a humorless chuckle escaping her lips. "Looks like we match now, eh?"

Susan's eyes narrowed, her gaze shifting from the wig now in Colleen's hand to the bare scalp beneath. "What the hell are you doing, Collin?" she demanded, her voice hoarse but strong in her confusion.

She sighed, pulling a chair close to the bed. "It's Colleen now, Susan. I've ... I've been going through my own changes too."

She stared at him in disbelief, a mix of anger and confusion painting her gaunt features. "So, you're a crossdresser now? Is this some kind of a sick joke, Collin? One last jab at your dying wife. Haven't you pissed on this family enough?"

"No, it's no joke. And yes, I am Colleen now," she said quietly. "A lot of the bad things I did, a lot of the hurt I caused ... I think it was because I was denying who I truly am. My aggression toward woman was just jealousy. They could be how I always wanted to be."

"So, you're blaming your mistakes on ... this degeneracy?" Susan hissed, her hand waving vaguely in the air, "You've always had excuses, Collin."

Colleen nodded. "I know, and I'm sorry. I'm not saying it's an excuse, it's an explanation. There's a difference."

"And what's next? Are you going to tell me you have a boyfriend now too?" she asked, her voice a bitter mix of derision and mockery.

Colleen hesitated for a moment before replying softly. "I have a partner of sorts. His name is Baker. He's a good man."

Her eyes flickered at that, a grimace crossing her face. "Baker, huh? What are you going to tell me next, he's black?"

"Yes, he is," Colleen replied evenly.

Susan laughed harshly, each chuckle sending a shiver down her cancer eaten frame. "Well, isn't that just perfect. A black man and a tranny. What a pair you make."

"I'm a transgender woman, Susan. And Baker is a person, just like us. His color doesn't define him," Colleen couldn't believe the words that came out of her mouth.

Susan was silent for a moment before speaking again. "I want a divorce, Collin. Or Colleen, or whoever the fuck you are now."

"If that's what you want, Susan, I won't fight it. You deserve to live your life as you wish, just as I deserve to live mine."

"Get the fuck out of here. I never want to see you again," howled Susan, summoning the last bit of her energy.

Colleen wanted to say many things but knew it was better to remain silent than to jeopardize a winning position. She simply grabbed the wig, letting it rest askew on her head, as she turned around and wobbled back down the maze of memories and drove off.

She grabbed her mobile phone and hit the number for the family attorney. "It's McFadden ... I just saw Susan ... How is she? Sick and dying. But the good news is we're getting a divorce."

The attorney raised all sorts of challenges as to why this was totally bad optics for McFadden's business future. He expressed long winded and insincere worries about McFadden's mental health. And he ranted that leaving a wife dying of cancer wouldn't play well in the press.

"Listen here. She wants to divorce me because she can't accept my real identity as a trans-woman," Colleen shut down the attorney, "As to what the news will say? They will say what we tell them to say — the truth. She was a bigot and racist and rejected the real me — Colleen Mc-Fadden. That's the story."

17
GRAVE DEAL

"Behind every exquisite thing that existed, there was something tragic." - Oscar Wilde

▟▊ Dafuk is this crazy shit?" said Baker glaring down at Mikey's limp body. A pool of syrupy pee was forming underneath him mixing into the oil slicks.

The hustler hadn't even hit him that hard but judging by the boy's emaciated, bruised, and marked up body he wasn't in the best of health to begin with.

Baker could see two other men peering out the door confused. He waved his gun in their direction. "Come on, drag his ass back in the room." He coaxed them with the gun barrel. "For real, don't be stupid, quickly."

The older, huskier one glanced over at the smaller one that looked like the last apple in the bargain bin with Muppet hair glued on. The shriveled man just shrugged and nodded.

The two went over and looked down at Mikey. "You get his feet," said the captain. They picked up the listless puppet and drug him over the gravel, cigarette butts, and broken glass back into the room. The few hanging outside the motel paid no mind:

It wasn't the craziest thing that was going on.

By the swimming pool — now a murky pond — a man in an oversized trench coat was dealing in exotic pets out of his suitcase. Ferrets, sugar gliders, and even a baby alligator sloshed around the shallow pool among used condoms and water bottles.

Across the parking lot, a beat-up old van was shaking rhythmically. Cackles of laughter and occasional exclamations in a language that was not immediately identifiable emanated from the vehicle. A neon sign, barely clinging to the side of the van, announced **MADAME ROSA'S CRYSTAL THERAPY AND THAI MASSAGE**.

"Easy," said Baker as he entered the room. The two men huffed and puffed and then simply dropped Mikey next to Laquinta. "Easy," he repeated. He knelt next to the prostitute and rested his fingers on totally the wrong place. It didn't matter. He already knew she was gone.

Including Cindy, he had lost two hoes in one day. Normally he would lose his shit. He felt that old 80's gangster rage rushing through him. The body pile in the hotel room was liable to grow. He even started to say, "Muthaf—" but got interrupted by the chime of his mobile phone.

Baker kept the gun on the two men while he fished his phone out. "McFadden?" he mouthed out loud, "Just one second. Business call." He kept the gun pointed in the two men's direction.

McFadden started talking quickly about some rap prodigy he found called Pizza Boy and having to bail him out of jail. He talked on about the Transition Studios and asked Baker to assemble a team for recording, even asking him to get this "Dre" he had been hearing about (a decade too late).

"You and me, buddy," said McFadden.

"Okay, I'll holler at you Collin," said Baker, ready to get back to the business at hand.

"It's Colleen," said McFadden. "Collin is a dead name to me."

Baker didn't give it another thought as he put the phone back in his pocket. Colleen? What was the white boy tripping on? But the conversation did remind him that he was transitioning out of the street scene into the life of a studio gangster. He checked his rage.

"So what the hell happened to her?" Baker asked the two men. The bug-eyed man simply deferred to Jay Mackie's lead with a nod. "And who the hell are you two ..." he looked down at Mikey, "You three?"

"We don't know him," lied Jay Mackie. "They just bought drugs from me."

Baker raised an eyebrow. "Drugs?"

"Only the best," said Jay Mackie. He nudged the man next to him. "Show him." The smushed faced man grabbed his briefcase and opened it up revealing an overflow of bottles and bags.

Baker surveyed the assortment, a thinly veiled expression of distaste crossing his features. "Best, huh? Looks like a bunch of cheap thrills to me."

Jay Mackie didn't respond immediately, but after a brief hesitation, he said, "They get the job done."

Baker snorted. "Yeah, I can see that." He gestured towards Mikey's limp form and Laquinta's lifeless one. "Really quality work."

Ignoring the sarcasm, Jay Mackie simply shrugged. "Not my problem how they handle it. They wanted the stuff, they got it."

For a moment, Baker considered pressing the argument, but he knew it was pointless. Drug dealers were a dime a dozen in the streets, and they weren't in the business of caring about the aftermath of their actions. It was all about the immediate profit.

He took another look at Laquinta. In truth he was gonna be done with her anyway. She hadn't made much for him lately and he suspected what little she did bring him was simply the leftovers of her massive drug habit. If anything, they had done him a favor.

"So there was a matter of payment," said Baker.

"Oh, yes," said Jay Mackie. "Don't worry about the cost of the drugs she took, I feel it is only right that we cover those ..."

"Cost of the drugs?" Baker snickered. "How about cost of the girl? You paid her for the night?"

Mackie nodded and grabbed her handbag, tossing it over to Baker. He turned it over emptying it out on the bed: A few crumpled bills, a half-empty pack of menthol cigarettes, a broken compact mirror, a used neon orange lipstick, a lighter, a couple of tampons, and an assortment of pills came tumbling out.

Baker sneered at the pathetic contents, picking up the crinkled bills and the half pack of Newports. "Was this what her life was worth to you?" he asked, his voice devoid of emotion.

Jay Mackie, unperturbed by Baker's display of senti-mentality, shrugged. "Life's cheap on the streets."[33]

The shriveled apple man remained silent, eyes darting between Baker and Mackie, his fear palpable. The situation was quickly escalating beyond what they had envisioned.

Baker lit one of the cigarettes with Laquinta's Sagittar-ius BIC lighter.[34] He exhaled minty smoke and turned his gaze back to Mackie. "Let's talk about compensation."

Jay Mackie swallowed hard. He knew Baker wasn't talking about a few measly bills. The question was, how much was it gonna cost?

As Baker set the terms, Jay Mackie knew he was in deep. If he didn't comply, he had a feeling he'd end up on the pile with Mikey and Laquinta. If there was one thing he'd learned in his years on the force, it was when to push, and when to fold. Or had he learned that from Kenny Rogers? It didn't matter, it was time to fold.

"Let's start with fifty grand," Baker said, watching Jay Mackie closely. "Think of it as ... a reparation."

---

33   It was a line he pulled from one of his crime short stories, "Love, Lies, and Lunacy"
34   She was actually a Gemini.

"Fifty grand?!" Jay Mackie looked aghast. "I ain't got that kinda cash just laying around."

Baker shrugged nonchalantly. "Not my problem, man. You figure it out."

Harrison was pale, sweat visibly beading on his bulging forehead. "Why don't you just take the drugs?"

"You can keep that shit. If you don't have the cash then you probably shouldn't have messed with my property," Baker said.

Jay Mackie was silent for a moment, then muttered, "We'll figure something out."

"Damn right. Let's figure out what you have in your wallet," said Baker, gesturing with his gun. "Come on."

The two men fished their wallets out of their pockets and tossed them on the bed next to Baker. The hustler reached over and picked them up, taking out the few loose bills and the scratch off lotto ticket Jay Mackie had stashed. "$50,000 first prize. Let's hope this is a winner for your sake, Mr ..."

Baker flipped open the wallet flap to look at the ID and his face went slack. "You some kind of cop?" And as quickly he looked at the other wallet pulling out a DOD Top Secret Access badge. "The fuck is this shit?"

"Listen, I can explain," said Jay Mackie.

Baker was already backing out of the room. "I don't know what you spooks have got going on but I don't want no part of it. I wasn't here, you hear? Just make sure this mess gets cleaned up."

With that he turned around and left the motel leaving Jay Mackie and his accomplice at a loss what to say. But the other man quickly found something to fill the awkward silence.

"Fuck you, Mack," Harrison spat. "What kind of fucked up situation did you get me into?"

"I'm sorry if you don't have the balls for true-crime, non-fiction," Jay Mackie snapped back. "Why don't you go back to your lab rats?"

"I think I will," said the doctor, stuffing his things in the briefcase. His hand drifted over the heap of journals. "Just a bunch of bullshit, all of it." He pulled one from the stack and waved it at the captain. "This entire one is just the word apple over and over again."

He began to leave the room when Jay Mackie stopped him. "Wait? What are we gonna do with the bodies?"

The man's caterpillar eyebrows raised. "I'm leaving and you are going to do whatever cops do with inconvenient cadavers."

"No way," said the captain. "You gotta take them. Don't you ever have to get rid of a failed experiment or two?"

"Yes, occasionally we have human biohazard that is incinerated but all of that is carefully inventoried. There would be no way to sneak this whore into the system."

"But what about Mikey? He's in your inventory. Just say something went wrong upon delivery. He's got fentanyl in his system. It's cut and dry."

"I don't know," said the doctor.

"Come on," Jay Mackie urged him. "I take her; you take him. One each. It's fair. Don't fuck me—"

"Gay Chris," murmured Mikey from the floor, interrupting them.

Both men looked over and mouthed "what?" in the most jinx you owe me a Coke way.

"Gay Chris," repeated Mikey, wiping his eyes. "He'll know what to do with the body."

"Who is Gay Chris and how does he know how to get rid of evidence?" asked the captain.

"Because I left him here with Jessica's body and it wasn't here when the detectives came so I guess that means he might know what to do with Laquinta."

It was a real moment of clarity for Mikey even though he had no idea if Gay Chris was even alive. That would all depend on if Charlie had somehow made it out.

Mikey woke in a narcotic fog, sprawled ass-up in the back-seat of Jay Mackie's Subaru. Harrison yanked a needle from the junkie's butt cheek. Mikey jerked with a yelp.

"Just a little 'get up and go', Mr. May," Harrison said as he cast a concerned look over to Jay Mackie.

As the cocktail of vitamins and uppers flooded his veins, Mikey rocketed upright. He was no fan of speed, but the burst of positivity that pulsed through him was undeniable. The sun seemed brighter. Life seemed ... better.

"Get dressed," Jay Mackie tossed a plastic bag stuffed with clothing back to Mikey.

Mikey rummaged, his hands emerging with an array of what appeared to be women's clothes. "What is this, some thrift store haul?"

"That's Laquinta's stuff," Mackie replied, "Wear it till we find you something decent."

Mikey delved deeper into the bag, drawing out an array of mismatched clothing. There were sequined tube tops, leopard print hot pants, a knock-off Bart Simpson t-shirt, a few neon lace bras that could have doubled as eye masks, and a pair of thigh-high latex boots.

"Did she dress in the dark?" Mikey muttered, holding up a neon pink tutu.

The *pièce de résistance*, however, was a loud, 80s inspired, red leather jacket with zebra-striped fur lining. It was the kind of garment you'd find in the wardrobes of faded rockstars.

Mikey considered the carnival of clothing before him, the humor of the situation doing little to dampen the sobering reality of their origins. He finally opted for a slightly less outrageous outfit — a neon-green tank top, a pair of the less scandalous hot pants, and the red jacket.

"Oh, and don't forget the boots, Mike," Jay Mackie chuckled from the driver's seat. With a sigh, Mikey slid his feet into the latex boots, grimacing at the tight fit.

"Perfect," Mackie drawled, starting the engine. "You're the image of subtle discretion."

"Not bad," Mikey replied at the outfit that had the style of an escaped glam rock drag queen.

"That's where we're going," Jay Mackie said, pointing to a towering glass building that glittered in the early afternoon sun. The Sky Lounge — one of the most exclusive spots in Beverly Hills. It was where Gay Chris usually held court amidst his harem of strung-out, pretty boys.

Mikey swallowed hard, apprehension curling in his stomach. Chris was a dangerous man to cross. And showing up at his favorite hangout uninvited, that was like suicide. He had been cool that night over the death of Andy, but Mikey couldn't test his generosity. There was no telling what he had done to Charlie — something awful.

Jay turned to Harrison in the backseat. "You're the man for the job, Harrison."

"Huh? Me?" Harrison squeaked. He was obviously surprised and not pleasantly so. "Why the fuck do I have to do it?"

Jay shrugged. "You're a doc. You've seen it all. And you've got that ... bedside manner."

Harrison's face turned an interesting shade of green. "I'm not doing that. No way."

Jay shot him a side glance. "Well, we're not asking you to marry the man. Just ... get friendly."

"But I—"

"But nothing," Jay Mackie interrupted, a wicked grin spreading across his face. "You're going to fluff Chris and get the information we need."

The Sky Lounge was awash with midday sunlight pouring in through the floor-to-ceiling windows. A cluster of pretty boys loitered around the bar, sipping on their cocktails. Amid them was Gay Chris. His expensive silk shirt clung to his portly frame, a chunky gold chain resting on his ample chest, the leather jacket crinkled with every move. His thinning hair was slicked back, his sunken eyes darting around the room like a hawk's.

Harrison gathered his courage as he approached Gay Chris. Amidst the crowd of youthful devotees, the man lounged like a sultan in his seraglio. Harrison knew Chris had a taste for young, broken things. He was neither. He had to play a different card.

"Chris," Harrison extended his hand, summoning his professional charm. "Dr. Harrison. You don't know me but we have mutual acquaintances."

Chris appraised him from head to toe, a slow grin spreading on his face. "A doctor, huh? I could use a good physician. These boys bring all sorts of trouble. Half of them have STDs."

Harrison pushed forward. "Actually, I came here with a proposition, more of a trade."

Chris leaned back and stroked his soul patch. "Go on."

"I can offer you medical services, no questions asked. Pharmaceutical supplies too, top shelf stuff, antibiotics for the clap, you name it," Harrison explained, his voice hushed. "I just need some information in return."

Chris's laugh echoed across the lounge. "My dear doc, I can buy any drug I want."

Harrison felt a knot forming in his stomach. He wasn't ready to play his last card, but he had no choice. He leaned closer to Chris. "What about something ... more personal?" he whispered, his cheeks flushing.

Chris's eyes glinted. "Oh? Do tell."

"I need to know what to do with a dead body." Harrison gulped. "Maybe you'd run across one or two before?" His eyes cast over to some of the boys that were so strung out they looked like they had both feet already in the grave.

Chris rested a hand on Harrison's thigh. "What are you talking about, doc?"

He gulped and whispered, "Mikey, sent me."

An hour later, Harrison emerged from a private room. He felt dirty, used, and utterly humiliated. But clutched in his hand was a card. The climax was coming; he could taste it.

Slinking back to the car, Harrison tossed a business card onto Jay Mackie's lap without a word.

"Aw, you're blushing, Doc," Jay Mackie teased, plucking up the card to examine it. It was simple with just a phone number. "You're a good sport. Always have been"

Ignoring him, Harrison settled into the passenger seat, trying to forget the past hour.

Mackie dialed the number on the card. The recording that greeted him was bizarre, starting with a robotic, "Press 1 for Spanish, Press 2 for English" followed by a litany of prompts that seemed out of place.

"Pickup or delivery?"

Mackie, assuming they were going to dispose of the body, answered, "Pickup."

The recording continued, "Dark meat or white meat?" It asked, then went on to inquire, "How fresh?"

Jay Mackie did his best to answer correctly, but the prompts kept coming, growing increasingly cryptic. There were odd, coded questions about pizza toppings and crust preference.

Mackie was soon frustrated. He began pressing '0' repeatedly, shouting "Operator" into the phone. But it led nowhere and only changed the automated prompts to Serbian. With an exasperated groan, the call clicked off.

"We're going to have to figure this out," he said, tossing the phone on the dashboard. His eyes flicked over, catching Harrison's still flushed face. "Or Doc here will have to go back and offer more 'services.'"

Harrison groaned and went back to looking at the card.

The flying saucer printed on the card tripped Harrison's memory. He jerked Mikey's 'apple' journals from the back seat. Rifling through, he found it. A doodled flying saucer. The name 'Stephen' under it, over and over again, written till the ink ran dry.

Mikey went apeshit seeing it.

Old, gnarly demons clawing back up.

Mackie slammed him with questions, pressing the wound. Jessica was on the line. Mikey clammed up, shame making him choke.

But Mackie wasn't having any. "Doc, juice him," he snapped.

"Only got the trial stuff, Jay," Harrison tried.

"Do it," Jay Mackie growled. He pinned Mikey to the seat, like an animal under a boot.

Harrison did it. Needle in, plunger down.

Mikey's eyes glazed over. His mouth started churning, words pouring out like vomit ... Traded his brother to aliens for a Nintendo ... The extraterrestrials took him away and never brought him back.

Mackie was livid. "More goddamn horse shit!" he barked at Harrison, blaming him for fucking up the dose.

In the middle of Mackie's tirade, Mikey howled "Stephen" and started spitting numbers like a busted slot machine. Harrison told Mackie to shut it, jotting down the numbers.

The screams petered out into gutteral sobs. Amid the numbers they had caught the putrid scent of a house of a thousand rotting corpses.

18

A DANCE WITH THE DEVIL

Los Angeles 2018

"The only way to make sense out of change is to plunge into it, move with it, and join the dance." - Alan Watts

The sun was setting on the imposing concrete structure of the city jail, casting long shadows over the scene as a young man stepped out. He squinted in the waning light, his baggy clothes hanging loosely off his skinny frame.

Colleen McFadden sat in the backseat of her sleek black BMW, watching him with shrewd eyes. Beside her, the sharp attorney who had masterminded Pizza Boy's release was already onto his next case, barely suppressing a yawn.

She tapped on the window, rolling it down as the Pizza Boy approached. "How did you hold up, kid?" she asked. "Didn't lose your virginity in there, I hope?"

The Pizza Boy shrugged, but his hardened gaze spoke volumes. "Had to fight a little, but I handled it." He flexed his hand. "You should see the other guy."

A smirk tugged at the corners of Colleen's crudely painted lips. "I believe you. Now, I've got plans for you, big plans. Come with me to Transition Studios. It's time we talked about your future."

He hesitated, glancing back at the jail house. What choice did he have? It was either embrace fame and fortune or get buttfucked for the next five to ten years.

As they drove through the city, the broad warehouse

that was to house Transition Studios in Boyle Heights soon loomed into view. The echo of construction and refurbishment resounded through the vacant streets, an emblem of change amidst the urban landscape.

Upon reaching the site, Baker was already there, leaning against his Cadillac, scrutinizing Colleen's ensemble with a sly grin. "You're dressed worse than one of my girls," he quipped, his eyes raking over her designer clothes. "You undercover?"

"Collin is dead. Meet Colleen," she retorted with a sharp edge in her voice. "And the attire, it's not a disguise. It's real."

Baker smirked, shaking his head. "Hip-hop and gender fluidity?"

"No, it's evolution, Baker," Colleen corrected, pacing the gravel lot, her heels crunching with authority. "Hip-hop has always been about challenging norms, giving voice to the unheard. It's about time we use it to do more than glorify drugs and violence. The prisons are full. There's no money in it anymore. We need to be on the next thing. That requires a new identity."

The attorney opened the car door and Pizza Boy stepped out, blinking in the bright light, his nervous energy palpable. Baker and Colleen exchanged a glance before moving towards the young prodigy.

Colleen was the first to speak. "We want you to be part of the new wave, a fresh narrative," she pitched. "You'll rap as a woman, embody the unheard voices."

Pizza Boy bristled. "I just want to be real. To be me."

"But who are you, really? No one knows you." Colleen asked, not unkindly. "Who we are is defined not just by what we say, but by the stories we tell, and the roles we play."

Baker, chewing on a toothpick, jumped in. "Look, kid, it's show business. Tupac, the king of gangsta rap? He was a soft theater kid before he started playing the role of the thug. Eminem was a toothless hick from Kentucky who had to take vocal coaching to sound like he was from Detroit. What about Ice Cube? He was an engineering student from the suburbs. What matters is the persona."[35]

Hesitation flickered in Pizza Boy's eyes, but before he could voice his doubts, Colleen, with a knowing smile, revealed the *pièce de résistance*. A McLaren 720S Spider, gleaming and formidable, was driven in. It was a car made for the fast and the furious, one that spoke of speed, power, and recklessness. It was also a message; an unspoken promise of the future. The only thing was that it was Pepto Bismol pink.

Pizza Boy's eyes lit up at the sight of the vehicle, his mind churning. The world of hip-hop was one of powerful beats and poetic rhythm, but it was also one of image, of illusion. And the promise of being part of the new narrative, of transforming the genre, was a powerful draw. But mostly it was about the motherfuckin' money.

Baker jumped in, "How about I sweeten the deal with two front row tickets to the Lakers game tonight. It's how all the big hip-hop artists get noticed."

"Alright, alright. I'm in. But there's one thing we gotta talk about before I sign anything."

Gunner paced around his cell. The kid had no reason to keep his end of the bargain. He couldn't fault him for bailing. What was four grand and a loose promise of protection versus whatever the record deal was worth?

He thought about all of this for the morning and he thought about this through his bologna sandwich and grape Kool-Aid lunch and he thought about this through the dinner Salisbury steak with some weird brownish blend of many Kool-Aid flavors that he merely pecked at before giving it to the drunk that had replaced the Pizza Boy.

---

35   One of those examples was a lie. Baker didn't know which.

He was halfway asleep on the verge of not thinking about this while also thinking about how lovely it would be to be a dolphin with a rainbow afro having a beach party in Polynesia and other happy dreams.

The party was just getting good when the rattle of the bars awoke him. A cop gestured him out. He went reverse through time through the check in some backward get your watch back and your belt and your shoestrings and your dignity because they didn't even bother to look up your asshole to see if you were smuggling anything out type shit.

He felt a sigh of relief until he saw Colleen McFadden in the parking lot standing in the most unladylike way and yet still tapping a size 13 flat in her best impersonation of an irritated, sitcom housewife.

"Pizza Boy tells me you are his entourage," said Colleen with a brusk that she hadn't quite shaken off.

"That'd be me. Security. Bodyguard," Gunner launched into an impromptu job interview that no one had asked for. "I'm a vet so I don't know if that gives you any tax benefits but I'm good with a gun ... heavy artillery ... special forces ... explosives. Good hand-to-hand ... of course you found that out ... er ... yeah ... did I mention war veteran?"[36]

"Can you pass a pre-employment drug test?"

"Depends on how long I have to study for it," said Gunner.

"Any past problems we should know about?"

"I sometimes have *incidents*."

"What kind of incidents?"

"The sexually charged, violent kind," snipped Gunner. McFadden had already experienced one of his incidents. He was lucky to get this far with her.

McFadden thought for a moment and said, "You got the job until you pay back my lawyer fees for getting your

---

36   Gunner didn't understand that being a vet only got you cred at a podunk VFW until they found out you 'weren't there, man' when it came to 'Nam.

ass out. After that we can discuss the salary. But you gotta protect him at all costs."

"Who?" grunted Gunner.

They were interrupted as the Calamine lotion colored McLaren roared and skidded into the parking lot. It nearly clipped a light post as Gunner darted out the way. The heavy bass from the car's audio system shook the ground like an earthquake.

"Pizza Boy. You're his driver and bodyguard. His life is in your hands," yelled Colleen to be heard over the pounding beat.

The Pizza Boy killed the engine and jumped out waving a bottle of Moet-Chandon at Gunner. He had changed out of the grimy Romeo's delivery uniform into a Lakers jersey and he had an iced out slice of pizza on a gold rope chain hanging around his neck. Gunner secretly wanted to choke him with it.

"Did I come through for you?" the kid asked. "Like even after I kicked your fuckin' ass in there ... Did a homey hook you up?"

"Thank you," mouthed Gunner, which was difficult because he was simultaneously trying to swallow everything he really wanted to say at the same time.

"Get in," said Pizza Boy as he tossed him the keys. "We got places to go, people to be."

Gunner jumped in the driver's seat and Pizza Boy climbed in and tossed a glass over at Gunner which he slightly fumbled and then caught. He tried to pour Chandon and got about 62% in the glass, 20% on the seat, and 18% on his pants.

Gunner hoisted the drink up all the same. "Cheers, kid. Here's to the next ... thing."

The Pizza Boy laughed, hit a pinch hitter, coughed, took a drink of sparkling to clear his throat, coughed more, hit the pipe and stifled another cough and then erupted in maniacal laughter for a long spell and then said "Wait ... wait ... wait ... wait."

Gunner took a swig of the wine which was kinda flat from all the jostling. "Cheers, kid," he repeated for lack of anything better to say.

"No, wait," said the Pizza Boy. "If you are my body-guard, shouldn't you sing that song?"

"What song?"

"*I-I-I-I-I-I will always loooovvvve youuuuu,*" the Pizza Boy shrilled and giggled. He might be good at rapping but even autotune couldn't cure that tone def throaty take on Whitney Houston post-crack.

"So about that meth?" Gunner had a one-track mind and "have sex" had just been covered.

"What about my four thousand?" said the Pizza Boy.

"It's at my apartment."

Gunner drove the car to a rundown tenement building, a grim behemoth squatting in the grimy urban landscape. Gunner led the way, his large frame dwarfing the scrawny Pizza Boy who trotted behind him.

They stepped into the building. It reeked like the guts of a rotten elephant, a cocktail of decay, cheap booze, and piss. The walls were a sad mural of desperation, colors drained like old bloodstains.

Gunner's place was a bleak hole on the fourth floor. Unlocked, the door creaked open, revealing an interior as lifeless as a grave. It was comfort mocked — a sofa patched together from neglect, a static-buzzing TV teetering on a wooden crate.

The kitchen was a cruel jest. A worn-out counter, a protesting mini fridge, a lukewarm hot plate. One bar stool patched with duct tape, as uninviting as a cactus in an asshole, completed the picture.

This was Gunner's hole, his sanctuary. It was a crumbling edge of a life about to slide into oblivion.

Gunner's bedroom was a shrine to loneliness. Just a tired bed, a battered dresser, and an ancient military trunk decorated with old Charlie's Angels stickers. He cracked open the trunk, plucked out a wad of cash. Counted four thousand. Handed it to the Pizza Boy.

His eyes fell on an old uniform, worn and faded. Ghosts of a soldier's past life. He changed into it. Badges glinted under the weak light, medals strained against his chest.

Under the uniform lay an arsenal of firearms. He chose two Glocks. Checked their weight. Slid them into his arm holsters. Grabbed extra ammo. Then grabbed some more.

Gunner transformed. His depression was a shed skin, his purpose now was steely. The uniform wasn't a costume, it was an identity. He was a soldier ready to march into war.

"All set," he grunted, his eyes were fire. The apartment seemed less grim. The Pizza Boy was silent, not knowing to laugh or salute.

As the L.A. skyline dwindled in the rearview mirror, Gunner couldn't shake off the unease slowly uncoiling within him. He was behind the wheel of the Pizza Boy's new car, a machine more beast than vehicle, its interior awash with soft leather and sleek, touch-responsive screens.

Funded by the fresh influx of his signing bonus, the Pizza Boy lounged in the passenger seat, his gleaming grin mirroring the car's polished exterior. "Good, huh?" He was unable to contain the smug satisfaction that colored his words. "You gotta take some pics of me in it for my Insta ... and my Tinder. I'm going to be an influencer. Fuck yeah, I'm gonna get some pussy."

"Feels like I'm in a fucking spaceship," Gunner grunted, shifting uncomfortably on the plush seats that seemed to swallow him whole. Everything was too polished, too clean — an alien world compared to the grit and grime of his low-rent LA apartment they'd just left behind.

Desperate for a familiar anchor in this sea of luxury, he reached out to the radio. The screen blinked back in response, glowing green icons swimming under his touch. The soft beeps were a poor substitute for the satisfying clicks of a physical dial. "What in the hell is this?" His growl echoed through the car, frustration simmering beneath the surface.

The Pizza Boy's amusement was a palpable entity, an irritating buzz in the background. "Relax, old man." He chuckled, reaching over to tap a few icons. The car immediately came alive with the pulsating rhythm of an underground hip-hop beat, a buzzing, beating soundtrack that filled the space between them.

"You don't have any rock? Maybe some Zeppelin, or AC/DC?" Gunner asked, his voice barely masking his distaste. "I'd settle for Rush."

"Nah, man. Only the good hype shit. Underground hip-hop. Gotta stay connected to the scene," the Pizza Boy replied, his voice thick with misguided pride.

Gunner grit his teeth, opting to swallow down the retort that threatened to spill out. The last thing he needed was a pissing contest. The road stretched out ahead, an asphalt snake slithering through the underbelly of L.A.. The pulsating beat continued to echo around them, a discordant metronome marking their journey into hell.

A decorated veteran and a pizza delivery boy turned aspiring hip-hop artist. It sounded like the plot of some low-budget dark comedy. But this was no joke, and the punchline, Gunner knew, was waiting for them at the depilated trap house.

Pinto's house loomed ahead of them, the typical L.A. setup: a dingy two-story nestled between other worn-out residences. Gunner cut the engine, plunging the car into an unsettling silence that sat heavily between him and the Pizza Boy.

As they approached the entrance, the front door swung open. Pinto was leaning casually against the frame, his lips curving into a lazy grin that didn't reach his eyes. "No crusty pizza today, fool?"

The Pizza Boy shot him a look, his bravado a stark contrast against the nervous energy stinking on him. "Nah, man. I ain't about that no more. We're here to score, not deliver."

Pinto let out a laugh, a low rumble that echoed around the quiet street. "Is that right? What're you after?"

"*Escante*," Pizza Boy blurted out, a little too quickly. The silence that followed hung heavily in the air. "4k worth."

Pinto's eyes widened, surprise momentarily breaking his cool facade. "Big step up from shitty pizzas and *molta*, huh?" He mused, regarding them both for a moment.

This was the point of no return, the precipice overlooking a deadly plunge. Gunner felt the familiar weight of tension settling on his shoulders as he took a step forward. "So, you got the stuff or not?"

Pinto eyed Gunner. "You brought the army with you?"

"He's my entourage."

Pinto pushed away from the door frame, a smirk twisting his lips. "Come in, fools. Let's see if you can handle the heat."

Gunner followed the Pizza Boy into the house. As the door closed behind them, Pinto's laughter echoed ominously in his ears. Inside the house the hum of fluorescent lights was the only sound. Gunner and the Pizza Boy stood facing Emilio and his henchman Flaco across the length of the table. The money was counted, verified, the deal seemingly done. But the tension was a live wire, sizzling between them.

Gunner, a stony look in his eyes, took the first step in diffusing it, "Deal's done. Let's have the stuff."

Emilio smirked, leisurely pulling out a package wrapped in black plastic from a cabinet. "Sure, right here. Four grand worth of primo."

But as he extended the package towards the Pizza Boy, Flaco started tweaking out, "Wait, Emilio, you remember what happened with that fool Charlie last winter, right?"

Emilio's hand froze mid-air, his eyes narrowed. "What's that got to do with anything, Flaco?"

The tweaker shifted uneasily, his fingernails dug into his arms. "Just that ... well, you know. He tried to scam us with that fake money."

Emilio rolled his eyes, "That's different, homie. This is the fucking pizza delivery boy—"

But Flaco had already turned his suspicion onto Gunner and the Pizza Boy. His hand rested on the bulge in his waistband, his nervousness slowly turning into aggression.

Gunner, sensing the change in the room, reached for his own piece. "Hey, easy there, big boy. We're not looking for trouble."

"What if you are, though?" Flaco challenged, drawing his gun and pointing it at Gunner. His mouth twisted into a toothy grin.

Gunner felt it — a gut twist that teleported him to the blood-soaked streets of Baghdad. He was going

His heartbeat jolted like he was wired to a car battery.

His reality morphed — this dingy, drug-soaked house melted into a past battlefield.

Dusty streets, deadly gunshots, suffocating fear under the heat of the desert sun.

Burning skin.

Rotting guts.

It was enough to make a vet's dick hard.

He blinked. Pushed away the phantoms of his past. This wasn't Iraq. It was a different war. Flaco's jitters were the first battle cry. Twitchy, ready to pop. His hand was on his weapon.

Flaco made a move, Gunner was faster. Trained reflexes kicked in. His Glock was out, firing before Flaco could draw.

Chaos exploded. Gunfire, dust, blood. Gunner dove for the black gold - the meth. A bullet grazed him. It felt like a cheerleader, egging him on. Behind cover, Gunner snorted a quick line.

A lightning bolt of power.

Popeye with his spinach.

He was unstoppable.

In contrast, Pizza Boy was a freeze frame of fear. His tough talk was just that — talk. While trying to pull out his gun he shot himself in the dick, a total Tupac move gone wrong.

Gunner barely noticed the pitiful scream. He was in his element, thriving in the mayhem. Things really went off when Emilio emerged with a flamethrower causing Gunner to recoil behind a flaming couch. Peering around he could see the devil tattoo on the gangbanger's neck, bloating and distorting like some kind of frog as Emilio cackled.

Gunner charged out, tucked, and rolled. A movement that he was way too old and slow for but it was enough to sink a single bullet right between the Devil's eyes. As the guy flipped back his flame thrower went wild catching the curtains and the ceiling which went up in a blaze. The Pizza Boy tried to kick and crawl away from it but he could barely move.

Gunner moved fast, picking him up and cradling the young man in his arms as they rushed out the front door.

It was a touching cinematic Kevin Costner kind of moment. So touching you could almost hear Whitney Houston singing up from hell.

In the car, the Pizza Boy was ghostly pale. He was bleeding out. The engine roared to life. And he didn't mind the music selection in the space mobile. They left the burning house behind along with their burning four thousand and burning methamphetamines.

"You saved my life, man," said the Pizza Boy.

"Just doing my job," said Gunner.

"But for real if I write some bars about this, I was the one doing the killing and you were the one that shot yourself in the dick."

"Whatever, kid." Gunner gripped the wheel.

"Yo, I got front row tickets for the Lakers tonight from McFadden. Take 'em." The kid worked the blood-soaked tickets out of his pants pockets groaning and cursing.

Gunner accepted it even though he hated basketball. He felt his hardness against the military fatigues. This was his war, his battle. And he was going to win. He hit the accelerator and spun the tires toward the hospital. McFadden wouldn't be happy.

19

HORRORS BEYOND COMPREHENSION

SIMI VALLEY 2018

"The process of delving into the black abyss is to me the keenest form of fascination." — *H.P. Lovecraft*

The trio of Jay Mackie, Harrison and Mikey left L.A. toward the unassuming plains of Simi Valley. A once thriving Chumash Indian territory, now a semi-arid expanse stretched out before them, interrupted only by the skeletal outlines of gnarled, old trees. The sun was setting, painting the horizon in deep hues of orange and red, casting long shadows that danced over the craggy hills and dales.

"You sure we're heading the right way?" asked Jay Mackie after he took a draw from his cigarette.

Harrison waved the smoke away. "Sure? Hell no. But this is where the coordinates lead."

Mikey was in the back, slightly bouncing up and down and moving his fingers in wild motions. He was still intoning the GPS coordinates underneath his shallow breath like a psychotic chant.

"Cigarette, Mikey?" offered the captain.

Mikey took the half-cigarette and quickly sucked it down until he scorched the filter only to go back to mumbling the string of numbers.

"Harrison, can you calm him down?" said Jay Mackie as he worked the radio to find any kind of music reception. There were a few choices in the middle of nowhere and he settled on a faint, crackling broadcast of Johnny Cash's "Ain't No Grave."

The doctor looked back at Mikey and said, "Better not." He checked his watch. "He should be coming down in a couple of hours ... I hope."

Jay Mackie's map app led to the end of a dirt road. "Shit," he swore. "There's supposed to be a road here."

"We're not far," said Harrison surveying the landscape. "Maybe the girl's buried out here somewhere."

"I guess we're walking," said Jay Mackie.

The three men got out and began to hike as Harrison used a GPS app. "This way," he said, gesturing toward a hilly incline littered with boulders and scrubby brush. The dying sun's fiery glow bathed the landscape in a sinister red hue, casting long, monstrous shadows that looked like dinosaurs.

Jay Mackie glanced at Mikey, his jittery figure a stark silhouette against the red horizon. He was muttering to himself, lost in his world. The bug-faced man seemed to pay no mind, simply trudging on with a grim determination etched onto his face.

An eerie silence fell over the desolate landscape, broken only by the crunch of gravel under their boots and the distant howl of the wind. As they crested a hill, a sight emerged that seemed like it was ripped straight from the pages of a Lovecraftian tale.

An ominous castle-like house towered over them, its gothic architecture a stark contrast to the unremarkable Simi Valley landscape. A sickly aura seemed to emanate from it, tainting the air with a palpable sense of filth. But the most startling aspect was its incongruity — an architectural anomaly planted squarely in the middle of a barren, forgotten landscape.

"This has to be it," Harrison confirmed, looking at his phone.

"Let's get this over with," Jay Mackie said, leading the way. A flock of crows cawed ominously from a nearby dead tree as they approached the dark, foreboding structure from behind. They first came upon a stone garage and the captain peered through the window. His gaze focused on a 1976 Dodge Panel Van parked inside, a garish UFO airbrushed on its side. The odd vehicle served as a disquieting welcome mat.

Harrison opened the garage door with a loud woeful creak. When Mikey saw it, he muttered, his voice barely a whisper, "That van ... That night."

In the eerie silence that followed, Jay and Harrison exchanged glances. Then, before either could voice their concern, Mikey stumbled towards the van. Jay and Harrison caught up to him as he yanked open the door. The interior was as stark as a surgical suite, all steel, and chains. The gray alien masks scattered in the backseat only heightened the chilling reality.

"We need to document this first," Jay Mackie, ever the detective and the writer, declared, swallowing his initial horror. He pulled out his voice recorder and began to drone into it in a detached, almost academic tone, weaving a narrative of their grim discovery.

"Here we stand," Jay Mackie began in a husky voice, aiming his voice recorder at the van, "at the scene of a nightmarish tableau, as if ripped from the pulpy pages of a 1970s sci-fi horror comic book."

The captain's eyes scanned the scene, soaking in every haunting detail. "A 1976 Dodge Panel Van, once a symbol of freedom, now an artifact of dread. Its paint, faded and weather-beaten, bears the image of a flying saucer, a crude and garish design that belies the terror it must've held for those who found themselves inside its cold, sterile interior."

His gaze then fell on the seats. "The van's backseat has been stripped bare, replaced with stainless steel benches.

Chains, ominous and rusted, are bolted to the walls, their purpose frighteningly clear."

"The oddity," Jay Mackie's voice trailed off, almost choked, "does not end there. Littered across the bench seats are masks. Not just any masks, but masks fashioned in the likeness of the almond-eyed invaders. The implication of their presence here is as chilling as the desert night."

Jay Mackie clicked off the recorder and stared at the van a moment longer. "We need to keep moving," he said.

But Harrison and Mikey had tuned out his monotonous narration and set their sights on the foreboding castle. Their journey led them to the cellar.

Jay Mackie kicked at the rusted lock until the hinges broke off. He beckoned them on but Mikey was fading fast.

"Come on, kid," the captain muttered, casting an impatient glance back at Mikey. But the kid was planted firmly on the ground, staring blankly at the rusted iron door of the cellar.

The sight of the house had jolted Mikey back to the past. A wave of terror washed over him and his waning heart jackrabbited. His breathing became ragged, and he could barely hear Jay Mackie's reassurances over the rushing sound in his ears.

With an encouraging nod from Harrison, Mikey followed the captain into the cellar. The sight that greeted them inside was beyond their wildest imagination.

Jay Mackie took a deep breath and flicked on his flashlight. A cold, damp gust of air greeted them, followed by the grim spectacle of what could only be described as a charnel house.

Fucking furniture made out of bone.

The thought crossed Jay Mackie's mind, followed by a visceral shiver. Skulls and bones of indeterminate origin had been polished to a shine and meticulously arranged into grotesque versions of everyday items: chairs, tables, even a grim chandelier made of femurs and vertebrae.

"What the hell?" Jay Mackie muttered, his flashlight beam dancing over the grim decor.

If he had hoped for Mikey to answer, he was disappointed. The boy was too engrossed in his own shock.

Suddenly, the silence was cut by the creaking of the cellar door. All three spun around as the eerie glow from the house above streamed in. Framed by the light, a tall figure emerged, with a lanky, awkward gait, as if unused to his towering height. He moved like a newborn deer covered in afterbirth.

The man was wearing a ridiculously small He-Man t-shirt that was stretched taut over his muscular frame and shorts that were too short, exposing knobby knees and shins covered in coarse hair. Most disturbing of all, his face was hidden behind a child's pillowcase, two holes cut out for eyes. The surface of the pillowcase had been crudely marked with a marker drawing of a boy's face, the wide, innocent eyes and curly hair a stark contrast to the hulking figure beneath.

Slung over this grotesque man-child's shoulder, was a frail old man, ancient and cadaverous. His bony fingers clung to his carrier's shoulder while his sunken eyes roved over the intruders, finally resting on Jay Mackie.

"Martin," the old man croaked, "Why didn't you tell me we had guests?" His tone was reprimanding, but his gaze was manic with excitement.

Martin, if that was indeed the name of the pillowcase-headed behemoth, stood silent and stoic, only adjusting his grip on the old man when directed.

"Come along, come along," the old man cackled, clapping his hands together, "You boys mustn't mess with the Halloween decorations. But since you're here, why not join us for pie? I insist."

With that, he urged Martin to turn around and head back up the stairs, leaving the trio in stunned silence.

"Did ... did he just invite us to have pie?" Harrison finally stammered, breaking the silence.

"Okay, you two go up," Jay Mackie said, his hand fumbling at the stone wall for a light switch. "I need time to take a look around here."

Harrison hesitated, looking at Mikey. "You sure, Captain?"

Jay Mackie nodded, his face set in a grim expression. "Just be careful, okay?"

With that, Harrison and Mikey began their reluctant trek up the winding, rickety staircase, leaving Jay Mackie alone in the dimly lit cellar.

As they ascended, Harrison and Mikey found themselves navigating through a vast collection of porcelain masks, each more grotesque than the last. The walls were lined with dark and twisted oil paintings depicting nightmarish scenes. The whole house felt like a monument to a demented, creative mind — a sort of Addams Family meets Ed Gein aesthetic shit out by John Waters.

Meanwhile, Jay Mackie's investigations took him to a hidden door in the cellar wall. With effort, he forced it open and found himself staring down a tunnel, leading to a cavernous expanse beyond.

The cavern was like something from a Hardy Boy's nightmare — a subterranean cathedral dedicated to some dark, unknown god. An altar dominated the center, adorned with symbols of a cultic nature. A knife lay by its side, its blade dark and stained, coiled ropes, candles, and an assortment of other ritualistic paraphernalia strewn about.

And amidst it all, a collection of Elvis Presley 45s and an old sound system sat incongruously. The records were neatly stacked next to the player, their covers yellowed with age but lovingly preserved. Jay Mackie picked one up, flipping it over in his hands. "Hound Dog," he read out loud. He could almost hear the echo of the King's voice, providing a bizarre soundtrack for whatever dark ceremonies went on here.

The main dining room was a dark, cavernous space, dominated by a heavy mahogany table. At the head of the table was a woman, tied to her chair, a porcelain mask obscuring her face. Her body was still, lifeless.

"This is my wife, Barbara," the old man introduced her to Mikey and Harrison with an eerie casualness, "And my boy here's Martin. Can't you see the family resemblance?"

It was a grotesque mockery of a family dinner scene. Martin gently set the old man down in a chair next to Barbara, and with a surprising dexterity, moved to the kitchen to retrieve the pie.

As Martin served the pie, the old man chattered on, reminiscing about family memories as though they were just a regular family at dinner. His stories were punctuated by fits of raspy laughter, his gaze darting between Mikey and Harrison with wheezy glee.

Mikey did the only thing he could think of; he began to eat the pie and hoped their might be milk.

Harrison, however, was more cautious. He picked at his slice, his fingers shaking as he lifted the crust. His worst fears were realized when he found a piece of human finger and what looked like human flesh, nestled among the apple filling.

Fucking penis pie.

The old man, noticing Harrison's hesitation, grew irritated. "Look at you," he barked, "You're a picky eater. I can't stand picky eaters."

The old man gave a nod to Martin, who had been standing ominously silent by the old man's side. In response, the masked man moved around the table with swift, predatory grace and slammed Harrison's face into the pie.

The room filled with the old man's dusty laughter. "No television until you finish your dessert!" he crowed, his voice echoing through the room as if scolding a misbehaving child.

Harrison spluttered, lifting his face from the pie, pieces of crust and apple and presumable penis sticking to his hair. His eyes met Mikey's across the table, shock and horror reflected in their depths. This was more than they had bargained for; this was madness.

Just as Harrison spluttered, lifting his face from the pie, the doors to the dining room slammed open. Jay Mackie stood in the doorway, his face drawn and serious, his handgun steady in his hand.

He had seen enough. He was ready to end this sick charade.

The old man's laughter ceased instantly. His eyes narrowed to slits as he regarded Jay Mackie with a newfound hostility. "Father Gary," he spat, his tone venomous, "you've come to ruin our family dinner."

His rage was palpable, a living thing that hung heavy in the room. He turned to Martin. "Get him!" he ordered, "Throw him in the fire!"

Martin charged towards Jay Mackie like an amped up psycho. The gun went off, the shot echoing through the room, but Martin was too fast. He knocked the gun from Jay's hand and went for it. As Martin turned the gun towards Jay, Mikey sprang into action.

With a feral cry, he picked up a large femur from the table and swung it at Martin's head. The impact was solid, the sound of bone meeting bone echoed in the dining room. As Martin crumpled to the floor, Jay Mackie scrambled for the gun, leveled it at Martin, and pulled the trigger.

The whole time, the old man cackled, his mad laughter bouncing off the walls as he threw curses and rants against "Father Gary."

"Well," Mikey said, panting heavily, "Let's see who you really are." (It was a real Scooby-Doo moment.)

He bent down and yanked the pillowcase off Martin's head. The face that stared back at him was young, blonde, and disturbingly familiar. "My name's not really Martin," the young man muttered, his voice weak, "I know my first name is Stephen."

Recognition slammed into Mikey like a punch to the gut.

Stephen, his younger brother.

His missing brother.

Harrison turned to the woman tied to the chair. Gently, Jay Mackie lifted the porcelain mask.

Jessica. It was Jessica.

The relief was short-lived. Jessica was in bad shape, her face pale, her eyes vacant.

She had been gutted and her breasts carved off.

But it was Jessica. Jessica.

Jay turned the gun on the old man, his voice steely as he said, "It's over."

The old man glared at him. "Damn you, Father Gary," he spat, "Damn you to hell for taking them away from me again." His teeth looked like moldy candy corn.

Mikey fled, tearing through the house, out into the yard, and into the waiting van. The engine sputtered to life and the van swerved away, leaving a cloud of dust in his wake.

20
THE FINAL SCORE

Los Angeles 2018

"In the end, we'll all become stories. Or else we'll become entities. Maybe it's the same." — Margaret Atwood

The van barely made it to the outskirts of Los Angeles when it began smoking and belching thick black exhaust. Finally, it popped loud with a terrific rattle that caused Mikey to veer over to the shoulder. It hadn't helped that he was burying the speedometer needle to put as much distance between him and that castle in the desert. It all didn't even feel real. It took on the haze of some kind of drug induced nightmare. He had seen Stephen many times before in tortured REM sleep along with the inky eyed visitors. It seemed all too typical.

But there was no time to think about that. The only thought was to get high, pass out, and wake up into another dream or another nightmare. Anything was better than that moment. He grabbed Harrison's pharmaceutical case and walked over to a grimy pub. He'd get high and he'd get lost. He'd always wanted to go to Alaska and hunt a polar bear or the bear might hunt him; either way it was a fitting end for a writer such as himself. Hemingway would at least be proud of his moxie.

Mikey entered the bar and quickly ordered a drink next to a man dressed up in a soldier's uniform. Mikey didn't bother to wait for the Coke as he beelined toward the restroom. In a dingy stall he fished through the case until he found the amazing kick-in-the-lungs powder Harrison had given him. He sprinkled some on some tinfoil reminding himself to go easy. He still had some things to do before he took that final heroic dose.

As the vapor kissed his lungs, he felt a euphoric ease wash over him. The world became hazy and everything was just fine. The castle and the flying saucer drifted back into junkie fantasy. Mikey pulled out a Sharpie and added to the collection of drunken musings on the stall door:

MIKEY MAY GOT HIGH HERE — 4-2-18
He underlined his name for emphasis.

He inspected his handy work and then wished he had brought his journals in with him. He always wrote better high. Instead, he decided to make the pee splashed bathroom wall his notebook:

"**DEAR STEPHEN**," he began in his usual manner:
"**YOU'LL NEVER GUESS WHAT I SAW TODAY! IT WAS A FLYING SAUCER, LIKE THE ONE THAT TOOK YOU AWAY THAT DAY. THE ALIENS SAID THEY'D BRING YOU BACK AND THEY DID, BUT YOU HAD CHANGED. SO THEY TOOK YOU AWAY AGAIN. BUT IT WAS GOOD TO SEE YOU. I'M SORRY I GAVE YOU AWAY FOR A NINTENDO. I WISHED YOU COULD HAVE PLAYED DOUBLE DRAGON WITH ME. YOU WOULD HAVE LIKED THAT. I HOPE THEY HAVE BETTER GAMES IN OUTER SPACE. I MISS YOU. I LOVE—**"

His marker scratching was interrupted by a loud knock on the stall door. "I'm kind of busy in here," he said.

"Hey, this is gonna sound like a crazy question," said a voice that sounded like a mouth full of gravel. "Would you happen to have any meth?"

Mikey didn't know how to answer that but he slid out the briefcase.

"Thanks. Mine burned up with the Devil." Gunner popped open the briefcase and was startled to see a bunch of vials, pill bottles and containers of unknown content. There were no real labels except for odd barcodes and cryptic inventory numbers. It reminded him of the experimental stuff the Army gave him during the war. He chose a couple of brownish powders that kind of had 'that smell' and 'that taste' before he tapped on the door again. "Sorry to bother you buddy but do you have a piece of foil?"

"Hang on," said Mikey. Soon a couple of pieces of thin metal and a lighter slid out under the door.

Gunner tapped out a mixture of the two powders onto the foil, hoping that at least one might be some kind of amphetamine. He torched it and inhaled the vapor. It didn't give him the kick of meth but his grimy surroundings came into clear focus. He felt he could literally see the pubic hairs and roach turds that littered the floor.

The stall door opened and out stumbled the junkie with a glazed donut look and a small smile spread across his face.

Gunner was starting to shadowbox. "How much do I owe you for ... whatever those two things are?"

Mikey looked at the powders resting on the sink. He shrugged. "I dunno. Just pay for my drink."

Gunner stopped his bobbing and weaving. "Cool. They call me Gunner."

"I'm Mikey May, you may have heard of me from bathroom walls and the television news."

Fucking celebrity, thought Gunner as he exited the restroom with Mikey, each lost in their own chemically induced world. The atmosphere in the pub was familiar and grimy, filled with an eclectic mix of patrons. Gunner sat at the bar, nursing a beer as he half-listened to the chatter of the nicotine yellow alcoholics. It was an affable hole in the wall where a man could drink without having to bump into a big deal or negotiate expensive bottle service. The only bottles here were domestic piss water — perfect for Gunner's pissy disposition.

He had come there to wait for McFadden to visit the wounded Pizza Boy in the nearby hospital. He had hoped to score and was excited to see the faded young man carrying an expensive looking briefcase. His pale face was drawn tight, and his eyes were glassy, symptoms of withdrawal already clawing at him. Gunner didn't know what he had smoked but Mikey May was his new best friend.

Mikey slid onto a stool at the end of the bar, the buzz from the fentanyl dulling the edges of reality. His eyes, however, were fixated on the news, an eerie sense of familiarity crawling over him. In this claustrophobic pub, both men existed in their own miasma of misery, their paths crossing but never quite intersecting. And throughout the evening, they continued to exist side by side, their individual stories unfolding in the hideous heart of a grungy Gomorrah.

Gunner's gaze was immediately drawn to the news broadcast. It was talking about some alleged serial killer that was found in Simi Valley. The news lady said the actual crime scene was too gruesome but did show scenes of intricately painted porcelain face masks. The old rage simmered, his grip on the beer glass tightened.

The evening news continued blaring from the old television set perched above the bar, showing a perp walk of an elderly man. As the announcer spoke, the face filled the screen, skin drawn taut over the skull, eyes dead and remorseless.

Both Gunner and Mikey stared at the visage, frozen, their drinks untouched on the counter. Each word struck Gunner like a punch to the gut. That face was the face from his nightmares, the one that haunted him for years. His knuckles were white around his beer, rage bubbling up within him. His high turned sour, the images on the screen warping and distorting.

Mikey blinked, trying to clear his vision, to rid himself of the images. "Turn it off," Mikey shouted. "Change the channel."

Colleen McFadden entered the pub then, bringing with her an air of authority that she couldn't shake off, even in a dive bar. She looked at Gunner, concern etched on her face. "The kid's gonna make it, Gunner, but ... he's not gonna be the same."

Gunner turned to her, the rage giving way to relief. He had started to like the kid. "What do you mean?"

McFadden grimaced. "He ... might lose his ... you know, his manhood. Doc said the bullet did a number on him. Shredded it like pulled pork."

Gunner was silent for a moment, then shrugged. "Guess you'll have to rebrand him as the Pizza Girl then."

"Great minds think alike." McFadden chuckled, reaching over to pat Gunner's shoulder. The physical contact made him feel strange. He hoped no one would mistake the two of them for a couple. He had marginally better standards.

Gunner fished the blood-stained tickets out of his pocket. "Pizza Boy had these tickets for the game tonight. I'm not much for sports—"

Colleen rebuffed him. "I need you with me. We've got front-row seats and we will look like losers if we don't have an entourage. We might even need you to fight somebody."

Gunner grinned hoping for trouble. Getting paid to beat some asshole to a pulp was too good to be true. Especially when he knew Colleen had the legal muscle to get him out of any future 'incidents.' "Can I bring a plus one?"

"The more the merrier," said Colleen. "Bottoms up. It's almost game time and we need to meet up with my partner, Baker."

Bottoms up indeed, thought the war vet as he drained

his beer and walked over to Mikey. He slid the ticket over to him. "Don't know what's on your mind tonight, but maybe you'd want to catch the Lakers?"

Mikey eyed the ticket and suddenly knew how his story finished.

Back at the crime scene, Harrison and Jay Mackie stood side by side as a flurry of police officers descended upon the area, armored up in raid gear like Teenage Mutant Ninja Turtles. The old man, cackling and ranting to the end, was cuffed and led away, his laughter echoing hauntingly in the chill desert air.

Harrison was on his phone calling the home office. "Yeah, having some crazy adventures out in the desert ... Camping trip with an old army buddy ... Listen there is someone that was just arrested that might be a good study candidate ... Yeah, his name is ████████████ ... Watch the news tonight." Already the news choppers were swooping in from above like vultures.

Exhausted, they trudged back to their car, the adrenaline rush subsiding, leaving them drained and a bit shaken. Once seen, some horrors were not easily forgotten.

And there was still the question of Mikey, but he could easily be found. It wasn't easy to conceal such a garish van. Mikey wasn't exactly street smart for all his hard lessons.

"Damn it," Harrison swore, peeking in the window, "Mikey took my case."

Jay Mackie glanced at him. "Your drugs?"

"Yeah," Harrison admitted. "Had some heavy-duty stuff in there. Experimental pharmaceuticals. If those end up on the street—"

Jay Mackie sighed. "Probably for the best. Mikey's on a fast track to an overdose anyway. I figure all our problems will be solved by the end of the night."

Harrison frowned. "He took the journals too, Jay."

Jay Mackie shrugged. "So what? You said it yourself. They're just junkie gibberish. No real value. Complete and utter horse shit." He pointed to his temple, smirking slightly. "I've got the real story all in here. I'll remember what I can't remember, I'll make up. That's my writer's gift."

"Did he take Laquinta?" Jay Mackie hoped out loud.

Harrison peeked into the back of the Subaru and recoiled from the smell. Her body had been baking in the sun, oozing and spilling out toxic organs like an overripe tomato in a manure pile. They should have remembered to roll down the windows.

"I'll take that as a no," said the captain.

He and Harrison pulled out the body and dumped it in a nearby ravine. Jay Mackie used his pocketknife to crudely carve some of the symbols he had seen in the underground dungeon into her bluish-black skin. "The cops will find the body or they won't," he explained. "What's one more victim? She won't be the last they dig up around here."

They climbed into the car and drove away, leaving the grisly scene behind. The two were almost to L.A. when the fetid smell finally began to fade. He'd have to have the car detailed. Or he'd just buy a new one with the book advance.

"Shit, Jay, stop," yelled Harrison abruptly.

Jay Mackie hit the brakes and skidded the car next to the UFO van parked on the shoulder. "I told you we'd find him," the captain said. "Fuckin' Mikey May. Dumb as a box of bullshit."

The two looked through the van but found no trace of the junkie, his journals, or the drugs. The neon glow of a bar sign beckoned in the distance, so Jay Mackie steered towards it.

"Let's go check it out" the captain suggested, "If nothing else we can get a drink and celebrate."

Though there didn't seem much to celebrate it was

shaping up to be a banner day. The police chief had a man-gled niece to bury (or at least a good 73% of her, give or take.). Mikey's parents would be reunited with their son Stephen in a similar way — pale and lifeless. It would be for the best as no telling what the kid had been through in many years of living hell with the old man. No amount of therapy would ever fix that. But there was some kind of closure in just having a body to dump in the ground and mark with an epitaph. It wasn't pefect but it was an end-ing — at least one that Jay Mackie could write about.

Inside they did a quick look around and not seeing Mikey decided to ask the bartender if he had seen a junkie. He chuckled, "seen plenty," but there was one a while ago. Left with someone in an army uniform.

"Harrison, looks like one of your buddy's already came and got him."

"I'm so fucked," mumbled Harrison, running his hands through his greasy Muppet hair.

"Me too," laughed Jay Mackie. He slapped his hand on the mahogany bar top. "Might as well just get more fucked."

Harrison didn't argue and they ordered drinks. As the doctor got out his wallet for the first round, he paused, cursing under his breath. "Baker took all our cash."

Jay Mackie's eyes were fixed on the television screen, a Lakers game in progress. He turned to the bartender, a twinkle in his eye. "I'll bet our drink tab that the score ends up 83-83."

The bartender smirked, shaking his head in amuse-ment. "Sure, buddy," he said, taking the bet. An NBA game ending in a tie? That was one he was confident he'd win.

Gunner drove McFadden's BMW to Boyle Heights to meet up with Baker. His eyes started to blur around the edg-es and everything had a bit of a ripple to it but he was otherwise laser sharp and focused. His heart was beating at a steady 180 BPM and his cheeks were flushed.

At the Transition warehouse, Baker, the newly minted music mogul, was busy working his angles to get the studio up and running. His gapped tooth smile clicked with delight. "I got Killary Klinton to agree to come from San Francisco to talk."

"Killary Klinton?" said McFadden, not understanding.

"The tranny that pissed on you in that one music video. You know the one that had that hit song. Her real name's Bethany. " Baker smiled. "Took some convincing too. She's scared as shit it's some setup to get even."

McFadden smirked. "Good but I hate the stage name. That won't play well in the media."

"What about Tranzista?" suggested Mikey, stumbling up and rubbing his bloodshot eyes.

"This is Mikey. He's part of our entourage tonight." Colleen pointed at Gunner in the driver's seat of the BMW. "And that's Gunner. He's special operations, demolitions, bodyguard, and driver."

"What's Mikey do other than turn a phrase?" asked Baker.

"I carry the drugs," Mikey explained and shook the case, the pill bottles rattled inside.

"Good idea," said Baker in approval. He got some cocaine out of his Cadillac and handed it to Mikey. It made Mikey feel important to be so trusted.

The odd foursome took off to the Staples Center. It was almost showtime.

As they neared, McFadden cast a sidelong glance at Gunner and Baker. "Should we leave our heaters in the car?" he asked, hoping he used the lingo correctly.

Baker scoffed, his gap-toothed grin flashing in the dim light. "Nah. A gangsta without his piece is like a ho without her pussy — useless."

McFadden raised an eyebrow but didn't argue. They

followed Baker to a particular VIP security checkpoint around back where a beefy guard stood. The guard, clearly known to Baker, let them through with just a nod, not bothering to check them thoroughly, only giving a cursory pat down for show. Gunner was waved through because it was hard to refuse a man in uniform even when his eyes had turned to pinholes looking in two different directions. He did stop Mikey who was lugging in the chrome briefcase and a box of journals, but Baker interceded, "He holds the drugs. He's cool." The guard nodded and waved him through.

Once inside, their front-row seats made them an immediate focus of the omnipresent cameras. Baker, with his sharp suit, McFadden, now Colleen, in head-to-toe Lakers gear, Gunner in his crisp military uniform, and Mikey in Laquinta's garish hand-me-downs made for a unique spectacle. The cameras panned towards them again and again, broadcasting their images to the millions of people watching the game from the comfort of their homes.

When Baker and Colleen appeared on the big screen, she gripped his hand and leaned closer to him.

"What are you doing?" Baker whispered through his forced, gap-toothed smile, feeling all eyes on him. No telling how many of his homies were watching at home. He hoped she was passable.

"Go along with it, partner," she whispered back through ruby painted lips.

Baker leaned over and gave her an awkward kiss on the cheek. He'd been with less attractive and at the end of the day he reckoned a woman was a woman.

Back at McFadden's home, his ex-wife, seated on the couch with a glass of merlot, recoiled as she caught sight of her former husband and his new companions on her large flat-screen TV. A mixture of anger and disgust marred her usually composed features. She even shouted 'that word' at the screen. Bernita was unfazed by the outburst. She had heard 'that word' many times.

Meanwhile, in the sterile environment of the hospital, the Pizza Boy, now rebranded as the Pizza Girl, propped up in his bed, trying to put pen to paper. The TV in his room was tuned in to the game, and he jotted down words, weaving them into hot bars about his recent encounter with Pinto:

The Devil thought he was hard, thought he was a pearl,
But he ain't got nothin' on the Pizza Girl.
Dodgin' bullets, McClaren ridin' fast,
Life in the rearview, livin' in the past.
Livin' the hustle, got the world in a whirl,
Got the pie spinnin' round the Pizza Girl.

Each word flowed into the next, his shaky handwriting laying out her truth, her identity, her new life.

At the dive bar, Jay Mackie and Harrison's eyes widened as they spotted Mikey on the screen. Adorned in Laquinta's outrageous wardrobe, he was an unmistakable splash of color against the Lakers' court.

"Damn, we gotta go," Jay-Mackie muttered, standing up. But the bartender's gruff interjection stopped them in their tracks. "Tab's not settled, fellas."

Out of cash, they reluctantly returned to their seats. The game, and their fates, hinged on an unlikely tie.

As the second quarter was underway, the game was an intense back-and-forth affair. Julius Randle, driving the Lakers' offense, powered through the Kings' defense and threw down a statement dunk, nudging the Lakers ahead 14-13. The Lakers seemed to be finding their groove.

They embarked on an 8-0 run, with well-coordinated passes and dynamic offensive plays that had the home crowd on their feet, roaring their approval. By the end of the first quarter, the Lakers led 22-16, looking every bit the dominant force they were expected to be. But the Kings were far from out of the contest, keeping pace and ensuring that the game remained tightly contested.

Meanwhile, Gunner was fighting his own war. A personal battle that raged inside him with every passing second, fueled by the war-induced PTSD, the overwhelming meth rush, and shocking revelations from his past. The ripples of his vision were suddenly forming odd, twisted shadows. Amid the roar of the crowd a white noise whisper was trickling into his ears. He nudged Mikey. "Bathroom break?"

Mikey grabbed the briefcase and followed the camo-clad man to the restroom. A couple of dudes gave them a curious but knowing eye as they both ducked into the same stall. Neither gave a fuck riding high on the chemicals, adrenaline, and general feelings of VIP imperviousness. They were superstars.

Gunner took some white powder from Mikey. He snorted what he hoped to be an upper, desperate for some semblance of control over his fraying senses. He beat his chest rhythmically like a war drum.

Mikey smiled as he crushed up the rest of the pills and powders, stirring them with a little bit of toilet water, in a discarded plastic nacho container.

Gunner eyed him with what remained of his waning fucks left. "That's a serious dose. You know what the fuck you're doing?"

"I'm blasting off tonight." Mikey smiled and sucked it up into a vet-sized syringe. "Beam me up, brother."

The veteran nodded in a kind of understanding. "Til' the wheels fall off," he said and snogged up an even larger line. "*Oh, I've been through the desert on a drug with no name ...*" he began to sing.

As the third quarter was winding down, the tension in the game was palpable. A surge of energy from the Kings had them claw back into contention; the intensity of the game mirrored in the nervous anticipation of the crowd. Sacramento's Nigel Hayes. capped off a 10-2 run with a three-pointer, giving the Kings a 60-58 lead.

But the Lakers would not be outdone. Josh Hart and Channing Frye responded with back-to-back 3-pointers, and the Los Angeles side wrestled back the momentum as the third quarter buzzer sounded. Despite a few missteps, the game was neck-and-neck, as they headed into the fourth quarter.

Gunner, meanwhile, was descending deeper into his own mind, the arena and its spectators transforming into an eerie spectacle of porcelain masks and writhing body parts. The roar of the crowd, the tension of the game, the buzz of anticipation — all of it faded into a distant hum as he navigated his hallucination.

Mikey, on the other hand, was laser-focused on his suicide plan. He felt the weight of the syringe in his pocket, a chilling reminder of the macabre spectacle he intended to unfold. But with each passing second, as the Lakers and Kings traded blows on the court, the nerve he had been building seemed to waver, the uncertainty creeping in.

In Gunner's ears, the white noise became a repeating chant growing louder with each passing second, "Gregory ... Gregory ... Gregory ..." His name echoed in his mind, bouncing off the walls of his consciousness like an uncaged animal. It mixed the persistent hissing that accompanied the name, morphing into an unbearable static that set his nerves on edge.

His heart pounded in his chest, a brutal, cannibal island rhythm that threatened to consume him.

He could feel his sanity slipping away.

He was caught in a horrific hallucinatory loop, a nightmarish vision of his past brought to life by the potent methamphetamine rush and his own torturous memories.

His mom was swinging — just a swinging.

Meanwhile, Mikey was ready. Ready to meet whatever came after life, or nothing at all. It didn't matter much to him as long as he was adored and immortalized. It wasn't too much to ask:

The Legend of Mikey May.

Clutching his concocted suicide cocktail, he navigated through the labyrinth of spectators and concession stands, making his way towards their big-time front row seats. His heartbeat pounded in his ears, each thump a ticking time bomb, counting down the moments before:

3 — 2 — 1 ... blastoff!

As the fourth quarter kicked into high gear, the Kings and Lakers continued their fierce back-and-forth. As both teams pushed into the eighties, the outcome of the game felt more and more uncertain. Gunner, lost in his own world, barely registered the escalating excitement of the crowd.

However, Mikey's resolve was wavering. He looked at the pulsating crowd, the players giving it their all on the court, and he felt a pang of something he couldn't quite place. Was it regret? Fear? Or was it a desperate yearning for a different ending to his own personal game?

With the score tied at 80 and seconds ticking down, an opportunity presented itself. A timeout was called and the players huddled around their coaches. Mikey felt the syringe weighing heavily in his pocket. With a sudden rush of adrenaline, he made his move toward the floor just as the Lakers managed a three-pointer, pushing their score to 83.

But before Mikey could make a move, Gunner made a move of his own. The vet in a meth-fueled, PTSD-induced rage, storming onto the basketball court, a firearm in hand. The first shot went off as the Kings, in a disoriented scramble, managed to sink a desperate three-pointer just as the buzzer sounded, tying the game at 83-83.

Panic ensued. The players scattered like frightened birds, spectators shrieked, ducking and diving for cover, popcorn and drinks flying. Some shit themselves.

Gunner didn't seem to see anyone or anything but the demons in his own mind. He fired randomly, his aim unsteady, yet with military accuracy.

Among the chaos, Baker, always ready for a fight, pulled out his own gun and aimed at Gunner, his shot grazing the soldier's leg. But Gunner, unfazed, turned and delivered a fatal shot, nailing Baker.

Shit, thought Baker as he bled out — shit.

McFadden cowered behind the seats, a look of sheer terror etched onto her face. Mikey saw his chance. Dropping his suicide plan, he sprinted towards Gunner, an injection filled with the lethal cocktail poised in his hand.

With a yell, he lunged at Gunner, managing to drive the needle into the beast's jugular before being thrown off. The bullet that followed hit Mikey squarely in the chest, silencing him forever.

But the damage was done. Gunner stumbled, disoriented by the cocktail of drugs coursing through his system, his eyes glazing over.

McFadden, mustering up all her courage, rose to her

feet, her antique pistol trembling in her hands. With a firm squeeze of the trigger, the tiny metal sphere left the chamber, flying straight towards Gunner. Like a scene from an old biblical tale, Gunner, the hulking, drug-fueled Goliath, dropped to the floor, a small stone lodged in his forehead, his reign of terror ended by the unlikely David — Colleen McFadden, music executive.

As Mikey lay on the polished wooden court, the blaring lights above turned hazy, their intensity wavering like distant stars. The scoreboard, looming above him, morphed in his last gasp mind into a colossal spaceship, descending from some distant, psychedelic cosmos. Its face displayed the final score in glowing numbers — a dead heat, 83-83, a cosmic balance, life and death.

Through the hallucinatory haze, he saw a face that tugged at his guts. Stephen. His brother, so young and carefree, oblivious to the cruel circus that life could be. They were children again, stargazing and looking for spaceships.

A profound sense of peace washed over Mikey. It was as though he was floating, untethered from the sordid reality of his life. The tumult around receded into a distant hum. As the corners of his vision started to darken, he let out a silent chuckle. His ended on a whimsical hope:

They better have some damn good space drugs.

A junkie always needs more junk.

EPILOGUE

PALABRA

"This is a rare moment for me when I am actually terrified of death. I'm smart enough to know that copious amounts of drugs and alcohol will only make the situation more unmanageable. But at this point it's what is expected from me, it's the "poetic ending."
— Ryan Leone

The aftermath of the Lakers tragedy left the media scrambling for a single antagonist. Gunner, the actual shooter, was a decorated war veteran, making him a challenging subject. His role forced uncomfortable questions about war veterans' reintegration and the VA's handling of their mental health. The optics were all wrong.

The mainstream news reshaped the narrative: Mikey became the shooter, Gunner the defender against a suicidal junkie. The execution required careful editing, but amidst the chaos, it appeared plausible. Blurry cellphone videos from the scene only added to the confusion. It became easier to vilify Mikey, already the primary suspect in Jessica's murder and potentially his brother Stephen's. However, the question remained: how did Mikey escape from state prison and land front-row Lakers seats?

It was the prison captain, Jay Mackie, who would end up taking the fall for that. It took a lot of Scotch whiskey before his 'writer's gift' gave him Mikey's fanciful escape plan. Known for his habitual drug use, Mikey overdosed and went into a coma-like state. He was transferred to the morgue within the prison grounds, awaiting official pick-up and autopsy. Mikey came out of his coma and simply walked out the unlocked door.

The prison officials thought it was just a case of a missing body but it wasn't until the Lakers broadcast that they realized what had happened. It was a shitty story but commonly accepted as the alternatives were too insane to comprehend — Occam's Razor.

Jay Mackie had his career almost gutted. His loose oversight of Mikey's escapades earned him more than a few harsh glances from his superiors. Only his tenure, connections, and the role he played in finding Jessica's body spared him jail time. Hoping for a redemption story, he poured himself into a new endeavor — writing a true crime novel based on Mikey's chaotic life, dubbed "The Ballad of Mikey May". But his narrative, full of conjecture and embellishment, pinned Jessica's demise on Mikey but left so many unanswered questions and plotholes that it failed to resonate with readers. (Average Amazon rating 2.23 stars.) It was far from the *In Cold Blood* caliber success he had envisioned.

As the next couple of years passed, Mikey's posthumous reputation took a bizarre turn. His journals, leaked to the public following the cleaning crew's discovery and sale on eBay, sparked a wave of conspiracy theories and underground fandom.

(One janitor also stumbled upon an unclaimed lottery ticket that Mackie had bought on a whim and had been dropped by Baker. They turned it in the final chance drawing for losing tickets and were overjoyed with a $50,000 windfall. Unfortunately, a misguided bet on the Lakers saw the custodian's luck run dry, his newfound fortune evaporating as quickly as it had materialized.)

The Mikey May historical revisionism really kicked into overdrive with the discovery of the journal he hid in the cave near his family home in which he stated that Jessica had simply died of an overdose. YouTube handwriting analysis "experts" believed that the journal was likely the work of Mikey, while various debunking websites ruled the journal a hoax by an overzealous fan.

The same conclusion was made the bathroom graffiti attributed to Mikey that fateful day and, even more surprising, a bizarre crop circle that appeared in Idaho depicting Mikey and his brother Stephen as children. The final nail on the legend of Mikey May was an ill-fated biopic called *Savage* starring Johnny Depp, subject to de-aging CGI, portrayed Mikey in an uncanny valley light, burying Depp's career under a landslide of negative reviews and a Razzy award.

It was perhaps Colleen McFadden who caught wind of the times. The white walls of the old world were crumbling and those that held on would soon be buried in irrelevancy. The future was about wild reinvention. To keep up you always had to be the next thing. Her heroic actions at the game caught national attention and she somehow bridged the gap between increasingly polarized political parties. Right-wing media lauded her as a poster child for Second Amendment rights, while the left celebrated her as a trans woman champion—very brave and strong. Colleen went on the media circuit and not bothering to contradict the narrative talked about how she had taken down Mikey after he gunned her beloved partner Baker down in cold blood. (She would usually tear up at this moment to really sell it to the public.)

Simultaneously, Transition Records and their breakout stars, Pizza Girl and Tranzista, soared to new heights with award-winning tracks like "Snip, Slip, Snatch" and "HRT" and the compilations "This is REALLY Trap, volumes 1 through 4".

Whenever an album got a poor review, McFadden's flacks went on the social media warpath decrying detractors as alt-right bigots, homophobes, and Trump supporters. Eventually, all the influencers would champion the label and gold and platinum records followed.

Colleen would have many ornamental boyfriends and

girlfriends but continued living with Cindy. She moved her to a swank Malibu mansion and watched in horrid fascination as the ex-prostitute ballooned up indulging in pizzas. When she lamented her lost looks, Colleen was always quick to comfort her with words like, "Baby, in the olden days people would pay to see a body like yours."

The "body positivity" movement did encourage Cindy to start an OnlyFans for which she got a moderate following. She was never top-10 but her plus-sized bedroom photos and pictures of her eating would earn enough income to supply her obsession of hoarding vintage Cabbage Patch Kids — perhaps the only pleasant memory of her past.

The assumed dead, Gunner surprisingly showed great fortitude and the small round had only embedded in his skull and simply rendered him unconscious. What Mikey had hoped was a suicidal dose also did not kill him. However, the two gave him serious brain damage and caused him to become even more unhinged. In his asylum he would howl and moan and scream at images of porcelain masks, hanging lifeless bodies, and the twisted old man that cackled and whispered "Gregory ... Gregory ... Gregory."

Harrison kept the sick old pervert from Simi around in a separate unit to be studied but mostly tormented. The mad doctor found it a great revenge to decorate the serial killer's containment with crucifixes, Catholic icons, and photos of the Pope. Like some kind of modern day vampire, they always seemed to send him into a rage and he cursed "Father Gary". Sometimes he would wheel him into Gunner's room for "further study," which amounted to just letting the two fuck with each each other. One day they would both be dead and incinerated with the human biowaste but in the meantime, he found it to be good sport.

Elsewhere, Mikey May danced on the dark side of the moon with no regrets, delighted that people were still talking about him — the perfect poetic ending.

ABOUT THE AUTHOR

Ryan Leone (August 3, 1985 — July 2, 2022) was a gifted storyteller whose life was a testament to love, resilience, and justice. Despite facing the challenges of addiction and enduring eight years of incarceration for nonviolent drug offenses, Ryan's indomitable spirit shone through. During his time in federal prison, he channeled his passion for storytelling into *Wasting Talent*, a literary gem that touched the hearts of thousands.

Upon his release in 2013, Ryan became a beacon of hope and inspiration, using his captivating storytelling abilities to connect with the marginalized and dispossessed. Through YouTube, Patreon, and other platforms, he encouraged and supported those struggling with addiction and long-term incarceration, fostering a sense of community and empowerment.

Ryan's influence extended beyond his literary accomplishments as he fearlessly advocated for a more compassionate approach to addiction and the reform of the criminal justice system. His dedication culminated in the establishment of The Ryan Leone Foundation: Paul's Project, which aimed to combat opioid overdoses and save lives in high-risk areas. Ryan's enduring legacy lies in the lives he touched, the hope he instilled, and the profound impact he made on those he encountered, leaving an indelible mark on the world of literature and social justice.

ryanleonefoundation.org
patreon.com/Karinafranco :: youtube.com/@ryanleone5805

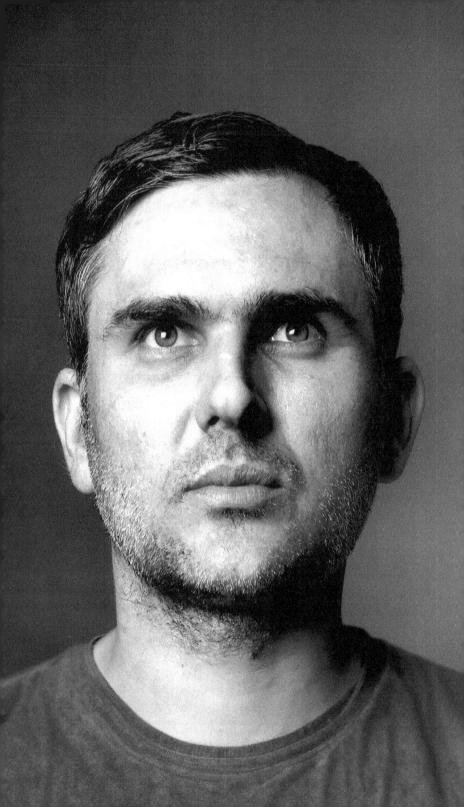